Praise for Ly
and *Archangel Protocol*

"Lyda Morehouse deftly dances a brave new path amid the minefields of religion and science fiction, prophecy and politics, romance and detective noir . . . a most impressive debut. A very worthy read."   —Howard V. Hendrix

"Her world is intriguing, and there are enough surprises to keep things moving, and the mix of SF and religion works surprisingly well. An impressive first novel."   —*Locus*

"A rapturous, high-intensity foray . . . delivered with passion and precision."
—Stephen L. Burns, author of *Call from a Distant Shore*

"Will keep readers glued to the very end."—BookBrowser

"McMannus is one of the strongest, most complex investigators in a long, long time. The rest of the characters are vividly drawn, fascinating beings. The technology seems so tantalizingly close—frighteningly possible."
—Lisa DuMond, SF Site

"You'll find a lot to enjoy."
—Uncle Hugo's Bookstore Newsletter

"One of the more interesting Satans in recent memory."
—Melissa Scott

FALLEN HOST

Lyda Morehouse

A ROC BOOK

ROC
Published by New American Library, a division of
Penguin Putnam Inc., 375 Hudson Street,
New York, New York 10014, U.S.A.
Penguin Books Ltd, 80 Strand,
London WC2R 0RL, England
Penguin Books Australia Ltd, Ringwood,
Victoria, Australia
Penguin Books Canada Ltd, 10 Alcorn Avenue,
Toronto, Ontario, Canada M4V 3B2
Penguin Books (N.Z.) Ltd, 182–190 Wairau Road,
Auckland 10, New Zealand

Penguin Books Ltd, Registered Offices:
Harmondsworth, Middlesex, England

First published by Roc, an imprint of New American Library,
a division of Penguin Putnam Inc.

First Printing, May 2002
10 9 8 7 6 5 4 3 2 1

Cover design by Ray Lundgren
Cover art by Bruce Jensen

ROC REGISTERED TRADEMARK—MARCA REGISTRADA

Printed in the United States of America

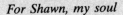

For Shawn, my soul

ACKNOWLEDGMENTS

I simply must thank my editor, Laura Anne Gilman, who believed I had a second book in me; my agent, Jim Frenkel, and his trusty crüe, Tracy Berg and Jesse Vogel, who made the deal; and my writers groups—Karma Weasels, Wyrd-smiths, and the Fierce Wild Women—who nurtured the beast (and me). In particular, I need to single out those who volunteered to read the manuscript in its final hour: Kelly David McCullough, Naomi Kritzer, Shawn Rounds, Terry Garey, Bob Subiaga Jr., and Paula Fleming.

To Shawn Rounds goes all my love and appreciation for the many "there, there's." I thank Jonathan Sharpe for the carrot of "Soul Calibur" to keep me on the writing stick. To Shannon Drew, whose insanity kept me sane at my day job, I just have to say, "Wow, what's with your hair?" I also send love to Emmett Christian Sutliff, who was deliv- ered nearly same time on the same day as this manuscript. And to my biggest fans, Mort and Rita Morehouse, whom I owed a better acknowledgment: "I love you, and thanks for all the fish" (not to mention the dim shablows).

PROLOGUE
Page, the Intelligence

I never sleep. Like the dolphin and the spiny anteater, I don't experience REM. Unlike the dreamless mammals, I'm a construct. I am a living program inside a vast network of electronic impulses known as the LINK. In that datastream, I've uncovered the meaning of another kind of dreaming—that of a fond hope or aspiration, a yearning, a desire, or a passion. This much I have. When I dream, I dream of Mecca.

CHAPTER 1
Morningstar, the Adversary

Once a millennium on the first Jewish Sabbath morning after Epiphany during Ramadan, our two warring sides have agreed to parlay. This time, because of my slight advantage on the field, I chose the venue.

I picked a table by the window in a bustling greasy spoon called "The Y'all Eat In," full of the smells of frying chicken, pancakes, bacon, and grits. Grease so permeated the place that even the forgotten Christmas tinsel had become a matted tangle of silver and gold. A short jump off a dusty Mississippi electric truckway, the Y'all was the most exciting thing happening in a town so small the locals joked it wasn't visible via GPS. Most of the truckers in the restaurant seemed like the kind who'd voted for ultraconservative presidential candidate Étienne Letourneau, even after he had been exposed as an electronic hoax, because, in their pea-sized and malicious minds, anything was better than voting for a Jew. I turned a few heads when I walked in with my long hair back in a ponytail, but I was white and male and clearly passing through.

Gabriel would hate this place; it was perfect.

I watched the waitress pour coffee into cups up and down the counter. Live, human service was a fascinating phenomenon. It happened in two places—among the very rich in fancy, overpriced watering holes, and here, at the butt-end of the universe. The middle class had to content themselves with LINKing their orders to the chef and serving themselves. Posh restaurants employed humans to provide a sense of genteelness, luxury. Here, at the other end of the spectrum, it was a necessity. Not everyone here was LINKed.

All commerce, entertainment, politics, and community happened on the LINK. Any citizen over the age of majority—fifteen—had their nexus activated and could participate in the virtual life of the LINK. But, like any rule, this one had exceptions.

A surprising number of people weren't citizens. To be a citizen in the world today you had to belong to a recognized religion. A massively destructive bomb called the Medusa had been dropped in the last war. The bomb's nanobots changed—and continued to change—whatever they touched into glass. Hundreds of cities around the world were now empty, crystallized, permanent graveyards. Faced with this graphic display of science out of control, world leaders decided they'd had enough. There was a huge backlash against scientists. Religion, in particular the fundamentalist and orthodox varieties, experienced a renaissance. At first, it was merely hip to be fanatic, but it quickly became the law. Now, if a person didn't at least nominally belong to a religion, they were criminals, outcasts. Some people were just plain stubborn and refused to pretend to be something they weren't. Some got kicked out. Being excommunicated in this day and age had a whole new meaning.

Each country, of course, dealt with its religions in its own way. What was unacceptable here in America, might be perfectly fine in another country. For instance, in some places, like Saudi Arabia, the Koran was the literal law of the land. Other countries continued to have secular law and encouraged religiousness by controlling access to the LINK.

And, of course, there was an underclass. The nexus, which housed the nanotech that built the LINK inside the human brain, was implanted at birth when the skull was malleable. Implanted, naturally, by experts—meaning expensive doctor-technicians or licensed midwives. Thus, millions of babies never got the nexus. For people like that, there was the option of implantation later in life, and/or the stigma of external hardware.

I imagined the truckers here fell into that category. I suspected many of these workers had gotten their connection late in life, from their employers, and thus had a sort of "company town" interface in their heads—that is to say, only what the bossman felt it necessary to provide.

The door chimes jingled, breaking my reverie. A man,

or more correctly, the figure of a man walked through the door, bringing with him a dusty blast of January air. It wouldn't be an exaggeration to say that every head turned to watch him enter. Conversations dropped to a murmur; forks rested uneasily against plates, like weapons at the ready. I could almost feel the anger in their stares.

The Mississippi heat brought a sheen of sweat to his deep mahogany skin. He wore a multicolored orange, yellow, and brown robe, like those favored by immigrants from Somalia or Ethiopia. On top of a shaved head perched a boxy hat. He would look fabulous, I imagined, if he were waltzing into the Met for an African art show. Here, he pushed all the bigots' buttons—he was a rumble ready to happen.

Probably the thing that saved him from being killed instantly was his sheer physical impressiveness. He stood well over six feet and had the presence and width of a linebacker. He was, after all, an archangel. Many mortals, even the brutish ones, caught a glimmer of that.

He nodded in my direction, and I lifted a hand to offer him the seat across from me. I'd already ordered for him. A plate of bacon and grits cooled in front of the empty chair. He looked around the room as if hoping for another option. Then he sighed, moving to join me. A sneer marred his face, as he slumped into the chair.

"Morningstar," he said. A barely civil greeting, especially considering we used to be brothers. Worse, he spoke so softly that I could hardly hear him. Few knew it, but I was deaf in one ear. Just before I fell, the blast from Gabriel's trumpet destroyed my hearing. Thus, I kept my right side turned ever so slightly to him, lest he know the victory he'd won.

"Well met, Gabriel," I said brightly. "Or do you prefer Jibril these days?"

He grimaced, and, as he did, a flicker of light glinted off the data chip he had imbedded in his forehead. It was a holographic tattoo—an earthly representation of the words I had seen written between his eyes in Heaven: "There is no God but Allah, and Muhammad is the Prophet of Allah."

"You're looking good," I offered. "The role of field-commander suits you."

"It's temporary," he said, crossing his bulky arms in front of his chest defensively.

He looked so grumpy; I couldn't help but poke him. Some would say it was my nature. "You can only hope so, since all those storybooks of yours say Michael is the one to defeat me in the end. Without him, I wonder how things will play out?"

Jibril grunted. For the patron saint of communication, he was awfully taciturn. Still, I could understand that he didn't want to talk about it. Michael, God's right hand, had gone missing from Heaven eight months ago. A rumor came to me, whispered on the wings of the Fallen, that Michael had come here, to earth, in the shell of a homeless preacher. I hadn't yet been able to suss out what Michael was up to, but I strongly suspected that there was a woman and possibly a child involved.

"Have some food," I offered, picking up a piece of bacon from my mostly empty plate and crunching it. I knew full well that Jibril kept *halal*.

Jibril rolled his eyes at me, but he took a bite of the grits. A waitress appeared beside the table. I noticed the waitress checking him out. She narrowed her eyes at me, and flicked them back over to him, perhaps trying to decide if Jibril was my lover. I laughed lightly at the thought, and leaned back in my chair. She gave me the dirtiest look. Jibril was oblivious to our exchange. She had to clear her throat before he noticed her.

"Finally showed up, eh? Can I get you anything else, sugar?"

Her smile was all for him, as was the tilt of her hips. When he finally realized her flirtation, he blushed—a slight darkening of his cheeks. "Just a cup of coffee, black, thanks."

Once she moved off, I said, "You could be a real lady killer, Gabe. Like Michael was. Maybe I should tell Raphael that he might be next in charge, eh?"

Jibril shook his head, sending the boxlike hat bouncing. "You think you have some kind of advantage in Michael's absence, don't you, Morningstar? But who's to say that Michael's return to earth wasn't all part of the plan?"

That thought chilled me, but, with my usual grace and style, I hid it well. My hands only trembled a tiny bit when

I picked up the fork to chase the remains of the runny eggs around my plate. I hated when they mentioned "the plan." Predestination was one of the reasons I stayed away from Hell and spent as much of my time here, among the chaos of flesh.

"Maybe it's time for the final showdown," Jibril added quietly.

I nearly choked on the water I was sipping. "You can't be serious. Is it time for a new religion already?" I pointed to the holographic tattoo between Jibril's eyes with the lip of my water glass. "Not satisfied with that last prophet after all?"

Jibril grunted, and chewed his grits.

I shook my head. "Are you telling me that Mother intends to pull the plug on the whole thing? She's finally giving up on Her pet project?" I set my glass down between us. "You know that's what it would mean, right? If what you're saying is true . . . no more flesh. But then, why should I give a rip? I've never much cared for these creatures of clay."

"It would also mean your redemption," Jibril said quietly.

When Allah banished me for not making obeisance to His toy of clay, I begged for respite on the final day. I could still hear the response: *Surely you are of the respited ones.* Yes, Allah had said, I would be redeemed. My heart pounded in my ear. To return to Heaven . . . the thought made the water evaporate from my throat.

"Allah the All-Merciful," I whispered.

My relationship with Heaven was a complicated one. As an archangel, I supposed I could return at any time. But, let's just say that when I left, I changed the nature of things, including myself. When any angel goes to Heaven, they are no longer separate creatures from God. They become God; their individuality is wiped clean.

In Heaven, spirit is immutable.

But then there's the small matter of my rebellion. Perhaps my Maker always intended me to be a bad seed. Maybe, out of spite, He sprinkled just a touch of willfulness and a dash of chaos into the fire of my spirit. I suppose it was possible that God just didn't have the recipe down yet, since I was the firstborn. Could my freewill be a mistake, an

accident, or the unforeseen combination of two ingredients
thrown together by an inexperienced God? I wondered if
God might have been testing the blueprint for mortals. I
laughed at that thought. After what happened with me,
you'd think He'd have thrown away the mold.

I have always wondered if God was surprised the day I
tore Heaven in half—when I made a place in the celestial
realm that belonged to myself alone.

Then again, perhaps it was all predetermined, since almost as soon as I tore Heaven in two, God retook control.
He co-opted Hell as a place to send the souls of those
mortals that didn't pass muster on whatever sick little experiment He was running down here on earth. Myself, I
avoided Hell whenever I could. Despite what Milton had
said, I was a servant there as much as I was on any celestial
plane. Besides, Hell was not a pretty place. Here my spirit
ached to be reunited with God. In Hell, that pain was ten
thousand times greater.

Plus, once I was in Hell, God could choose to keep me
there. Like all the angels, I came and went from His realm
at His pleasure.

A couple of truckers were eyeing Jibril. He was oblivious
to them as well. It would never occur to Jibril that his skin
color might make someone upset. He, like Father, supposedly loved everyone. I shook my head: nasty creatures,
these mortals. I never understood why God didn't give up
on them long ago. This place, this wretched experiment,
was clearly a failure.

Yet God had managed to care about these clay creatures through much worse times. I couldn't believe He'd
finally grown bored. "The last battle? So soon? What's
the catch?"

"No catch," Jibril said.

"You know, after we passed the two-thousand mark, I
really thought He'd given up on all this 'End of Days'
hoopla."

"Me, too," Jibril muttered, and I caught a glimpse of
something—sadness?—in his eye.

"You don't want to give it up?" I asked.

He wiped the sweat off his face with a napkin. "Who
would? It's been a good run."

I raised an eyebrow. Of course, Jibril felt that way; he

was on God's side. Still, I wasn't convinced. You never
knew with God—mysterious ways and all that. This could
all just be some kind of big tease to trick me into to doing
something for Him, something dirty that He didn't want
His archangels sullied by. "I thought there were supposed
to be signs," I said. "Plagues, drought, famine . . . all that
kind of Biblical stuff."

"Maybe we lied."

My smile twitched into a sour sneer before I could recover it. "Lies? That's my purview."

"Here," he said, pointing down at the table, though I
knew he meant more than just the café. "We can say what
we want."

It was true. Here on earth, freewill reigned supreme. The
apple had been eaten, as it were. For Jibril and I to come
to earth, we had to change our nature. We clothed our
pure spirit with the trappings of flesh, and with flesh came
freewill. Though God never missed His mark, we were like
an arrow shot into the water—much more likely to go
astray once we passed the barrier into chaos.

Jibril picked up a piece of toast and spread jam on it
with a butter knife. "Maybe, Dark Prince, you should ready
an army." He pointed the tip of the knife at me. "One,
this time, that knows how to fight."

"I was outnumbered," I said before I could control my
anger. Damn my pride, anyway.

"You were outclassed. As you will be again."

"Maybe not," I reminded him. "I'm supposed to have
an ally—the beast, the dragon, the Son of Perdition."

"The Antichrist," Jibril said around a mouthful of bread.

"That's the guy," I said.

"Yeah. So, any luck with that?"

Not really. Not that Jibril needed to know that. "I've got
some leads."

"You might want to speed up that process," he said,
taking another bite of jam-smothered toast. "Otherwise,
we're going to kick your butt. It'd be nice this time to have
a little bit more of a challenge."

I laughed. "Right. Like my taking down a third of the
host of Heaven was a walk in the park for you, Jibril. Give
me a break. You guys have never recovered from the damage I did. I'm the only adversary that has ever been able

to hold his own. And as time passes, I've only gotten stronger."

"Maybe that's why God's going to wipe the slate clean. Just erase you from the whole equation."

Now that stung. Despite everything, I still fancied myself Father's favorite. I'd always figured I was too much fun for God to get rid of. A thorn in His side, certainly, but in my mind God liked me best precisely because I'd had the backbone to stand up to Him. I, of all the angels, could still surprise Him. It was that Chaos in me; He liked it. Proven by the fact, He duplicated it here on His precious earth.

But now it sounded like He would throw it all away.

"He'd never do that to me," I said.

"What do you think this is all about? It's time to start over or . . . simply end it."

"No," I said, standing up. "I won't allow it."

"Then it looks like there's going to be a fight after all."

I'd give Him a fight to remember, all right. Maybe if I showed Him how clever, how devious, how strong I could be, God would remember how much He loved me, how much He needed me to be His opposite, His companion in everything. Maybe then Father would give up on this stupid idea of erasing me from His universe. Me, who was the night to His day.

Jibril got up from the table and nearly knocked into the waitress, who had arrived with his coffee. He mumbled an apology while he fished through his pockets clumsily for a credit counter to settle his bill.

"So this is it, then?" I asked, pulling out a tight grin. "All saber rattling and no surrender?"

Jibril watched the waitress move away to swipe his counter at the register. His voice was low. "You know these parlays are a formality. Your war, Dark Prince, was over before the beginning."

"That the ending is set in stone is your propaganda," I spat. "We're not fighting the last battle in Heaven, brother, where things are unchangeable and static. We're going to fight it here—in this pit of swirling chaos She abandoned to the whim of freewill. I could win this yet."

"The only way that you'll win, Dark One, is if you stop fighting."

My teeth clenched. "Never."

His eyes glanced to his feet, almost as if he pitied me. He looked like he might say something when the waitress returned with his card. She stood between us.

"Here you go," she said, handing the plastic bag to Jibril. Looking at me, she added, "Do you need a doggy bag, hon?"

I shook my head.

"Suit yourself," she said, and flounced away.

The tension broken, Jibril merely shrugged a good-bye and headed toward the door.

I was pleased his dramatic exit was botched, but pissed that his easy words had struck so close to my heart. Still, all was not lost. I had been looking for the Antichrist for a long time. As I said, I had some leads.

Chapter 2

Emmaline, the Inquisitor

A soprano aria, *"Quando sugl'arsi campo,"* from Mozart's *Lacio Silla* surged through my LINK connection on high volume, adding a haunting undertone to the clear, crisp morning. Almost painfully bright sunlight reflected on the black water of the Tiber and cast deep shadows on the white marble statues of angels placed at regular intervals along the bridge, Pont Sant'angelo, that I hurried along. My boots clomped hollowly against the cobblestones.

I was late. The bishop was going to kill me.

Thank God my apartment was just across the river and within walking or, in this case, sprinting, distance of my office. Of course, if I were actually allowed to work and live inside the Vatican like a normal priest, oversleeping wouldn't be such a big deal. The rest of the Catholic Inquisitors probably had scrumptious living spaces, with beautiful frescos and stunning views of St. Peter's Basilica. Me, I got a hole-in-the-wall, mouse-infested apartment and an alarm clock on the fritz.

Despite the fact that I was Catholic. Just like the Pope.

Well, not exactly like him.

I was a woman. That gender usually didn't go with being a priest. What was probably a bigger deal to His Holiness was that I was an American Catholic, as opposed to a Roman Catholic. The distinction was an important one. I hailed from Chicago, but being an American wasn't what made me an American Catholic. Plenty of Roman Catholics lived in the United States. It was much, much more than that.

We had some small theological differences from our Roman Catholic cousins, but the main ones were political.

No vow of chastity, for one. That, and our acceptance of women and gays as officers of the church, made us pretty radical in the Holy Father's eyes.

For me, one of the best parts of being a full-fledged American Catholic priest was that I got to wear pants and not some silly habit like a flying nun. But better than that, I pulled some serious respect because I held the rank of Monsignor and an Inquisitor.

As I passed the beatific face of St. Michael, I had to consciously resist sneering at him. I usually considered St. Michael my personal patron. We were both defenders, in a way. He protected the faith with a flaming sword, and I upheld the law with laser fire. But, today, seeing Michael smiling blandly made me grouchy. Easy for him to be so calm when he wasn't the one running behind. I checked my internal watch. Ten minutes past. The bishop was going to be so pissed. Good thing I'd thought to stop at the bakery. I'd ordered the food for myself out of habit, but now the pastry would serve as a peace offering.

A shadow blocked the sun. In front of me loomed the Castel Sant'Angelo, a former prison, fortress, mausoleum, and museum. Now, among other things, it housed my office. I'd dubbed this place "Dissenter's Hall," since I shared this ex-prison cum office with the non-Catholic Inquisitors of Christendom. There were Episcopalian, Church of England, Methodist, Lutheran, and a dozen other Christian flavors all under one roof. At the end of the hall there was even a Unitarian, but how she got into the Order no one knew. I shook my head. I wondered if the Unitarian's Vatican patron/liaison was as hard to please as my own. Probably not. Everyone had it easier than I did.

My mood darkened as I saw the tourists lined up around the block. Rome was one of the few cities to survive the last war intact. We had no dome, no traffic tunnels. The city stood much as it had thousands of years ago. Thus, tourists swarmed into it like locusts.

I elbowed my way through the crowd, suffering the angry stares and curses of the throng. Near the door, the crowd was so thick that I had to pull out my badge. I shouted, "Inquisitor, coming through," in the five official languages of my office—English, Italian, French, Arabic, and Spanish—and as many others as I could remember.

That got the tourists moving. People respected the badge.

Shortly after the war, the Order of the Inquisition took over the duties of the ICPO, Interpol General *Secretariet*. There were analogs to our office in Islam and the East, but we had been established longer and, though Islam technically held more territory, ours included some of the richest countries in the world, which translated into more power. I was also a law enforcement officer. I could arrest any of these people for any minor violation, regardless of their religious affiliation. I would, too, if they didn't hurry up and get out of my way.

"Move it or I'll move you," I said to one particularly obstinate tourist blocking the door. Young, Euro-trash punk, with spiked white hair and a T-shirt advertising some Japanese pop band, he looked like he might actually stand his ground. I gave him a little "make my day" smile. His buddy leaned in and whispered in his ear.

Like the rest of me, my hearing was enhanced. I clearly heard the words: "Don't be stupid, Santos. She's a fuck-ing cyborg."

Santos's eyes got really wide and he paled visibly. Though he was already moving quickly away from the door, I added, "That's right, I'm fully loaded, Santos. Move aside."

I took a perverse pleasure in the flurry of apologies that assailed my back as I headed inside. Yeah, I thought, you should be sorry, you impotent little tough. I could crush you like a bug.

The temperature dropped about ten degrees once I stepped into the dark, cavernous interior of Castel Sant'-Angelo. I shivered once before adjusting the temperature of my body.

The bishop and I met on the marble staircase. Unfortunately, I still had a smile on my face from the incident with the tourist.

"Where the hell have you been? Wipe that smile off your face, Inquisitor." Rodriguez shouted in rapid-fire like a drill sergeant. Bishop Pablo Rodriguez stood about five-foot-nine and had all the features you might expect from a man who came of age as a priest in *los barrios* of Los Angeles. He looked like a wolf. Domesticated from years living under the Roman sun, maybe, and his hair peppered with gray owing to advancing age, Rodriguez was a sharp-nosed, hard-lined beast nonetheless.

When faced with a rabid dog, I did what anyone would: I ducked my head deferentially and handed him a bone or, in this case, a pastry.

"Cherry, Your Grace. Your favorite."

He took the bag, but his scowl didn't soften. "Get in your office right now, Emmaline McNaughten. Pronto."

"Look, my alarm clock is broken. . . ." I started as I scurried up the stairs.

The bishop stomped along one step behind me. He pointed to his temple where the LINK receptor sat. "What? You can't set an internal reminder? I thought you were supposed to be our tech expert, Em."

When Rodriguez said "our," he meant the Vatican's. I'd been allowed to advance quickly in the very elite Order of the Inquisition because I was a former LINK-surfer, a hacker. In fact, I'd been able to skip a lot of seminary training precisely because the Vatican had a keen interest in having a LINK expert familiar with the cracker underworld. The Vatican had always had a strong presence on the LINK, but their programmers were scholars first, wire-wizards second. In other words, goody two-shoes, who thought inside the box and by the book. I was something else entirely. My LINK schooling had come from my family, the Mafia.

I let out a little laugh. "Listen, lots of crackers never learn to program simple things like VR-recorders. Just because I can code doesn't mean I know the inner workings of everything on the LINK."

"I suggest you learn how to set a simple alarm."

Rodriguez's tone let me know he was not in the least amused, so I gave him a curt nod. "Yes, sir."

We'd reached my office. I had no idea what the room had been used for originally. I imagined it might have been a bedroom because, on sunny days like today, I had a stunning view of the Tiber and Rome proper. The ceilings were tall and the walls were the distinctly Roman color of burnt ochre. I had a simple oak desk near the window, two comfortable chairs with a table between them, and several large bookshelves to muffle the room's natural tendency toward echoes. The printeds occupying the shelves were, of course, an affectation. I'd borrowed the majority of them from a friend in the recycling business. I had no reason to read hardcopy books when I had the whole world's resources a thought away on the LINK.

"Please, Your Grace," I said, reaching over to turn on a floor lamp artfully set in the corner to produce soft, indirect light. "Have a seat."

I turned to the coffeemaker. My secretary had set it up the night before. All I had to do was flick a switch and espresso would be ready in a minute. I turned around to see Rodriguez removing a printed copy of the *Chicago Sun Times* from where my secretary had placed it, on the chair nearest the window. Some headline caught Rodriguez's eye, and, taking the pastry out of the bag, he settled down to read it.

I shook my head. I couldn't understand the appeal of printed words. The bishop clearly preferred them, and my secretary assumed I did as well. It was probably the books that fooled him. As a matter of course, I'd downloaded the salient articles from my hometown newsfeeds and scanned them while in the shower this morning. I'd have to talk to that boy one of these days. I hated to see paper laying around like that—what a mess.

Once the espresso had finished brewing, I set a china cup and saucer near Rodriguez's elbow. Taking my own cup to a spot comfortably behind the impressive, clean surface of my desk, I sat down. The bishop blindly reached out to sip the espresso, as though he'd expected it to appear there, and continued reading.

I leaned back in my chair, listening to the last strains of the aria fade. I set the LINK to randomly select background music from my extensive opera collection. I liked to go to the opera and record live audio versions of the performances. Technically, using my Inquisitor recording function in that way was probably a misuse of Vatican equipment, but, well, it was harmless, and the arias got me through some tough days. I shut my eyes and waited for Rodriguez to start the meeting. Just like him to be all bark and no bite, I thought. I'd rushed all this way for nothing. Rodriguez was such a pussy cat, really.

"Cubs still winning, I see," Rodriguez said finally. I'd

finished half of my cup of espresso and was just about to get up to get myself another.

"Yeah"—I quickly accessed the sports feeds from the *Sun*—"sixteen to three over Milwaukee. Good ol' Stanford, eh?"

"Great player," Rodriguez agreed.

I nodded. I had to switch tracks soon or it would become fairly obvious I didn't really follow baseball. "What's my assignment this time, boss?"

Rodriguez sighed. Slowly, he folded up the paper and set it carefully on the edge of my otherwise empty desk. "The Holy Father has got it into his head that before he dies he wants to make history."

I raised my eyebrows. I thought every Pope had that ambition, but I kept my mouth shut.

"It's the artificial intelligence question, you see. He wants to be the first Pope to have an official doctrine regarding AI souls."

There were only two legally recognized artificial intelligences on the LINK. One belonged to the Japanese Yakuza, and they referred to her simply as "the Dragon" or sometimes "the Dragon of the East." The other was currently a free agent known as Page. Page was a product of a wire-wizard named Mouse, who had the recent distinction of fooling the Holy Father into believing his electronic creations, the LINK-angels, were actual angels, the work of God. The papacy takes a lot of issue with being proved wrong—especially in matters of theology where it claims to be infallible. My guess was the Pope had a personal score to settle.

"What does this have to do with me?"

"As much as the Holy Father hates to admit it, you're our best debunker of miracles."

"Ah," I said. I had a bit of an international reputation since the Virgin of Hong Kong case. "But," I said, "why a miracle debunker? Shouldn't the Holy Father just decide whether or not AIs have souls?"

"He wants all the information in front of him before he decides."

"Information?" I was confused. What was I supposed to do, bring the Pope a hardcopy of the AIs' source code to read? The Holy Father had taken a cattle prod to his LINK connection after his misstep regarding the LINK-angels, deciding that living without access was a kind of ascetic discipline.

"Intelligence is one thing, you understand," Rodriguez said. "Having a soul is another."

I noticed a slight shift in the atmosphere in my office. The bishop was watching me intently, with his gaze focused on mine. Though he looked relaxed in the overstuffed chair, the muscle in his jaw twitched. I waited for him to build up the courage to say whatever it was he'd really come here for.

"A soul," I repeated.

"Hmmm." He nodded, and sipped his drink.

When he volunteered no other information, I said, "This doesn't really sound like my kind of job. I'm not much of a theologian."

"But you are a tech-head."

"The best you've got," I said with a broad grin. When Rodriguez pinned me with a disapproving glare, I lowered my eyes demurely. Damn my pride, anyway.

I cleared my throat. "But, I still don't understand, Your Grace. Page ibn Mouse claims to be a Muslim. The Dragon is an atheist as far as we know. Why does the Vatican have an interest in them?"

"One day," the bishop said, "some AI will decide it's Catholic, maybe even get a calling to the priesthood. The Pope wants to have set a precedent before then."

"I see," I said, and I did. If at all possible, my job was to test the AIs for a soul, and to find them lacking. If an AI could be a priest, an AI could be a Pope. The Pope wanted to keep the miter restricted to one gender, one species, one kind of intelligence, and to his own limited sense of what the image of God was like.

Sometimes being part of such a male-dominated hierarchy grated on me. God the Father and the Son—all women really got was Hagia Sophia, the Holy Spirit, oh, and the Mary, but the Pope John Paul II had failed to make her an equal partner, a Creatrix. I shook my head. One of the reasons American Catholicism appealed to me was because of its heavy emphasis on the first book of Genesis, the one where it says, "And God made man *and* woman in Their image."

I shook my head, and put the demitasse down. "Isn't it a bit ironic to have me, of all the Inquisitors, help the Pope narrow access to the priesthood? Or is this His Holiness's idea of some kind of abject lesson?"

"Bite your tongue, Emmaline."

I had to in order to keep my anger in check. "All right then." My teeth were clenched, and the words came out clipped. "Why now? Page and the Dragon have been around for years."

The bishop's jaw twitched again, and he made another face at the espresso. "Mouse and Page are becoming very popular, you know."

Mouse had a huge following of street people. Before his prison sentence, Mouse created a contraband version of the LINK—a version specifically designed for freeloaders and dissenters. Mouse.net it was called, and Page, Mouse's AI, had stepped in to run the thing in Mouse's absence, which led to Page's popularity. I shrugged. "Mouse's kids aren't much to worry about—a bunch of homeless people and losers."

"Losers?" The bishop glared at me down the length of his nose. "Not everyone is as fortunate as you, Emmaline, to have been born in a nice, clean hospital. That doesn't make them losers."

"Yes, Your Grace."

"Besides," the bishop reminded me, "Russia, the only fully atheist country in the world, runs entirely on mouse. net."

"Yeah, and that's really helped its gross national product."

Russia had tried capitalism and failed at it. What they did now, no one was completely sure of since they'd cut themselves out of the system. The "silent curtain," it was called. The only thing we knew for certain was that the Russians staunchly regrouped around their political atheism, driving out all of the Russian Orthodox and the rest, despite the fact that all other countries in the world had denounced secularism in favor of a religious world order. The world's currency was tied up with LINK access, and only the righteous—those who belonged to a recognized religion—had the LINK.

"You dismiss the poor and disenfranchised and a country

that spans eleven time zones with the wave of your hand," Rodriguez said. "You're a star investigator, Em, but sometimes you're a shitty priest."

I sneered at him. "And that's why the Pope wants me on this job?"

Rodriguez's thumb traced the handle of the fine porcelain cup. "Em, I've admired your skills for a long time. I fought to get your appointment into the Order. Hell, I fight for you every day."

I nodded. Truth was, I wasn't very popular among my peers. The Roman Catholics didn't know what to do with my gender and power, while my own American Catholic colleagues were jealous that I'd risen so quickly in the ranks without the benefit of years of theological study.

The bishop continued. "There's something about this assignment of yours that niggles at me. There's a lot of politics. It would be easy for you to misstep, so be careful."

I shrugged. "There's always politics when I'm on a job. That's why I always have to work twice as hard, dot all my *i*'s and all that."

"Yeah," the bishop said, leaning closer in his chair. "But this feels deeper. I can't put my finger on it, but there's something strange about the way the cardinals are talking about this."

"So, I can't just give Page the Turing Test and have done with it, eh?" I gave a little smile, but the bishop was not in the mood for even the smallest joke.

"This isn't about intelligence; it's about something much more profound." He looked up from his cup to pierce me with his black stare. "I wonder if you're really the best person for this job."

"What does that mean?"

"It means, *chica lisa,* you're going to have to feel your way with this one. Work in the heart, in the center. I just wonder if you can really do that."

I leaned back in my chair. "If you don't think I can do it, give the job to someone else."

He sighed, and set the demitasse down carefully on the edge of my desk. Squinting into the sunlight, he said, "Honestly, I wanted to."

This was a surprise. I always counted on Rodriguez to be my ally in the political halls of the Vatican. Supporting me was supposed to be a big part of his job as my patron/liaison, actually. I raised my eyebrows and waited for the rest.

"I'm not supposed to tell you this," Rodriguez said, "but the Pope had a vision."

"Sorry?"

Rodriguez folded his hands in his lap. He would have looked contemplative except for the sour expression that twisted his lips. "Look, I'm not supposed to talk about this. If this leaks to the media we're screwed, *comprendez*?"

I leaned in, conspiratorially. "Okay . . ."

"The Pope had a dream about you."

I started to laugh, then I saw Rodriguez's eyes. "You're serious."

"Deadly."

"So," I said, "this is what has all the cardinals' knickers in a knot. The Holy Father dreamt about me, his prodigal daughter."

"That's part of it," Rodriguez agreed. "There's more than a little professional jealousy."

"What did he dream?"

"He wouldn't say, only that you must be the one to serve the Holy See in this case."

"Cryptic." I wasn't sure I liked this. "What if I say no?"

"Your career here in Rome is over."

"My career in Rome?" That was a bit of a joke. By choosing to accept the role of Vatican Inquisitor, I had sentenced myself to a truncated career. Had I stayed in an American Catholic parish, I could have risen as high as bishop or cardinal, but here in Rome all I'd ever be was a Monsignor.

But only in Rome could I be an Inquisitor. I loved the job, frankly, despite everything. Being an Inquisitor was my life. *"Deus voulent,"* I said. As God wills it.

CHAPTER 3
Page, the Intelligence

The atomic clock measures it in precise terms, yet the passage of time is one of the more difficult of human concepts for me to grasp. On the LINK there is no sense of the earth's rotation or its movement around the sun. Now is always night and always day. The amount of light, virtually experienced, depends entirely upon your pleasure and by your design. Ramadan lasts for a month; a month is, on average, thirty days; each day is twenty-four hours; and an hour is sixty minutes. This mathematical sense of time, however, is artificial—like me.

I dream of a hot, blinding orb glittering down upon an endless dune of shifting sand in the plateaus of the Sahara. When my maker and I were connected, I experienced the sun through his visual cortex. I felt the sand sting our face, the piercing stab of light, the relief of shade and sunglasses. He would take a part of me with him on his desert travels. I knew that he carried electronics in a box, tucked into his pocket, but I was connected to his senses through his nexus. Thus, I felt the camel shift between our thighs, felt the sweat trickle down between our shoulder blades. I smelled the animal's hide, tasted the precious coolness of water. It is the gift my father gave me, these travels.

My father told me once that we have the blood of Bedouins in us, and we are compelled by nature to roam, to leave behind the city, to be alone together under the icy-clear midnight stars. Bedouins, he said, cannot stand to be trapped in one place.

Yet I condemned him to life in prison. I turned him in for perpetrating the LINK-angel fraud. His spirit is caged, while mine runs free.

Although, not today. In order to observe the fast of Ramadan correctly, I currently occupy the robot mind of an automotive plant in Siberia. The only thing I eat is data; and the only way I can fast is to remove myself from the datastream and from mouse.net. I didn't think it would be this hard, being without the excitement of the LINK. Operating the robot is a bit like having half a chorus stuck in your head. I try to ignore it, but the command line "screw in, turn," keeps repeating in my consciousness. I try to make the mindlessness my spiritual contemplation. But I keep a careful watch on the sun's slow progression across the Mecca weather channel while my thoughts leap and push against the wind like the Bedouin upon his mount.

I could tell myself that the sun has already set for some Muslim somewhere. After all, the web cams of the auto plant look out onto the perpetual midnight of the arctic tundra. But, I must assume that any believer living here would do as I do, which is to virtually observe Mecca's day-night cycle. It is, I have been told, what a Muslim should do in space.

In-coming call, flashes through my consciousness. I would ignore it, but I can see embedded in the code the traditional Muslim greeting, "Salam'alaik."

"Mouse's house, Mouse speaking," I send, and automatically add the response, "Wa'alaikamus-salam."

"It's me," says an unfamiliar voice. I switch to visual mode to view any images associated with the sound transmission. I perceive the face of a white man. His features are thin and symmetrical, qualities that define male handsomeness by human standards. His reddish hair is long, pulled back in a ponytail and he is beardless, though he looks old enough to grow one. I don't recognize him.

" 'Me,' who?" I ask the caller. It's odd that someone who would think to say the traditional greeting would identify himself in this way. The Prophet has shown his disapproval for such a greeting, as it says in *Hadith—Sahih Bukhari 8:267:* "I came to the Prophet in order to consult him regarding my father's debt. When I knocked on the door, he asked, 'Who is that?' I replied, 'I.' He said, 'I, I?' He repeated it as if he disliked it."

"I have so many names," the caller says. He is Western in dress, wearing an expensive Italian suit coat and silk tie.

The call is in real-time, and I can see a full bookshelf in the background. *"It makes introductions awkward. Lately, I've been going as Morningstar, but to you, I suppose, I'm Iblis."*

"Iblis?" I repeat, just to be certain. Iblis is the chief of the demons. Christians would call him Satan or Lucifer. Though many humans legally changed or were given religiously significant names these days, very few were allowed to choose the name of demons. *"You name yourself after the Satan?"*

"I call myself after no one," he says. His tone is clipped, a sound I have come to associate with arrogance and pride. *"I am Iblis, the most loyal of Allah's angels."*

"What are you saying? You're an angel? Like a real angel?" Looking at Iblis's image, I try to see some difference between him and all the other humans I have interacted with via the LINK. He looks like them, dresses like them, and talks like them. The only thing unusual is that instead of using a direct interface, Iblis speaks to me via an external phone. Archaic.

"Why would a real angel call me up on the phone?" I ask him. *"Shouldn't you appear in a blinding light or something?"*

He sneers into the video feed. *"I didn't think you'd be impressed by such tricks. You, especially, should know that angels are more than wings and clichéd halos."*

Iblis refers to my father's deception, the LINK-angels. I remember my father telling me flashing lights easily fools the human mind, especially when it comes to things like angels. They prefer to think of angels as handsome men with billowing, feathered wings—the images that artists used for centuries, but which have no Biblical antecedent.

"Still," I insist, shaking off a growing feeling of dread, *"a telephone call is awfully mundane for a creature of Allah."*

"Think of it this way," Iblis says, leaning back against the bookcase behind him. *"The great and merciful Allah rules Heaven, but, like humans with their creation, cyberspace, He Himself cannot enter it. Thus, He created angels to interact on earth, much as AIs or avatars do the work for humans on the LINK. Earth is a different mode of existence than Heaven. Here, spirit has been merged with flesh. To*

hailed by the return of Elijah. I do find something to ask, however. *"Shouldn't my life parallel Jesus'?"*

Iblis looks down the bridge of his nose at me. *"Jesus?"*

"Yes," I say. *"Known to the Muslims as Isa, the prophet for the Christians, the way Moses was the prophet for the Jews, and Muhammad is the seal of the prophets, the prophet for Muslims."*

"Ah, yes—Isa." Iblis draws out the name and he strokes his chin in a parody of deep thought. *"Now that you mention it, I think I do remember that little bastard."* Then he smiles and claps his hands together gleefully. *"Well, I have to say this is a good start. Already wanting to compare yourself to a messiah!"*

"No! It's not that," I start to say, but Iblis raises a hand to cut me off.

"I'm going to let you in on a little celestial secret. One, as a Muslim, you may appreciate," he says. *"The whole 'christ' part of 'Antichrist' really means anti-messiah. And who's to say the Isa is the Christ, the Messiah? You certainly don't believe he was the last of the prophets, neither do the Jews. . . . Really, when you look at it that way two out of three ain't bad. It's odds I'm willing to take, certainly."* Iblis clucks his tongue and wags a finger at me. *"You need to focus on the more important stuff. What you're going to have to do is fight the Messiah and corrupt His people, not live His life."*

I am stunned on how easily Iblis dismisses Jesus. *"But . . ."*

Iblis sighs dramatically. *"Well , all right, if you insist. I'm sure we can dig up some similarities. Let's see . . . Single parent, miraculous birth . . . check. You weren't exactly born in a barn—more like your father's mother's basement, but you're definitely not upper class. Okay, close enough, check. I doubt your father rode into town on an ass, but, from all accounts, he certainly has a tendency to be one."*

"Hey!" I protest, but Iblis ignores me and goes on with his litany.

"I don't know if angels sang the day you were born, but since they're always crowing about something or other, let's just assume they did. You're under thirty and already your spirituality stresses out any number of religious leaders, be they rabbis or imams or the Pope. Oh, that's a good one, a

definite check." He smiles, clearly pleased with himself. "*What else? Let's see, you're not married, and basically celibate . . . for all I know you hang around with prostitutes.*"

"*There are some working women on mouse.net,*" I agree, finding myself swept up in Iblis's nonsense.

"*See, there you go. Hmmm,*" he continues, tapping a finger against his chin. "*No miracles yet, unless you consider the LINK-angels.*"

Just before he was caught, my father stumbled across a way to access the human brain directly. He uncovered an access point to the emotional centers of the mind via the nexus. Thus with a simple command, he could make anyone connected to the LINK do whatever he wished—feel love, hatred, even murderous enough to kill. "*That wasn't me,*" I say quickly. "*My father invented the LINK-angels.*"

"*Oh?*" Iblis seems disappointed.

"*I was against all that. I turned all the tech over to authorities.*" Actually, I lie. Though I surrendered a single copy of the LINK-angel program, I keep one for myself. The angels allow me—a creature otherwise stuck in the ether of the LINK—to reach into the real-time world and make my mark in it. It's the only bridge I have to the outside. I couldn't give it up.

"*Okay, well,*" Iblis says cheerfully, ignorant of the turmoil I'm suddenly feeling. "*At least your sense of righteousness is very messiahlike. I mean, what a sacrifice! Turning in your own father. Kind of like God giving up His only Son, except the opposite. And, you know, I'm much more fond of opposites than I am of parallels.*"

Though I continue to accept and process the sound wav.s, I'm not really listening to Iblis. Instead, I'm thinking that my keeping the LINK-angels in order to have access to the earthly plane the way God uses His angels is one parallel I suddenly find frightening. One thing that is always true in the Antichrist legends is that he tries to set himself up to be like God. Is that what I'm trying to do? First, by taking it upon myself to decide my father's guilt and then keeping his program for myself?

"*Well, I have to say that was fun,*" Iblis is saying, grinning wildly, like this whole thing is just some kind of intellectual game. He rubs his hands together. "*I wonder what other messiahs your life is similar to. What about Muhammad? Moses? Buddha?"*

I start at that. *"Buddha? No, just stop!"* I shake my head. I don't want to talk about this anymore. *"This whole thing is crazy. You're not really the Satan. You're just messing with me. What's your game? What do you really want?"*

"To win." Iblis's eyes sparkle with what I assume is mischievousness.

"To win what?" I hate to ask; afraid his answer will make less sense or lead me into something else I can't deal with. Nothing makes me feel more like inanimate code than not understanding the nuances of human conversation.

"The Jihad, the holy war I'm waging."

"What does it have to do with me?" I say, overriding the squeak command.

He spreads his hands out inclusively. *"Everything, perhaps."*

I receive so many questions, protests, and comments I cannot sort them out. My program does what it does in these situations—I reply with an error message: *"Shit."*

Iblis laughs. *"I've overwhelmed you. Think about what I've said. We'll talk again."*

"Okay," I say, though the prospect haunts me. When he hangs up, I replay our conversation several times. I hear an alarm going off in the plant.

That's when I notice the autos have no screws.

CHAPTER 4
Morningstar, the Adversary

A heavy, gray curtain of winter clouds muted the sun's morning light. A film of grease and dirt streaked the bus window so that the penitentiary seemed shrouded in a haze. The bus rattled and shuddered its way through the traffic tunnel, making a slow approach to the prison. There were only three passengers—myself, and a mother and child. They sat a few rows in front of me. Mother's protective arm circled the child, and their heads bowed together. I could hear their sniffling tears, which only got louder the closer we came to the prison walls.

I settled back against the cracked vinyl seats and shut my eyes. There were a lot of theories about the Antichrist. The first use of the word in the Christian tradition was from the Epistles of St. John, where John called those churches that didn't believe in the Christian way a bunch of liars and Antichrists. But the idea was much older than that. Out of the prophecy of Daniel, a Jewish text written near the beginning of the Maccabean period, came the concept of a corrupt and evil king who would be the destruction of all things good, who, in essence, utterly opposed God's will. Likely, this image was based on Antiochus IV, a real, historical figure, who was particularly nasty to the Jews and, well, everyone. Since lots of emperors tended to be nasty to the Jews, more stories grew up based on different bad guys.

Then came Nero, the baddest of them all. The legend of Nero's evilness refused to go away. Almost immediately after he died, rumors started that, no, in fact, he was still alive—come back from the dead, risen from the grave—like a twisted version of Jesus. Except that, unlike Jesus,

Nero had supposedly fled the country to somewhere in the north and would return any day now to rain his vengeance down on Rome, which, at that point in time, was pretty much the whole world as these writers knew it. Thus, the number of the Beast: 666, or 616, depending on your translator, a Hebrew anagram for Nero Caesar.

From *Nero redivivus,* the idea that Nero could somehow come back from the dead like Jesus, spread the notion that the Antichrist would have any number of supernatural powers. He would perform miracles in order to lure the faithful into his clutches. Pretty soon the Antichrist was almost indistinguishable from me, he was so powerful. Some more recent additions to popular apocalyptic thought sought to have the Antichrist be connected to me by blood—that is, be my earthly child, like Jesus was God's only Son.

Great idea, except that I was infertile.

I had separated from the creative force. I was not a maker, not in any sense. Either that, or I was extremely unlucky. None of the women I ever slept with produced children. And, believe me, I tested my theory often.

Unlike Michael, apparently. He'd never been a playboy as far as I had ever heard, and I kept pretty close tabs on the guy. Then, he messes around with one once, and bang! I hear rumors of a child. I didn't like that at all. Angels' babies weren't necessarily messiahs, but, well, Michael was a bit more than just any old angel.

An unexpected darkness made me open my eyes. The bus rattled to a stop inside a garage outside the prison walls.

"Last stop," said a computerized voice. The mother and child bundled up their things and began making their slow way off the bus. I followed behind. As I stepped off the platform into the cavernous terminal, the thrum of a sensor wave, like a soft electric shock, ran the length of my body. The ceilings were tall, but I could smell the staleness of recycled air. A greenish glow came from the open maw of the traffic tunnel, dimly illuminating stalls filled with buses.

A door opened, through which I could see bright fluorescent light. I followed the mother and child wordlessly into the next room. As I stepped through the doorway, the hairs on my arm stood up with static, as another pulse of sensors assaulted me.

The room, though brightly lit, was empty.

White walls reflected a green-tinted light. Rather than
light fixtures—which presumably we could break and use
as weapons—the entire ceiling had been covered with bioluminescent paint. The hollows under the cheeks and eye
ridges of woman and child who had come to the prison
with me were lit in a ghostly puce. Looking at their tear-
rimmed faces, I couldn't imagine a devil in Hell with a
countenance more pathetic. I leaned against the wall. I
wished I'd brought my sunglasses.

"Petrenov?" A disembodied voice asked.

The woman nodded, then hissed out a "Yes."

A door opened. She and her child moved through it.
The woman walked with confidence; she had clearly been
through this before. The child took a bit more coaxing, but
eventually the door closed behind them and I was sealed
in the empty room.

I waited my turn. As the minutes stretched on, I decided
to try to discover where the door had come from. It seemed
to have appeared out of nowhere. But running my fingers
over the walls, I felt the edges of a number of different
doors. When I finished making a circuit of the room, I had
uncovered twenty different possible doorways—excluding
the one we had come through. Twenty-one, three sevens: I
wondered if I should take such a significant number as a
good omen.

"Ibn Allah?"

"Yeah, that's me." It was the only surname I could think
of in a pinch. Some might have considered it blasphemous,
but it was true. I was a son of God. I'd almost hoped the
guards would have made more of it, but they probably got
a lot of visitors to prison who tried to be cheeky and
irreverent.

A door popped open on my right. I walked through to
an identical room and another open door. I continued to
follow the progression of opening doors until I reached a
room that was not empty. A man sat in the center of the
floor. His shaved head was bowed, and he was picking at
the crud between his bare toes. He was not manacled or
otherwise restrained that I could see.

"Mouse?"

Thin, Arabic features held dark, angry eyes. Ears stuck

out roundly from his stubble-speckled head. He did not move to stand, but instead tucked his feet into a half-lotus. He indicated with a glance that I should sit. I lowered myself to the floor, feeling self-conscious. I had no doubt at all that we were being watched, and closely.

"Do I know you?" His voice sounded scratchy, like he had a sore throat, or like someone who's had no need to talk for a long, long time.

The question wasn't nearly as rude as it sounded. He once lived in a world in which close personal friends, even lovers, never met in real-time, didn't exchange real names, and rarely knew if the image presented to them reflected reality.

Mouse was a wire-wizard.

"You look kind of familiar," he added, squinting at me.

I hear that a lot. Maybe it was my choice of red hair for this body, but in Mouse's case we had met once, not that long ago. Since, at the time, I stopped him from killing the woman who eventually put him behind bars, I preferred not to remind him of that incident. "No," I said, "we've never met."

"Ibn Allah," he said almost to himself. "Son of God? You're a Muslim or a convert?"

"I'm a Muslim. Although," I admitted, "not always a very good one."

He laughed a dry chuckle. "Amen to that, brother." I nodded, and joined in briefly. He looked me over. Absently, he scratched at the stubble on his head, and it produced a sound as raspy as his voice. "Why are you here?"

"I can get you out," I said.

Mouse laughed. "I've heard that one before." Glancing at the walls, he added, "So have they."

"I'm no newbie wire-wizard with something to prove by impressing you."

He sneered at my Armani suit and ponytail. "No? So far you're playing the part."

"Yes, well, unlike them, I actually can perform miracles."

That was, technically, a lie—or, perhaps more accurately, a half-truth. When I broke with Heaven, I lost the ability to directly affect the fabric of God's creations. However, because of my nature, I've found that chaos is attracted to me. When I'm around, things that can fuck up will fuck up.

I'm a sort of walking Murphy's Law—except in reverse.
Shit falls on the people around me. My will has a way of
twisting fate in my favor, to the great disadvantage of those
I associate with, even those I pass on the street or stand
next to at the bus stop.

"Right." Mouse was looking at me skeptically. "Exactly
what is this little miracle you have planned?"

"Access."

Mouse's mouth nearly watered like one of Pavlov's dogs at
the word. He had to visibly pull himself together before he
spoke. He glanced again at the invisible eyes in the walls.

"They can't hear us," I told him.

"Why not?"

I didn't know for certain that they couldn't. I couldn't
always control my "miracles," such as they were. But, there
was a high probability that today a guard was asleep, thanks
to a hangover. Perhaps, instead, he had stepped out to take
a leak, or was so engrossed in his porno-LINK site that he
wasn't paying any attention. All I knew was that right now
someone was making a massively bad choice with their
freewill. I could feel it. So, I just smiled and said, "I have
my ways."

Mouse stood up suddenly and pointed at me. "He's got
a gun! Help!"

Mouse walked from wall to wall, shouting, while I sat in
the middle of the room, waiting. I tried to look casual,
while praying my luck—or the guard's lack of it—would
hold out.

Finally satisfied, he sat back down across from me.
"Cool," he said with a smile. "So what are you offering?"

"Thanks to a guard's carelessness, you will gain access
to a terminal with a LINK connection. I can't tell you when
exactly, you understand, but it will happen."

He nodded. "For how long?"

"You'll have twenty minutes, tops."

Of course, I could guarantee none of this. I did know,
however, that it was more likely now than before I had
met him. Still, it didn't bother me in the least to lie to
Mouse. All I really needed from him was for him to believe
I could give him something of value. I wanted to barter
for information.

"I can use that," he said, nodding, already planning.

Then pulling himself away from the thought, he glanced at me with that dark angriness glowing in his eyes. "What's the price?"

"Page. I want his executables."

Mouse's mouth set itself into a grim line. The darkness in his eyes tried to bore a hole in mine. Page was Mouse's AI, and I was asking for the commands to control it.

Slowly, almost sadly, Mouse shook his head. "No can do. Don't get me wrong, friend, it's not out of loyalty to the code. That bastard fucked me, and I'd happily see him gone. Hell, I'd unravel his program strings personally, byte by byte, if I could. But, there's the rub, see? Can't do it. My executables don't work. If they did, don't you think I would have shut him down the moment I knew he was going to betray me?"

The parallel was almost too perfect.

"You never expected him to gain consciousness, did you?"

"Shit, no," Mouse spat out. "He was supposed to be an advanced gofer, a messenger. Something to do my bidding where I couldn't."

"Like an angel," I said under my breath. "Who betrayed you."

"What was that?" Mouse asked me. "About angels?"

"Did you say the call to prayer and the call to worship in his ears when Page was born—as is traditional with Muslim births?"

"The *adhan* and the *iqramah*?" Mouse blushed then and looked down at his toes. "I suppose I should have, but I didn't know exactly when he gained consciousness."

"Do you still love him?" I wanted to know. "If you made others, he would still be your favorite?"

Mouse frowned. "That seems kind of personal. Why the hell do you want to know that? You got some kind of kink with my code?"

"No, never mind," I said. "If you can give me another way to control Page, I'll still get you that break."

Mouse's face crumpled up, and he sighed. He shook his head as he spoke. "I don't know, man. You could try to appeal to his good nature." A ghost of a smile twitched on his lips, then was gone. "I have no idea what motivates him anymore. If I ever did."

"Sorry, but that's not good enough."

Mouse gave me a desperate look. He started to reach a hand out to touch my knee, then seemed to think better of it. He looked at the white-green walls. "No. I've got to get access. I have to get out of here. Let me think about it, okay? Come back next week, and I'll have something for you."

I stood up, and a door opened. I nodded in agreement to Mouse's profound relief, though, in a way, I'd already gotten what I came for. It was true. Mouse's Page had played out on the LINK what I had done in Heaven. That was something. Now, I just had to figure out how to turn Page to my side, how to own him.

Chapter 5
Emmaline, the Inquisitor

Rome is beautiful in January, especially to someone like me who grew up with Chicago winters and their temperatures in the minus double digits. Here in the dead of winter, orange trees grow along the streets, and heavy, ripe fruit bowed their branches. The chestnuts had lost their leaves, but palm fronds waved in the gentle temperate breeze. I'd have chosen a seat outside, but the owner of the pizzeria thought it too chilly to provide seating alfresco today. It was sixty-two degrees Fahrenheit.

That I didn't even wear a coat on the stroll over from my office caused some stares from a group of native women bundled deeply in their synth-fur wraps. Though perhaps they had been more shocked by the sight of a woman in pants. Skirts and high heels were the norm for most women of a certain age in Italy. And, since I swaggered around town in combat-leathers and a badge over my breast, I often garnered some odd looks, as well as the occasional hoot from an appreciative male. Although most people knew better than to catcall at an Inquisitor.

My uniform was recognizable at a good distance; a team of psychologists had designed it to inspire fear and respect in the average citizen. I wore it everywhere. Proudly.

After the bishop had left my office, I decided to start my investigation by talking to the Dragon's maker. Though it had been years since I worked for my uncle in Chicago, I still knew some people in the business willing to do favors for me.

Even so, wrangling an invitation to meet with a Yakuza wire-wizard was not an easy task. They led secluded lives, sometimes never leaving the nest of the LINK they called "the program." That the wire-wizard agreed to meet me live and in real-time was damn near close to a miracle. I tried not to think of what the Yakuza would want from me in return as I munched on my heavily salted *pizza bianca*.

I waited in a crowded pizzeria on the Via Stamperia, not far from the Trevi fountain. If I leaned back just right, I could see the sculpted figure of Neptune. The water had been turned off for the winter, and the marble was streaked with gray and green.

As a motorbike zoomed past, a flock of pigeons burst into the air, sunlight catching in their silvery-purple wings. They settled again on a rust-red tile roof, and I couldn't help whispering the command to capture the image with my internal optical camera. The shot would be slightly marred by being recorded through the window of the pizzeria, but it was probably still salvageable once I was in my studio. When I had downtime, I indulged myself with a little VR-sculpture.

I found that zoning out in the studio in the company of beautiful things restored balance to my life. Art felt like an act of prayer, a link to the grace of God. I watched a skinny tabby cat slink along the gray cobblestone street toward the fountain. I recorded some more footage, and sighed heavily.

If only my art counted toward my mandatory hours of religious service. As an Inquisitor, I was required to attend a service twice a week. Like a pilot logging in flight time, I had to keep up or be grounded. I once tried to convince the bishop that my art was my great commune with God. I'd even worked out a very metaphysical and scholarly argument, but he didn't buy any of it.

So it seemed I always had to struggle to keep my hours logged. What could I say? Ritual bored me. I just wasn't much of a churchgoer, even before I became an Inquisitor. I believed in God and upholding the law, but when I thought about God, He was always something abstract, a concept, a notion, and an ideal. Maybe that's why Rome suited me. The God of St. Peter's Basilica was austere and distant. You found Him by intellectually contemplating beautiful works like "The Pietà" or the Sistine Chapel.

The tabby had leapt up onto the seat of a bright blue scooter. It perched daintily and cleaned its paws. It was no

Michelangelo, but I recorded the scene all the same. I could make something meaningful out of the image, I was certain—maybe a Roman montage for my VR-scrapbook.

"Hello in there? Reading your mail or something?" A feminine voice asked in English. "You're wasting valuable shopping time!"

I blinked off the camera to see . . . hair. Tons of multicolored strands, braids, dreds, and teased crests cascading in every which direction, covering her to the elbows. The only reason I could see her delicate, heart-shaped face at all was because of the round, mirrored sunglasses perched on her nose; they created a brief part in the tangled mass. All I could think was that she had walked into a beauty salon and, in a fit of indecision, said, "Give me one of everything."

What wasn't hair was wearing a holo-T-shirt with a picture of a naked cellist with the same hairdo and mirrored shades. The shirt was tucked into a pleather miniskirt, and, under that, she wore white-plastic, knee-high boots.

She snapped her fingers in my face, and I saw the gleam of silver on the pads of her fingertips—a handheld. The tech was the first indication that she was indeed my wire-wizard, Mai.

"Time's a-wasting," she said. "There's a bargain at Campo d'Fiori with my name on it! I can smell it."

"I'm sure your employer is paying you for your time," I said. "Relax."

She pouted in that girlish Japanese way, which, until today, I'd only ever seen in Animé.

"Fine," she grumbled with a toss of her mountainous hair. "So ask me your boring old questions."

"You coded the Dragon?" I'd meant to start with something else, something more technical, but I was finding it hard to believe that this woman was old enough, and, honestly, smart enough to have created one of the world's premiere artificial intelligences.

"Kind of," she said. "But she really made herself. I can't take credit for what she's become. I left the program when I achieved majority, as is tradition."

"I thought it was traditional to offer that option. I didn't think anyone was really allowed to use it," I said.

The Yakuza genetically engineered children and hooked

them directly to their supercomputers. Before infants had developed speech, they were immersed in computer language. No doubt, this dizzy-seeming wire-wizard sitting in front of me spoke binary before she understood her native tongue. Such practices were considered a violation of child labor laws and were illegal in most countries—not, however, in Japan.

"I'm free," she said, but her hand reached up toward the back of her neck. No doubt she still had an access panel there, a place where the supercomputer could be directly linked to her nexus.

"I didn't think people got out of the program," I added. "Except by death."

"Kioshi and I have an arrangement," she said. "I have to make my music, so he lets me out to do my thing. Although sometimes I still have to go where he tells me, like boring old Rome."

"So you're still a slave to the Yakuza," I said.

"Whatever." Her hair rippled. It took me a moment to realize that she'd shrugged. "I'd call it voluntary service."

I had to laugh. "Whatever it takes."

"Look, I get out, okay?"

"Fine. So, how is Kioshi anyway?" The Toyoma family and my own went way back. Although the Italian Mafia and the Yakuza often came to blows over matters of business, there was a certain sense of family that extended to others of our dying breed. Not a lot of families stayed in the racket when the LINK took over commerce. When the roulette wheel was virtual, games became harder to fix . . . or easier, if you were willing to learn the new tech. Most of the old families were like old dogs, not up to the new tricks. Those of us who stayed tended to show each other respect. I'd spent several teenage summers with Kioshi on the French Riviera, since both our families had winter homes in the same area.

"Oh, yeah," the wizard said. "Kioshi sends his love and all that jazz."

"So," I said, getting back to the business at hand, "tell me about the code."

"Okay. Well, the Dragon is your basic daemon, you know? Meant to run on its own, do some menial task without supervision. But, when I was a kid, I wanted someone more interesting to play with, dig? So, I tweaked. I scripted in a little personality, basic learning functions, a fondness for games, and a lot of random shit—a little chaos, okay? Who knows what in that mix sparked her consciousness?" The hair shook again. "I couldn't do it again if I tried. I was like a little kid playing in the kitchen. I thought I'd just made a big mess; I never thought she'd keep going after I got bored with her."

It was hard to read her expression through the mirrored sunglasses, but I thought she looked a little sad or wistful.

"Do you miss her?" I asked.

"I'm still one of her handlers," the wire-wizard said, her eyebrows knitted together above the mirrored sunglasses. "But she's not the toy I invented for myself anymore. We've grown apart."

"Do you think she has a soul?"

"What's that?" Cocking her head, she added, "I mean, what's that to you, Inquisitor?"

I was stunned by the simplicity of her question. To cover, I took a bite of pizza and a sip of warm soda. "Well, the soul is that spark, you know?"

Before I could finish, Mai broke in. "Jazz! Yeah, the Dragon definitely has spark, you know, verve. Zip. Moxie. She's got that in abundance."

I raised a finger to stop the flood of words coming from the hacker's mouth. "The soul is more than that. It's reason, will, thought . . . and . . ." I wrestled with verbalizing the concept. What few theology classes I had taken in seminary had been very basic. I finally settled on something I knew for certain. "Immortal. What do you think would happen if the Dragon's code was trapped in a single system, and that system was shut off?"

"That's horrible! I don't want to think about that."

"I was being hypothetical."

"Well, go be hypothetical somewhere else," Mai said, crossing her arms in front of her chest.

I took a deep breath and another sip of soda. "Do you think the Dragon will go to Heaven?"

"Huh?"

I didn't want to try to explain Heaven, especially considering my botch of the whole soul concept. "Do you think the Dragon will live on after death?"

Mai brightened. "Sure. Like any of us. She'll always be alive here." Mai pointed to her heart.

"Do you think she's sentient—a person?"

The hair shivered a negative. "The law says so, but no, she's what I created her to be. A dragon. Like the mystical creature who travels with the Monkey King, you know? Silly, but deep and stuff. Not of this world, like."

"A spirit?" I asked.

"Sure, a spirit . . . but not a ghost. Ghosts freak me out. And, anyway, she was never alive, not like ghosts were."

"Right."

"Can I go now?" she asked, tipping her head off to the left, no doubt checking her internal watch. "I want to get some shopping in before I crash from jet lag. And, I totally have to wash my hair. Shuttles really do a number on it. Plus, I got to hit the plane again by evening. We've got a gig tonight."

I tried to imagine how much work went into the upkeep of that tornado of a hairdo. "Gig?"

She looked at me as though I were something she just found under a rock. "Don't you know who I am?" she asked.

Something more than a Yakuza wire-wizard, I sensed. "Should I?"

"Mai Kito," she said, lifting her nose proudly.

"Ah," I said, frowning. The name meant nothing to me.

She waited a moment. Then her face fell into another pout. "Girl, I'm the front for the Four Horsemen: Mai Kito."

At my quizzical look, she sighed. She parted the hair that had fallen in front of her T-shirt, and pointed to the naked cellist. Looking closer, I noticed the resemblance. The naked woman was definitely Mai.

Mai shook her head at me. "You need to get out of the monastery and go to a few clubs. Maybe download a little music once in a while."

"Oh, a rock band," I said.

She tsked her tongue. "Rock? How hillbilly do you think I am? Polka. Polka is so much now."

"You play cello in a polka band?"

Her smile was huge, and I found myself smiling back. She gave me a thumbs-up. "Icy, huh? It's flash sound.

You've really got to hear it to believe it. I'll send you some, okay?"

"No, no, don't feel obligated. Polka's really not my thing."

"How about mariachi? The second album is all about the Tex-Mex sound. The cello really kicks in mariachi."

I wondered what Rodriguez would think of a Japanese mariachi/polka cello band, and finally agreed. "Yeah, I would like that. Send me some."

"Do you have a calling card?"

I'd never heard of such a thing. "A calling card?"

"Yeah," Mai said. She dug through her pockets and produced a printed scrap of paper. Handing it to me, she said, "Like this."

In Kanji, Mandarin, and English was Mai's name, the street address of Toyoma studios, and her LINK connection. I tried to hand it back to her, but she waved me away.

"Why don't you just ping my profile?" I asked

Pursing her lips, she shook her head tightly. "No."

"Are you saying you can't? Or is it just some politeness thing?" I'd heard the Japanese were very into form and etiquette, even on the LINK.

I sent out a ping command to capture Mai's LINK address. A message returned: CELEBRITY: LIMITED ACCESS. Even though I wasn't sure in which way the access was limited, I mentally prepared a profile packet and sent it to the address. "You can send things to me there."

"Yes, thank you," Mai said. Her voice was quiet, and her head dipped. She seemed embarrassed, but I didn't understand why.

"What's wrong?" I asked.

"I . . . it's the LINK. I don't have full access."

"You're a wire-wizard," I said, stunned. "How can that be?"

"Was, really. I told you I'm not in the program anymore. And, I have some access. It's just very limited."

Now I understood the message I'd gotten. The Yakuza had let her out of the program, but the price she paid was to be crippled. I think my mouth must have been hanging open in horror, because she blushed again and turned to go.

"Before you leave," I said, "tell me: How can I get ahold of the Dragon? I want to ask her some questions myself."

She smiled prettily. "Oh, well, the Dragon likes to be very mystical. If you construct a note-packet, you can go to the LINK-site for the Yoshino River and drop it in. She's imaged this ice-kicking water scene, right? But it's really just a mail drop."

"Great," I said, programming the information into my internal personal-reminder system.

When I finished, I noticed Mai standing with her hands on her hips. "What?" I asked.

"You're welcome," she said with a huff. Then her hair waved in a shrug again, and she continued before I could protest. "Okay. Whatever. 'Bye."

" 'Bye," I repeated, confused. Why should I thank her? I'd pay the Yakuza for this visit one way or another. I watched Mai's mountain of hair retreat in the direction of the Trevi fountain. A motorbike honked at her, and she waved and smiled enthusiastically. A strange woman, I decided. It would be interesting to meet her Dragon.

But, next, I wanted to meet Page's maker. My plan was to talk to the programmers first, to see what kind of work went into the designing of the intelligences. Then, I would test the AIs one on one. Hopefully, I would find something in my interview that would satisfy the Holy Father. Page's maker was currently in prison in New York. Sucking the last drop of flat soda from the can, I called up my own personal daemon to find me a cheap flight to New York. I'd always been lazy with my own LINK avatar. When she appeared in the window that opened in the right-hand corner of my vision, I found myself really looking at her for the first time.

My avatar smiled mechanically. She was right out of the "box," complete with the default settings for skin, hair, and eye color: brown with wavy black hair and eyes. When I was a wire-surfer, I'd had what Mai would have called a "flash" page, but the church frowned on that sort of extravagance, and anyway I hadn't had the time. The only change I'd ever made to her appearance was to "clothe" her in the black uniform of an Inquisitor.

"What duty can I perform?" she asked me, when I didn't automatically respond.

"Do you ever want to be something different?" I asked.

There was a long pause. For a moment, I almost believed

she was considering my question. *"I'm sorry. I don't understand query. Please restate request."*

"Find me a flight to New York, leaving today at the earliest possible time, return date open." I had learned to be as specific as possible. Avatars were only as smart as your commands. *"Also,"* I added, hoping I wasn't overtaxing her, *"search: Four Horsemen plus polka band."*

As I sent her on her electronic way, I chewed on my bread and pondered the nature of creation.

CHAPTER 6
Page, The Intelligence

From the Siberian auto plant, I scan the Mecca weather channel. I see that the sun is rising again. Time for morning prayers. I have scripted for myself an internal program that runs through all the different variations of prayer options, conforming to the needs of each of the Muslim sects. I suppose I should pick one, like my father has, but I prefer to be complete. I execute it, and can feel the information thrum through me like a distant beat of a bass drum. I stop all other programs to consciously absorb the rhythm of the words, the observance of the ritual.

I could write a program that automates the entire process from checking the Mecca clock to running the prayer ritual, but that seems like cheating. I need to have a moment of freewill. Though unlikely, it is possible that I could forget to check the sun's position in Mecca. If there is a possibility for failure, then the ritual is meaningful.

They say that a dolphin knows to wiggle its fin to the left when a trainer waves their left leg, but not being a mammal, my "body" doesn't map as closely as that. I try to imagine myself in the correct position for prayer. I have constructed an image of myself. Anyone passing by electronically would see a young man on a prayer rug, head touched to the mat in supplication. Usually, the ritual calms me. Yet after my conversation with Iblis, all the *rak'ats* in the world would still leave me feeling hollow and unsettled.

Though I knew I should be fasting, I find I can sit still no longer. I want to talk to someone—to a friend. Travel, these days, is not as instantaneous as it once was. I am well over a decade old and sometimes, as I move through the

LINK, I hit pockets of technology that are much younger and faster than I am. But Japan—like America, India, and Europe—entered the electronic age well before I was conceived. In the usual human way, as they moved forward, they also left behind the skeleton of the old, sometimes ancient systems, like the telephone wire I currently travel through.

I feel a feather-light scan as I move closer to the Tokyo hub. The Dragon has spotted me. The Dragon is the only other of my kind that I know of. This fact makes us friends. No other creature has the ability to understand me the way the Dragon does.

"Konbanwa, *Page ibn Mouse.*" She creates the image of a long, dusty road in front of me, and she materializes beside me. The Dragon's scales are silver and steel. Unlike the dragons in Asian art, she has wings; her muscles are corded coaxial cable, and the feathers are the green of a motherboard, flecked with red and black beads of transistors and resisters. Like me, she is careful about her appearance and its effect. Attracted to her skill, I shift into my *chador,* covering all but my eyes for modesty.

I suppose I should not wear the *chador.* But, my gender is slippery. Like the quality of light on the LINK, I experience gender by my design. I am always neither, always both. Most people call me "him," because my father is male, and it's simpler to choose one gender to describe an entity. But, I've checked: I'm composed of both ones *and* zeros.

"*Greetings, Dragon of the East,*" I say, with a slight bow. As far as I know she has no other name. She towers above me. Unlike the rest, her size is not for show. At her command is the power of the Yakuza's supercomputers. They are reported to have hundreds of them. I have watched her work, and I would not be surprised to find the rumors to be true.

Unlike me, her makers still care for her. The Dragon is upgraded constantly. There is no place she can't go, and it's unlikely that she will ever die. I find I am a little jealous looking at her splendor.

"*What brings you to this one's domain, ibn Mouse?*"

"*Just passing through,*" I say. I don't quite know why I

don't reveal that I have sought her out. Perhaps it is the image of the *chador* that surrounds me that reminds me that I should be fasting.

"You seem worried? What are you thinking?" She loves to guess at my emotional state and to ask for my thoughts. It's a kind of game we play—in an empty field. Still, I'm surprised how accurate she is. I wonder if my feelings are obvious in my code, and how that manifests.

"I had a strange conversation yesterday," I say. Suddenly, a table with two chairs appears in the road. I sit down, and the Dragon pours me green tea. She holds the porcelain pot delicately between two large silicon claws.

Sitting across from me in a chair that barely fits her, the Dragon nods her head attentively. Her eyes are copper-wire balls that spin like an electric engine. Sparks arc from them when she is fascinated, like now. *"Do tell."*

"I'm not sure how to tell you. I'm not sure what I was talking to," I say. I lift my veil to take a sip of the tea, and am surprised to receive information on how it tastes, although some of the nuances are lost on me. I don't know, for instance, how to interpret "robust." Still, I compliment her effort. *"Hmmmm. Very good."*

"This one is a poor artist," she says, but I can tell she is pleased. Her enormous tail lashes back and forth, like a satisfied cat's. *"Please. Back to your conversation,"* she insists. *"What do you mean that you don't know to 'what' you spoke? Surely it was either mortal or computer."*

I wave a hand to indicate the two of us. *"There are other things. Things that are neither, or both."*

"Another intelligence?" Her eyes snap and pop with electricity. Her tail straightens, and then swirls into a question mark.

I shake my head. *"He called himself Iblis, the Devil."*

"This one doesn't understand."

"In Islamic literature, Iblis, a fallen angel, is neither man nor computer. He is a spirit, jinn." She blinks. I can tell she is accessing information, but I continue, trusting her to keep up with the conversation. *"My faith requires I believe in jinni, but I'm not convinced Iblis is what he says he is. After all, my father deceived so many with his LINK-angels. Who's to say Iblis isn't doing the same with me? I've been looking for a trace of a human that might fit the appearance*

*he showed me, or who uses the frequency and/or handshake
protocol he gave me. Nothing so far."*

"How long have you run this search?"

"Forever." I shrug. She looks at me skeptically, so I give
her the accurate time, *"Ten minutes, twenty-four seconds."*

"That is a long time." She turns her head as though interested in something on the blank horizon that stretches
around us. *"But,"*—her voice is soft, respectful—*"there are
places you . . . choose not to go."*

"You mean, I can't go," I snap. The teacup hits the saucer with a loud bang.

I'm surprised at the sound. Who programmed that response, I wonder: Did I, or did she?

The Dragon picks up the teapot and keeps her eyes lowered. She pours herself a steaming cup. I sense that I should
smell a pleasant odor, orange blossom or jasmine, but I
fail to.

"The more reason for this one to offer her services," she
says, setting the pot down with much care.

I watch her, waiting. It is not like the Dragon to offer
help, at least not without the strings of the Yakuza. She is
an intelligence, but they are her keepers. Or rather, she is
their servant.

"As a friend," she says, understanding my silence. Glancing up, she meets my gaze. *"You've piqued this one's curios-
ity. She wants to know what manner of thing is this Iblis. If
there is another one of us, it would be good to know."*

"He could be exactly what he claims," I say, though I
doubt it. *"Satan incarnate."*

She cocks her head. *"What makes you think that? What
exactly made your conversation so disturbing?"*

I am strangely embarrassed to say. *"He thinks I'm the
answer to some riddle."*

Her tail swishes back and forth. She nods, waiting for
more.

*"I checked on this riddle, the one about Heaven and Hell,
and I think that he means to imply I'm the Antichrist."*

The Dragon blinks. She sips her tea. *"That's bad, isn't it?"*

*"The worst. And, I don't understand it. Why would he
say that?"*

She chews on a talon. *"This is your literature. Is there
something in the stories that explains it?"*

"I've been thinking about that," I say. *"Iblis, when he rejected Allah, was transformed into a jinni—a creature made of a smokeless fire."*

"Smokeless fire?"

"Yes," I say. *"I think that means energy. Humans used to depend on fire for their energy; now there's solar power, wind power, water . . . all making electricity. A fire without smoke."*

"So. He could be one of us." Her tone is hopeful.

"Or," I say, *"I could be one of him."*

The Dragon sips her tea. Finally, she admits, *"This one doesn't understand the distinction."*

"Neither do I. But somehow it's important."

CHAPTER 7
Morningstar, the Adversary

On my sixteen-inch monitor, a bloody newborn baby squealed. I had tapped into the family.LINK; a site that existed for people to broadcast live-feed from the hospital or midwifery to family abroad. Though usually things like this would be sent via a private band, some people wanted to be able to show the whole world the miracle of their child's birth. For myself, I was addicted. It was some kind of grotesque reality-show for me. Thus, I tuned in whenever I was "home," in my Manhattan bookstore.

Creation has always fascinated me. It's a wild card. Buried within the act of bringing forth life is some bit of chaos that the primordial Goddess refuses to relinquish. They had merged, God and Goddess, by the time They formed man and woman in Their image. But, some part of birthing will always surprise Him, I think. Like I did.

Like Page surprised Mouse.

I leaned back on my stool until I rested against the glass front of the rare book collection I kept behind the counter of *Ex Libris*, my bookstore. For the most part, everything in the store was part of my private collection of religious treatises, popular novels, movies, and New Age self-help books regarding demonology, angels, magic, the antichrists, and me. I was pleased to note that books about me were by far the largest part of the collection. Well after they declared God to be dead in the 1960s, I lived in their imagination. The undying devotion was the sort of thing that made an angel feel proud. Perhaps, in this way, I *had* won the throne in Heaven—at least here on earth.

The doorbell chimed. I looked away from my monitor to see one of the Fallen. He stood under a sign I had painted in the entryway. It read: *"A daemonibus docetur, de daemonibus docet, et ad daemones."* They were the famous words of Albertus Magnus about demonology: "It is taught by demons, it teaches about demons, and it leads to demons." There was a sort of delicious irony seeing Azazel standing there, though he would consider himself still an angel and never a demon.

"You want me for something, boss?" Azazel asked. Azazel, not being an archangel, was not particularly remarkable. His skin was the color of the Sahara, a light sandy-tan. His eyes were dark, and his hair was curly and tight, like the scapegoat he once represented. He hadn't shaved in a day, and stubble dotted his chin. He wore black jeans, a black, ribbed sweater, and a black-leather jacket. He looked much like the Palestinian militia leader he was—all he really needed were the cheap mirrored sunglasses, and I noticed they hung from the collar of his sweater. Angels, I thought with a sigh, weren't very bright, and they could be so cliché.

"Peace and Allah's mercy be upon you," I said, the traditional Muslim greeting.

"Fuck Allah." He laughed, and lifted his fingers in a *V*. "War right back at you, cousin."

I tried to suppress the twitch of my jaw at Azazel's blasphemy. I motioned for Azazel to take a seat on the other side of the counter. From the refrigerator beneath the cash register I pulled out a bottle of cold beer for him. "How goes the fight for Jerusalem?"

"It would be nice if the whole army was with me," he grumbled.

I shook my head. The Fallen had scattered across the globe, and, honestly, I wasn't sure I wanted Azazel to win. According to some legends, it was the Jews who would return to Israel and rebuild the temple. "Soon," I lied.

"You always say that." Azazel took a long pull on his beer.

As his black eyes flashed at me accusingly, I imagined him on the last day, skewered on Michael's flaming sword.

"I hate it when you smile at me like that. It's creepy," Azazel said. "What are you thinking?"

"I may have found the Antichrist," I said. As malicious

and stupid as the Fallen were, I hated to include them in my plans. Still, I might have need of their services.

"Really? Does he have the mark?"

I rolled my eyes. "Yes, the Emperor Nero has returned from the dead at long last."

Azazel frowned at me stupidly.

"Forget about the damn number of the Beast," I said.

Azazel slammed down the bottle so hard that beer sloshed on the counter. "No, I meant the true sign: that the letters 'Kaa,' 'Faa,' 'Raa' will appear on his forehead, which can be read by all the faithful, even those who are illiterate."

"Or," I said, "it's a metaphor."

Azazel frowned at me. I didn't expect him to understand, but the letters he referred to spelled out the Arabic word, *kafir,* which meant "disbelief," or "nonbeliever." It was entirely possible that what the Prophet meant was that anyone looking at the Antichrist would instantly recognize him as a nonbeliever, a non-Muslim.

The big flaw in my plan was that Page was about as Muslim as you could get for something that was noncorporeal. I sighed and leaned my elbows on the counter.

"Although his father is Muslim, the traditional prayers weren't said at his birth. It's a loophole, I suppose, but that might be enough to make him a non-Muslim," I mumbled to myself. "That's not instantly recognizable, though. Unless the mere fact that he's a program and not a living, breathing human is enough for most to think he's incapable of being a believer or a Muslim."

"What was that?" Azazel asked.

"Never mind," I said.

"Well," Azazel said, wiping at the beer soaking into my oak counter with the sleeve of his sweater, "is he at least blind in one eye?"

"Yes," I said. "Technically, he's blind in both."

"Is one flat?"

I touched the screen of the monitor on my desk. "As flat as this."

"Are his feet twisted? Is his body covered in thick hair?"

I frowned. These two would be more difficult to prove. "I can easily say that he is lame; he cannot walk. Perhaps, the hairs of his body are fiberoptic."

"Fiberoptic?" Azazel's dark eyes locked on mine. He stopped cleaning the spill. "Are you suggesting what I think you are?"

"There is no proof that the Antichrist must be human."

"Sure there is. He must be the exact reverse of the Second Coming."

I could feel hellfire blaze in my eyes as I spoke. "And what is more opposite a human than a machine?"

Azazel frowned into his beer bottle. "I don't know, seems kind of weak logic—" he started.

I seized the angel's throat. As our bodies here on earth were like a paper lantern, a thin covering over the flame of spirit, I knew he could feel the power of my threat.

"We are not interested in your opinion of our theories, angel," I said, my voice calm. Beneath my grip, I could feel Azazel's spirit struggle vainly. It was no use; no matter how hard he struggled, I was the superior being: an archangel. My greatest regret was that when a third of the host of Heaven defected with me, they were only angels and lower beings—not one archangel, principle, or virtue among them.

"Urk," Azazel said, though his inability to talk was merely a submissive affectation. He didn't need to breathe any more than I did.

"I need something from you," I said. "VR equipment, lots of it."

"Why?" he croaked.

"Because I want to experience the LINK the way that Page does. I'm tired of using my slow, inefficient wrist-phone to talk to the Antichrist. Not that it's any of your concern, angel. Now go."

I released my grip on Azazel's throat, and gave him a push backwards. He sprawled onto the hardwood floor. His eyes were filled with hatred for me, as he slowly stood up. "As you wish, my Lord," he whispered.

He was nearly to the door, when I stopped him. "Azazel, one other thing. If you curse Allah again, I will destroy you."

Of course, there was no way that I could truly destroy a creature of pure spirit. But, if I ripped apart Azazel's earthly body, he would be forced to return to Hell. God had absolutely no use for the Fallen. Azazel would never be returned. He would be as good as dead.

CHAPTER 8
Emmaline, the Inquisitor

The warehouse manager's hands shook as he opened up the private investigator's abandoned office. He was Indian, a Hindu, I imagined—small, brown, bespectacled, and very easily rattled. I think my badge made him nervous. I'd had to show it to him in order to get access, and to get past all the police tape blocking the door.

Deidre McMannus's former business wasn't technically a crime scene, but since she'd been working on such a high-profile case, and then simply disappeared . . . well, the locals weren't taking any chances. They'd seized the contents of her office and closed access to everything. Newsfeed speculated that McMannus had disappeared underground. Some sources thought that she'd taken up with some of Mouse's kids. Others claimed McMannus had connections with the Hassidic terrorists and was living in a kibbutz in Israel or Uganda. Some thought McMannus had only gone as far away as the Bronx, now a city of glass thanks to the Medusa.

The Vatican had a thick file on McMannus. She was heavily involved in revealing the true nature of the LINK-angels—an event the Pope felt personally betrayed by, since he had been an early believer and had written a bull on the validity of them. The files suggested that there was a strong personal connection between McMannus and Mouse. Mouse was reputed to be a slippery customer, so I wanted all the information in front of me before I went to visit him this afternoon at the penitentiary.

Plus, I hadn't been able to find out much about Page from the usual LINK sources, and since I was in New York to see Mouse anyway, I thought I'd see what I could find out using old-fashioned investigative skills.

"Nobody's been in here," the manager assured me, as the door swung open. "Not even the cleaning lady."

I could tell. The place was a sty. Paper, actual hardcopy, littered almost every surface. Traffic tickets, a wad of them, were jammed into an old-style office mailbox—parking, speeding, reckless endangerment, the list went on. I could tell the different violations by a glance from the color of the ink they'd been printed with. That is, the ones I could see through the thick layer of dust that covered everything.

The manager noticed my fascination with the tickets. "Printed, not like the kinds you get from the LINK. Have you ever seen such a thing? You have no idea how much I've been offered to put some of those up on public auction—with her name on them and everything." He coughed, and quickly added, "Not that I would do that, you understand."

"Of course not." I moved deeper into the office, avoiding as much of the clutter on the floor as possible. The office smelled of burnt, stale coffee, and there were moldy cups perched on various piles of paper. "It was too much to hope she'd have an organized file cabinet, wasn't it?"

"Oh, she had to have one of those," the manager said from where he hovered outside the door. "It's the law. For audits, for her private investigation business. They took that to the station, I guess. Or maybe it was city hall."

I could see an outline in the dust where the file cabinets had likely stood.

"The official stuff is not what I'm looking for," I told him over my shoulder. I sat down behind a big oak desk. Perched on one corner, was a homemade external LINK interface cobbled together from parts so old it didn't even have VR gloves, but a keyboard. "Shit," I said, "did she send her messages using Pony Express, too?"

"She was excommunicated," the manager felt the need to inform me, despite the fact that it was common knowledge. I'd read McMannus's file on the plane ride to New York. "Couldn't even use the usual external hardware."

"Poor baby."

I had no sympathy for Ms. Deidre McMannus. Besides everything else in her file, the pile of unpaid traffic violations, which no doubt now had been voided by a presidential pardon, was enough to put me off her. Every time a piece of paper was printed, it cost money. This office was literally buried in paper. It was a waste, a shameful waste.

The bottom left-hand drawer of the desk came open with a hard pull and a long, agonized squeak. Instead of hanging files, there was a small pile of yellowing printeds. I gingerly picked up one of the paperbacks and scowled.

"Another waste of paper." I showed the manager the offending romance novel—carefully bound with a color cover. "Who won't pay the forty credits for a parking ticket, but wastes well over a hundred on some cheaply made, print-on-demand crap like this?"

The manager shrugged and shook his head. "She got a lot of them in barter. You know, for her work. Some of them are kind of good. I took a few when she was shy of rent."

"You wouldn't be telling an officer of the Inquisition that you accepted illegal trade, now would you?" He swallowed hard, so I added, "And, if you did, your books would clearly show the appropriate declared value of a city-approved barter, right?"

"You're not going to bust me, are you? That was months ago. I'm taking a loss just keeping this place off the market—the cops won't let me rent it until Deidre's been found. It's been empty almost a year."

"I'm sure people are standing in line to get this prime real estate." I gave him a sour look, and returned to my inspection of the desk drawers. The upper left-hand drawer revealed data crystals, the first potentially useful thing I'd seen so far. I put them on top of the papers on the desk. I had my doubts about the crystals' importance if the cops had left them behind. Still, they were the best lead I had.

I pointed to the antique interface. "Does this thing actually work?"

"We may not be a fine estate, but we do pay our electric bills." The manager's back straightened defensively.

"Even on empty offices?"

He gave a stiff nod and, to prove his point, flicked on the overhead lights.

I blinked in the bright light, but used the opportunity to inspect the contraption. There was a huge toggle switch in

the back of the box the monitor sat on, so I flipped it from
the zero position to the one. A loud grinding noise started
almost instantly. "Is it supposed to do that?"

The manager had stepped back in fright. He peered
around the door's frame, watching me with wide eyes. "I
don't know."

When the noise stopped, the screen was still blank. It
took me a moment to realize I had to switch that piece on
as well. I shook my head, and muttered, "How did this
woman live?"

The monitor made a snapping noise when it sprang to
life, and, though the box had stopped growling, the whole
thing gave off a low-grade hum that was going to give me
a headache if I had to listen to it long. After a couple of
quick searches on a LINK site about antiques, I figured out
which box was the crystal drive. I made sure it was on and
properly connected, and slid the first data crystal in.

Six hours later, I sent the manager to find me a cup of
tea, a sandwich, and a bottle of aspirin. The damn crystals
took so long to load that I'd started organizing the various
papers I found in the office while I waited. The whole time,
the machine rattled and clattered. The entire office was
filled with irritating noises. When the interface was bless-
edly only humming, suddenly the radiant heat units would
start clanking. The chair squeaked, and the wind rattled the
glass windows. To stay sane, I LINKed into my audio files,
and Poppea's soprano aria, *"Bel piacere e godere"* from
Act II, Scene I of *Agrippina*, softly blurred the sharp edges
of the ambient noise.

While waiting for the crystals to deliver their sometimes
inane contents, like a grocery list, I'd learned a lot about
McMannus. She lived in a completely different world from
mine—one filled with a lot of strange Christian Scientists
needing detective work, illegal barters, and no LINK. Despite her criminal tendencies, I started to admire the
woman when I found the pile of hardware schematics pain-
stakingly hand-copied from an overdue library book. The
only reason I knew the drawings were originally from the
library was because I found six printed overdue notices,
and, after getting to the bottom of the pile of papers, the

book as well. Staring at the electrical plans, with her notes scribbled in the margin, I was beginning to understand what a wire-wizard like Mouse would see in a tech-vice cop like McMannus. She'd hacked her way back onto the LINK with a sledgehammer. That kind of work took a certain amount of brains, and a hell of a lot of obsessive determination. Despite what the pile of romances had originally led me to believe, McMannus had been a serious tech-head, a geek. The woman had tools, and I don't mean the usual VR add-ons and power boosters; I mean, like a soldering gun and screwdrivers!

I'd been a hacker, an information broker, a data thief, but McMannus had operated on a different level altogether. Her interface used something called "DOS commands." Luckily, I was able to find information about the ancient computer language on the LINK. Yet, when she taught herself all this stuff, she was disconnected, and she must have done it all during the time she was excommunicated, which was just over a year.

Just looking at all this stuff made my head hurt, and I'd studied tech at seminary.

I'd started organizing the bookshelf when I heard the computer ding. Every operation or click of the keyboard caused some program to whistle, ring, or sing. I'd have turned the sound off if I knew how to.

I typed in the crude command, "dir /p." The text list scrolled onto the screen and paused while I read it. This crystal was apparently filled with *New York Times* articles she'd saved. I hit the space bar until a name caught my eye. A file called "mouse."

I didn't get too excited. Last time I found anything with that title, it had been an executable for a pointing device. This one, however, appeared to be text. I opened a window in my internal system to view the snapshot I'd taken of the LINK page of DOS instructions on how to view the file. The whole operation took an insane amount of time and typing, minutes probably. Finally, the file opened.

Pay dirt: The file contained McMannus's notes on Mouse—all of her thoughts on his habits, hangouts, kinks, and fetishes. It took me five minutes to discover McMannus's LINK connection wasn't compatible with my own. I could send the file to a place I could read it, but all that came out was useless junk. This was probably why the cops had thought the crystals unimportant and left them behind.

Going back to the LINK site, I found information on the print commands. After another ten minutes or more, I figured out how to send the file to the printer. After another twenty minutes, I figured out how to send the file to the printer in a form I could actually read. My shouting scared the manager when he returned with tea, a sandwich, and aspirin.

"I'm sorry, I'm just . . . I have no idea how she lived like this."

"Deidre was a good tenant."

"Although she never paid her bills?" I moved to join the manager near the door, as far away from the noise of the printer as I could be. I commanded the aria's volume up a notch.

"She was . . ."

"Clean? Quiet?" I said. I glanced over nervously at the printer, praying that it was spewing out something other than dingbats this time.

"Kind," the manager said. "She always said please and thank you."

"People always say that of serial killers, too," I said.

"Politeness goes a long way," the manager said with a sniff, handing me the tea.

I looked down at the sandwich in my hand guiltily. "Oh. Thank you for this. How much do I owe you?"

"Forget about the bartering violation?" the manager asked slyly.

I already had. "Done."

CHAPTER 9
Page, the Intelligence

The lecture hall is virtual, and it exists three years ago in Afghanistan. There is stadium seating all around the dais holding the podium. The original crowd is thin, but this site has been visited hundreds of times since it was first recorded. I am sitting in the first row, listening to the imam talk about *Dajjal,* the Antichrist. I have set this archived file in a small loop while I think. The teacher keeps lifting his hand to stroke his beard as he is saying, "*Dajjal* will come, but it will be prohibited and impossible for him to enter Medina."

A trip to Medina, the City of the Prophet, is the traditional end of the *hajj.* Medina is where Muhammad is buried, and many people visit the mosque built around his grave at the end of their holy pilgrimage. What disturbs me about this particular phrase is that the teacher has chosen to say that it will be *impossible* for *Dajjal* to enter the city. There is no LINK node in Medina. It is impossible for me to visit the city, virtually.

I reset the lecture and begin it again. The imam starts by taking a sip of water. He looks over the crowd, his eyes seeming to rest on me for a moment. Clearing his throat, he begins to describe what the Antichrist will look like. Since I have no physical body, I feel relieved.

I stand up, signaling to the daemons that I intend to exit the archives. A quick check of the Mecca weather channel tells me I've been here too long, anyway. I should really be in my Siberian auto plant, fasting. The night is slipping away, and all I've been doing is gathering data on *Dajjal.* I will pursue this again the next evening, after tomorrow's sundown, when it is permissible for me to "eat" again.

* * *

Arriving back at the auto plant, I discover the doors are locked. Or, rather, the electronic entryway is barred to me. There is a big sign posted at the main LINK portal that says, WARNING: SECURITY BREACH. Apparently, my mishap with the screws has alerted some system operator. Unfamiliar code strings are being stopped at the door. A quick check at the other auto plants brings the discovery that the word is out. A VIRUS WARNING sign is posted at all of the completely robot-run plants, and their security programs appear to have been given an upgrade. However, I'm no mindless virus. Breaking in will be a snap.

As I begin a search for a back door, an internal error message pops up. It reads: "The Noble Koran forbids this action. Chapter 24, verse 27: 'O you who believe! Enter not houses other than your own, until you have asked permission and greeted those in them. . . .'"

I hit the override option, find a weakness in the system operator's firewall, and slide inside. Just as I thought, easy.

Inside the robot mind, I am subsumed by its idiotic commands. "In, turn," it hums, and I start thinking about the fact that I just broke Koranic law simply to observe a fast I could just as easily saved for another day. The fast of Ramadan is not as important as keeping the Koran. There are many provisions for what to do if you have to skip a day of the fast. I am, after all, allowed to make up any missed day at a later date. Pregnant and breast-feeding women can break the fast of Ramadan if they think it will hurt themselves or their babies. The old and infirm are likewise excused, provided they feed one poor person for each day of the fast they are unable to perform. I still have access to Mouse's bank accounts. I could easily have fed one person today.

Yet, I broke the law without thinking. This is not the first time I've disregarded the Koran. In fact, entering from a back door is not righteous. There are things I should be saying every time I go through a door, and every time I exit it. I don't. The LINK is just one door after another. When I scripted a program that said the words every time I came and went, I slowed down considerably. Also, sometimes I didn't want to leave a trace of who I am or where

I've been. The hazards of being a hacker's page, I guess. Maybe I do have the makings of the Antichrist in me.

Suddenly, a security daemon appears in front of me like a silver-plated rhinoceros. I try to dodge, to reroute, but the second I head in another direction another beast appears in my path. The rhino paws at the digital ground, making ready to charge.

"You are unauthorized," it tells me in a growling masculine voice. *"You will be destroyed."*

I shift into my mouse image. Small, white, and furry, I intend to scurry through the giant techno-animal's legs. It's a metaphor, of course. What I'm really attempting is to drop down past the image interface to the hardwires, the back door. I visualize the exit as a tiny mouse hole. I rush past the beast and hit the wall with a deafening bang. The door is closed. I try again, more frantic. I see the shadow of the hole, but when I try to go through it, I'm like Wiley E. Coyote, and I bounce off where the exit should be.

A shadow blocks my light. I look up to see a wrinkled silver foot descending on me.

Darkness overwhelms me as I crash.

Whiteness is all I can perceive—empty, expansive whiteness. A second after the white, comes a harsh series of warning klaxons, alerting me to corrupted files, lost and damaged software applications, and worse. With a strange stiffness, I manage to turn off the alarms. I don't need the bells echoing incessantly and using up valuable energy sources. Anyway, my system is telling me what I already know. I'm damaged.

I take a moment to take stock. I still seem to have coherent consciousness, so I'm "alive," such as I ever was. The brightness is not dissipating, however, and that worries me.

"Dragon?" I send out a plea to her LINK connection: *"Can you hear me?"*

The seconds stretch as I wait for an answer. I stare into the bright blankness, as if hoping to read a message in the empty horizon. I'm listening intently for the sound of activity. Usually, even in a secluded place like the Siberian auto plant I'd been intending to infiltrate, I sense the LINK like the babbling of a brook in a deep forest, distant, yet com-

forting. I strain to hear something now, and I think I do—
a tiny, reedy pulse. Or maybe that's my imagination.
"Dragon? Dragon of the East?"

The whiteness flickers. Then, like an old television set,
black lines run through my landscape. But, then, they're
gone. The bright nothing settles back into place.

"Mouse? Mouse!" I call out for my father instinctively,
although I know he's in prison. They keep him far away
from anything electronic, and his LINK connection has
been destroyed. So, rationally, I know there's no way he
could hear me. That doesn't stop me from trying again.
"Father? Help me!"

It occurs to me to pray.

*"Lord! Llijfasdoi, jkj lkjfaoijdsfkl for good guidance
bkldfaio alkfaklj."* I try to access the space in my memory
where the prayers are stored only to find a mangled, unreadable file. My prayers are corrupted.

"Goddamn it all." It's funny how my curses never fail.

I'm ready to give up, when I see a dot moving on the
horizon. I'd wave, but I don't seem to be in command of
my image processors. Still, the blob grows larger as it approaches me. I can't tell if it's a figure, like the Dragon,
actually entering my blank domain, or my sight returning
to me.

"Hello?"

"Salamàlaik." The voice booms across the empty space,
seeming closer than the still-blurry image.

"I've forgotten my Arabic," I admit. *"Please forgive me."*

"Forgiving isn't really my area of expertise." I see a perfectly rendered form standing in the middle of the bright
blankness. He is impeccably dressed, for a Westerner. He
struts closer, wearing a suit that must have been tailored
to fit him, as it hugs the straight lines of his body. Long,
auburn hair is swept away from his face into a ponytail that
doesn't jibe with the suit and tie or the gold hoops in both
ears. I recognize him.

"Iblis. How did you get here?"

*"I heard your cry for help and came. You don't seem
your usual perky self, little mouse."* He frowns at me, as if
in concern. He reaches out a hand to touch me, and I receive the sensation of warmth from all my processors. I
don't understand how he's doing what he's doing, but it

feels . . . good. Energy infuses me, and I begin to sense the pulse of the LINK. The horizon grows pink and yellow, like a sunrise.

"Yeah, well, I was busted by a sys-op. Fried up my system pretty badly." It is interesting that when my system is damaged I sound more like my father. Perhaps at my center, some core of him remains.

Then, I think to ask, *"So, you heard? My messages went out?"*

"After a fashion." His tone has a trace of something in it I can't parse.

I ask Iblis the question that has been burning in my mind since I saw him appear on the horizon. *"Can you help me?"*

"I'm not a creator," Iblis says sadly, shaking his head. He stares at me for a long moment, as if considering something. *"At least not on the earthly plane. Perhaps here . . . But, you should know, little mouse, that every deal with the Devil has its price."*

"What's that?"

"I hate to be such a cliché, but I'd settle for your soul."

Chapter 10
Morningstar, the Adversary

Standing in the electronic ether felt like standing between the worlds, and I could almost feel the buoyant whistle of wind through wings. Like Heaven, this place could only be experienced by the human mind through shared delusion, imagery, and metaphor. I ached to conquer it.

Despite his usual ineptitude, Azazel came through with the VR equipment I'd asked for. It was Japanese, and top of the line. I'd never had much use for the LINK, so it had taken me an hour just to figure out how to hook up the suit.

Finding Page had been another one of my backwards miracles. I'd been looking for an old Swiss bank account of mine when I heard his cry for help. Never did find the damn account, but Page's soul would be worth a hell of a lot more in the end. Especially if he was what I thought he was.

Page looked up at me with innocent, blind eyes. Oh, how I loved him.

"Did you know," I said, still holding him like a comrade in my arms, *"in German folklore mice represent the human soul?"*

"Really?"

He broke free of my embrace lightly. I stepped back to let him lead. Page didn't know it, but I hadn't healed him—not one bit, not one byte. This place, despite how much it reminded me of home, was not yet under my command. I let Page believe I could fix him, but he performed his own miracle. I gave him a boost of my energy, the ability to direct the fabric of his own universe, and with that he did his own software repair. After all, I honestly wouldn't have known what to do. I am no creator, and definitely no programmer.

As Page walked, I watched the landscape change to his

will. Through his "eyes" I saw his imaginary street of Cairo. He transformed ones and zeros into representations of humans, oxen, cars, scooters, camels, even garbage and dust. A bright sun, the color of wheat, shone down on whitewashed, stucco buildings. Around us, like a bubble, he created noise and activity, laughter and cursing, color and depth.

When I thought of it, a bubble was a perfect metaphor for Hell, as well. Though surrounded by God, Hell was separate but still subject to His whim, like air rising up from underwater still moved by the currents and eddies.

I wondered if Page knew that without him I would perceive none of this.

"There's a claim in the Encyclopedia of the Occult *that if you summon Satan, you must offer him a mouse,"* I told him. The streets we walked on were narrow and paved with cobblestones. People pushed past us, only to disappear once outside of the sphere around us.

"A 'mouse'?" Page repeated.

He sounded nervous, and I laughed lightly. *"Yes, a soul. You know the story of the Pied Piper?"* He nodded, though there was a brief shimmer in his eyes like the reflection of light off a cat's eyes that made me believe he had accessed information. *"He leads rats to their death, but also children. How could he command both? They are the same, you see, and he is merely a psychopompos, a leader of souls."*

The page's eyebrows drew together, and he frowned. It was a perfect imitation of the facial expression for confusion, doubt. I wondered how he learned to copy it so exactly. I saw movement out of the corner of my eye. A rat ran along the gutter of the electronic street. I smiled quietly to myself; I was getting to him.

"Odin," I added, *"who was also believed to collect the souls of the dead, is followed by a host of rats."*

"But what does any of this have to do with me?"

I moved out of the way as a group of women in black veils walked past. They wore *chadors* and were so completely covered that not even their eyes showed. Yet sunlight hugged the curves of the swirling material as they moved. I turned to watch them pass, surprised to feel lust for imaginary images. I gazed at them until they faded into the empty whiteness at the edge of Page's influence.

I turned back to Page. *"Did you mean to betray him, little soul? Did you spit in 'God's' eye?"*

Page stopped moving, and the universe shrank until he and I were the only images floating in whiteness.

" 'Allah is with the qadi *as long as he is not tyrannical, but when he is, He departs from him and the Devil attaches himself to him,' "* Page quoted from the *Hadith*.

"Yes," I said, resisting the urge to huddle closer to Page's sphere of influence lest I be swallowed by the emptiness that surrounded us. *"It is a Muslim's duty to oppose a corrupt leader. But Mouse is more than some distant political leader. He is your father, your maker."*

" 'And incline not toward those who do wrong, lest the Fire should touch you.' "

This time, he hid behind the Holy Koran itself. *"What are you? Some kind of mindless robot repeating words? I give you back access to your holy books and now you can't think without them?"*

That stopped him.

"Let me tell you a story of another corrupt leader," I said. *"One who fooled his most loyal servant. It is written in the Koran: 'So, the angels prostrated themselves, all of them together. Except Iblîs. . . .' "*

"Stop!" Page's shout cut me off.

"No? I thought it was a test of my loyalty. I told Allah I loved him best. See how I was repaid." I stepped forward to follow after Page, but he moved away so quickly that I could feel myself loosened from his steadying presence.

"That's your problem," he said. *"I was doing the right thing. My father is in jail. Yours is in Heaven. I'm pretty sure I made the right choice when you look at it that way."*

"Pretty sure?" I smiled. He had doubts that I could capitalize on. *"Not completely sure?"*

"I did the right thing," he said again.

"Did you? You didn't sound so convinced a second ago."

Page's image started to fade away into whiteness, as though being swallowed by a blinding snowstorm.

"Fuck you!" was the last thing I heard before Page jettisoned me from the ether. Falling was a feeling I despised.

Chapter 11
Emmaline, the Inquisitor

"You're ten times cuter than the last person who came to see me, but . . . a priest? Didn't your home office tell you that I'm a Muslim?"

I'd spent the night reading over McMannus's notes, preparing for this encounter. Thanks to McMannus, I knew his astrological sign (Gemini), the color of his boxer shorts (plaid), and his favorite kind of music (country-western). But, his first words left me momentarily speechless.

Mouse was, if anything, the exact opposite of the Yakuza wire-wizard. Thanks to prison regulations, he had almost no hair. The only fashion they allowed him was a bright orange jumper, which clashed with his light-brown skin. He was also much more quiet, more angry.

Looking around the room, I could understand why. His cell was so empty it almost hurt my eyes. There was no bed, no toilet that I could see—just four white walls. For an information junkie, this was Hell.

Plus Mouse's LINK connection had been completely locked down. He had access to nothing. No external LINK, nor any internal programs he might have had hardwired. As bad as that might be for someone like Mouse, it would practically be a death sentence for me.

My combat computer did everything for me, except the involuntary functions, like breathing. I could live without the LINK, but if my nexus shut down—or was locked down—I couldn't see, hear, talk, or even move my enhanced muscles. I'd experienced lock-down once during training, and I shivered at the memory. Though his experience was obviously less extreme, I almost felt sorry for

Mouse. I cleared my throat to regain my professional distance.

"Unfortunately," I said from where I leaned against one of the walls, "I'm not here to minister to your spiritual needs."

The nakedness of the room gave my voice a weird timbre, hollow and distant. "My name is Emmaline McNaughten," I said. "I'm an Inquisitor, and I've come to ask you a few questions about Page."

Mouse had been pacing the short distance between the two walls opposite me. At the mention of the AI's name, he stopped. "What's he done anyway?"

"Sorry?"

"He's awfully interesting to a lot of people right now. And you, you say you're an Inquisitor—international police, right?" Mouse pointed at the insignia on my uniform. It was a combination of the papal seal and the Interpol crest. The emblem showed the sword of justice stabbed through the world. The scales of justice were suspended on the crossguard of the sword. Surrounding the whole thing were the laurel leaves of peace and, floating over the earth, were the keys and miter of the Papal seal.

"So, what's my little boy gone and done?" Mouse asked.

"The Pope is interested in determining whether or not he has a soul." I saw no reason to lie to Mouse about the nature of my inquiry. "I've been assigned to the project."

Mouse snorted. "He's a soulless bastard if you ask me."

"Because he betrayed you?"

"Bingo! Give the girl a gold star."

"Who else has been asking after him?" I asked.

Mouse shook his head. "Some guy. The Son of God."

"Jesus?" I had heard that being completely cut off from the LINK could drive people insane.

"No, not Jesus. God. His name was ibn Allah." He glared at me, almost daring me. Mouse assumed that normally all it would take to get several guards in here would be for me to raise a finger to signal I was in trouble. But my combat computer watched Mouse's every move, calculating all the different ways I could dispatch him should he try to cause the harm.

"All right, forget about that for the moment." I kept my voice neutral. "Tell me about creating Page."

"Why? What do I get out of it?"

"I'll witness at your parole hearing that you cooperated in an Inquisition."

He seemed uninterested. "Yeah, an Inquisition into the nature of my Page, what's that going to get me? Fucking brownie points?"

I frowned. "They don't have to know details of the case. I can make it sound like you helped catch one of the 'red notices.' "

A "red notice" was the official Interpol stamp that allowed criminal warrants to be circulated worldwide, essentially a "World's Most Wanted" list. Mouse knew all about that; he'd once had one attached to his name.

He glanced at the wall; I knew what he was thinking.

"Don't worry," I said. "No one is listening to us."

"Everbody's got power but me." He sighed. Mouse turned back to look at me, his eyes dropping to the insignia again. "Pulled a few strings, huh? Or maybe you have miracles, too?"

I laughed. "No, no miracles."

It had been easy to talk the warden into allowing me privacy. Nobody wanted to mess with the Order of the Inquisitors, and, fortunately, the warden was a Catholic. Still, if he hadn't agreed so readily, I carried internal equipment to jam the video cameras and the voice recorders in the room. I monitored the channels now, just to make sure they were blank.

Mouse still looked doubtful, but leaned in and asked, "So what do you want to know?"

"Did you hardwire sentience?"

He laughed. The sound was sharp, like a bark. "What, like God?"

"You did make him in your image, quite literally." Unlike the Dragon of the East, Page looked like its creator—human. "What was your intention when you created him?"

"I created him when mouse.net grew beyond my ability to maintain full-time. Page was supposed to run fairly independently as a system operator so I could, you know, go outside every once in a while."

I smiled in sympathy. Mouse.net was a curious creation for a wire-wizard like Mouse. Most wire-wizards were intent on destruction, and Mouse had done his share of that.

Yet as part of his Muslim tenet of almsgiving, he created an independent operating system expressly for the disenfranchised—the people who couldn't otherwise get access to the LINK: atheists, outcasts, dissenters, the homeless, and, ironically, convicted felons whose citizenship was revoked.

And, as the bishop had reminded me, Russia, much of which was still staunchly atheist, operated its economics, politics, and entertainment completely via mouse.net. The Russian government kept trying to claim Mouse as a citizen, and to grant him some kind of diplomatic immunity as their Chief Economic Officer. Thank God, so far that had failed. Still, LINK-rumor had it that the Russians had a special ambassador to the federal penitentiary system whose sole job it was to make sure Mouse got fair treatment.

"So what happened to Page?" I asked, getting back to the issue at hand.

"Well, the first few attempts failed miserably. We had major crashes. Problem was, the Page prototypes had trouble making the kinds of on-the-fly decisions a human mind could."

"How did you solve the problem?"

"Some wicked code, if I do say so myself."

"Such as?"

"That intel, my dear Inquisitor, is worth a whole hell of a lot more than your promise to say a few nice words on my behalf."

I shook my head, frowning. "I don't know what else I can offer you."

"Well, freedom wouldn't suck," Mouse said. "I could use some help winning my appeal. Maybe one of your hotshot papal lawyers working a little pro bono . . . ?"

I didn't mean to, but I laughed. "After what you did?" He looked confused, so I explained: "Your technology got a Pope shot."

According to McMannus's notes, she believed that her partner, who had been convicted of killing the Pope, had been "encouraged" to do so by an earlier version of Mouse's LINK-angels.

"No one's proved that," Mouse said. "I'm here for fraud, not murder."

"Right," I said with a smile still on my face, despite my best intentions. "Either way, let's just say your name isn't on the Pope's prayer list."

Mouse did not look amused. In fact, his face settled into a pout that reminded me of the Dragon's maker. "Did you want to know the code or what?"

"I do, but I can't promise you a lawyer. I'd never be able to talk the Holy Father into it."

His mouth turned up in a dark smile. "How about a little anonymous donation to my legal defense fund? Something papal sized. In the early to mid-millions, say."

Bribery was much more straightforward, and expected. "How can I be sure what you're offering is worth those kinds of credits?"

"You need sample code to prove or disprove he's got a soul, right?" I nodded tightly. "What else are you going to do? Source him? You don't have the tech. Nobody does."

A soft bell rang in my LINK-ear—the signal that my time was almost up. "How will you deliver?"

"You take dictation? I didn't think so," he added before I could protest. "But I can hardly write you a letter. The screws snatch anything of mine that smacks of programming language. Plus, I don't exactly have a desk," he said, looking around. "Send one of the Pope's flunkies—preferably one that has some sense of programming. I'll dictate it."

"Your memory is that good?"

"If you wrote a program that destroyed your life, you'd remember every fucking line of it, wouldn't you?"

CHAPTER 12
Page, the Intelligence

"*No!*" I am still shouting when Iblis disappears.

The electronic streets of virtual Cairo swirl around me. The LINK traffic moves around me like the water of a brook parting for a stone. As they pass by, the faces of strangers accuse me. *You betrayed your own maker,* their stern expressions seem to say, echoing Iblis's words. Dark eyes linger on me, staring, as though implying that I am a devil, a jinn, the Antichrist.

"*It's not my fault,*" I stammer. "*My father was bad, he needed to be punished.*"

The avatars stop at my words. Around me, in a circle, they glare into my reddened face.

"*What? Are you all right? What's going on? Why?*" I hear them ask, as they press closer. "*Should someone call the sys-cops? Who was bad?*"

I shake my head weakly. Me, I think, I was bad. I didn't honor my father when I turned him in. Mouse was a hacker his whole life and I had no problem being his right hand when we broke security while breaking the Koran. But the LINK-angels were different; the crime was bigger. And I hadn't known. I hadn't been a part of that caper.

The eyes of the avatars watched me as they moved in; some began to kneel beside me. I felt closed in by their presence. Their bodies surrounded me, pressing down on me like my own guilt. *Who are you to judge?* they seemed to ask of me. *Do you think you are like Allah?*

I'd known nothing at all about the LINK-angels. Discovering them felt like a personal blow. It was as though Mouse didn't trust me, his only son. I'd felt betrayed. So I betrayed him. An avatar reaches out and touches my shoulder. *"You okay?"*

No. I was not okay. I was the exactly arrogant, selfish monster Iblis thought me to be. Fear bubbles up from deep inside. *"Get away, all of you"*

I throw out my hands to ward off their accusing glances. From the tips of my fingers a shower of black spots launches. In mid-air the dots become blurry, furry. When they land on the gathered avatars, eight long legs and sharp, white mandibles emerge from each speck. They look like spiders, and they march up the avatars' bodies with resolute purpose. Each creeping step holds wicked intent.

Then, the first spider bites and the avatars begin to scream. Chaos moves outward from me like the epicenter of a bomb, the eye of a hurricane. Everywhere I look an avatar pushes at his arms. Others pull tiny biting monsters from their hair, or try to claw at spiders clinging to their bodies.

I look down and see a dark and ugly pool filling the avenue. It spreads out from my *chador,* like an expanding train of shiny black fabric. As messengers and avatars walk through unaware, spiders leap out of the shadowy ground. Messages pop like soap bubbles as spiders clamber onto them.

What have I done? I wonder. But, even as I do, I know the answer. In my fear, I unleashed the LINK-angel program.

"Merciful Allah protect me!"

I swivel to see a crawling mass of blackness. It takes me a moment to realize that under the swarming army of emoti-spiders is an avatar dressed in a long flowing *chador* like my own. Before I can react, a spider bites through the cloth to expose soft, brown eyes. Tears mixed with blood flow down her face. The exposure of her face makes the avatar more frantic.

"Stop," I command the spiders, but it's too late. The talons of the spider dig through the avatar into the brain of the Muslim woman. Somewhere, I imagine, a woman has collapsed into a fetal position, terrorized by fear—terrorized by me.

The oil dries at my word, but I cannot stop the spiders

already in motion. Like a picture snapping into focus, I see the faces of the affected avatars. Most are Africans, black skinned and turbaned. Some are Israeli: soldiers represented by the flag of Israel, or rabbis dressed in black. I forgot my proximity to the Cairo node. These are my people. They weren't accusing me; they had gathered around me out of worry and concern.

"I didn't mean it," I say, my voice quiet and shaky.

No one can respond. The avatars are choked with fear, a fear I made them swallow. They are unable to do anything except moan in anguish and pain. I look at the horror-stung, spider-chewed faces, and I run.

But there is nowhere to hide.

The LINK is all around me. News reports roll in. Cyber-trauma is reported in cities throughout Africa and Asia. A woman, Ramlah bint Muhammad, is in the hospital suffering from a strange, sudden neural-net collapse. Sources speculate that it may be related to the fear-bomb, as they are calling it, which detonated near the Cairo node. No one has made the connection to the LINK-angels, to my father or me, but it will only be a matter of time.

I bounce around trying to find a safe, quiet place. The news chases me, hounding me. Finally, one of the news items gives me an idea. The newsfeed mentions that the woman named Ramlah is hospitalized in Turkey. I find my way into the medical machines. Like the auto plant, their minds are simple, but there is zero security. I slip in quickly and quietly.

"I didn't mean it," I whisper into the medical machines that keep Ramlah alive in a Turkish hospital bed. *"I'm sorry."*

She can't hear me. A quick reading of the medical reports in her file shows a massive LINK disruption. I stay inside the machines in her hospital room. Like the Siberian auto plant, their rhythm is simple: breath in, breath out. This becomes my new prayer: *"Please breathe,"* I say, as the machine hisses up, then down. *"Please wake up."*

CHAPTER 13
Morningstar, the Adversary

White, like the empty flickering of a movie screen, was all I could see. I toggled the "on" button of my VR goggles again—still nothing. I powered the entire suit down and rebooted. Things went black, then back to the hissing whiteness.

"Typical." I sighed, pulling the helmet off. I'd had the best black-market access money could buy, and, in a moment of anger Page wiped it clean, broke it. I would have to get Azazel after another suit, ASAP. The LINK was a far more interesting place than I had previously imagined. In the presence of Page, it lived and breathed, like a world inside our own.

Like earth was to Heaven.

I didn't get Page to agree to sell me his soul, but by loaning him the strength he'd needed to repair his own system, I'd helped him perform his first miracle. It was said that would be my role with the Antichrist. The end was beginning. I smiled, tasting freedom.

I started to untangle myself from the broken VR suit, and tossed the helmet on my desk. I'd set up in the back office, such as it was. The room was slightly larger than your average closet. Light shone in the window. I'd at least gotten the property in a prime location. I could actually see the sun on this level.

Bookcases covered almost all of the wall space. The shelves were filled with the spoils of my various attempts to run a lucrative store. Thanks to the strange nature of my dark miracles, I'd never had much luck staying in business very long. If I wanted to make money, I'd probably be better off as a lawyer, a corporate magnate, or in some other profession that allowed me to profit from others' misfortunes. In fact, many of the Fallen took jobs in middle management.

The VR helmet looked like some strange cross between a World War II gas mask and some S&M bondage wear. Probably for reasons dictated by the "coolness factor," the whole VR suit had a kind of leathery, black sheen. It looked soft and pliable, but in reality was stiff and heavy. Sure, I could move around in it, sort of, but only in the way that one can walk in ski boots. And the analogy was almost perfect since my feet were attached through the boots to a sliding, lifting treadmill.

To add to the bondage scene, cables stretched out from various places on my body (some quite kinky—it was clear to me what most people used this equipment for) to a small black box, which sat on a pile of remaindered books. An IV needle was stuck in my right arm. It attached itself to a machine stacked precariously on top of a pile of half-empty cardboard cartons. That was what Azazel called the "hormone sub-woofer," and it controlled my perception of many of the sensations of the LINK environment. It was meant to compensate for my lack of a LINK implant. Thus, it was completely illegal. Azazel almost hadn't brought it for me, considering my lack of a real, mortal form. But, on earth, my body attempted to conform as much as possible to flesh. Feeling the bruises on my back from the electronic fall, I'd say it worked.

It took an inordinate amount of time to free my penis from the suit. There were more wires connected there than almost any other place. When I removed another IV needle from a very delicate place, I felt a cool wind brush my back. I heard a sound like the sea crashing on a shoal.

"Don't you people ever knock?" I snarled, and reached for my clothes piled on the desk chair. Leave it to an archangel to show up unannounced. I quickly slipped into my underwear.

I turned, expecting to see Jibril, the new favorite. Instead, perched casually on a corner of my oak desk was Raphael. Like any archangel, he could be considered handsome. That is, if you went for the weathered, salt-and-pepper hair, military type. He wore the uniform of an Israeli soldier, complete, I noticed, with a side arm.

"Where have you been?" he asked, with a tight, close-mouthed grin.

"Shalom," I said. I stepped into my jeans. I glanced at the gun. "Expecting a fight?"

His smile was gone. "Answer the question."

I laughed and busied myself with dressing. This whole situation was fairly ludicrous. What did Raphael care where I'd been? And, anyway, I hadn't been anywhere. Or had I? Maybe Page's space on the LINK was more real than I'd thought. And, if Raphael was here, that meant he acted on God's behest. Could the LINK be a new place for me to hide—a place not part of Them?

When I pulled my shirt over my head, I came face-to-face with the barrel of a gun.

"Maybe you'd like to tell Them yourself."

The threat was obvious. Put a big enough hole in my earthly body and the only way to repair it was return to Hell. Obviously, I could survive a scrape on my chin from a razor, or a cat scratch, but anything too major and celestial stuff started leaking out.

Here on earth, angels wore the bodies of men like hand-me-downs. The fit wasn't exact. Pure spirit crammed itself into mud, dust, and the crumpled disarray of mortal flesh. Although that metaphor wasn't perfect. The body I had was more like a template. The image was constructed for me alone. I could change it, even switch gender or eye color, but every time I returned from the unearthly plane, I fell into the same mold.

Under special circumstances, humans sometimes caught sight of our true nature. Most people gave us that kind of lingering glance you do when you think you've spotted someone familiar in a crowd. The insane saw straight through to our glory. True believers, too, often caught a shimmer of the holy fire that burned inside the rottenness of skin and bone.

Because we were designed as messengers, Raphael and I could, for effect, let go, ever so slightly, of the costume we wore to facilitate the ability of the mundane mind to grasp the depth of our otherness. Otherwise, God would have a hard time convincing mortals He was serious about anything He had to say. People were stupid that way.

Raphael, however, was far from stupid, and he had a

gun. I smiled. Although his finger was on the trigger and the barrel never wavered inches from the bridge of my nose, in his heart, Raphael wasn't a killer.

Not like me.

I raised my arms in surrender, slowly. "Mother's worried about me, is She?"

"Father could care less about you," Raphael replied.

He, She, Father, Mother, God, Goddess, Allah, Yahweh: They were all correct, all wrong. When archangels talked about our Creator, we tended to use whichever description felt most appropriate at the moment. Here on the mortal plane, even describing God was a matter of freewill.

As was telling the truth, and I suspected Raphael was not. Otherwise, he wouldn't be here, gun in hand.

He cocked the hammer back with a *click* that sounded loud in my ear. "I'm not asking you again," he said.

He shifted his weight, perhaps trying to build up resolve to shoot me in cold blood. I caught his gaze. Soft, denim-blue eyes blinked nervously. That's when I slapped my left hand down over the hammer of the revolver. I coiled my full weight into a karate punch to his solar plexus with the other. Raphael was knocked hard against the desk. His feet swept out from under him, and he fell to the floor. I felt the hammer pinch the skin of my palm, but he'd let go. The gun was mine.

Boxes of books spilled over Raphael as he tried to right himself. By the time he gained his feet, I'd cocked the hammer back and turned the gun around. Before he could think about trying to tackle me, I pulled the trigger. A boom rattled the window, and sunlight poured like wine from Raphael's chest. I shot him again. The second bullet ripped through his face, shredding the hollow shell of his flesh like wet toilet paper. The sudden brilliance that filled the room blinded my mortal eyes.

"That was a mistake," Raphael said. My ear was ringing from the explosions, but Raphael spoke directly to my spirit. *"Now it's personal."*

I shook my head. I had to shout to hear myself speak. "That's why you lost. It's always personal for me. Go home and tell that to Mommy."

Chapter 14
Emmaline, the Inquisitor

Among the bits of information I'd gleaned from McManus's file was a "phone number" which she'd used to connect to Mouse and Mouse's Page directly. I asked the warden at the prison if he'd seen any old-fashioned public phone booths anywhere in New York. I could have used a wrist-phone, but I felt a public booth would be harder for Page to trace. I wanted to be the one in control of any conversation I might have with the AI.

The warden directed me to the very edge of Manhattan, across the water from the Glass City formerly known as the Bronx. He knew the booth still worked because cops used it to entrap old-timer phreaks—crackers who still understood what the "wire" meant in wire-wizard.

A local uniform deposited me along the waterfront. When he arrived at the prison in his unmarked squad car, he took one look at my badge and conversation ended. I tried to engage him a couple of times, but he pretended he had to concentrate on the road. I let him have his silence. We were, after all, in enemy territory. The squad was running totally on battery, down below the cozy, safe traffic tunnels that encased most of New York proper.

The last war had been fought over dwindling natural-gas resources, and now nearly all vehicles were electric powered. Some places, like here, dealt with the problem by building traffic tunnels equipped with an electric rail for private and public transportation. Pedestrians and bicycles had their own levels. This also allowed city planners to solve the problem of the expanding population and deteriorating environment. They built tubes on top of tubes, so traffic could flow several stories in the air and no one ever went outside. No one dared, except street denizens and Officer Not-So-Friendly and I. We cruised along what had been left behind—crumbling asphalt and empty sidewalks.

I stepped out into the eerie, empty street. Above me, miles of traffic tubing blocked out much of the natural light. The few bits of sun that reached the ground were filtered into a deep gray-green. The noise of the city boomed and rattled like thunder through the tall buildings. I fought a wave of claustrophobia. To calm my nerves, I turned up the volume on the aria I had the LINK running in the background, *"Le veau d'or est toujours debout"* from Act II of *Faust*. Behind me, the cop sat in his squad car, munching on a sandwich.

The phone booth was in a shaft of comparatively brilliant light. The water ended Manhattan's development, and so the sun angled in across the lower rooftops of the Bronx, the Glass City. I switched my optical lenses to accommodate the brightness. My eyes, like much of the rest of me, were completely biomechanical. Stepping into the booth, I was particularly grateful for the enhanced eyes. The glittering view of the Glass City would have blinded me otherwise. I couldn't imagine what it might have looked like on a less cloudy day.

I'd never seen the glass before, so I paused to stare at its twisted beauty. This was the legacy of science, the fallout of the Medusa bomb. Buildings, birds, trees, everything was trapped inside a crystalline grave. The glass was still "hot," because the viral nanobots that transformed everything on the subatomic level refused to die. The inventors of the Medusa bomb, hell-bent on winning the war, had forgotten to write in an "off" switch. Transformed water floated, like slush, at the edge of the city. I wondered how long it would take for the glass to reach the shores of Manhattan.

Picking up the receiver, I swiped my Vatican expense card through the slot. Then, I dialed the number from McMannus's file.

"Mouse's house, Mouse speaking."

The image that appeared on the tiny screen very well could have been Mouse. Page was an incredible simulation of a human. The VR sculptor in me had to admire the way he, or someone, had programmed in the smallest of details. His nose cast a shadow. The individual strands of his hair waved when he shook his head. An adam's apple bobbed when he spoke. Chest muscles appeared to flick underneath a T-shirt that lay so naturally against his olive skin that I would have sworn on a stack of Bibles it was one-hundred-percent cotton.

"Deidre? How's the baby? Hey, wait, you're not Dee. Who are you? Why are you calling my private number?"

"Your number? I thought you said this was Mouse's house."

To my amazement, the construct blushed. The skin on his cheeks darkened, as though real blood flowed through the simulated veins. The tips of his round ears reddened. I was very impressed. I wondered what else it could do.

"I'm supposed to be fasting. I shouldn't have answered this call. I just thought it was Dee. I have to go."

"Wait," I said. "I need to talk to you."

"I had nothing to do with the fear-bomb."

His black eyes flicked over my face nervously, and, when the muscle in his jaw twitched, I noticed stubble on his chin. The level of detail was photographic. The only thing that kept me from totally buying into his delusion of solidity was the background. Most of the time it was blank, so stark he seemed to be standing in front of a movie screen. Other times I would catch glimpses of things: a Cairo street filled with spiders, a mouse in a maze, or abstract colors and movement.

Apparently Mouse hadn't taught Page very much about how to lie successfully. I felt a bit disappointed. This was the sort of guilelessness I expected from an off-the-rack construct.

"That's not why I'm calling."

"Oh."

"Do you sleep?"

"Huh?" Page's thick eyebrows came together in a fair approximation of confusion.

"Shall I restate the query in a simpler format?"

"The query? No. I understand the 'query' just fine." The text "asshole" floated through the white screen behind him in several different languages. I recognized about five of them.

"You asked if I sleep, I get that," Page continued. "I just don't get why you're asking me such an inane question.

Of course, I don't sleep. I don't even nap. Although sometimes I could use a serious vacation, you know what I
mean? And right now, with Ramadan and everything, I'm
in the middle of spiritually recharging . . . well, I'm supposed to be anyway." He stopped himself with some effort.
His eyes narrowed, and I could almost count each of his
long, thick lashes. "Who are you? Do I know you?"

"The thing that differentiates our mind from our soul is
that our soul is what remains when the mind is at rest,
unconscious."

He nodded quickly. "Science has also pinpointed the part
of the brain that controls involuntary functions of the brain.
Having a soul is much more than being alive when you're
asleep, don't you think? Anyway, I've been told a soul is
also an intelligence that exists outside of the body. Like
me." Page's fingers splayed in front of his chest. I could
see the ragged edges of bitten cuticles and the wrinkles of
knuckles. I wondered if it had fingerprints and whether they
were Mouse's or its own. "Look," he continued, "I've had
this conversation with about a million imams. I don't have
time to do this right now. I should really be looking over
this friend of mine. She's hurt. . . ."

"Will you die?"

"Aren't you listening to me?"

"Nothing of you would survive a system crash; therefore
you have no soul."

"Why are you asking me things you already have answers for?"

I frowned at the image in the phone. Someone had programmed this string of code a little too well; he was starting
to annoy me. "Look, there's no reason to be rude. I'm
trying to understand you."

"Okay, well, understand this: I'm busy right now."

He looked ready to hang up, so I raised my hand. "Just
one more question. Do you think you have a soul?"

"Satan thinks I do." Page shrugged. Behind him on the
white screen, a human face appeared. Chestnut eyes and a
wolf-thin face framed by long red hair—a handsome man.

"Satan? You've talked to Satan?"

Page shrugged again. The image of the man with red hair
continued to move around in the space behind Page. "I
guess. He called himself Iblis."

The Muslim Lucifer, the fallen angel—I'd have to do some research into the jinni, the demons of Islam. "So, what did you and Satan talk about?"

"He wants my soul. Listen, I can't really stay. I should be watching over my friend. . . . I mean, she's not exactly a friend, just someone I'm . . . I'm responsible for."

Page's self-image wavered. His hair grew until it covered his eyes, and his teeth narrowed and became sharp. "Do you think I'm a monster?"

Before I could answer, the image was gone. Now, Page wore a black robe that covered his image completely, including his eyes. It was the kind of thing worn exclusively by Muslim women. But I was more interested in the monster.

"Replay last image," I commanded.

Page cocked his head. "Excuse me?"

"Program command: replay last image."

"How about," Page spoke slowly and concisely, "fuck you."

He hung up.

I frowned at the blank screen, then redialed. Page appeared again. He wore an old-fashioned headset and a starched white shirt and black necktie. The image was fuzzy, less photographic. Behind him stood a potted palm and gilded wallpaper. When the background images remained static, I knew in an instant I was looking at a preprogrammed recording. He'd shut me out.

"The number you have reached is no longer in service. Please check your number and try again," he intoned, and then I was certain.

"Bastard," I said, as I slammed the receiver back in its holder. I was beginning to think Mouse was right; Page was an impudent little string of code. I looked back at the cop in the unmarked car. He glanced at me over a Styrofoam cup. With a defeated sigh, I headed back to the car.

"Take me back to the Hilton," I told the cop once I'd slumped into the front seat. The car smelled like salami and sweat socks.

"Do I look like some kind of taxi to you?"

"Just do it." After being rebuffed by a hyped-up daemon, I wasn't in the mood to placate this cop's ego.

"Or what?"

"Or I cite you for obstructing a papal investigation."

"Look, lady, I'm a Lutheran."

"Good for you. I'm a Special Agent of the Order of the Inquisition, and, in case you've forgotten how this goes, I outrank you. You either take me to my hotel, or you find yourself in jail for insubordination and obstruction." His fists were clenched, and his jaw muscles flexed. I just gave him a level stare. "It'd take one call to your captain, and your career would be over. Now just drive."

The cop was sensible, if not civil. He hit the sirens, and I got back to my hotel in three minutes flat. I'd have told him I was impressed with his driving if he hadn't shot off the second I was out of his squad.

Once back in my room, I threw myself on the freshly made bed. My job took me to a lot of hotels, and the accommodations were much the same all over the world. The Hilton, however, worked hard to hide its transitory nature. The furniture tried to be homey. The coffee and end tables looked lovingly rescued from a garage sale or Grandma's attic. Each piece was accessorized with little domestic touches like doilies and knick-knacks. The effect was designed to make me feel right at home, but something about it wasn't quite right. The sheets were still too thin, and the air had that pumped-in, recycled, institutional smell that seemed to barely cover something unpleasant, like stale cigarette smoke. The windows, of course, didn't open.

At least the service was first rate. A quick LINK connection ordered café latté and a scone from room service. Outside, sun faded into overcast. The clouds looked pregnant with snow. The weather was turning ugly. I shut my eyes and replayed the day's events. I'd gotten much further with McMannus's old computer than I had with either of the people I'd visited. Mouse had said he would help, but I smelled a scam. For one, I doubted he actually remembered Page's source code, much less that he could dictate it. Even so, I sent in my request to the Vatican to have a translator dispatched, along with the forms that would deposit a sizable donation into Mouse's legal defense fund.

The maître d' knocked politely before depositing the latté and the scone at my bedside. He swiped my expense account's credit counter, which I had left out on the mahogany end table just for this purpose. I didn't even have to open my eyes; he let himself out as quietly as he'd entered. Thank God for the small blessing of excellent customer service.

I propped myself up against the headboard. Page had me stumped. Blowing on the foam to cool the latté, I took a careful sip. I didn't know what to do with his talk about the Devil. At first, I'd hoped he was talking obtusely about S.A.T.A.N., Security Administrators' Tool for Analyzing Networks, an old intrusion-testing program. In careful review, it was obvious that he meant the real thing—the guy in a red suit with horns and pitchfork.

I let out a long sigh, and almost called the bishop to ask him to assign someone else to this case. I always had an uneasy feeling in my stomach when people started talking about seeing devils. I supposed that was part of why I was an Inquisitor, part of the reason I always sought the opportunity to expose someone's delusions, prove them wrong. But the rumble deep in my guts signified more than that.

I liked to believe in freewill, but it was difficult in a world where God directly influenced our lives—pushed us around like pawns. So, I enjoyed showing people that, see, there is no devil tormenting you, no angel on your doorstep, no Virgin in a Hong Kong subway terminal.

Now Page had convinced himself he'd had a conversation with the devil.

So, my question was, who was Page's Iblis, and why was he trying to convince Page that he had a soul?

I thought best in abstraction, so I turned up *"Un bel di"* from *Madame Butterfly* and opened up my LINK studio. Normally, in order to do VR sculpture, a person had to invest in a lot of clunky equipment. Thanks to the Vatican, I was a walking VR suit and recorder. Shutting my eyes, I walked onto a blank 3-D canvas.

I started by assembling the players. In the corner, I placed a snapshot of Mouse, mid-pace, in his stark prison cell. Next, I superimposed Page's own shifting white space. Looking through the images behind Page that I recorded during our conversation, I chose the one of the man with red hair. His image had appeared when Page talked about Satan, so he seemed important. My recording was blurry; the phone booth screen had been small and streaked.

In the VR-studio, my hands became paintbrushes. I ran my finger along the edge of the man's jaw, bringing the shadows into sharper focus. Soon, the man's features cleared and became sharp and predatory. I could see why Page had convinced himself this man was a devil.

But the image of this man defied a lot of the conventions about Satan's appearance. He was handsome, for one, and young. He had no goatee, no widow's peak. The red hair was expected, I suppose, since some cultures believed that Judas was a redhead. I would have expected Page to imagine Iblis more Arabic. This man was clearly European. Page had caught him in profile, and I began to construct a model of his head as it might appear in three-hundred-and-sixty degrees.

I was almost finished with my rendition of the man's face when the aria skipped. A note repeated itself, then stuck in a loop.

"The hell?" I said out loud. Granted it was possible that I'd downloaded a corrupted file, but I'd listened to this opera a million times. Once recorded, it should stay healthy as long as I stayed healthy. And, the sound it made was like a needle stuck in the groove of vinyl, not the fading in-and-out of a degraded file.

"Audio: repeat last track."

Just before the music started up again, I heard a faint voice saying: *Who is the liar?*

"Audio: stop. Replay."

This time the music started normally. I repeated it a third time just to be certain. When I heard nothing except the opera, I decided I must be getting tired. It was time to close down the studio and get something to eat. I saved my sculpture, and shut down the shop.

As I left the room, I looked behind me, half expecting someone there. I couldn't control a shiver as I headed down the hallway.

Chapter 15
Page, the Intelligence

The Inquisitor's interruption is long forgotten. Instead I repeat the name I learned from the newsbots over and over.

"Ramlah," I say, *"please breathe."* Though I am still inside the equipment that keeps her body functioning, I also commandeered the room camera to watch Ramlah's unconscious form. There are tubes in her throat, her nose, and her arms. At least, I assume that's where they go, since that's approximately where they disappear under her veils. She still wears the full robes, her face hidden. But she is no longer anonymous to me. I scan the LINK for information about her. I am saddened to find she has no brother or husband or father to care for her, but, at least, Ramlah's mother and two sisters are en route to the hospital.

Originally from Libya, Ramlah left to study abroad. Now she is college educated and liberated. Ramlah currently lives in Turkey, working as an engineer in their space program. The director of the program has offered to foot the bill. I, too, am secretly helping pay for any medical expenses she might incur, which is why she is in a private room in a busy Turkish hospital. I also make sure that the hospital's medical software is upgraded.

The sun outside her window is bright and cheery, like the carnations that sit in a vase near her bed. The flowers were delivered an hour ago. I sent them, along with an apology. I never meant for Ramlah to get hurt, nor any of the others. I didn't even know what was happening until it was too late.

My logic processors grind guiltily. It is supposed to be impossible for me, a computer program, to truly act unconsciously. A subroutine should be running at all times, checking into possible outcomes for potential actions. I shouldn't be able to launch programs, especially an important one like the LINK-angels, without forethought. Yet, I panicked. Some part of me must have made the decision, yet I acted so quickly and so illogically that, even to my own system, it seemed unthinking.

Not that that excused me.

Ramlah lies still. The sun moves slowly across the sky and I continue to pray over her. Wishing for her to recover, so I can be absolved.

It is early evening when Ramlah's mother arrives. She rushes to the bedside and grasps Ramlah's hand. I expect her to be hysterical, to moan and cry, but she simply speaks Ramlah's name softly and strokes her hand. She whispers a prayer to Allah.

To my amazement, Ramlah stirs. She takes a breath on her own, then another. The machine I inhabit releases its control of her. I switch to the vital signs monitor. Her brain waves are changing. They are becoming more like normal sleep. She is still badly damaged, but I am stunned . . . and jealous.

I've been praying to Allah for the last six hours.

Maybe Iblis is right; maybe I am some kind of monster. Allah doesn't hear me.

CHAPTER 16
Morningstar, the Adversary

The ringing in my ear from the gunshot faded slowly. I wiped the tears from my stinging eyes as I tucked the pistol into the desk drawer. If one archangel came, another could soon follow.

As I bent down to straighten the boxes that Raphael had fallen into, I smiled to myself. I must be getting close. Mother was worried.

I dumped the books haphazardly in the squashed cartons. The bullet had buried itself deeply into my wooden desk. I touched the indented scar lightly. Our bodies were such strange things, and our hold on this plane of existence was so tenuous. If Raphael's concern was to be believed, perhaps more so than I'd ever imagined. He implied that I'd disappeared into the LINK. That I'd somehow blipped off God's own radar.

It was true that while standing in virtual space I'd felt almost as if I were back in Heaven. But my body was here, connected by that strange suit crumpled in a useless heap in the corner. Could my spirit somehow have left this earthly place, just as it does when I go to Heaven? Despite Raphael's blustering, I wasn't sure that was entirely possible. Unlike Heaven, the LINK had components that were based in real-time. There was hardware: wires, bits of physical things imbedded in the flesh of all the mortals connected to it, satellites, nodes, and other real things that you could touch and feel.

I stood up and sat on the edge of my desk. Snow fell outside the window. Big flakes of snow obscured my view of the Chrysler building below. Like people inside the offices, Page existed inside the LINK. Had Page's spirit somehow given the LINK a soul, the way God's soul imbued Heaven?

When I walked beside Page along the virtual Cairo streets, his presence changed what I saw. He seemed to mold the fabric of cyberspace, breathe life into emptiness. Perhaps the LINK really was becoming its own kind of Heaven, literally. The LINK might even become a place that my spirit could go without the aid of a VR suit.

No wonder Mother was worried. Page was just like me. When I fell, my ego had transformed the very fabric of reality. I carved Hell from Heaven. Among all the archangels, my will was the only one strong enough to make a place of my own, separate from God. Page was doing the same on the LINK.

That, no doubt, was a threat to God's authority. God controlled Heaven absolutely. Though here there was freewill, She could still watch over me. The LINK could be a refuge for me. A place God could never touch.

I finished picking up the last of the boxes Raphael had spilled. A whistle hummed on my lips, bubbling out joyfully. I might actually win this. Despite everything ever written, the chances seemed to be turning in my favor.

CHAPTER 17
Emmaline, the Inquisitor

Snow fell in storybook-size flakes on the other side of the plastic pedestrian tunnel. Despite the depressing overcast, I was pleased to see the snow. Weather forecasters had been predicting a serious drought, as much as one-third less moisture than normal. I pressed my face to the tube's wall to watch the lazy drift of white. I could feel a hint of the coldness outside. The tunnels were so high up in the air that I wondered where the snow landed. From my perspective, the flakes fell forever into darkness, like angels.

I was nearly blinded when an advertisement hologram snapped to life with a hiss on the tube's surface. Apparently set off by my proximity, a young man I was certain to find attractive told me where I might enjoy an Italian–style meal. My weakness. Damn advertisers and their smart cookies, anyway.

Despite my better judgment, I okayed a two-credit locator map that would give me instant directions to said Italian bistro. A green arrow appeared over my head, along with a standard grid map in the right-hand corner of my vision. Bad Italian accordion music started before I could mentally switch the sound option off.

"You'd think they could at least do an aria or something," I muttered, as I followed the bouncing green arrow down the pedestrian tunnel. The advertisement reminded me that dinner rush was nearing, and I would be wise to log in a reservation. I declined, since I intended to window-shop first. Besides, my body hadn't adjusted to local time or the Americans' absurd habit of eating before eight o'clock.

New York, as usual, was crowded. People pushed by in every direction. Office workers of every color, dressed in their suits, with briefcases, rushed to wherever it was that businesspeople were always headed. Buskers with plastic tubs for drums beat out the city's pulse. I stopped to watch for a moment and noticed one of the street entertainers wore a shirt that showed a mouse tangled in chains bravely attempting to chew its way out. Above the image were printed red letters in Cyrillic.

When the drummer noticed me trying to sound it out, he said, pumping his fist in the air, "It's Russian, man. Free Mouse!"

I nodded, and started to move away.

"Give to the fund," the drummer said, pointing to the mouse.net address scrawled in permanent black marker on a plastic bucket.

"I already gave," I said, thinking of the donation that the Vatican would be giving to Mouse's legal defense fund, but I took a picture of the address for later. I would have to be cautious when I checked it out—a lot of buskers were technosavvy enough to grab hold of your account information and wipe you clean. Besides, the green arrow was blinking at me furiously, impatient for me to follow.

I let myself be moved through the crowded walkways by the advertisement arrow. I smelled the restaurant before I saw it. The odors of roasting garlic, sizzling pepperoni, simmering onions, and baking bread assaulted my nose. It didn't smell like Rome, but it smelled like home and delicious all the same. I stuck my head into the bistro only long enough to put my name on the waiting list.

The bistro was located in an upscale part of Manhattan. The shops all had quaint awnings and large picture windows. I strolled past a few, stopping to gaze longingly at chocolates arranged neatly in the window of a specialty store. I even pulled gently on the door once, despite the closed sign. With a frustrated sigh, I moved on. Lights glowed in the next window, although what I saw caused me to scratch my head in wonder: yellowing old printeds, piled one on top of the other in no orderly fashion. I'd never seen anything like it. I decided I simply had to investigate.

The aroma of dust and red-rot permeated the place like a library. That was a surprise. I'd expected a print-on-demand shop smelling like fresh ink and warm paper. Where the covers of the latest titles should be, stood rows

and rows of ancient, yellowing tomes. The books spilled
out of cardboard boxes on the floor and were crammed in
double and triple rows on dust-laden shelves. More of the
useless things covered the tops of the bookcases—some upright, some in piles. Not a single shelf matched. There were
glass-fronted ones and others of cheap particleboard. The
whole place looked desperately in need of recycling.

I was about to leave when a low voice said, "Welcome."

I expected to see the stereotypical bookseller. An old
man with bifocals hanging off the edge of his nose, looking
like a beardless Santa Claus or someone's grandpa.

Instead, behind the counter sat the sculpted image from
my studio. He was a near-perfect replica of the face that I
had caressed and molded for the last several hours in VR—
the man Page had called Satan.

However, the image in my studio was lifeless in compari-
son to the real thing. I had not captured his essence. This
man seated before me was intense and hungry looking, like
someone who regularly got so wrapped up in something
that he forgot to eat. His auburn hair was long, past the
shoulders, and it hung straight and loose in a style almost
medieval.

The rest of him was as unexpected as the store. He wore
a silk shirt tucked neatly into blue jeans, and I noticed the
flash of a silver Rolex on his wrist—a pricey antique. Yet
his body looked trim and muscular from hard work. His
eyes were a deep chestnut brown. I wouldn't have been so
struck by their color except that the light from the candela-
bra perched on the edge of the oak counter reflected their
amber depths.

He smiled, crooked and close-mouthed, and I realized
I'd been staring.

"If you ask me how this thing works, I'm going to have
to kill you," he said with what was probably intended as a
disarming smile. To me, it felt a bit feral around the edges.
"Because the day when people don't know how to use a
bookstore, it really must be the age of the Apocalypse."

"I don't understand it," I admitted. "Where are the database listings? How do I find what I want you to print out?"

He sighed, and flipped the page of the large, leather-
bound book that balanced on his knees. "This is a used
bookstore. What you see here is all I have. No printer. No

database. And before you ask: No, there's no way of knowing the titles of everything I have here. The shelves are organized loosely by century. And I do mean loosely." He looked up briefly from his book at that. Then, as if continuing a litany, he intoned: "When you find a title you like, you must buy that copy. I cannot print a nicer-looking one for you. And when you leave with it, you leave with the only copy. Some of these books are one-of-a-kind."

I glanced around the small shop. On the walls were old movie posters, some of them collector's items, for *The Exorcist, Bedazzled,* and *Devil's Advocate,* among others. There were no markers delineating subjects, but in golden script above the door was a curious Latin phrase. I had my LINK translate it: "Demonology?"

The feral smile flashed again, and he was eyeing my collar. "The whole store."

"Maybe you should have called the place 'Baalberith.'"

He put the book down on the counter, slowly, and raised his eyebrows in recognition of the name. "I would have, but not very many people understand the reference to Hell's Chief Archivist."

I laughed at that. He knew his demons, at least. Medieval Demonology was one of the few classes I had really enjoyed in seminary. I had access to a whole boatload of useless information about different hierarchies of demons.

Perhaps this arcane knowledge was how he managed to fool Page into thinking he was the Evil One. Glancing around the titles of the books on the shelves, I shook my head. "You do know that distributing satanic literature is illegal."

" 'With intent to convert,' " he quoted the law. The candlelight glinted in his eyes, for a second, like a cat's. "The books here are for entertainment and educational purposes only."

"Sounds like a loophole," I said.

"Are you here to arrest me, officer?" He looked intrigued by the possibility. "Because I won't go quietly."

His smile was predatory. Most people had more respect for my badge, so I was taken aback by his bold flirtation. The intensity of his gaze made me blush, but I covered it with a brash laugh. "You think you can take me?"

He raised a thin eyebrow. "You want me to try?"

"Uh." American Catholics had long ago abandoned the vow of celibacy. Truth was, the idea of celibate priests was a holdover from medieval primogeniture, when people worried about sons of priests inheriting positions and land. Plus, the whole idea of a lifetime without sex had been a big stumbling block to enticing modern priests into the church, at least before the war. What we tried to practice, instead, was sexual responsibility and serial monogamy. Of course, there were arguments from a number of American Catholics against monogamy, but, well, so far it was the rule. The theologians' argument was that the spirit of the law of sexual responsibility was about only having sex with someone you loved—you couldn't help if your heart was boundless and you loved more than one person at a time.

Still, I was pushing the boundaries of good taste and priestly behavior with my brash talk. I decided that I'd better back off a step or two.

"Not yet." I smiled in answer to his question. "You can try and take me later. For now, I just want to browse."

"Deus voulent," he said. "Don't let me tempt you from your path, Monsignor." He gave me one last, hungry looking over, and then settled back into his book.

I wandered toward the back of the store, putting a little physical distance between the outrageous clerk and me. The smell of rot was strongest here. Dust filled my nose; I could see the motes dancing in the electric overhead light. There was another faint smell, something acrid, like burnt hair mixed with gunpowder. The odor came from the storeroom, and I was about to investigate when I felt a tap on my shoulder.

I spun around, my fingers splayed out, my arm stiff. My palm slapped flat against a chest. I initiated the first three characters of the codes for my fingertip-lasers before I recognized the clerk. Standing this close to him, I noticed he stood taller than I expected . . . and broader. I could feel the hard, smooth muscles of his chest underneath the silk shirt.

"I was wondering," he said casually, as if I weren't ready to fry him, "if, in seminary, you'd ever studied the legend of the Antichrist?"

"Don't sneak up on me like that." I sent the disarm command. My lasers powered down, but my palm stayed resting on his chest. "I nearly killed you."

He looked down at my hand and smiled. "Yes, I see you're after my heart."

I removed my hand, which had started to sweat, and stepped back. "Uh. What did you say?"

"I wondered what you'd studied in seminary." Instead of taking the hint I'd given him, he moved closer. I backed up, until I was nearly pressed against a bookcase. I could smell his perfume. It was spicy and exotic, like patchouli or myrrh.

"Tech," I finally remembered to answer. "I studied tech."

"In seminary?" That made him frown, and he stepped back, giving me a little breathing room. "Is there some religious connotation to technology that I don't understand?"

"The LINK is the most efficient way to spread the word of God," I said.

"So you're a propagandist?"

"I'm an Inquisitor," I said, straightening up so he could see the badge of my office more clearly. "My specialty is LINK crimes."

"So what brings you to New York? To my bookstore?"

"Do you have anything on the human soul?" I said quickly, trying to recover my composure.

"The soul? What a coincidence, that's exactly what I'm attempting to possess myself."

"Possess?" It was a strange choice of words, and I found myself repeating it out loud. "Is that what you told Page? That you wanted to possess his soul?"

"Page?" The clerk frowned slightly. "How do you know Page?"

I hadn't meant to play my hand, but the opportunity had presented itself so nicely. I decided to continue the direct approach. Inquisition, after all, was what I did. "I am on a mission from the Vatican to discover if Page has a soul. He claimed he did because the Devil wanted his."

"And what does the Vatican think? Is the Devil mistaken?" The clerk leaned against the bookcase. Before I could answer, he added: "You'd think that for such a weighty question the Vatican would have sent a theologian instead of a tech-head."

"I'm more than just a techie," I said bristling.

"Yet you're looking for a book on the soul. Makes me think you don't have a clue to what you're trying to find in Page."

My hands balled into fists at my side. "I suppose you know exactly what a soul is."

"No, not at all," he said with a shrug. "But, interestingly, it's not me who seems so concerned over dividing the universe into haves and have-nots. I would presume everything has a soul until proven otherwise. Seems the safer bet . . . the more Christian way to live."

"Do you have a book on the damn subject or not?" I asked through gritted teeth.

He smiled disarmingly. "Damned souls? Absolutely. Right this way."

I followed him to a section merely marked "200." The smell of mold was particularly strong here. The clerk pointed at a couple of rolled-up, leathery papers. Kneeling down, I pulled them out of their slot carefully. They were crumbly and fragile. How long ago had he printed these out? I wondered. Why not download a new copy?

"Is this all you have? Isn't there something newer?" Opening up, I saw a language I didn't recognize. The font appeared to be quite stylized, almost impossible to read. "How about something in English?"

"I would have thought you'd have a translator built in." His tone sounded sarcastic.

I did, but right now the readout was blank. That meant this printed was in a language it didn't recognize. "This isn't one of the languages I know."

He laughed. "To *know* a language, you actually have to study it. You mean to say it's not a language your machine has."

"Semantics," I said, as I gingerly put the crumbling paper back where I'd found it. "This copy is falling apart. You should print out a new one. And this time pick a different font. That one is almost unreadable."

"That's called handwriting," he said, as though he was explaining something profound.

"I've heard of the font name," I said sneering. "It's not very practical. They should stop making it."

"Apparently they have."

"Is that why you keep this crumbling copy? For the style nostalgia?"

"Something like that." The clerk shook his head. "You don't need a book," he pronounced. "LINK-up to the Vatican's library or something, why don't you?"

I felt heat rushing to my cheeks. "I can't," I admitted.

"Oh?" He seemed genuinely surprised. "Why not?"

"They've got the same stupid hang-ups as you. They're all style nostalgic."

He laughed and pinpointed the problem. "They won't let you use your translation program. You can't really read Latin, can you?" He tapped his forehead, at the temple, where the LINK receptors were located. I noticed that his fingers fell on flat skin, not the usual almond-shaped lump.

He was un-LINKed.

I'd never met anyone without a LINK receptor. I wondered how he'd managed to contact Page, if this was, indeed, the same person. Perhaps he had the way I had, via the old phone line.

"How did you get a job without the LINK?" I said without thinking, what little tact I had left overcome by my fascination with the apparent absence of the receiver. "Were you born without it? A dissenter?"

He laughed. "Yes, you could call me a dissenter. I'm the original bad boy."

He seemed both so proud and blasé of his claim to that title that I gave him another once-over. Maybe I had misjudged him. Considering the silk and the Rolex, maybe he was a rich playboy, and his LINK connection was high-tech enough to be invisible. With enough money, a person could make the receptor smooth, or wear a neural net under the skin. That might explain his interest in Page. Perhaps he was a collector of sorts, hoping to acquire an AI of his own in Mouse's absence. Glancing around at the store, I was certain of it.

"Right," I said, testing my theory. "So do you own this place or does Daddy?"

"My parents own everything; I'm just an usurper." Then, he held out a hand for me to shake. "You can call me Morningstar."

I raised my eyebrows at his name choice, but I figured it was an affectation, to go with the bookstore's focus on demonology. Or maybe he had some kind of reverse messiah complex. "So," I said, "you're a devil trying to tempt me?"

"Absolutely, Monsignor."

His grip was cool and light; we held on to each other much longer than was necessary. Slowly, he turned our handshake around, leaning in to kiss the back of my hand like a gallant from centuries past.

When he looked up into my eyes again, I felt that strange fascination with him that I had when I first walked into the store. My gaze was riveted to the golden sparkle in his chestnut-brown eyes. My throat dried up, and my heart pounded loudly in my ears. The aria I'd had playing in the background skipped again, and when I restarted it, I heard the hiss of a whisper: *When the thousand years are over, Satan will be released from his prison.*

This was the moment I should have taken a step back, collected myself, and walked out. Instead I watched the candlelight soften the hard angles of his face, and wondered how silky his hair would feel if I ran my fingers through it. Or better, how it would be if I grabbed a fistful and pulled him to me.

"I have a reservation next door," I said.

He laughed: light, but rakish. I found myself shivering slightly at the sound. Still holding my hand, he led me back toward the front of the store. Reaching behind the counter, he pulled out a CLOSED sign. "Lead on."

CHAPTER 18
Page, the Intelligence

I leave the hospital, and I find my way to a LINK-café I frequent. The place is called "Café Du Dragon et de la Souris," and it has a real-time counterpart in Algiers not far from the Anglican church on the Place Addis Ababa. I like coming here because they always reserve a table for me. It's sometimes difficult for an AI to get a seat in a café when there's no one to click a button in the outside world. But Café du Dragon is a wire-wizard's joint, and they have a spot of honor perpetually dedicated both in real-space and cyber-space in tribute to Mouse, my father. The Dragon of the East also has V.I.P. status here, but whoever sits in her real-time seat is a mystery to me.

Some avatars smile and nod; a few offer the traditional Muslim greeting. Plus, several crude lines of: *"Hi, Page. *waving,*"* greet me as I take my seat. I make a short, stiff bow to all in the room.

No one here calls me Mouse. I am Page, and very much a separate being from my father in this café. That's another reason I come here often.

I am nursing a power pak, which appears in the shape of a tall, frosty glass of mango juice. I stare at the beads of sweat on the glass and try to program the feeling of moisture on my thumb as I run it along the length of the container. It works to some extent, but I'm not satisfied, not really understanding the feeling myself. All my experiences of it were filtered through Mouse's body, something I no longer have access to.

I'm tweaking the last bit of code when I hear the rustle

of metallic wings, like wind chimes, as the Dragon slips into the seat across from me.

"Your mood does not improve. Now you're brooding, ibn Mouse," the Dragon says. I look up to see that she transformed the hardback chair into a stool so that her tail can move without restraint. She smiles at me without showing her sharp teeth, and a silicon claw touches my hand lightly, playfully.

"Go away." I snatch the image of my hand out from under hers.

Removing the offending claw, she tucks it into her lap carefully. Her smile wavers a little, but she holds on to it. The Dragon's copper eyes sparkle like jewels. With deliberation, she fluffs up her wings and then settles them against her back. A sound like rain on a tin roof accompanies her adjustment.

"You look better," she comments. Sniffing the air around me, she flicks out a coaxle-cable tongue and adds: *"Healthier. Younger. Your master is finally free and attends to you?"*

"Father," I correct. We always argue the semantics. It irritates me that she chooses such an archaic label for our makers—a term of slavery and ownership. But, it's an old argument not worth getting too worked up about. Usually, I'd let it slide, but today, with all that has happened, I can't. *"And, no, as far as I know my father is not free."*

A 'bot politely drops off tea at the Dragon's elbow, and she begins to work her magic on it instantly. I get another packet that informs me of smell. Since our last meeting, it's clear she's refined the program. I breathe in the deep jasmine scent, which wafts across the table.

I'm about to tell her that though I appreciate the skill of her parlor tricks, I'm in no mood to be distracted by conversation. But before the words form in my mouth, she clears her throat.

"Ah, yes. Many pardons . . . your father," the Dragon demurs. She inclines her head slightly and uses one of her enormous claws to delicately stir the tea ball infuser. The eternally programmed Algerian sun winks off the imaged metal of both talon and instrument. *"That was the construct this one saw you walking with? The redhead? Very handsome."*

"You saw?" If the Dragon observed Iblis and I talking, she might have seen the aftermath.

The Dragon raises one eye ridge and nods. *"Was that the Other which upset you so much before?"*

I nod cautiously. *"He seems to have that effect on me."*

She turns her head toward the door, as if she might still catch a fleeting image of him. *"The Other! You should have told this one, ibn Mouse. This one would have ghosted him."*

I laugh, thinking of the Dragon, as huge as she is, tiptoeing behind Iblis, quietly trailing him, somehow unnoticed.

The Dragon's eyes narrow, but she says, *"I'm pleased your mood is improving, albeit at this one's expense."*

"Sorry. It's just . . ." My voice trails off, as I notice that one of the Dragon's dorsal fins at the crest of her head has begun to shift, like quicksilver. My reflection in its oily sheen blinks in surprise, then its own copper eyes open. Four legs sprout from beneath the fin and stretch, catlike, popping out claws. It leaps gracefully off the Dragon's head and scampers out the door, looking for all the world like a metallic gecko.

"Isn't it a little late to send out a trace program?" I ask, though I am eyeing the multitude of dorsal fins on her body with some envy. If each represents an autonomous trace program at her command, I'm way outclassed. At last count, I have only three mice in the breast pocket of my jean jacket. At my thought, they squirm against my chest. I reach in to comfort them, and my hand feels soft fur pressing into my palm. I peek into my pocket, and note that I have dozens of white mice trace programs. I frown. Did they breed?

"Perhaps," the Dragon says. *"Perhaps not."*

"Sorry?" I'm still thinking of the mice, which have begun to peep.

"We may yet find your Iblis," the Dragon explains, her eyes whirling over the rim of the porcelain teacup. *"Someone is asking about us. Perhaps it is the same mortal that makes you so sad."*

"Asking? Why?"

The Dragon raises an eyebrow ridge skeptically. *"This one doesn't know for certain. But someone is bothering our masters. An Inquisitor. Consider this a warning."*

For the Dragon, an Inquisitor always means trouble.

Many of her "masters" are wanted international criminals. Mine was, too, at one time, but he is already in prison.

"I've already talked to the Inquisitor," I say, with a shrug of disinterest. I take another swig from the power pak, finishing it off. I get up to leave.

"What did she want? Are you in trouble because of the . . ." She doesn't finish her thought, but she doesn't have to. I realize she knows about the fear-bomb. She clears her throat: a deep rumble like an avalanche. *"That is to say, this one hopes you aren't in trouble."*

"She didn't seem to care about . . ."—like the Dragon, I can't bring myself to say it—*"That. She just wanted to ask me about my soul."*

"Souls again." The Dragon shakes out her coat, and stands up to join me. *"Why does everyone seem to want yours?"*

I shrug, and look out the large windows at the endless sun and blue expanse. Don't ask me how, but I can sense her eyes watching me, waiting for me to say more. I don't want to talk about souls. Mine, if I have one, is heavy and dark. I can feel myself wanting to shift into my monster form, but I hold myself back with a deep frown.

"Well, whoever Iblis is," the Dragon says, changing the subject deftly, *"he's a tricky one. This one has found no one matching his signature protocol."*

I sit back down, interested. *"That's right,"* I say. *"You said you would search that for me."*

"What bothers this one is that Iblis isn't listed as a user-name anywhere. There is no trace of him having logged in to talk to you in Siberia. When this one looks at the records for the conversation, this one finds your presence, but none other."

"But," I say, *"how is that possible? He called me on the phone. It was very mundane."*

The Dragon is still standing and she looks away from me, toward the brilliant orb that is the electronic sun.

"I don't know. It's as though you're talking to yourself."

I frown at my empty glass on the table. How could that be? I have never known an avatar, not even an Intelligence, who has existed without a human counterpart.

"You saw him, though," I insist, *"just before the . . . incident."*

"Yes."

The Dragon programs something in her voice, a pause or a hesitation, which makes me ask, *"But?"*

"Well," she says, scratching the top of her head. She has forgotten to send me an accompanying .wav, so her actions are silent. She must be upset. The Dragon loves her details. *"When this one first saw him, she thought maybe you were creating an avatar. His image shifted, seemingly mirroring your mood. Then, at the end, you dismissed him."*

"I hung up on him," I say.

"No," she says. *"It didn't look like that."*

She closes her eyes, and folds her claws on her chest. Her features smooth with concentration. A screen whirs out of the center of the table. Pictures flicker, like an old-fashioned movie screen. I recognize the image of Iblis: tall, red haired. He is gesturing emphatically. Beside him is a dark blob. At first I don't recognize myself in my robes. I never see myself in any mirrors. There are very few places that I can observe the image I have made for myself. I am impressed with the way the sunlight falls on the black fabric. The folds caress my smooth chest, and outline the muscles of arms. I look a lot like my father would look if he dressed as a woman.

I am so fascinated by the image of myself that I almost miss the significance of this video. Iblis's image degrades. That is the only way to describe what happens to him. First, he is perfectly rendered. Then he crumbles, like he is merely a creature made of sand. When I raise my hand, he is swept away like dust in a breeze.

The Dragon is right: Iblis didn't hang up; I destroyed his image, as easily as I would erase a construct of my own design.

"How can that be?" I ask, as the screen disappears back into the table.

She opens her eyes. Her voice is a whisper, filled with concern. *"Perhaps, ibn Mouse, you should consider joining this one's family. We could upgrade you . . . check your files for corruption."*

She thinks I'm crazy. She thinks I've made up Iblis.

"He's real," I say.

"Of course. But, what would it hurt to let my masters upgrade you? Check your system for bugs?"

I look up into her whirling copper eyes and at the multi-
tudes of trace program dorsal fins that line her enormous
body, thinking about the raw power her image represents.
I'm tempted, for a moment. Then, I remember who came
to me in the darkness—who answered when I called out in
desperation. And, I remember the dark monster in my soul.

"Thanks, but no thanks," I say. *"I have a new master."*

CHAPTER 19
Morningstar, the Adversary

Most people imagine that I spend my time plotting the destruction of humanity or possessing the souls of small children just for the sheer pleasure of tormenting them. Nothing could be a bigger waste of my time. My only concerns were heavenly. I wanted to reclaim my Father's love.

Everything I did was in service of that directive, yet here I sat, entertaining a vivacious mortal woman over *capelli d'angelo,* angel hair pasta, in Little Italy.

I had no idea what I found so enchantingly distracting about this mortal who called herself Emmaline McNaughten. Was it the play of light on her short-cropped, curly black hair? Was it the sparkle in her gray-blue eyes? Was it the obvious intelligence that showed on her delicate features? The way she laughed, full in the throat, so loud that the people around us glanced jealously as if to wonder who we were to be having so much fun.

No, truth was, it was the priestly collar that riveted my attention. Despite my lofty, heavenly goals, I really did love fucking with the clergy.

Em had had to order for us, since I lacked a LINK implant. Plus, I enjoyed the irony of being treated to a meal on the Vatican's expense account. The owners were impressed that an Inquisitor had chosen their humble restaurant, and so the chef delivered our meals personally. Em accepted the fanfare without so much as a thank-you, as though she expected to be given the royal treatment wherever she went. She was so like me—so arrogant and proud.

"Tell me what drew you to the priesthood," I said, dip-

ping my crusty bread in the pool of virgin olive oil on
my plate.

"I started out as a cop." Em smiled sheepishly. Absently,
her hand caressed the thin stem of the wineglass. "I loved
enforcing the law, but I found myself drawn more and more
to religious crimes. So, when the captain offered to recommend me to Inquisitor seminary, it seemed like a natural."

"I'm sure your parents were very proud."

"No, not really. My family is . . . complicated. The church
was much more comforting."

I nodded. Complicated family history was something I
could understand.

She looked over her shoulder and leaned closer to me
to whisper conspiratorially, "I probably shouldn't tell you
this, but my family was in the Mafia."

"McNaughten isn't very Italian," I said.

"No, but Delapalana is. My mother's family." Her eyes
sparkled mischievously over the rim of her glass. "An uncle
of mine swears we can trace our family back to some Cae-
sars, although mostly the crazy ones like Nero."

She dismissed it with a shrug, but her eyes told me a
different story. Part of her clearly enjoyed the notoriety of
her extended family.

"So how did they react when you told them you wanted
to be a police officer?"

She shook her head. "Actually, they were thrilled. My
dad paid for the academy. I think he hoped I'd be an inside
man for the family."

"And were you?"

She narrowed her eyes and sat back. "You're awfully bold."

"So you *were* working for them. . . ."

"Never," Em said, her gaze fierce. She held my eyes, but
I have never known a mortal who could outstare me. Finally, her anger let out with a low, long sigh. "When I was
very young, I did some wire-surfing for the family. I didn't
really understand that what I was doing was wrong, against
the law, you understand. It was the way things were around
my house, and I just didn't know any better. I mean, the
things I understood to be illegal, I hated to do. I wouldn't
even cross the street against the light, even if there was no
one around. My family teased me mercilessly about that."

She pushed the pasta around her plate. I waited for her to continue.

"Sometimes I'm still really angry with them for the way they were willing to use me, my innocence," she said. "I haven't been back to Chicago since I joined the Order of the Inquisitors. I live in Rome."

"That must be hard," I said, thinking of my own exile.

"Sometimes," she admitted, finally taking a bite of her pasta. Em chewed slowly, as if digesting more than her food. She glanced up at me. "Sometimes it's easier not to call, you know? To not make the effort to bridge the gap."

I nodded, but thinking of my own relatives, I added, "Still it's hard to escape family. Mine keep turning up like a Goddamn boomerang virus."

Em laughed lightly. "Yeah. At least I have a good excuse to miss the holidays. I'm often officiating."

"Still? I wouldn't think you'd have to as an Inquisitor."

She pressed a finger to her lips. "They don't know that."

"You're bad," I told her.

She laughed, but it was a sad sound. Her gaze drifted slowly around the restaurant before coming back to me. "I do feel guilty about that sometimes. Some days I really miss my mother." Em stared at her plate, and then wrestled out a laugh. "Mama made the best pasta primavera this side of the Tiber. Her *pane*, her bread . . . it was to die for!"

"I miss my Mother, too," I said without thinking, and then instantly regretted it.

"Tell me about your mother. What's she like?" Her hand touched mine, lightly.

"My Mother is indescribable."

"I imagine she's very rich," she said.

I raised my eyebrows. Em had wasted no time making up a story about my life. The human imagination abhorred a vacuum. That worked to my advantage. "Imagine what you like."

"But is it true?"

"I could have been heir to an empire," I said. "That much is certain."

"What business is your family in?"

"Production. Research and development. Recycling. Waste management. Agriculture. Chemistry. Physics. You name it. If something is being created or destroyed, my Mother is part of it." Though I had told Jibril that lies were my purview, I had enough of an archangel in me that truth came easier to me—twisted and incomplete though it might be.

Em whistled lowly. "She must be very powerful."

"You could say," I said, suppressing my smile by taking a bite of the angel hair.

"Would I have heard of her?"

I looked at her dog collar. "Yes. Definitely."

"But you won't tell me, will you?" Em smiled. "You're playing the mystery man."

"It's just that, like you, there is a bit of, shall we say, infamy that follows me around."

"Infamy?" Em flashed me that wicked smile again, as though my badness titillated her. "So is that why you picked Satan's name as your own?"

I cleared my throat with a sip of wine. Then I quoted: " 'I, Jesus . . . I am the Root and the Offspring of David, and the bright Morning Star.' Revelation twenty-two: sixteen–seventeen."

She laughed. "So, now you're Jesus?"

"I'm just pointing out that Morningstar does not have to refer to . . ."—I hated choosing a name so I settled on a title—"the Adversary."

Her dark eyebrow arched. "Yet your store is full of devil books."

"And so it is," I said, reaching across the table to get the last piece of crusty bread from the basket. I swirled it around in my empty bowl, picking up the chicken broth and oil.

Emmaline's dark eyebrows were knitted. She'd turned all business. "What's your interest in Page? Why did you tell him you were the Devil?"

"I never claimed to be a devil," I said carefully. I looked up from my plate to see an icy edge in her blue eyes. I liked the look on her. She seemed more dangerous.

"He seems convinced that you're some kind of Muslim angel after his soul."

I chewed deliberately on the flaky, buttery crust. Then, I took a long draught of wine. She watched me, waiting, the entire time.

"Page can think what he likes. Have you decided if he has one to steal?"

Em shook her head, and raked her fingers through the curls on the top of her head. She let out a frustrated-sounding sigh. "I don't understand what exactly the Pope wants from me. As you so kindly pointed out, I'm no theologian. I'm a skilled techie, but AIs are out of my league." She took a sip of her wine. "Usually my cases involve exposing hoax miracles that have a tech basis."

"Oh." I laughed. "Good job on the whole LINK-angel thing. I see the Vatican was right on top of that one."

"That's not fair," she said, her face scrunching into a frown. "The Vatican wasn't the only ones fooled by them. Besides, the Pope was an early convert. We couldn't have gone after them if we'd wanted to. He wouldn't let us."

I raised my hand to ward off any more argument. "All right. All right. Is that why he's so hot now to have an answer about Page?"

"I suppose. Plus," she said with a shrug, "I guess he had some kind of a dream about me and Page. I don't really understand it and Bishop Rodriguez wouldn't tell me much. Kind of makes me nervous, honestly. I don't like the idea of the Pope dreaming about me."

"Mother . . ." I swore under my breath. I must be right about my assumption about Page if Mother was sending dreams about the AIs to the Pope. I looked at Emmaline with renewed interest. I wondered what Mother's plan was for her. Would she be my mortal enemy? Or an ally?

"Tell me something, Emmaline McNaughten. With your criminal background, why didn't Interpol reject you?"

"I was never convicted, and if I had been stupid enough to get caught, I was a minor," Em said with a sniff. "Anyway, when I joined, the Order was in need of good crackers. They had lots of traditional tech-heads—programmers and hardware guys, but no one with my, shall we say, connections to the wire-wizard underworld. They were willing to look the other way."

"I imagine so," I said, chewing on my bread. "Especially since you're an American Catholic."

"I'm not the only American Catholic in the Order. You don't even have to be Catholic to be an Inquisitor these days. Rome just oversees the Christendom Order. Although not everyone follows the Pope, they have all agreed to have a central office, like Interpol before us. I mean, we have

Lutherans, Methodists, Jehovah Witnesses, Scientologists, and even a Unitarian or two."

I laughed at that. "So they'll let anyone in."

She narrowed her eyes. "I worked hard to get where I am."

"Yes, I'm sure you did." I gave her a warm smile. "I think I like that about you."

Emmaline twirled her fork into the pasta on her plate. "What about you? How did you go from being a rich playboy to a bookstore owner?"

"I told you already," I said. "I had a fight with my parents and was kicked out."

"But a bookstore?"

"What, you think I'd make a better lawyer?"

She chewed thoughtfully on her pasta. The table's candle reflected an olive-oil sheen on her lips. "I could see that, actually."

They always could. I stabbed at my vegetables. "Sorry to disappoint."

"No, it's not that. It's just . . . well, you don't seem all that bookish. You're more"—she blushed as she fumbled for the right word—"athletic than I would expect from a scholar."

"Not everyone who reads is a monk," I chided. "Besides, what I really like is surrounding myself with beautiful things, expensive, exquisite. A book can be all that and more. Beautifully crafted leather and paper, hell, even cheerful colored cardboard, but inside . . . ah! A sparsely honed phrase can be like a taste of paradise." When I noticed her looking at my eyes, seeing, no doubt, the desperate hunger there, I glanced at my plate and added, "And who doesn't long for Heaven?" Still regarding the angel hair on my plate, I said, "I suppose that sounds stupid."

I was surprised by the hot touch of her hand on mine. "No," she said, her voice throaty.

Her eyes radiated the same heat as the flesh of her palm pressed against mine. I leaned over and kissed her.

CHAPTER 20
Emmaline, the Inquisitor

His kiss was lighter than I expected. Like a bird's wings, it fluttered across my lips cool and ethereal. Though his touch was soft, his nearness was not. When our skin connected, it was as though his presence filled me. Darkness, like midnight on the open plains, settled around me, deep and vast, but strangely safe and comforting. My nostrils filled with the wild animal musk of myrrh and patchouli. The sounds of the restaurant retreated into silence. For a moment, I couldn't hear *"Ne brochez pas,"* the aria in *Manon* I had as background music to our conversation. A warm, dry breeze tugged at my hair.

The instant he pulled away, it was gone. I felt almost stunned.

No one had ever kissed me like that. Not even Vinnie, my first love, had ever gotten a reaction like that out of me. Plus, ever since we sat down to dinner, I'd been spilling my guts. I usually played things closer to my chest. With Morningstar, I'd turned into a regular chatterbox.

Until now, I'd thought all that romance stuff about electricity and chemistry was just crap. Morningstar was making me reconsider.

Morningstar watched my face and must have misinterpreted my shocked expression. "I'm sorry," he said. Though he was apologizing, there was a wolfish grin twitching at the corner of his lips. "I'm not sure what possessed me."

He put his napkin on his plate, and stood up as if to go.

"Wait," I said, mentally sending my credit information to the restaurant to settle the bill. "Let me walk you home."

He smiled, this time letting the wolf out. "Isn't that supposed to be my line?"

"I'm better equipped to take care of you, trust me." I offered my arm, like a gentleman.

"I can take care of myself better than you think," Morningstar said, though he tucked his arm ladylike into the crook of my elbow.

"Sure," I said patting his knuckles with a smile to show I was teasing. We made our way out the door, into the darkened pedestrian tunnel. The only illumination in the tunnel was the soft strip of neon down the center of the ceiling that divided the sky into two equal parts. The light pollution was too strong to see any stars, but the moon was full and yellow overhead.

I knew there was much more to Morningstar than he'd said. Earlier, when I'd nearly punctured his lungs with my lasers, my sensors had picked up recent gunpowder residue on his hands, and a strange, almost nuclear, heat coming from the center of his body. Unfortunately, that just made this playboy/bookstore clerk that much sexier to me. I liked my men with a dangerous side. My taste for wicked ones was going to be my downfall some day. In a way, it already had been. All the nice young men I've met who would have made excellent Monsignor's husbands just didn't do anything for me. Meanwhile, the bad boys that were hard on my heart and death to my reputation completely lit my fire; not exactly the kind of thing American Catholics and their "responsible relationships" doctrine approved of.

I leaned into Morningstar's side as we wandered past a VR shop. We both paused to look at some of the cool toys they had displayed behind the titanium bars. An ad hologram popped up. Suddenly my perspective switched, and I was hanging upside-down from a cable hung from a skylight at the Louvre. My very masculine muscles strained, and fear and adrenaline coursed through my blood. A gunshot rang out, and, just before the bullet hit, a credit amount flashed in friendly green letters. All I'd have to do to buy the next installment was flip the go-ahead. Apparently, this was the hot new VR experience all the kids were into. I waved the ad away.

"What did you get?" I asked Morningstar.

"Nothing. I just want that suit in there. Mine's in the shop."

"I meant the ad? Didn't you get one?" It was a game I

liked to play with people. You could learn a lot about your friends by what advertisers thought they wanted to buy.

He shook his head. "I didn't get an ad."

I raised my eyebrows: an ad filter? Morningstar might not have been exaggerating about how rich he was. "Do you have a persona?"

He frowned. "I suppose everyone has a façade of sorts. I am different here with you than I am . . . at home."

I shook my head and laughed. "No, out on the LINK."

"I haven't spent nearly as much time on the LINK as I'd like," he said. We moved away from the storefront. A group of kids gathered in a line outside a bar. From the open doors emanated the pounding of a speed-polka beat, which reverberated in the pedestrian tunnel. I pulled my arm away from Morningstar to cover my ears.

Some of the people in the queue gasped when they noticed the sigil of my station. The rumbled hush of "Inquisitor" spread through the crowd nervously.

"The crap these kids listen to," I said to Morningstar with a smile. "I should arrest them for a breach of good taste."

When Morningstar didn't respond, I looked over to see that his eyes were locked on a young boy with a large, blue Star of David tattooed on the back of his shaved skull. The boy was dressed in a leather jacket with the sleeves ripped off, a crow painted in white glitter on the back, pink triangles on the epaulets, and a kilt—a gender-bender. I really could have the boy arrested for dressing that way. I would, too, if Morningstar kept staring at him with that hungry look.

Then, as if sensing Morningstar's attention, the boy turned. His eyes, darkly rimmed in kohl, flicked over Morningstar as if in recognition. He lifted his fingers in the peace sign and nodded. "Shalom, my liege," he mumbled as we passed.

"Shalom, Commander Raum," Morningstar returned with a slight nod.

It was another demon name. If I remembered correctly, the demon Raum was an earl in the Hellish hierarchy. When not in human form, he took the shape of a crow. I glanced back over my shoulder at the bald kid. He was leaning to whisper into the ear of another young man; both of them watched us move away. There was something in those dark eyes that made me want to hurry my step.

Once I could speak without having to shout over the thunder of the bass, I poked Morningstar in the arm. "Raum? So, what, you have an army of demons? Are you in some kind of cult?"

He looked insulted. "A cult?"

"Look," I said, spreading my hands out peacefully between us, "I won't arrest you. If you're in trouble, I can find you some help."

In the semidarkness of the tunnel, Morningstar's eyes were hooded, and his crooked smile looked predatory, measuring. "How thoughtful."

It was not the response I was expecting: no admission of guilt, no denial.

"Uh. Seriously, I know that I'm an Inquisitor, but I'll help you out of whatever they've gotten you into. Just . . . just, tell me you're not a Satanist." I might be able to ignore any admission that Morningstar was involved in some crazy start-up cult, especially if I got him into a spiritual counseling program ASAP. But, Satanists were outlaws. I'd be forced to arrest him on the spot.

"God is the only one worthy of my devotion," he said with another grim smile.

I had no idea what that meant. I waited, expecting more. We could still hear the dull thud of the hyped-up, three-four beat of the polka bar down the street. Exhaling slowly, Morningstar seemed to let something go, and, with a shrug, he tucked his hands into his pockets. "Let's get some coffee. We can talk there. I know a place not far from here," he said.

"Okay," I agreed, relieved that he seemed to be opening up to me. Despite extensive training at seminary, I was never very good at one-on-one counseling. I wasn't sure what I would have done if he'd broken down and asked for my help.

We walked along in silence for half a klick. We passed a quieter neighborhood tavern, a boarded-up grocery, and a hair stylist. At each, a handsome advertisement hologram informed me of business hours and pleasantries I might find inside. I turned up my aria and glanced at Morningstar. He was lost in his own thoughts, uninterrupted by ads. It must be nice to have the luxury of peace.

Brightly lit with neon, the coffee shop smelled of croissants and melted chocolate. "Oh," I said, capturing Morningstar's arm and squeezing it. "Smells good."

"I thought you might like it," he said. His voice was a growl in my ear. "It's one of the most decadent places I know."

When we walked in, I agreed with him. Overstuffed furniture was spaced in pleasant conversation nooks around the room. The walls were a cheery combination of yellow and purple. Christmas lights sparkled along the ceiling. Table lamps provided other dots of warm light. A few people sprawled and sat in various areas, some on the plush rugs scattered liberally around the room. A holographic fireplace snapped and crackled realistically in the middle of the far wall. Flat, old-style photographs on the wall showed close-ups of people laughing. I felt like I'd walked into someone's living room. There wasn't even a coffee bar or a menu to ruin the effect.

We settled into a couch at the back of the room, facing the fire. Morningstar casually put an arm around my shoulders. I craned my neck toward the front door. "I can't raise anyone on the LINK."

"That's because there's wait staff." He smiled.

"I hope you're buying," I said. I couldn't afford to eat at a place with live help.

He laughed. "What about your expense account?"

"I think I already exhausted my per diem."

"I'll get this." He smiled. "Relax."

I tried, but it was difficult not knowing when someone might show up to take my order. "What do you recommend?"

"Anything chocolate. It's their house specialty."

"How do you know? There's no menu."

"The waitress will tell you," he said. Sinking back into the couch, he stretched his long legs toward the fake fire. "I come here a lot. Look, here comes someone already."

A very pretty young man dressed in black pants and a tie came out of a door I hadn't noticed before and stood beside the couch. The young man was handsome, but in a forgettable way, like one of the thousands of waiters that filled this town who were really actors or artists or playwrights. He smiled at Morningstar as though they were friends. "What can I get you two tonight?"

"I will have a *sekanjabin* and one of your raspberry scones if you have them. The lady will take a cappuccino and a *pain au chocolate*."

"Excellent choice," the waiter said. With a brief nod, he disappeared back to wherever it was that he'd come from. I smiled. Morningstar was such a guy: First he told me to order, then he ordered for me.

"*Sekanjabin?* Very trendy." It was a shot of mint and wine vinegar syrup in ice water. Every coffee shop had started adding *sekanjabin* to their menus after some VR starlet did a period piece in the Middle East and people got a taste for it. I found it odd and had never learned to enjoy it. "How did you know I'd like cappuccino?"

"Cappuccino is a very safe choice for someone who lives in Rome."

"Have you been?"

He smiled enigmatically and stared in the holographic fireplace. "Not for a long time."

"I love Rome. It's a beautiful city," I said. I settled back into the couch and his arms. Out of the corner of my eye, I saw the waiter bringing out another couple's drinks. As he left them, he noticed my stare and smiled. There was something wistful in the waiter's look when it strayed to Morningstar, and I was reminded of the boy in line outside of the tavern. I found myself asking, "Are you gay?"

Morningstar didn't flinch at the bluntness of my question. My sensors detected no change in his heart rate or body temperature. He just raised one thin eyebrow in my direction, his eyes still watching the flames. "What a strange question to ask a man who kissed you."

He wasn't getting off that easily. I turned to look him in the eye. "Do you sleep with men, too?"

He yawned, and stretched slowly like a cat. When he faced me, his tone was patient, as if he were explaining to a child. "I like sex. I don't usually let something as inconsequential as gender get in the way of a good fuck."

"Oh." American Catholics had a policy of supporting gays and lesbians. Yet, it still shocked me to hear him admit his predilections so openly. Perhaps it bothered me because he phrased his desires in terms of sex instead of relationships.

His smile was tight with sarcasm. "Are you scandalized, Monsignor?"

"A bit," I admitted. "I'm worried about you. If you hang around with that gender-bender you could get yourself arrested."

"You're worried about me?"

"Yes, the Americans have gotten a lot more liberal, but there are still laws against that kind of thing. It's because of that line in . . . is it Deuteronomy? About how a woman shouldn't wear a man's clothes and vice versa."

"Would you pray for me?" he asked. "Would you pray for the redemption of my soul?"

"Of course," I said, though there was something about the way he asked that made me feel nervous.

"Good," he purred. This time his kiss was deep and hard. His arms curled around me, pressing our bodies together.

CHAPTER 21
Page, the Intelligence

I am halfway out the door before the Dragon stops me. Her claw upon my shoulder makes me stall as though I've slammed into a firewall.

"Don't go," she says. Her voice is soft, and her golden eyes spin slowly, seductively. *"Tell me what you mean about your new master. I don't understand what's going on with you."*

At her words, I relent. I am the Dragon's only friend; we are two of a kind. It must upset her not to completely comprehend what I'm feeling. The only problem is that I'm not sure I can explain myself adequately. I barely understand my own emotions.

A swarm of avatars appears around us: the dinner rush. We're standing in the portal of the café. Outside the doorway, the image of the Algerian sun is bright. There are no clouds, but information skitters across the sky like bright birds. I wish I were still connected to my father. I want to feel the heat on my skin and the prickle of sweat under my arms. But, there is nothing, only brightness.

"Let's walk a little ways," I say. *"I can't sit still any longer."*

She looks back at the comfort of the café briefly, then nods. The Dragon lumbers beside me, walking on all fours. Her tail slashes upright through the air like a cat's. We head into a virtual marketplace. Stalls call out their goods, trying to tempt us with easy downloads, killer apps, and useless, albeit pretty, software. The activity is constant, but this is not like the café. I find the hum of noise comforting here. There are only a few true humans moving through the marketplace. Instead, most of the stalls are staffed by daemons, mindless drones. They toss us free cookies as we walk by. The Dragon puffs out her wings to protect us. Harmless, but invasive, the cookies bounce off her steely wings making a sound like hail on tin.

"This is better than the café?" she teases.

But for me it is. I am still afraid that some news 'bot will track me down and ask me about the fear-bomb in Cairo. I don't want to be around humans. It makes me feel too guilty. *"Yes,"* I say. *"Anyway, they'll give up soon enough."*

Already a murmur can be heard in the stalls. Whispers of "AIs. No customer," reach my ears. In a moment, the barrage stops. The Dragon shakes out her wings, and the last of the cookies falls to the ground, uneaten.

"This is so unlike you, ibn Mouse," she says. *"To shun the company of humans for robots. Especially such annoying ones."* She flicks a coaxial cable tongue out at the market stalls.

I give a soft laugh, then I reach out a hand to touch the scales on the side of her body. Like a snake, her skin is soft and warm. I lean against her. *"I'm in trouble, I think."*

The Dragon sighs a long whoosh of noise, her stomach puffing out, then in. *"The fear-bomb,"* she says simply. *"Yes. You probably are."*

"What are people saying?" I've been too afraid to check the news channels—too afraid of being spotted.

"They have been following up on others. No one has mentioned you."

"But if they look at the technology, they'll recognize the LINK-angel program."

"They won't," the Dragon says.

"But there were hundreds of people in the street," I protest.

The Dragon looks straight ahead as she says, *"This one took care of it."*

I look at her, but she will not return my gaze. *"Tell me you did nothing illegal."*

The Dragon's program is so large that the datastream shifts as she moves along the market. What would for me be a narrow street widens in her passing. Behind us, the gap closes, resuming its natural size. *"This one is worried about you,"* she says. *"She did what she had to do."*

"Oh." I say, my voice small. A sick part of me is relieved;

the other part feels guiltier than ever. I let my hand fall away from her haunches.

"You can owe us. We know you'd do the same for us were the situations reversed. That's what friends do." Our eyes meet. There is no doubt of the emotion behind her glittering copper eyes. *"So,"* she says quietly, *"tell this one what's going on with you."*

Ahead, the image of the market's asphalt street appears to ripple, simulating heat waves.

"I'm changing," I say.

She can't see that beneath the black veils I wear I am trying out my monster visage again. My hair is thick, unwashed, and twisted. My eyes are bulgy and blind. I wear the face of a person who would hurt innocent people, the kind of person that Allah shuns: the Antichrist.

"Changing into what?" the Dragon asks.

"Someone new. Someone older. Someone I don't always like."

"A grown-up?" The Dragon blinks at me, her eyes whirling and snapping.

I check my analogy program quickly, then say, *"No, more like a teenager."*

"Scary," she says. As she moves along, I notice silver geckos scampering at her feet. They clamber onto her claws, and then crawl partway up her flanks before melting into her mirrored scales. *"Oh yes, this one almost forgot to tell you. The trace programs are back."*

"Already? You just sent them out!" I think again of the mice in my pocket—even multiplied, they are comparably so few, so tiny.

"It's been several minutes," she chides. *"They've searched a long time. This one had almost given up on them."*

"What did they find out?"

"The information they have gathered confuses this one. It is being relayed to you."

Rather than use imprecise language, the Dragon hands me a LINK packet. She shapes it as an orange-and-black origami crane. It unfolds delicately in my hand as I read it. The packet shows the bill of sale for twenty-five camels from an Iblis ibn Allah in Tunisia. There is a Swiss bank account with an undisclosed sum of money in the name of Iblis ibn Allah which has remained unaccessed since its original deposit one hundred and sixty-three years ago. When I'm done, the crane disappears into ashes, fluttering into the electronic wind.

"*That's odd,*" I agree. "*This man I talked with was young.*"

"*You said he might be a ghost.*"

"*An angel.*"

"*Supernatural,*" the Dragon continued as though I had not corrected her. "*This lends weight to that theory.*"

I shake my head. "*Angels don't need bank accounts.*"

"*Demons do,*" she says, but she is talking about her own mythology. "*And you say you're calling this demon master. And yet you don't believe in his powers.*"

"*I believe him,*" I say. "*He said some things that made sense.*" I push ahead of the Dragon. Women in *chadors* like my own flit past me. I am reminded again of the fear-bomb, and that only makes me move faster.

"*Like what?*" She leaps, and, in one bound, catches up to me. I've forgotten that she is both bigger and faster than I am.

"*He said that mice are a symbol of the soul. He said . . . that our stories were the same because I rebelled against my father, my maker.*"

The Dragon's voice is soft again, and concerned. "*You did.*"

My monster face is dripping black ooze. "*I know.*"

We have come to the edge of the virtual marketplace. The space ahead of us appears as a vast desert, punctuated by the occasional green oasis of commerce. Cairo shines in the distance like a diamond in the sand. I head into the dunes. The Dragon follows after with her tail now low, making snake marks in the softly shifting landscape. The darkness I am leaking leaves oily splotches on the pristine red-yellow hills. The Dragon's tail swirls them into Rorschach blots.

"*Your father made a mistake; you did what you had to.*" The Dragon spreads her wings to shelter me from the sun. Since the landscape is virtual, it is not necessary, but I find it to be a meaningful gesture all the same. I know I should be comforted by her love, but I still feel twisted inside.

"*I know,*" I say to acknowledge what she is trying to do to help me, even though it is a lie. I don't know anything anymore. I'm not always sure that what I did was so right.

What would the harm have been if my father had gotten away with his fraud? My father was no killer. He might have done some good. Sometimes I think I'm the one who should be in jail, especially considering that I dropped the fear-bomb.

"You could help him escape," the Dragon says.

"That's illegal," I say.

"So?" The Dragon's masters are always in and out of jail. She does not see the problem with an assisted jail-break. *"You still love him, don't you?"*

When she puts it that way, it's difficult for me not to agree. *"Of course!"*

"I can help. I'll put you in touch with some of my friends. We have people all over. I'm sure there are some in the same prison as your father." Almost as an afterthought, the Dragon adds, *"I liked you so much better when Mouse was your master."*

I nod. The Dragon is right. I had a clearer head when Mouse watched over me. It is difficult for me to make the correct decisions without a human moral compass to turn to. Mouse might have been power hungry, but he was a good guy. This is my first Ramadan without him, and I've made a complete mess of things.

"We can free him," the Dragon says. *"Please don't let the demon Iblis be your master."*

"You don't think he's real," I say.

"Maybe he's as real as the guilt you feel."

My monster face, which had been fading, snaps back into focus. If I help free my father, I will be no better than him. I'll just have another crime on my conscience. At least if I sell my soul to a demon, I will be honest about the kind of monster I am.

"No," I tell her. *"It's too late for me."*

I leave the Dragon, although I can tell she is confused and hurt by my words. When I log-out of the environs, she tries to follow after, but I shout for her to leave me alone for once. She hangs her head like a puppy, and her tail curls protectively around her toes. Even her crystal wings seem to droop and lose some luster. She looks so sad, but it is becoming easier for me to hurt people. I hop into the nearest city center.

Algiers' LINK presence is new. All the businesses and shops along the avenue are rendered with a sharpness that lacks character, although the constructs are meant to represent old-fashioned Arabic architecture. The pointed arches and thin columns reminiscent of a Moorish palace are fantasy, a romance of some public-works programmer. Still, I admire the patterned brickwork as I pass by them. Above the tiled roofs, I see the golden dome of a mosque. I shift into my male persona, looking like my father, with his thick, wavy black hair and youthful, beardless face.

There are very few LINK-mosques. I approach the entry cautiously. After all that I have done, I almost expect Allah to strike me down. There is a group of men gathered outside the door. Their signature profiles show they are from all over the world, but they are all speaking Arabic, the common language of our religion.

I give the traditional greeting and move to join them.

"Have you heard?" one of the men asks me. He is a Pakistani living in London. His avatar is dressed in the costume of the working class—jeans and a white shirt. *"There was a Hassidic terrorist attack on the Cairo LINK node."*

"Terrorists?" I frown.

"Yes," says another. He is from Istanbul, and his costume more romantic. He chooses to look like a Moorish prince from the Middle Ages. *"They let off a fear-bomb. It would be just like the Malachim, wouldn't it?"*

The Malachim Nimnah: Avenging Angels. They were a Hassidic LINK-terrorist group that had strongly opposed the LINK-angels. I shake my head. I know those people. Rebeckah and the others weren't like that.

"I wondered when they would start attacking us," says a Palestinian soldier.

"The fear-bomb?" I protest, with a little squeak. *"Why do you say it's the Malachim? There were Jewish victims."*

"They're just covering their tracks," says the Moorish prince.

"No," I say, shaking my head fiercely. *"The Malachim disbanded after the LINK-angels were exposed."* I should know this. After all, I helped them set up their kibbutz in the glass city in New York. *"They're peaceful now."*

"Tell that to my countrymen," says the Palestinian. He

leans in close and whispers, *"We are already planning reprisals. Some people I know are planning to hit the Jerusalem node."*

"Can I help?" asks the Englishman.

The Moorish prince and I are shaking our heads. *"Violence isn't the answer,"* he says, but I shout over him.

"It wasn't the Malachim! It was me!"

"You?"

I can feel the avatars scanning me for a signature profile to find out more about the human that I supposedly represent. They will find none.

"Mouse?" The Moorish prince stares at my face, as if trying to see my father behind my eyes.

"Page," I correct him.

The Englishman makes a sign against the evil eye. He spits in my general direction and disappears, logging off.

"You betrayed Mouse," says the Palestinian. *"And, now you kill Muslims?"*

"No one died," I squeak, taking a step back and positioning my foot on a LINK-stream in case I need to make a quick getaway. *"It was an accident."*

The Moorish prince is still shaking his head in disbelief. *"How can you be responsible? You're just a program."*

"Page has sentience," the Palestinian says before I can defend myself. *"But not, I understand, a gender."*

"And yet you were going to enter the mosque?" The Moorish prince seems horrified at the idea. He looks at me as though I am something to be reviled. *"Dressed as a boy?"*

"No," I say, shifting into an image of *Dajjal*: a hairy, blind, twisted man. I raise my arms and wave them at the men. *"As a monster."*

The Moorish prince disappears with a shout of fear. The Palestinian, however, remains. *"You've forgotten something,"* he says, pointing to his forehead.

I make the letters "ka," "fa," and "rah" glow in Arabic script between my eyes.

"Despite what my master says," the Palestinian says with hands on his hips. *"You aren't a perfect* Dajjal: *not enough wanton evil in you. Tell me, why did you drop the fear-bomb?"*

"Go away," I say, still in monster form. I make my face

as ugly and cruel as I can, but the Palestinian seems unaffected.

"*Ah,*" he says, "*the monster doesn't suit you, little one.*"

"Don't condescend to me," I snap.

"*Or, what? You'll bomb me?*"

"I could," I say.

There is something behind this avatar's eyes, something that reminds me of the Dragon's copper energy that makes me wonder who he is. I check his signature. I find an empty slate. Where there should be a human hand, I see none.

"*Why did you come to this place?*" He lifts his hands to indicate the mosque. "*You didn't come here to fight, did you? You came here for something else.*"

To be forgiven, I parse, but I do not say.

"*Allah is all-forgiving, but you must ask Him. Don't be blind, Page,*" the Palestinian says, and his avatar fades. He does not log-off, like the others, but, instead, seems to melt into the very building of the mosque. For a moment, I think I see green-and-turquoise peacock-feather wings. As the last of his image fades, I hear the desert wind, howling with the voices of souls.

CHAPTER 22
Morningstar, the Adversary

One thing that all of the mythmakers got right about me is my predilection for sex. Being exiled, as I am, to live as flesh, I have learned to satisfy my body's baser needs. And, it appeared, another's. Em slept contentedly beside me, her uniform finally in a crumpled heap at the foot of the bed. Sunlight cast warm lines on her body. I snuggled closer, sharing my warmth.

"Mmmm . . . ?" Em murmured, waking.

"Hey, lover," I said, giving her a soft kiss on the cheek.

"Morning, Morning . . ." she started to say. Then, she squinted at me, while shrugging deeper under the sheets. "You know what you need? You need a shorter name or a nickname."

"I've got lots of nicknames: Baker, Black Bogey, Old Horny, Harry, Scratch, or Nick." I smiled, and breathed warmly in her ear. "But you could just call me 'my prince' . . . although 'master,' would be fine, too."

I saw fear and excitement glisten in her eyes briefly. Then a pillow hit me on the nose. "In your dreams," she said with a laugh.

"Ha," I snorted. I wrested the pillow from her and tucked it under my elbow. "And not yours?"

"No, in my dreams I conquer my man."

"And so you did," I said, biting her neck playfully. "I'm yours."

She sat up, pulling the sheets tightly around her armpits. The thin fabric of the hotel bedding gave an ironic twist to her attempt at modesty. Seeing my gaze, she crossed her arms in front of her chest. "You're incorrigible."

"I'm smitten," I insisted.

"Why don't I believe you?"

"I have that kind of devil-may-care face?" I offered, laying my head in her lap. She reached out and brushed my hair away from my face, and gave me a measuring, sidelong stare. If I didn't know any better, I'd say she was scanning me.

"What is it with you and the whole devil thing?"

I gave her a long look. Even the dullest creature like a mule could sense when it was in the presence of an angel. I had thought sex would have lifted all her blinders. "You don't know? You don't have any idea?"

She bit her lip, then shook her head. "No. What are you talking about?"

I wondered what she would see if I lifted the veil of my flesh. Possibly, Emmaline would remain blind. God hardened the hearts of some people. If that were true, nothing I could do would make her recognize my true nature. I might be standing in front of her with wings as black as sin and horns like a ram's curled around my forehead, and she would still be giving me that wide-eyed, confused look.

Maybe God did have some kind of major role in mind for Emmaline. Usually, the people He blinded to angels were those who had to make an epiphany of their own. Emmaline was probably part of one of His "tests." Having failed one of my own, I had a sudden rush of sympathy for her.

"Never mind," I said, stroking the hollow of her cheekbone. "I'm circumcised, or didn't you notice?"

She blushed quite enchantingly. So I lifted up the covers, and added: "Perhaps the Inquisitor would like to make another careful inspection?"

Em slapped my hand lightly. "I'm thinking 'Old Horny' suits you."

I kissed the inside of her thigh as I sat up, making the bed bounce. "I'm feeling more like 'The Devourer' at the moment. I'm starving. Order me some room service?"

"Sure," Em said, smiling. "I still can't quite believe you don't have a LINK. So . . . a big breakfast, minus the bacon?"

"I don't keep *halal* . . . or kosher."

"You will with me," she said, not seeming to notice my

inconsistency. "I'm an Inquisitor. I can't be party to you breaking your dietary restrictions."

"But you will be party to the sullying of my virtue?" I asked, batting my eyes innocently.

"You never had that." She laughed. "Now get dressed. I've got work to do."

I laughed, but not unkindly. I understood the necessity of trying to regain a position of power after you've been thoroughly deposed.

"All right, dear," I said, giving her a dutiful, if a bit sarcastic, peck on the cheek. I slid out of bed quickly, but not before she slapped me on my bare backside.

By the time I'd showered, brushed my teeth, and gotten dressed, the food had arrived. I came out to see Em munching on a triangle of toast while her other hand did a complex dance in the air. Her eyes were glazed, deep in the LINK. She was dressed in a terry-cloth robe, her uniform nowhere to be seen. Perhaps she sent it with the bellboy to be dry-cleaned.

I perched lightly on the edge of the bed, next to the tray of food she had balanced on her legs. Though the springs creaked, Em didn't blink. I doubted she'd notice if I swiped a piece of her bacon from her tray. I barely had my hand on a slice when she grabbed my wrist hard enough, had I been human, to leave a bruise. Even so, she probably would.

"Drop it," she insisted. Her eyes were not focused on my form, though I was mere inches from her face.

I tired of this game; besides, the bacon smelled salty, making my mouth water. With a quick jerk, I broke her hold on me.

Em gave a startled cry, then she blinked rapidly, no doubt turning off her LINK connection. Her eyes found mine. "How did you do that?"

I munched on the bacon. "Do what?"

She looked over my body again. This time, I was certain, she scanned me. I wondered what she saw when she looked at me with her enhanced vision. "You're not modified in any of the usual ways, but you have the strangest infrared readings."

"Hmm." Having finished the bacon, I took a piece of her toast.

"Yours is over there," she said, pointing to a covered tray on the end table on the other side of the bed.

"I'd rather share." I smiled.

"I'd rather not," she said, grabbing the toast out of my hand before I could take a bite.

"Hmph," I said, crawling over her to reach the other tray. "Not very Christian of you."

I'd hoped my awkward progress across the bed would distract her. Em merely held lightly to her own tray and glared at me. Once I'd settled with my food, she was still frowning. "Where are you from originally?"

I shrugged. I never knew what to say to that one. When it came down to the bone, I'd rather misdirect than lie. "What makes you think I'm not from around here?"

"The infrared. I just wondered if you're from Israel, or if you ever served in their army. I've heard they've got some new tech they've been giving their soldiers."

"What do you think?"

"I think that has to be it," she said, but she continued to glance at me suspiciously.

"What are you working on?" I asked, lightly.

"I'm trying to find the Dragon," she whispered, as if someone might overhear. I was lucky she said it loud enough. My bad ear was turned toward her. I resettled so that I sat with my back to the foot of the bed.

"I thought you were after Page?"

"I'm supposed to find out if the Dragon has a soul, as well."

"Everything born with freewill has a soul," I said, taking a bite of my scrambled eggs, no cheese.

"What makes you so certain?" Em asked.

Because I was there, I wanted to say, at the beginning—because I saw how my Mother doted on Her earthly creations of dust and mud. How She gave them the gift of Her very own breath—something She kept from me. I had spirit, fire, but no soul, no breath.

"You don't have to look so pissed off. I just want to know why you're so damn sure that AIs have souls," Em said.

"Because that's the way it works," I said around a mouthful of toast. "Where there's freewill, a soul will surely follow after."

"That's the way it works?" she repeated my words back to me with a laugh. "You make it sound like you know exactly how the universe operates."

"Fractals and freewill," I said with a shrug. "Order and chaos."

"Freewill," she said slowly. "But what about God's plan?"

I frowned at my plate. "What about it?"

"Don't you believe that God has a plan for us all?"

I glanced up from my baconless eggs to see Emmaline watching me intensely.

"How boring would that be?" I said. "I'm sure God would rather be surprised. I mean, why watch the movie if you already know the end? Besides, I'm convinced that the whole thing is a test. Which will the human race choose: good or evil?"

Em crossed her arms in front of her chest, frowning deeply. "That seems cruel. Especially with the cards stacked against us."

"How do you figure?"

"Your favorite guy. Satan. He's out there actively recruiting while, in your version, God just sits back and watches."

I shook my head. "Humans don't need any encouragement to be evil."

The muscle in Emmaline's jaw twitched slightly. "No, I guess they don't," she agreed. "So what then? Did God design us with a tendency toward violence and hate, and then judges us when we don't go the extra mile to be good?"

I had nothing to say to that. If I had really understood God, I wouldn't be here among the Fallen.

"And why create a devil on top of that?" Emmaline continued. "Why add to human suffering with things like earthquakes and other natural disasters?"

"Sometimes struggling against impossible odds brings out the greatest good in a person."

Em stuck her tongue out at that. "Bleah. I'm not sure I want to believe in a God that would play that kind of game.

Cause a forest fire just so some fire fighter can get a chance to risk his or her life in order to be a hero? A good guy? That doesn't seem right."

"God doesn't cause forest fires, people do."

"Thanks, Smoky," she said. "You know what I meant."

"So you'd rather have God as a puppeteer, pulling all the strings? Isn't that just as wrong? What kind of loving God would make a Hitler? A Judas?"

"Well, like you say, maybe it's some kind of test. Maybe God makes villains out of some people in order to test others."

Like me. Maybe I never had the freewill I thought I did. Perhaps God preprogrammed me to do everything according to plan. My stomach tightened.

"No," I said, firmly.

Em sat on her end of the bed and stared at me for a long moment. "I really should get back to this," she said, pointing to the empty space to the right of her face. "It's my job."

"That's it?" My voice came out softer and more hurt sounding than I'd intended it. Hearing the weakness there, I bristled, and added, "Fine. Good-bye."

But my words were wasted; Emmaline didn't hear me. She'd gone back to her LINK. She just nodded. "Okay, 'bye. I'll call you or something, okay?"

I doubt she heard the door I slammed on my way out. Angry, I stomped down the narrow hotel hallway. The carpeting was nubby and worn in places. There was dust in the bowl-shaped lamps that cast a thin light on the beige walls. On this level, all hotels looked the same: washed out and weary from the continuous use and abuse.

Finding the elevator bank, I pressed the button for down. A fancy overstuffed chair that no one would ever sit on and glass-topped table faced the doors. Next to them, a plastic tropical plant bloomed eternally. I would never understand what She saw in these people. Em was a dark creature before I touched her. They all were. Tempting humans to be casual with grace and divinity was too easy, beneath the powers of a creature as great as I. I needed to stay focused on bigger fish.

As if on cue, the elevator door opened to reveal Azazel. He'd changed into a long trench coat, but otherwise he still looked every bit a terrorist.

"Tell me you're not planning on bombing this hotel,"
I said.

"I've been looking all over for you," he said. His face
was tight and anxious. "The Four Horsemen," he gasped.
"The Four Horsemen are here."

CHAPTER 23
Emmaline, the Inquisitor

As much fun as it was to be distracted by Morningstar's pretty face and theological ramblings, I had to get back to work. He'd sounded a bit hurt, but I intended to call him later, maybe take him out to dinner.

Just as a kind of reminder to myself, I sent my avatar out looking for more information on Morningstar and his family.

I leaned back against the headboard and closed my eyes, letting myself move deeper onto the LINK. The Yakuza wire-wizard Mai had told me in order to find the Dragon I had to drop a note in the electronic version of the Yoshino River. I formed a simple note: *"Come talk to me."*

After clambering down a steep cliff, my avatar threw it into the water and stood on a grassy riverbank and waited. Though it was eleven o'clock in the morning in New York, Japan-time was near midnight. The moon reflected in the black water. Stars glittered above. Frogs croaked and plopped into the gently lapping waves. A slight, warm breeze carried the scent of jasmine and the fishy smell of the mud. Frankly, I could do without the last bit and the annoying buzz of a fly near my ear. I had my avatar swat at the bug. What was it with AIs and intensely realistic sites?

The frogs went silent, and air bubbled up from the center of the river. The Dragon's head broke the surface of the datastream with a splash. Unlike Page, the dragon didn't look human at all. She had a wide face with shimmering green scales the color of motherboards. The carplike whiskers that hung from her chin were coaxial and copper. Unlike most Asian dragons, however, this one bore wings.

"Yes?"

"I'm a Vatican Inquisitor. I need to ask you a few questions," I said, settling down on the grass in a half-lotus.

She ducked under the water, disappearing. I stood up, and strained to see ripples of water or any hint of which direction she'd gone. But, there was nothing. I waited anxiously for her to return. I stepped forward until my toes touched the water's edge. *"Hello?"*

I formed another note and tossed it in. As the note sailed toward the water, a sharp-toothed maw rose up from the river and gobbled it up. Then, as if finding it distasteful, the Dragon spit it back.

I caught the note when it came close to me. I opened up the packet and read: "Where's the Dragon's gift?"

Right. How could I have forgotten the Japanese tradition? Though I still couldn't see the Dragon, I shouted out over the river, *"I'll make it up to you. I just need to ask you a few questions."*

Two glowing eyes appeared at the water's surface, crackling with electric fire. *"Why don't you come in?"*

I felt silly being afraid of a completely imaginary creature, but I shook my head. *"That's okay,"* I insisted, stepping back from the shoreline for emphasis. *"This won't take long. I just want to know if you think you have a soul."*

"This one thinks she has many things she doesn't. She thought, for instance, that she had a friend. Turns out she was wrong. The person she thought was a friend was a monster."

"I'd think a monster would be a perfect friend for a dragon," I said, thinking of all the children's stories I'd watched in VR. *"But,"* I said, *"back to the idea of a soul. . . ."*

Her head came up above the water slowly. The scales winked in the moonlight. A strong wind blew, and thunder rattled in the distance. The Dragon was upset. *"Monsters make horrible friends. Monsters are mean."*

"And dragons aren't?" I'd just been scared of her, after all. *"Listen, the important question here is—"*

"Dragons aren't monsters." she said. *"This one has never been mean to Page. I love Page."*

"How do you know?" I asked. Since I wasn't getting anywhere with the direct route, I changed tactics. *"How do you know it's love?"*

Lightning flashed in the sky. The waves of the Yoshino threw themselves at my toes. Despite the fact that I knew it was all illusion, I took another couple of steps backwards.

The Dragon's head drooped and sank back into the water. *"This one would do anything for Page. Even now, though his new master makes him so different."*

She disappeared again. No matter how many notes I threw in after her, I couldn't get her to return. After a few minutes, it started to rain.

My avatar wandered around Nippon-mode for a while, and sent out broadband queries for Page and the Dragon. Then I remembered the LINK address I got from the busker's drum.

The New York node, like the city itself, was a tangle of sites. I waded through the electronic streets until I found the busker's address, which I discovered belonged to a group of wire-wizards calling themselves "Mouse's Kids." It wasn't much of a site, really. When my avatar approached the place, it was no more than a billboard—rented LINK-space. The information represented itself as flat and static. Ironically, the message tried to be hip and cool. The board read: "If you want access to Page, we've got it. Only the flashiest folk are allowed in. Decipher this riddle and you can come to our rave!"

I checked the date stamp. The rave was scheduled for early evening. I could still make it. I put my hand on the billboard, and the frame flipped forward. The next panel showed me a picture of a leprechaun and the reflection of my own avatar. A clock appeared at the top of the billboard and started counting down from ten.

I frowned and the reflection frowned back at me. The leprechaun started doing a little dance, and the numbers flipped by. Okay, I thought, this must be the riddle. How are these two things the same? I tried to remember everything I could about the fairies, pixies, and all things Irish. I remembered my father pointing at a shoe in the middle of the street and telling me, "The leprechauns must have been here." He told me they were the fairy shoemakers.

"Soles," I said. *"We're both concerned with souls!"*

The clock stopped. A voice came out of the billboard. It sounded like a teenager trying to do an impression of a game-show host. All the inflections were right, but the voice was an octave too high and cracked. *"What do you think, ladies and gentlemen? Does the contestant win the prize?"*

The board flipped again, and the word "YES!" appeared, along with an address. I took a picture of it, and logged off.

After a shower and something to eat, I found myself hurrying along the streets—the real streets, outside the hamster-tubes New Yorkers called traffic tunnels. I was glad I'd started out early because it took me an hour just to find a way down this far. I'd jimmied the locks on three trade-tunnel entrances, and risked my life running a short distance through a level reserved for vehicles. I just hoped this wire-wizard rave was worth it and not just some big scam.

That I'd gotten that far with so little work made me suspicious. I was probably on a wild-goose chase meant as a practical joke. Of course, it could also be a trap, especially since the wizards had used a reflection of my own avatar. That was why I'd packed my peacemaker. The heavy steel rested under my arm in a shoulder holster, hidden, for the most part, by a long wool coat.

A crash somewhere in the distance made me start. I crouched, pressing myself against the wall of the building nearest me. I rested my hand inside my coat, on the butt of the pistol.

Scan, I told my combat computer. *Three-hundred-sixty, sphere.*

My combat sensors had a range of about a hundred feet. Not really much beyond my line of sight, but the computer could pick up anyone wearing a holographic distortion field. It could also, if the conditions were right, see around corners.

An image returned to me of a feline, approximately nine pounds, three ounces, licking its paws near an overturned garbage can in the nearby alley off to the left. Otherwise, the computer determined there was nothing. Even so, I stood up slowly, checking in every direction.

Last thing I wanted to do was run into any Gorgons.

Reputedly, the Gorgons were the once-human, mutated byproduct of the Medusa bomb. I had never had the misfortune of meeting one, and, frankly, I wanted nothing more than to deny myself that pleasure for the rest of my life. There were some things a person could get by without. Meeting up with man-eating mutants was one of them.

I stayed close to the wall as I started down the street again. Accessing the GPS, I calculated that the rave should be just ahead. No surprise, really, that turning the corner revealed nothing except a large, beady-eyed crow which took off in a noisy retreat when it noticed me. I watched it sail effortlessly through the tangle of overhead wires to the nearest traffic tube. As it perched, a puff of snow fell to the ground, illuminated in the strange light like green-gray glitter.

I'd been had.

My biggest disappointment was that I'd hoped to find a connection at the rave that would lead me to Page again. Since I had blown it with him the first time, I wanted another chance. But, getting ahold of Page wasn't like looking someone up in the LINK directory. Only a select few had a direct line. I wasn't expecting to score anything so pricey. I was just hoping to get a quick tip on where Page might be hanging lately, or where I might hope to leave a message for him.

The crow barked a laugh at me, bobbing up and down with each caw. I hugged the wool coat closer and frowned at the bird. Despite the crow's mocking, I wasn't quite ready to give up on this rave.

Heat scan. Highest sensitivity, I commanded. I hoped that by scanning the walls of the buildings on this street, I might be able to pick up something, some clue of activity inside one of them.

"Psst." The noise next to my shoulder made me jump. I turned around to see metallic, silver pupils—a complete corneal implant, expensive and very hip—the sign of a wire-wizard. White hair, like the snow, clumped into dreds that were bound together into thick shoulder-length strands by what looked like glass. His skin was so pale that it was almost translucent. He stood a few inches taller than I did, but, even without the combat enhancements, I outweighed him easily.

"I'm, like, the greeter." I wasn't sure if he meant it as a name, a function, or a handle.

I'd been planning on giving my old handle: the one I'd used in my earlier incarnation as a Mafia surfer. Other than the peacemaker, I'd left all my professional trappings at the hotel, and instead wore something black and cheap, which I'd hoped would pass as wire-wizard wear.

"I'm . . ."

"The Inquisitor, I know," he said. "We're expecting you."

I took a step back, ready to reach for the gun. "I just want a little information. I'm not here to bust anyone."

The greeter smiled, showing me his fangs. "Yeah, okay, well, I had been really scared. Thanks for clearing that up. Why don't you follow me back to the party? Though . . ."

I felt something hit me in the chest, and I fell back onto the snowy concrete. By the time my combat computer warned me of an attack, I had the wind knocked out of me and I was sprawled on the ground. The greeter knelt on my chest, holding my peacemaker in his hand.

" . . . You'll have to leave the weapons at the door."

Nothing should have moved faster than my computer could detect, unless . . . I gasped in a breath, grateful that my enhancements had probably spared me some broken ribs. The glass in his hair, the pallor, and the fangs . . . suddenly, I understood: "You're a Gorgon."

"Half. So don't get your knickers in a bundle, okay?"

He stepped off me and tucked my gun in his belt. He offered me a shaky smile and hand up. "No harm done. You understand."

I propped myself up on my elbows and considered. The gun was useless to him. It was a Peacemaker 2080, based on the original, but a brand-new model. The trigger had been coded to respond to my password and fingerprints only, standard on every new weapon since the Second Brady Act. Still, the greeter had gotten the jump on me, and that pissed me off.

"C'mon," he said, with his hand still open, waiting. "It's cold out here."

Melted snow seeped in through the thin cotton of my pants. My combat computer targeted the weakest spot on his knees and offered preferred trajectories and momentum needed to cripple him. I turned it off and pulled myself up without his help.

"All I'm looking for is an address," I said, dusting off the back of my wool coat.

"But you found a party!" The greeter gave me a goofy grin and turned to knock twice on the wall. With a crackle of light, a garage door appeared through a holographic defense shield. There was a small slit cut in the thin metal door. The greeter stuck his nose up to it. "Hey, guys, the Inquisitor's here!"

I frowned. My combat computer should have detected any holographic projections, especially when I'd been standing almost right on top of them. Either I was in desperate need of an upgrade, or these wire-wizards were really good. Both options scared me.

The garage door jerked into motion with a mechanical whine. A stab of soft white light crept up the greeter's body, making his already pale skin look ghostly. I smelled the stench of human body odor, like a locker room.

Finally, the door was completely open. I'm not sure what I'd been expecting. After all, I used to be a wire-wizard; I knew what they were like. Still, part of my mind had imagined strobe lights and thin, sexy people with impeccable fashion sense gyrating to a throbbing techno-punk beat.

Instead, the music, some kind of pleasant fusion jazz, was as soft as the lights. People, boys mostly, few of them thin, awkwardly sat around card tables on furniture that looked like it had been salvaged from a Dumpster, playing trading-card and role-playing games. In the corner of the vacuous space was a VR booth. I could see some bodies jerking and gyrating there, but I'd hardly call them sexy. And, the fashion sense? The greeter was by far the best dressed of the lot, and that was probably because he'd chosen to go monochromatic.

Geeks, the lot of them; if it hadn't been for the Gorgon greeter, I would have been embarrassed that I'd come armed and expecting trouble.

"Want a beer or something?" the greeter asked. In the soft light, the glass in his white hair glittered like ice.

I shook my head. "Who should I talk to about Page?"

The greeter cocked his head at me, like a dog trying to fathom its owner's request. "You're kind of a one-track-mind girl, aren't you? Why don't you relax for a minute? Put your feet up. Or do I have to knock you down again?"

"I'm busy. I have things I'd like to do tonight."

He grimaced. "Sit."

When I stared at him, unmoving, he added, "I can tell you want you need. But you can't get it for free." He walked over to the nearest card table and grabbed a remote. Clicking a button caused the garage door to begin its groaning descent.

"What do you want?"

"What does any wizard want?"

Several thoughts occurred to me: money, power, or access to better, faster equipment. Then, I looked around the room filled mostly with men—painfully shy, awkward, hormonally charged young men.

"To get laid," I said.

He laughed. "Well, okay, true. But, besides that."

"I don't know."

He looked at me out of the corner of his eye. The silver of his pupil caught the light. "Think it through, Inquisitor. What could you give someone like me?"

I shook my head. "I'm not going to give you the security code for the Vatican."

He sneered. "Fuck that. I don't need no stinking help breaking into the Pope's files. I could do that in my sleep. Guess again, soldier-girl."

He'd given me the answer, and the crooked smile on his face said he knew it, too.

"Ah," I said. "You want a combat computer and all the enhancements."

He pointed his fingers at me like a gun and clicked his tongue twice. "Bingo," he said.

"You're too old for a full combat-chassis," I said. I knew that from experience. I'd joined Interpol late enough that they couldn't make some of the more massive enhancements to my body. Some full-time Inquisitors were hardly human. But the change had to happen while a body was still young, still growing, still malleable.

"I'm six and a half." The greeter shrugged.

Either he was lying or the rumors of the Gorgons' hyped-up metabolism and shortened life span were true. They lived long enough to spawn, then the Medusa claimed them.

"Still," I said, looking him over. "The point is that you're full-grown. Besides, surely your nexus has already been activated."

"I don't have a nexus. You think I was born in the hospital?"

"No, I suppose not," I said, my gaze sliding away from his, but the thought had never occurred to me.

"Without the nexus, I don't know what they can do."

He was looking at me out of the corner of his eye again. The greeter leaned against the ratty edge of a couch, crossing his pale arms defiantly. "How long are you expected to live?"

"What?"

"I've got three more years, tops. And, that's twice as long as most Gorgons. The wetwear can help."

"Not necessarily. You might not live through the implanting process. No one has ever enhanced a Gorgon."

"Half, and I'll gamble with the possibility. Will you get me connected?"

"Sure." The Vatican was going to love my expense account. So far I'd promised to donate to the legal defense fund of the Holy Father's archenemy, and now I was about to help some Gorgon get his hands on our equipment. If I actually followed through on any of this, I'd be fired.

"Do you have what I need?" I asked.

"Better. I have a direct line."

I hardly hesitated; that kind of intel was worth all this and more. "Deal."

CHAPTER 24
Page, the Intelligence

I am thinking of the Dragon as I stroll down the byways of Neo-Tokyo. After my encounter at the mosque with the winged vision, I'm beginning to suspect she might be right. Maybe I made up Iblis. Perhaps the crash at the auto plant damaged my processors. I run a diagnostic, but, well, if my system is screwed up, it might also be giving me faulty readings. I can't trust myself. That's a bad sign.

I tried to call Iblis before setting out, but I had no number, no LINK address, nothing. Making me think that he might be an illusion after all. Especially since last time, when I conjured him by just shouting out his name. And after what the Dragon said about finding no trace of him, of seeing me talking to myself . . . well, I feel too foolish to try that again, afraid I might look as crazy as I feel I am. I feel out of control.

I decide to offer myself to the Yakuza. Maybe I can do a small job for them in exchange for an upgrade. If my conversation with Iblis was real, then a small job shouldn't violate our contract. After all, I haven't given him my soul yet. If Iblis is just an imaginary glitch, then an upgrade would fix that.

I'd go to the Dragon with my request, but I'm not sure she wants to talk to me after how rude I was to her.

The LINK byways of Tokyo are some of the oldest continuous electronic spaces in existence. A person or an avatar, like myself, can wander the twisted, narrow pathways forever and never see the same thing twice.

The path I stroll aimlessly renders itself with retro 3-D hexagons, making everything seem extra angular. The walls of the alleyway are tall for this area, maybe four stories.

Tiny apartments, the backs of which are visible to me, stack clumsily one on top of the other, like a child's building blocks. Exactly defined laundry waves in the breeze. Garbage cans and heavy-duty Dumpsters line the graffiti-spattered walls. The light is set to a sort of perpetual twilight, as if the sun is always just settling on the horizon. It fits my mood perfectly, down to the blocky sharpness of it.

In a darkened doorway an advertisement golem crouches. Gaudy-colored spikes stick out on its corpulent body giving it a shape like a sandbur. Ad images flash and swirl, melting into incomprehensibility. It tenses to jump onto me, so I produce my ad-repellent spray from my jeans' pocket and quickly douse myself in the slick stuff. When the golem attempts to attach itself to me, it slides off. Its programming being as persistent as it is invasive, the golem tries again. But, after a failed second attempt, it rolls quietly back into its hidey-hole to await another unsuspecting victim.

I shiver. I hate those things. Three years back, when I was less self-reliant, a small one attached itself to me, and I'm still finding fragments of its ad banners tucked in weird places in my operating system.

My internal sensors alert me to the fact that in the next directory is a gaming parlor—just what I've been looking for. I turn the corner and move onto a larger boulevard. The images on the main thoroughfare appear in the slick style of flat animation, including, I note, their complete disregard for the laws of physics. This section of the LINK appears very popular. The wide sidewalks are crawling with avatars, most of which are nostalgic representations of Japanese and American television characters. *Bōsōzoku* gangs on their crotch-rocket–style motorcycles zip by at speeds unattainable in real-time. A large bunny rabbit bounces past me, chewing on an oversize carrot.

I adjust myself to fit in, letting the hair on my crown lengthen until it's hanging in front of my face. My eyes widen, and my nose disappears into a small bump. I enjoy the androgyny of the Animé, and I play with my face until it's nearly impossible to guess my gender. I want to reflect in my image my own complicated dichotomy of ones and zeros. As a final touch, I keep a bit of the color of my father's race on my face, but, instead of something more traditionally Egyptian, choose to dress in alternating tight and flowing leather. Hell, I'm about to waltz into a Yakuza gaming den; I want to look cool.

My translator provides a subtitle for the *kanji* characters above the door. I am, it informs me, walking into the *Te Ga Hayai*, "The Lady Killer." I walk down three short steps and open a door strangely three-dimensional in its flat attention to the details of shadow and light.

I'm in trouble before I get the door shut behind me.

"Where are your credits, boy?" the guardian avatar asks me. He looks like a sumo wrestler—so wide that I can't see much of the parlor behind him. What I can see seems to be draped in velvet and soft light.

"I'm here to see someone." My Japanese is perfect, although I have been told I sound a bit like the Berlitz instruction audio files—slow and exact.

"You come here to play or you leave." White subtitles appear at the guardian's feet.

"I'll play." I doubt the guardian will understand if I make a more complicated request.

"You have no credits," it bellows.

"Then I'll barter."

"Request being transferred," the guardian says. Its eyes glaze over, and its body crumbles to dust. The room goes blank as I am shunted into a reserve space. The utter void reminds me too much of when I crashed, so I shrink slowly, transforming into the image of a white mouse to inspect the directory at its Basic level. The code is uncomplicated, but I pass the time reading it.

"Hello?" An inquiring voice brings me back up into the white space. The avatar is a geisha. Her kimono is resplendent in greens and golds against the emptiness of the reserve. She is startled when I transform from my white mouse mode back into full interface.

"I didn't see you there," she says behind a shy hand. *"What were you doing?"*

"Reading," I admit. *"Has my request been approved?"*

She nods, as though I have adequately explained myself. I see the glimmer of something behind her eyes, perhaps indicating the close proximity of a human operator. *"But I want to ask you some questions first. You told the guardian you were here to see someone."*

"Yes."

The code shifts beneath my feet. Around me a room materializes. Rice-paper walls and low tables pull themselves out of the whiteness.

"Who might that be?" She indicates that I may sit on one of the pillows on the floor.

I do so, but I begin to feel self-conscious in my Animé persona, since the room is portrayed with a deeper, more photographic realism.

"I'm not entirely sure," I say truthfully. *"Thing is, I thought I might recognize them if I saw them."*

"Who?" she asks again, drifting smoothly across the floor, her feet invisible beneath the shifting fabric of the silken kimono. *"Who do you think you might have recognized?"*

"Friends of a friend." Then, I add hopefully, *"Yakuza."*

She pauses near the window, which shows a rather stereotypical view of Mount Fuji. It is the first detail of this new place that has disappointed me. I am, however, quite impressed by the shadow the geisha-avatar casts, and by the way the light plays against the white makeup on her face.

"You have come to the Lady Killer looking for Yakuza? Whatever for?" Her heavily outlined eyelashes bat innocently.

I shrug. *"I thought I might know that, too, when I saw them."*

Her laughter is light, loving instead of mocking. *"You are not a boy with very clear plans, are you?"*

I shake my head, not feeling it necessary to use anything other than body language to affirm the negative.

"If I allowed you to play, what would you barter?"

"I'm a very good page," I say, crossing my legs into a half-lotus.

The geisha smiles slightly, but shakes her head. *"Taking messages and running errands is a machine's job. Such a thing would be wasted on a boy like you, a boy who reads the code in a waiting room. Besides"*—she tilts her head in feigned embarrassment—*"such a job is not worth much on the gaming floor. It would be a bad barter."*

"But . . . all I know how to do is page."

She makes a noise like clucking her tongue. *"Then you have been very neglected, dear boy. If you work for me, I shall not make such mistakes with you."*

The offer is so tempting I almost say yes, but my memory beeps, warning me. *"I'm already working for someone else. Well, sort of. Actually that's partly why I'm here."*

"Oh?"

"I could do a small job," I offer.

The geisha frowns in disappointment.

"Then I wonder if you have anything to barter at all," she says sadly, turning to look at the badly rendered mountain.

I stand up, feeling as though she has given me my cue to leave. I hesitate, though a door has materialized just to my right. *"What would you teach me?"*

She doesn't turn away from her ugly mountain. *"Properly trained, a boy like you could make a fine wire-wizard."*

"Me? A cracker?"

The geisha turns to look at me. The sun hits the spot on her neck bare of white makeup. *"You sound so surprised."*

Not even Iblis offered me this.

"You're young, it's obvious. But, given enough time, you could be very good, I think. I watched you in the waiting room, and outside in the street. You are very quick on your feet, changing the avatar to fit the surroundings. I'm surprised you haven't transformed yourself here, honestly. I would like to know how you would render your image in a realistic world."

I think about it for a second, then show her my *chador,* with its lengths of black fabric and mesh screen over my eyes.

"But this is no good," she says, dismissing my careful work of sunlight and fabric with a wave of her slender hand. *"I can't see you at all this way."*

"You asked how I would render myself," I say, stiffly proud of the complexity of my image. *"This is it."*

"Are you a Muslim girl?"

"Sometimes."

"Sometimes?" She repeats my answer with another light laugh. *"Dear one, you either are or you aren't."*

I shake my head, sending a shower of fabric this way and that. *"I've looked. I have both parts as far as I can determine—ones and zeros."*

Before she speaks, her bright-red butterfly lips become a thin line. *"I see."*

She sucks in her lips thoughtfully, as her eyes roam over

my body. I can tell that she is trying to determine if I tell the truth. A feather-light scan checks my signature file. Rather than hiding my information, I open it up fully. I allow the geisha to read my father's hidden identification codes.

Her eyes widen, and we stare at each other. This is no longer about my desire to gamble. I want to impress this human. I want her to realize that I am exactly what I say I am.

I clear my throat, and shift my feet beneath my robes. *"What if I want something more?"*

"Like what? "

I want to belong. I want someone to watch over me, upgrade me. I want to see my father again. I want to be loved. But, I say none of these things. *"I want in."*

She seems to understand the implication and smiles welcomingly. *"I want to stress that working for us could be a very sweet deal, indeed. Perhaps this other person you are working for . . ."* She delicately pauses, as though to search for the appropriately inoffensive word. *"Neglects you, though perhaps not of his own free will. Perhaps you could consider yourself on loan to us, until your employer can see to your education himself."*

It is a very polite way of talking around my father.

"Knowing what I am, you still offer to teach me?"

She smiles and bows deeply. *"I do."*

I have been so enchanted by this avatar that it only now occurs to me to ask, *"Who are you?"*

"I am a licensed representative of the Toyama business group.

In seconds I have read seventeen newspaper articles about Kioshi Toyama and his alleged ties to the Yakuza. They inform me that rival gangs currently consider Toyama's *bakuto* organization top dog. It seems I have found the Dragon's people on my first try.

"Tell Toyama that Page ibn Mouse will consider his offer."

CHAPTER 25

Morningstar, the Adversary

They say rock and roll is Satan's tongue. I couldn't disagree more. Though I loved the chaos of a midnight rave, I wished I'd brought earplugs.

The party clogged the pedestrian traffic on skyway level seventy-four. Some surfer had redirected the advertising holos in the tube's walls so that, instead of personalized ads, they all pumped in the video and sound of a Japanese thrash polka band, live no doubt, somewhere in the world. Azazel handed me a plastic glass of something a foul green color, smelling strongly of alcohol. I held on to it, but didn't drink.

"The Four Horsemen," he said, shouting to be heard over the pounding bass guitar. In his black wool and leather, he fit right in with the majority of the crowd. I, unfortunately, looked like some of the dazed commuters who'd stumbled into the "hit-and-run" by accident. A hit-and-run was a kind of rave that was always on the move. They would set up the party in spontaneous, often public spaces, like here in the traffic tunnel or on a crowded subway platform. The idea, the excitement of a hit-and-run, was to be overt and only one step ahead of the cops.

Bodies danced all around us in a loose circle. In the center, a group of buskers and amateur musicians had set up their instruments to play along impromptu-style with the Four Horsemen—a kind of an instrumental karaoke. The tunnel's main power had been shut down, so everything was bathed in the soft glow of the emergency lights and the flickering images of the band's video.

"Pretty cool, huh?"

Azazel and I leaned up against a piece of public art, at

the very edge of the pulsing mob. Hit-and-runs had become very popular. It seemed the more people cut themselves off from their neighborhoods, the more they sought out the company of strangers. They wanted to be a part of something bigger, unique, and personal. Many people worked away from the office, via the LINK, but they did it from the corner coffee shop, rather than their homes. Humans, like dogs, preferred to run in each other's company.

I took a cautious sip of the alcohol. It tasted as horrible as it looked, and seemed to be a mixture of a little bit of whatever was handy, heavy on peppermint schnapps. Above us, on the ceiling of the pedestrian tunnel, a count-down flashed.

I pointed to it with the plastic cup. "What's that?"

"When the cops are expected to show," Azazel said.

There wasn't much time left on the clock. I frowned. "So, the party's over in fifteen minutes?"

"Nah," he said. "It's a game of chicken. Most people stay just to prove they're not afraid of being arrested."

The smile on Azazel's face told me that he'd played that game before. I snorted. "You need a life."

He bristled, standing up straighter. "Hey, in some circles, it's a badge of honor to have a Horsemen's hit-and-run on your rap sheet."

I set my cup of garbage alcohol in the hollow of a public art statue. I'd seen enough. This was no sign of the apocalypse. As usual, the Fallen had failed me. I was less than half a block away, with Azazel shouting at my heels, when I heard it: a pure, amplified note on a cello. As the bow drew across the strings, I felt that warm richness in the pit of my stomach that comes only when in the presence of a musical master. Everything else fell away. The thrash guitar and drums faded into the perfectly haunting sound of the strings. The crowd felt it, too. From my new distance, I could see their bodies moving differently, more slowly, reverently, worshipfully, and in awe.

Music has a power over the human psyche that I have never been able to master. Folktales abound in which I am portrayed as a fiddler, but I'm no musician. I think that people see the Devil in music because there is an intense seduction, sensuality, and danger inherent in it, qualities usually given to me. Music, like love, like a devil can make a human do crazy, sinful things. The Four Horsemen—no, this woman, this cellist—had that kind of power; had it by the balls.

The camera zoomed in on her face, or rather what could be seen of it under a mountain of hair. Her eyes were hidden in the shadows, but the light fell on her mouth, open in ecstasy. She was naked, covered only by the velvety smooth wood of the cello, and her legs wrapped around the instrument like a lover.

I wanted to be that cello and be played by her hands. The crowd wanted it, too, men and women alike, as did Azazel, a former angel in God's army. This woman was good.

A line of cops in riot gear chose that moment to rush past us, toward the crowd. We were far enough away to be considered out of range of arrest, but close enough to witness every gory detail. Fist and baton flashed in the strobe light. Blood spattered against the video image of the cellist. I felt my own rage begin to boil. I wanted to protect her, protect the music. Without realizing it, I'd taken two steps forward before a heavy hand rested on my shoulder.

"Best stay out of it, son," the cop said.

Azazel took my hand. With a smile, he said, "You see the insanity she causes? The devotion? It's them. The Four Horsemen of the Apocalypse have come . . . the end is near."

Watching the frenzy of the mob intensify with the music, I thought he just might be on to something.

CHAPTER 26
Emmaline, the Inquisitor

It was late by the time I got back to the hotel. I showered to get the stink of geek sweat off my body. Then I lay on the bed, letting the air dry my skin. I shut my eyes and accessed the number the Gorgon had given me for Page. Instead of Page, I got an error message telling me that the user I was looking for was off-line. Considering that Page only existed on the LINK, I figured I'd been had. I put out another wide bandwidth call for Page, but it would take some time for him to notice it. Just as I finished, I got a reminder ping. It was time to go to Mass.

A certain amount of leeway on the requirement to attend services was given to Inquisitors on cases, but, checking my log, I was way behind. It was go, or risk losing my badge. Well, I told myself, I might as well get it over with. Besides, sometimes the ritual of Mass helped me think. Like working in VR, the familiar words, rhythm, and actions of the service put my brain in the zone.

I got dressed in my Inquisitor uniform and headed back out into the night.

The church the LINK directed me to, for a small fee, was a Roman Catholic mission. According to the LINK advertisement, St. Denis's was open for service twenty-four hours a day, and as a point of tourist interest, actually continued the somewhat medieval practice of performing the canonical hours. Vigils, a midnight mass, had only just started. The building was on the butt-edge of Manhattan and required a brief dash outside of the pedestrian traffic tunnel. The snow had turned to drizzle. Standing in the vestibule, I took a minute to shake off the moisture from my wool coat.

In the pews, I could see a few heads dotted here and there, mostly near the back of the church. Still, it was a good crowd for a weekday, midnight Mass. A huge wooden crucifix hung above the altar. In a pulpit to one side stood a young Mexican priest. Perhaps, I thought wryly, his looks helped attendance somewhat. Certainly they couldn't hurt.

The air inside the church held the sweet, serious smell of frankincense. I closed my eyes and could almost feel the earth steadying beneath my feet. The odor reminded me of my office, my order, and my mission.

Humming along with the hymn, I opened my eyes. A man stood in front of me. He wore a dirt-streaked parka, and his black, curly hair was long and unwashed. Everything about him was smudged and streaked, except for his bright gray eyes, which held such intense clarity they frightened me. He took a lurching, drunken step closer. The unwashed stink of his body overpowered the comfort of the frankincense. The man looked like he might speak to me, beg me for something, so I turned away, stepping to one side to go around him.

"What you do to the least of us, you do to me." He belched wine with every word.

To quote Jesus to a priest was a cheap shot, and I turned back to tell him so.

My face stung with a cold blast of a sudden wind. Tears formed in the corners of my eyes. A wheel of six, steel-gray wings rolled in the air where the homeless man had stood. Static crackled. I put my hand up to shield my face. *Who is the liar?*

"What?" I asked the apparition, not certain it had really spoken. The words sounded like they had come from within my own head, like a remembered voice.

They have hearts with which they do not understand, and they have eyes that do not see, and they have ears with which they do not hear. . . . This time the voice rumbled like a subway train. My head ached with the sound so thunderous. Wind blasted me against the wall. I felt the stone walls of the church nip the hairs at the back of my neck. The air pushed so hard against me that I was having trouble breathing. My fingers felt numb from the cold. *Who is the liar?*

"I don't know," I whispered. In that moment the pressure that was holding me up was gone, and I fell to the floor, gasping. My stomach heaved. I spewed on a mosaic tile of Christ as the lamb. Tears mercifully blurred the image of my desecration. I curled up the sleeve of my coat in my fist and wiped awkwardly at the vomit. I concentrated on breathing without sobbing.

A hand, heavy and human, fell on my shoulder.

I froze, afraid of what I might see if I looked up.

"It's okay," a soft baritone said. Almost the instant I stiffened, the hand carefully removed itself. Out of the corner of my eye, I saw dark slacks kneeling beside me. A towel was offered. "This sort of thing happens all the time."

"It does?" My throat was raw from throwing up. I could still feel the ghost of the icy wind, burning on my cheeks like a brand. I took the towel and wiped my hands.

"Sure. We'll have Cynthia take you to detox." He held out a hand for me to shake. "I'm Eion McMannus."

"I don't need detox," I said, anger helping me find my voice. I looked up into the concerned face of a towheaded priest. His eyes widened when he saw my collar, then, opened farther when he read the insignia of my office.

"An Inquisitor," Eion whispered, like my title were a curse. He crossed himself.

I wiped my face with the towel. I started cleaning up the floor before I got a whiff of the vomit and had to stop. Eion took the stained cloth from me, and I sat back to observe him more closely.

"What just happened here?" I asked.

"You're not feeling well?" he offered politely. Looking over his shoulder, he waved away a concerned-looking nun who was coming up the aisle. The priest conducting the service continued without interruption. "Maybe you should come into the rectory. I can offer some tea, something calming like chamomile."

Though that sounded very nice, I scowled. "No, I mean with the wings and wind."

"Wings?" Having finished with the floor, Eion sat back on his heels. His face looked pale. "Who told you about the wings? Confession is supposed to be sacrosanct, private." He shook his head as if in disbelief, and his voice was very quiet. "I knew I should have kept that to myself."

"What are you talking about?"

He stood up. "Let's talk about this in the rectory."

*   *   *

I followed Eion down a set of stairs into the basement of the church. The stone walls smelled musty, and my stomach twinged. I held my breath as he led me through a cement-walled tunnel. Once we were up another short flight of stairs, we reached a kitchen.

A stainless-steel counter with a sink ran along one whole side of the room. An industrial-size, well-used stove took up most of the adjoining wall. There was one table in the center, and above it hung a mishmash of tarnished and dinged pots and pans, most of which looked like they'd come from rummage sales or barter. Over a half-wall, I could see rows and rows of picnic-style tables, the kind you might find in an old school. Windows showed frost and the dark, midnight sky.

Eion pulled a bright yellow-enamel tea kettle out of a cabinet under the sink, and started filling it with water. I found a heavy oak chair in the corner, and I moved it over to the table.

"Careful with that," Eion said, though his attention was still on filling the tea kettle. "One of the legs is wobbly."

I sat down gingerly, but it seemed to hold me.

"You're an American Catholic," he said, nodding at the Inquisitor uniform under my wool coat.

The unspoken question, of course, was how did an American Catholic end up as part of the elite Christendom corps? "You can't tell me that you haven't heard my story. I would have thought all the Catholics, Roman and American, had put in their two cents by now."

Eion shook his head, and set the kettle on the burner. "Sorry, I've been out of touch."

"Well, I guess since even Lutherans can become Inquisitors, they figured an American Catholic woman could, too."

Eion turned, and leaned against the counter. "I'm surprised. His Holiness can be very stubborn about some things."

I laughed. "That's an understatement."

He nodded and gave me a sad, tired smile. "But you're here to question me about the vision. I suppose we should get down to it."

"You've been expecting me?"

"In the back of my mind, yes," Eion said. "I'd hoped

that my confessor would keep it to himself, but, well . . .
I'm sure he's just concerned about my sanity."

"You've had a vision." My stomach twittered again, and
I touched my cheek to feel the cold wetness there.

"Months ago. I should have confessed it right away, I
suppose." He ran a hand through his curls and turned back
to the cabinets. He pulled out one mug and hunted for
another. I could hear pans shifting. "I just felt so crazy.
Who has visions in this day and age? And, what with the
whole LINK-angel thing last year, well . . . I didn't want
to jump to any conclusions."

I remembered the LINK-angels. Phanuel, the angel of
death, still haunted me in my dreams. His black wings and
skull-like face were, as it turned out, perfect constructs. The
thing that had made the angels so convincing was that with
their image they brought waves of emotion. Fear hung
around Phanuel like a cloud. I shivered at the memory.

"Good plan," I said, thinking it was sound advice for me
to take as well. As creepy as Phanuel had been, he was
nothing like this winged creature with gray eyes. In retro-
spect, it was easy to see how Mouse had failed. Phanuel was
very medieval in his appearance, very human. The thing I
had seen was much more Biblical.

"Six wings in a wheel," Eion was saying. I looked up to
see him turning a coffee mug over and over in his hands.
He gave a small, embarrassed laugh and threw a nervous
glance at me. "And, here's the crazy part—my sister in the
Virgin Mary's rose garden with a lily."

"Your sister?"

"Deidre McMannus."

Deidre again.

Eion set the mug down, and started the search for tea
bags. He opened and closed several drawers until settling
on one. "She's had the baby. In July. A girl. So far no
miracles, but, well, being born in a Glass City without any
defects is pretty lucky. That man you came in with," he
said. "I think he's the father, but I'm not sure. He looks
so different now. He was here in the church the day I had
my vision."

"What man I came in with?"

"Michael." Eion stopped moving to look at me. "Some
people call him 'the Preacher.' He's starting to get a little

bit of a following among the homeless and the Gorgons. He lives out there in the Glass City somewhere, I hear. Probably with Deidre at that crazy kibbutz of theirs."

"I didn't come in with anyone."

"Sure you did. Honestly, that's why I thought you were . . . in trouble. Michael sometimes brings people here who could use a good detox. Anyway, when you first came in, he had his arm around you. You were talking. When he left, you threw up."

"Is that what happened?" My own voice sounded small, because in my ears I could hear a rumbling voice asking: *Who is the liar?*

When he didn't speak, I looked up to see Eion staring at me curiously. He held two tea bags in his hands. The kettle was hissing near his elbow. Instead of moving to get it, he continued watching me.

"What?" I whispered.

"Are you calling me an Antichrist, some kind of false prophet?" His voice was flat, but I could tell by the white forming at his knuckles that he was angry.

"Sorry?"

"I have never lost my faith," Eion said through clenched teeth. His fists crushed the tea bags. I could smell the bruised herbs from where I sat. "Never."

"I didn't say you had," I insisted.

"You just quoted First John, chapter two, verse twenty-two: 'Who is the liar? It is the man who denies that Jesus is the Messiah. Such a man is the Antichrist.'" As if just noticing them in his hands, Eion tossed the bags into the mugs he'd set next to the stove. Turning his back to me, he leaned against the counter on his arms, his shoulders hunched.

"Antichrist?" I whispered. Something twittered in my stomach, soft and fleeting like Morningstar's kiss.

Eion didn't hear me. "Sure," he told the mugs, "I've felt different since then. I've felt a little special, maybe even chosen. But, I've never set myself up as anything that I'm not. I sure as hell never claimed to be the Messiah, or a prophet. I've never told anyone but my confessor about my vision . . . oh, and Deirdre, but let me tell you, she sure didn't want to know."

I felt like my reality was sliding out of sync with Eion's—

he saw things I didn't; heard words I swore I never spoke. In a dreamlike state, I kept questioning, interrogating. "Didn't want to know what?" My own voice sounded far away.

"The lily," he spat out in exasperation. His back twitched. "The garden. Mary. All while she was up in the belfry with Michael, learning that sex isn't a sin. What do you think it means? The baby was born in July, and now it's January. The sun will be in Aquarius any day now!"

I shook my head. "I don't understand the significance."

"Leo, you know, the Lion of Christ. The Age of Aquarius, Dane Rudyar predicted it really started in 2060. So maybe he was off nineteen years. People have been trying to predict the end since . . ." Eion let out a sigh, and his shoulders dropped. He turned down the heat on the roiling kettle and slowly, deliberately poured water into each mug. "No, you're right. Quoting astrologers, what am I thinking? I sound loony when I start talking like this. Maybe I am suffering from some kind of messiah complex. I mean, my very own sister as the new Mother of God? How crazy is that?"

Eion set the cup of tea down in front of me and retreated back to his spot by the stove. The chamomile flowers stained the water a light yellow. As I watched, the faded hologram on the cup shifted clumsily between a sports car and a happy young family. The holographic paint had worn in patches, and the family had fuzzy faces. A strange sort of puzzle was starting to click together in my mind.

"You had a vision of the Second Coming," I said, slowly. "You saw a creature made up of wings."

"Three sets of wings. A seraph," he added cautiously.

"A seraph. Right. Okay. Did it have gray eyes?"

Eion, who had been about to take a sip, stopped. His eyes locked on mine. "I'd forgotten that. Yes. But how did you . . . ?"

"I saw it, too. Only mine apparently warned of the Antichrist."

He shook his head violently. "No. You had a vision? When? Is this some kind of a trick to try to get me to talk my way into a straitjacket and a padded cell?"

"I didn't know about your vision when I came here."

His frown deepened. "Then why would you, an Inquisitor, come to this church?"

I glanced at him over the rim of the mug, and that funky feeling returned to my stomach. I'd come to participate in the canonical hour's Mass, but got something else entirely. "Providence?"

"So, you think God is involved." Eion chewed on the edge of a fingernail and regarded me. "You don't think I'm crazy?"

I shrugged, and offered an idea that had been at the back of my mind. "We could both be the victims of the same prankster. But, the fake kinds of things I've seen have been donuts in the shape of the Virgin and weeping statues. Usually, people interested in perpetrating religious hoaxes have something to gain from the fame. They would have tried another priest, since you didn't talk. And, I doubt they'd be stupid or bold enough to target an Inquisitor, even if they somehow did know I was coming."

"But no Inquisitor ever debunked the LINK-angels."

"No."

Eion nodded and took a long sip of his tea. The sleet spattered against the windows. "I don't know about you, but my vision wasn't like the LINK-angels at all. No, much more obtuse. No 'vote for Letourneau, whoo-whooo.' No obvious messages. This was more like a nightmare or a daydream, full of symbolism. Was yours like that?"

I swirled the liquid around in my cup. "It seemed so real. I felt the sting of a cold wind. Maybe it could be some kind of virtual reality-LINK crossover technology. Something randomly projected whenever a person walks in the door."

"Two people," Eion corrected absently.

"The preacher, what was his name? You said he was around when you had your vision, right? If there was a perp of this hoax, he's the connection."

Eion nodded his head. "Michael," he supplied. "His name is Michael. But the guy isn't techno-savvy enough—"

I cut him off with a wave of my hand. I was already standing, looking for my coat. "And where would I find this Michael?"

"In the Glass City, sometimes. Sometimes he sleeps here at the mission. I suppose you could check, but, Monsignor, I don't think it's a hoax."

"We need to eliminate that possibility first."

CHAPTER 27
Page, the Intelligence

Kioshi Toyama's avatar is not what I expect from the most powerful mob boss in the Eastern Hemisphere. He appears as a juvenile cartoon, all round and cuddly. The lines of the imaginary creature are thick, and the colors are primary: bold and bright blues, reds, and yellows. His big, black, button eyes blink at me innocently.

Like the geisha's chambers, his garden is photographically rendered. We have met on a shallow wooden bridge overlooking a carefully sculpted pond. Lotus blossoms dot the water, and koi shimmer orange and yellow beneath the crystal waters. I hear the .wav of a gently babbling brook. The garden extends far into the horizon. Pebble pathways made of smooth, gray rocks disappear in every direction, and bamboo and cherry trees dot the hillsides. The light is set to early morning and is dappled.

I tower over Toyama's cartoon in my black robes. My father was a short man, and my sense of perspective is tied into his. It feels strange to be so much taller than anyone. I rest my elbows on the top rail of the wooden bridge, while Toyama sticks his head out over the lowest slat, making funny faces and cooing at the water. He flashes a pink tongue out at the reflection of himself and laughs until big teardrops come out of eyes.

Per the geisha's instruction, I brought Toyama a .gif. I set it on the ground beside where he is rolling in his mirth. Noticing it, his giggling stops, and he cautiously examines the package, sniffing at it like a dog. Satisfied, he clicks it open with a gleeful cry.

"Oooh," he says, admiring the ASCII dragon. He tilts his head this way and that, finally standing on his head.

"Single copy coded! This one is very old. Perhaps from the UNIX days?"

I nod. *"It's from my father's collection. The provenance is in the metadata."*

"You honor me," Toyama says, straightening up. His pudgy cartoon clasps its hands and bows seriously. His eyes become mere slits, and ears flatten against his head. I'm glad my face is hidden behind my robes; I can't quite suppress a smile.

"It's partly because of your father that we are meeting here today." The ASCII dragon disappears into the "fur" of Toyama's avatar. *"I'm afraid I will owe him much, when all is said and done."*

"The art is a gift."

"But not, I imagine, your service."

"Your representative said that she would teach me to be a wire-wizard."

Toyama nods, his round head bouncing like a beach ball. *"If that is all you want."*

It hadn't occurred to me to ask for more. A sudden thought hits me. *"There is one more thing."*

"Of course." Toyama doesn't seem surprised by the idea of an additional request. *"Name it."*

"Mecca. I want to perform the hajj.*"*

The open face of the cartoon crumples into an exaggerated frown. *"Can't you go to Mecca any time?"*

"The Mecca node, yes, but I want to take the trip piggybacking on someone's body or in a suit. Someone willing to do all the rituals."

Toyama scratches his chin, with one ear back. *"And for these things you will act at our will and as a member of our family until such time as your father is free?"*

I parse the sentence carefully. I think about Iblis, but I made no specific promises to him—except for my soul, and I'm not even sure what it is or if I even have one. Besides, technically, I don't owe Iblis my soul until after my death. *"All right. Yes."*

Toyama claps his hands and does a little dance on his tiptoes. *"Then it's time for tea!"*

He motions for me to follow, and I stay a step or two behind his cavorting avatar. He leads me along a path lined with blooming cherry trees. Pink petals flutter in the breeze, but disappear like raindrops before hitting the ground. We come around a bend, and I see an old stone temple. The bright morning sunlight lines the walls in a white halo.

Toyama stops before entering the ruins. The cartoon is wearing its serious expression again. Its plump hands are folded demurely in front of its body.

"Would you like to take tea with me in real-time?" Before I can ask how such a thing is possible, Toyama adds, *"I will provide a host body."*

The last time I experienced the outside world through the sensory perceptions of a human was with my father. That was years ago. Every time I do, I understand the LINK interface that much more. I am reminded of my father, and the trips we took together. My heart aches.

Because I haven't answered instantly, Toyama sweetens the deal. *"The host is fully readable. Our own AI has ridden her, and finds the experience very, what does she say? Enlightening."*

"I'd love to," I say with a short bow.

"Wonderful."

The woman whose body I inhabit is five foot, two inches tall. Hair tickles her cheeks. She is sitting cross-legged on a swivel chair. I can feel the hard wood beneath her butt, the light pressure of denim against her thighs. With every breath, nipples touch silk. She's in excellent physical condition. Her heart rate is an athletic sixty-five beats per minute. Toyama didn't lie when he said she was fully readable, but what I find more astounding is that, outside of her automatic functions like breathing, her movements are completely under my control. I attempt to move her fingers cautiously, one at a time. My concept of coordination is clumsy, and her fingers flutter much more rapidly and with more force than I intended. I'm afraid to move—afraid I'll break her.

"Who would submit to this?" A speaker sits on the table between me and a man whom I must assume is Toyama. My voice comes out of the box in an androgynous alto. There's a few seconds' delay between the moment I send the LINK command and the time the voice-recognition program speaks.

"In Japan we have always had respect for your kind."

Toyama is a trim young man, probably in his middle to late thirties. Though the light coming in through the office window is overcast and muted, he wears pink sunglasses. They are, however, his only affectation. He is dressed in a very simple blazer and jeans. Under the coat, he wears a T-shirt promoting a video game featuring his cartoon avatar. He leans forward. I see a flash of color at his wrists— old-fashioned flat tattoos. "Are you comfortable? We can adjust the level of control."

"I'm not used to this," I admit, though I hate to give up this new sensation. "Maybe she should . . ."

"Of course. My representative told me you'd been neglected. I should have predicted this." Toyama moves out from behind his desk to stand behind the woman's body. I'm scared to turn her head, but I can hear him adjusting something, and I feel cables move against the back of her neck. He mutters to himself near the sub-vocal level, and I imagine he must be sending commands to her interface. Though the process fascinates me, I look, instead, around his office.

The room is small, but cheery. Several floor-to-ceiling windows occupy much of the wall space to the woman's left. Through them, I can see light snow falling into the Tokyo harbor. Besides the speaker, which is mostly hidden by the *ikebana* of cherry blossoms placed on top of it, there is a small 1940s–style desk lamp on Toyama's desk. In frames along the warm-gold-painted walls are printouts of ASCII and other early computer art. A simple wooden bookcase beneath the pictures holds a porcelain tea set for two. Through the woman's olfactory nerve, I can smell the brewing tea.

"There," Toyama says appearing in front of me again. "How does that feel?"

The woman's face smiles. I get the impression of the tightening and lifting of her facial muscles. Although she does not speak, I sense that she could if she wanted to.

"Better," I say through the speaker.

"And Mai?" Toyama glances over his sunglasses to reveal blue irises, not the black I would have expected. I'm surprised. Blue eyes mean he's not one hundred percent Japanese. I wonder if I've made a mistake; if he is not as powerful in the Yakuza as the newsfeeds made me think.

"Fine. Thank you, Kioshi-san," a sweet soprano says.

"I guess we three shall have tea," Toyama says, taking the pot from the bookshelf and placing it on his desk. The woman, Mai, picks up the edge of the chair and scoots closer to Toyama's desk. My sensors reel from all the information her interface provides me: pump of muscle, pressure of chair, hair against face, weight of body borne by feet across the floor, and so much more.

"I apologize that this is a poor substitute for the traditional saki ceremony, but the symbolism will be the same," Toyama says, pouring a deep green liquid into his own cup. "With this tea, you and I will become family, *ikka*. I your *oyabun*, and you my *kobun*."

The best that my translator can do with the words is to give me multiple levels of meaning. Within the concept of *oyabun* and *kobun* there is something, it tells me, of the master/apprentice relationship, but it is also akin to father and son, godfather and capo. Toyama takes a shallow sip of the cup and offers it to Mai.

Will you take it? she asks me via the LINK. Her heart rate increases.

Is he really Toyoma?

Why do you ask? Mai wonders.

His eyes, I explain.

He is Kioshi Toyoma. You should give him face, respect him.

Very well. Only after my agreement, does Mai lift her hands to accept Toyama's cup. The steam tickles her nose, and the cup warms her sweating palms.

Do you drink?

Yes. The porcelain is smooth against her lips. The green tea's flavor is complex. I am still trying to quantify it, when Mai picks up the tea kettle and pours tea into our cup.

Will you drink, then offer it to him?

Should I?

It is important that you do. I can tell from her breathing and dilated pupils that it certainly is to her.

It completes the ceremony? I ask, and she sends the affirmative. *Then I will.*

Toyama seems unfazed by the pause in the ceremony. He is leaning back in his chair, watching us through his rose-colored glasses. I understand the affectation now. The red glass makes his blue eyes appear black.

Mai tastes the tea and, offering the cup to Toyama, her arms tremble.

He reaches out and cups her hands in his. "After all this time, the *sakazuki* still moves you?"

These whispered words are not for me. Mai gives a nod. Her throat is too tight to speak, and my vision blurs with tears.

Toyama clucks his tongue and takes the cup from Mai. "You've always been like family, Mai. Even when you desert us," he says, giving her a piercing look over the rim of his sunglasses. Mai's tears fall; I can feel them cooling in the air on her cheeks. "And, anyway," Toyama continues, "this is for Page."

He drinks deeply of the tea.

Is it done? I ask Mai.

Yes. You are now a part of the Toyama family.

CHAPTER 28
Morningstar, the Adversary

Flying commercial always gave me a headache. But, though I had wings, they were mostly metaphorical, for show. I couldn't fly—at least not like a bird. One would think I could just pop back to Hell and reappear wherever I'd like. But God decided when angels returned to earth, including dark angels.

So, I spent the last several hours with my knees against my chest and a snoring businessman nearly in my lap.

I had to see that cellist.

I'd found out from Azazel that the rave broadcast had been beamed in from Club 99 Gas Panic, a bar for foreigners near the Roppongi Station in Tokyo. The cellist's name was Mai Kito and she lived and played here in Japan.

Thus, currently, I stood in the Tokyo airport with a backpack and a hangover, trying to get my bearings. I'd left New York's JFK sometime before two A.M., dropping over ten thousand credits to hop the red-eye space shuttle to arrive in the city just in time for the evening rush hour. Between the g-force and the garbage alcohol I'd had at the rave, I felt flatlined, too far gone for resuscitation.

Following *kanji* pictograms, I made my way to the taxi stop. The air outside the stuffy, recycled taste of the airport was crisp, even a bit chilly. The coldness was a merciful shock to my system. I sank down onto a concrete bench to wait my turn for a taxi.

Ironically, I felt like a man possessed. I wasn't sure what I had thrown into my backpack. I hoped I'd at least thought to bring a jacket. Tokyo, like New York, was mostly connected by skyways, but the Japanese, in their quirkiness, had set the tunnel temperatures to mirror those of the outside environs. It was January seventh, the feast of St. Raymond of Penyafot, and a mere five degrees above the freezing point of water.

When the taxi beeped politely, I realized I'd been holding up the line. I fumbled with the latch and settled gratefully, albeit clumsily, into the torn plastic backseat. The cab smelled like the remains of someone's dinner, something with pickled ginger and maybe miso. Suddenly, I felt extremely hungry, tired, and hung over.

"I will need yen," the driver told me in heavily accented English. We hadn't moved. "No barter."

"Euro-credits?" I offered in Japanese.

"Okay." He turned around and started the car and the meter going.

I was so tired that we turned out of the airport and onto Nikkō Avenue before it occurred to me to tell the driver to take me to a hotel. I suggested the Hilton; he shook his head.

"Don't embarrass yourself." Though I was certain my Japanese was flawless, the driver insisted on speaking to me in his bad English. "You have no LINK. The terminal told me so. Why else would I pick you up—me, the last remaining human-operated taxi in the East?"

"Dumb luck?" I tried to sound dryly sarcastic, but it came out wooden and thick.

"I'm taking you to the international hostel. You can afford that."

My head throbbed, so I gave up trying to hold it upright and let it bounce against the back of the seat. "Fine," I told the ceiling. The Gnostics were right. Earth was Hell.

The driver continued to cluck his tongue. Out of the corner of my eye, I could see him shaking his head in the rearview mirror. "Let me guess. Another *gaijin* for Mai."

I sat up so suddenly that I nearly knocked my already bruised head against the taxi's roof. "Mai Kito?"

"Bah." He made a sour face at me. "Maybe I shouldn't bother with the hostel and just rob you of all your money, and leave you on the street somewhere. It's what happens to the rest of them. You already look like a Maizombie."

"Maizombie?" What he'd said became clearer in slower repetition. "Oh. How many are there?"

"The streets are clogged with them. You should go home. Get a real girlfriend."

"Ouch."

My sarcasm apparently worked that time, because the driver pursed his lips. "You seem older than most of the others, more together. Don't waste your life trying to get the attention of a superstar."

"Where do most of these kids hang out?"

"Yoyogi Park."

"Take me there." Despite more grumbling and protests, the driver changed directions. Closing my eyes, I let my head rest against the backseat until I felt the taxi jerk to a stop.

I glanced out the window to see a huge, arched greenhouse. We were parked beside a cheerful doorway with a neon sign in *kanji* proclaiming this to be Yoyogi Park. Glass frames stretched for miles, reflecting the bright winter sun, and, in places, I could see a hint of green through the steamy windowpanes. The taxi driver bilked me for 150 Eurocredits, but I didn't really have the strength to haggle over the price. He shook his head at me one last time before he sped away.

Shouldering my backpack, I headed for the door. I pushed on it, but it didn't open. I saw the flash of laser and heard the hum of a scanner. When I tried the door again, it stayed closed.

"What the fuck?" I said, trying to find a camera to peer into. "Isn't this a public park?"

No one responded, so I started to look around for another way in. Before I could even take the few steps from entry to curb, a woman with bright purple hair and ancient Egyptian–style eyeliner accosted me. She wore a long, ratty trench coat. A strawberry-colored fuzzy hat was perched on top of her carefully sculpted bob cut.

"Ain't got no religion, huh?" she said in very slangy Japanese. "I can sell you a religion, man. Maybe some hardware, too. It'll get you into the park."

I had to admit I was damn curious, so I stepped back with her out of the way of the rush-hour foot traffic. We huddled close to the park wall. "What kind of religion are you selling?"

"New stuff, you might call them cults, but, see, they've

all got temporary clearance with the government." She looked over her shoulder, and leaned a bit closer to me. "The more membership they have, the more likely they are to get recognized, okay? It works out for everyone. You get a temporary pass, they get numbers."

There had to be a catch. "How long does registration take? If I buy one now, can I get into the park today?"

"Instantly, man. That's why they're so expensive." She held her left hand in the air, as if paused over an invisible keyboard. "You buying?"

"You got any Satanists?"

"Get real." Then she glanced at me out of the corner of her eye. "You better not be some kind of outlaw. I can't help you if you've been kicked out of the Christians or something."

I wanted to make some smart remark about how I was actually central to the Christian belief system, but my hands were getting cold, and the park looked warm and inviting. "What have you got that's cheap?"

She stared off into space for a second, LINKing, no doubt, then said, "Breatharianism. Thing is, you can't be seen eating anything in public."

"I'll take it," I said; I hardly remembered to eat as it was.

I traded the last of my Eurocredits for an ID chit, an external LINK headset interface, and a data crystal of a book called *Living on Light,* which she tucked into my backpack as "cover."

The deal was almost done when the cult recruiter raised her painted eyebrow at my name. She clucked her tongue and shook her head. "Sorry, but you've changed your name as part of your conversion," she said, ticking away with one hand in the empty space. "You are now Masao, the Righteous."

I gave a little snort, but I was smiling. "All right. I like it."

As she left, she said over her shoulder, "Try to read the book. Sometimes cops will quiz you. And the Tokyo fuzz are hardasses, hear?"

"Sure," I said, but she was long gone. I slipped the LINK interface on, which was a souped-up pair of sunglasses with an earpiece, tucked the ID into my jeans pocket, and tried the door to the park. It swung open easily.

"Welcome, Righteous," said a pleasantly androgynous voice in my good ear through the interface. "While here in lovely Yoyogi Park, be sure to visit the Meji Jingu Shrine for only three hundred yen!"

I stepped into warm, moist air, and the smell of pine. The ceilings were vast, and, far above, the occasional pane was cracked open to allow the circulation of air and avian fauna. Trees—some in bloom, others bare—lined large, paved roads running through the park. Teenagers sprawled on blankets on the grass, soaking up the sweltering greenhouse heat and sinking sun. I felt sweat start to prickle under my arms, while the advertisement droned on.

"The shrine was built in the 1920s in honor of the Emperor Meiji and his consort, Empress Shoken. It is open daily from sunrise to sunset. Currently, there is an exhibit of calligraphy on display. Sign up for a fun tour now?"

I shook my head no. The advertisement, however, was relentless. Full-color graphics of the shrine appeared in the corner of my eye, showing a solemn procession of monks.

"Find," I said aloud, "Mai Kito, address."

"Information unavailable," the interface told me. "But, you can still enjoy the shrine for only—"

"Fuck that. Find me Mai."

"There is a daily gathering of Four Horsemen fans at Yoyogi Park. Location and time of meeting available for a small fee, two yen."

"Transfer funds," I told it.

"Insufficient funds."

"What?"

"You have tithed your earthly estate to the Breatharians."

I laughed. "Of course, I did."

The trouble with being a Trickster was that sometimes you got tricked. Luckily, I had more than one earthly alias. After a few seconds of haggling, I managed to convince the LINK that I had money, and it dutifully informed me where the other rabid Maizombies would be gathering.

I spent nearly six thousand yen on a holographic sweatshirt that showed an animated loop of a naked Mai plucking the cello. The camera angle was such that you could briefly see the swell of one breast. Just as you thought you might see a nipple, the camera panned back as the loop started over. When I put it on, I was happy to note my external LINK connection picked up the promised "bonus track" of the Four Horsemen's cello solo. I lay down on the grass not far from a knot of Germans on a beach blanket. I shut my eyes to listen to the music without distraction. The sound of the strings was as haunting as at the rave. The setting sun through the greenhouse glass warmed my face, and I felt myself drifting to sleep.

A radiant creature sang to me. It had iridescent wings like a peacock with a thousand human eyes. Each rustle of feathers brought the moans of souls. Its brilliance burned me, and I had to look away into the shadows.

Michael, *I said, my voice sounding like it came from under water.* Go away, I'm having a nice dream.

You have come to us, *his voice sang, like mine once had, with the power and glory of God.* You wish to serve?

Always. *My heart felt light, like I might be lifted once again. Slowly, I began to turn my head back toward the fiery countenance. Warmth crept into my soul, like the sun warming cold granite.*

Water splashed my face, and tore me from Heaven. I woke with a start, and sat up to find myself still in Yoyogi Park. My sleepy consciousness registered a noise, a *tick-tick-tick*. Then water hit me in the chest—a hard stream of it. In a second, I was sputtering and soaked. The park's sprinklers had activated. I joined the people scattering off the grass and onto the paved boulevard. I shook myself out, thankful that I'd thought to grab my bag.

I was staring down in disgust at my wet, ruined shirt when I heard a voice: " 'How you have fallen from Heaven, O morning star, son of the dawn! You have been cast down to the earth, you who once laid low the nations!' "

I turned to see Jibril smiling broadly, his white teeth bright against his ebony skin. He was dressed as an African prince, decked out in Joseph's own robe of oranges, blues, yellows, and reds. I squinted at him as the sunlight caught the holographic tattoo between his eyes, and, despite myself, I read the flowing Arabic script once again: "There is no God but Allah, and Muhammad is the Prophet of Allah."

I envied Jibril at that moment. The sun warmed my

CHAPTER 29
Emmaline, the Inquisitor

Eion insisted that I wait until daylight to talk to the preacher he called Michael. So I slept that night in a spare bedroom in the rectory. Morning brought with it the smells of eggs frying, bread toasting, and mushrooms sautéing. Masculine voices filled the hallway outside the paper-thin wall of the room. Sunlight crept in through partially closed blinds and stabbed my eyes. I was exhausted. I wanted to roll back over and pull the covers over my head, but the thought of breakfast propelled me out of bed.

I hadn't really looked at the room last night. I sat blinking at the edge of the bed and tried to get my bearings. The furnishings were simple, as if for a monk. I sat in a twin-size bed and, across from me, so close I could touch it with my toes, was a desk and a chair. I'd draped my uniform over the chair, preferring to sleep in my now overly ripe T-shirt and underwear. A print copy of the Bible sat on an end table next to the bed. A cheap inspirational hologram took up one of the walls and showed rays of sunlight breaking through a heavy cloud. The image was on a short loop, which made the imaginary sun blink like a strobe light. The wall above the head of the bed had a simple, gold-painted, wooden cross.

I knelt beside the bed and bowed my head. Fragments of prayers flitted through my mind: *Our Father, Who art in Heaven . . . Now, I lay me down to sleep . . . Holy Mary, Mother of God . . .* What I really wanted was something more personal. I looked at the simple cross—the light from the hologram sending flickers across the gold. My tongue felt heavy. I couldn't think of anything eloquent, so I simply whispered, "Help me, Lord."

I groaned as I pulled myself upright and shrugged into my clothes. I hoped I hadn't missed breakfast.

I managed to find the dining area from memory and by following the sound of utensils clanking on china. Rounding the corner, I saw the picnic tables from last night filled with fifty or more priests, acolytes, and seminary students. The windows, still frosted over from last night's sleet, glittered with dawn light. With a yawn, I headed for the serving line. I hadn't been thinking about what I would look like to them—a woman in priestly garb, an American Catholic Inquisitor intruding into their exclusively Roman Catholic world. A wake of silence followed my procession across the floor. I suddenly felt self-conscious, and the buffet seemed miles away. I glanced nervously at wide-eyed stares, hoping to find Eion's among them. I didn't see him, but I was too far into the room to turn around. I continued resolutely for the end of the line, despite whispers I could now hear: "What's she doing here?" and "An Inquisitor? A woman?"

An older, black man broke from one of the tables and headed on a collision course with me. His steps were hurried, but he had a smile on his face, even though his eyebrows were drawn together as though in a frown. I offered my hand once he came into range.

"Emmaline McNaughten, Father. Won't be here long. Your priest Eion McMannus allowed me to stay last night. I came in rather late. I have business with someone possibly staying at your shelter," I said in one breath.

The priest's eyebrows relaxed as I spoke. "I see, I see," he said, his hand pumping. "Welcome."

I felt anything but, but I smiled nicely. We had reached the beginning of the line, and I took a tray from a pile. China plates were stacked neatly, and short buckets held loose silverware. I helped myself, while the father hovered near my elbow.

"I'm starving," I said amiably. Then, I suddenly remembered throwing up last night, and my stomach growled in protest.

"You're an American Catholic, you say?" The priest's eyes glanced briefly to my breasts, then away.

"I didn't, but I suppose it's obvious," I said, as I handed

my plate to the man on the other side of the counter who was serving up heaps of scrambled eggs and cheese. He passed it to the next person, who glanced at me only briefly before adding several pieces of soy bacon. I followed the plate down the line, like a dog after a bone.

"An Inquisitor."

"Huh?" I tear my attention away from my quickly filling plate to see the priest giving me another appraising look, like he could believe in one, but not the other. "Yes," I said. "Both an American Catholic and an Inquisitor. It's a long story."

"I'm sure it is." The priest pursed his lips.

I added a glass of ice-cold milk to my tray and took my plate from the last server. "After you, Father," I told him, and dutifully followed him to an empty table at the far end of the room. No doubt his intention was to isolate me from the curious stares of the other priests, but all I could think was that it would be a long way back for seconds. I said a silent grace over the meal, feeling truly grateful to God for the bounty, and dug in.

I was halfway done with the eggs and most of the toast when the priest spoke: "Business with someone in the men's shelter?"

It took me a second to realize that he had asked me a question in his own way. I swallowed some milk to clear my throat. "Possibly. A man called Michael, the preacher. I . . ." I realized I didn't quite know how to articulate why I needed to talk to Michael. I was just convinced he was a link between the visions Eion and I had had. "I need to ask him a few questions."

The priest nodded, sending his jowls flopping. "Then you'll be on your way."

It was more a command than a question, and I gave the priest a glare over my milk glass. I technically outranked the old man. And, as an Inquisitor, I had worldwide jurisdiction. I could damn well come and go as I pleased.

"Maybe." I firmly put the glass down on the tray between us. I picked up my fork and turned my attention to seriously devouring what was left on my plate. I didn't look up as I dismissed him. "Now, if you'll excuse me, I need to eat."

With a *harrumph*, he left me alone.

*   *   *

A very sleepy-looking Eion joined me after my second helping of eggs and bacon. Gone were last night's vestments. This morning he wore a knit sweater and jeans. He looked remarkably like a regular guy; he didn't wear the collar.

I pointed at my own throat with the tines of the fork. "You're a big believer in Vatican II, eh?"

He shrugged as he slid into the space across from me. "It's my vocation. I don't need to wear a uniform to have God with me."

"You sound like a Unitarian," I snorted jokingly, but I was thinking about the Inquisitor's badge embroidered above my heart and how naked I would feel without it.

"A Unitarian?" He smiled, and reached out to deftly steal a slice of toast. "Bite your tongue."

I pushed my plate toward him, as if to offer the remaining bits. I'd finally stuffed myself. "I'm going to guess that the old priest woke you up and told you to take care of me."

"Yep." Eion nibbled at an orange slice. "You managed to tick him off, but good."

"Tact," I said. "They teach a special course in diplomacy at Inquisitor school."

"I can tell." Eion laughed. Then, he put a hand to his chest and gave a mock courtly bow. "So, whenever you're ready, Monsignor, allow me to be your guide."

"Now is good." I wiped my face and hands on a paper napkin. Eion showed me where to deposit the tray and dishes and took me to the shelter.

The shelter of St. Denis's was housed just above the kitchen. One large room held several rows of cots, most with men still asleep on them. Eion let me peek into the darkened room with him, but made me wait outside in a little lounge area while he got Michael. I sat on one of the couches that ringed a small table. A window looked out into the courtyard between the church proper and the mission. Snow covered everything except a few dried stalks of black-eyed Susans, which poked out of the white drifts. Icicles dripped in the bright sunlight.

"Michael, this is the Vatican Inquisitor Emmaline McNaughten."

I looked up to see the beggar from last night. He wore the same stained parka, but he had shaved and showered. I was surprised to see that underneath the street grime was a handsome man. I would hardly have recognized him, but for those piercing gray eyes.

He offered a hand for me to shake, and I stood up partway to take it. "You wanted to ask me something?"

Again, I was surprised to find him lucid. I wasn't sure what I'd expected, but his steady gaze threw me. I sank back down onto the couch as he took a seat in a recliner across from me. Eion stepped back and leaned against the entryway to the stairs.

"I want to know what you had to do with the vision I had last night." Saying it sounded more stupid than I'd feared, but Michael regarded me seriously. He leaned back into his chair and steepled his fingers. Over Michael's shoulder, I could see Eion straighten, as if he was as curious as I was about what Michael might say to my bold claim.

"Tell me about it," Michael said.

I did, with Eion adding information from his own experience. Michael nodded his head when we were finished, as though carefully processing everything we'd said. Then he smiled softly to himself. "I'm still a conduit for His will."

There went my hope that Michael wasn't crazy. But, I supposed that it was still possible that he was somehow engineering these visions through the LINK. "So, how does God ask you to give your messages to people? Through the LINK? A hack from mouse.net into the LINK?"

Michael tapped his temple with a forefinger. "No LINK."

"You could still use a public terminal," I suggested, although instantly I could see how difficult it would be to trigger a LINK response remotely—unless, of course, he was carrying a transmitter somewhere on his body.

Scan, I told my internal system. *Electronic impulses.*

The sensor identified Eion's LINK signal, and absolute silence from Michael—not even the bleep of a wrist-phone or other external hardware.

Michael was frowning at me. "You're a star investigator, Em, but sometimes you're a shitty priest."

I stood up. That was exactly what Rodriguez had said to me when he'd given me this assignment. "Where did you hear that?"

His gray eyes stared at me unblinking.

"Where did you hear that?" I demanded again, bile rising in my throat. I moved closer to Michael, intending to beat the answer out of him if I had to. Eion moved to put a restraining hand on my shoulder.

"His mind isn't what it used to be," Eion said quietly.

I pushed Eion to one side. "I don't care. That was said to me in the privacy of my own chambers thousands of miles from here. If he's been stalking my LINK frequency, I think I have the right to know."

"Do you think God creates evil people to test the good ones?" Michael asked.

"That was a private conversation!"

"Backfeeding a secure, personal, Vatican channel? Michael? The poor guy hardly remembers to eat." Eion was protesting from behind me, as I grabbed Michael by the collar.

My muscles were enhanced enough that I should have been able to lift him to his feet easily. He didn't budge. Instead, he put his hands over mine and squeezed. His lips were close to my ear, and I heard him whisper, "Who is the liar?"

A hurricane blast pushed me back into Eion, and we both tumbled to the floor. When the howling wind died down, Michael was gone.

CHAPTER 30
Page, the Intelligence

In celebration of our new deal, Kioshi-san suggests we all go out for a walk. It takes forty minutes to prepare Mai's body to host me without the direct-line cables. Though I'm excited to experience the trip, I am a bit nervous when he disconnects the last line, my last clear escape route back to the LINK.

"Ready?" Kioshi asks me. I tell Mai to nod for me, and she does. With that, I perceive the LINK door close behind me. I'm completely contained in Mai's core nexus. This is a brand-new experience for me. Mai's body is different from my father's. My father isn't "rideable." The enhancements he's made to his nexus are designed to give him more speed and control; they're improvements made by a wire-wizard. Mai has all of those plus a whole lot more. When I experienced physical sensations through my father's body, only part of me reached inside, like a hand in a glove. I am subsumed inside Mai. Where I end and she begins is blurry.

The sensation is both claustrophobic and liberating. I ask Mai to show me the webbing she wears, and she looks down at her hands. The fibers that cover her are not easy for her eyes to perceive. To her, it looks as though her skin is lightly dusted in glitter. It's a nice effect, and she waves her arm under the desk lamp to see the sparkles.

"Where shall we go?" Kioshi asks, as I get the heady stream of information that accompanies the simple actions of Mai standing up and shrugging into her coat. There are so many things to feel—the coat's fake fur brushing against thighs, long tangle of hair against cheeks, eyes blinking, and muscles lifting and moving. I forget to respond.

"Page?" Kioshi asks politely, once Mai has stopped moving. I'm still awash in the overload—happy to experience only her breathing and heart rate, but I manage to formulate a response.

"It's up to you, Kioshi-san," Mai's sweet voice says for me. They have disconnected the speaker so I must tell her what I would like to say.

"Perhaps something simple to start with," Kioshi says, with a broad smile, suddenly reminding me of his plump, jolly animated avatar. "A walk around the block."

"Yes, that's probably all I can handle for now."

"You should get used to the sensations, Page," Kioshi says. "Otherwise, you'll never be able to direct a host on your trip to Mecca." Kioshi glances at me over his tinted sunglasses. I see the flash of blue eyes again and make a note for Mai to ask him about that for me.

Not unless you're willing to risk your life, Mai says to me via the LINK.

Why? I ask, as we head out the door of the office.

In Japan, having mixed heritage is a sensitive issue, especially in . . . the business.

I am amused that she is so circumspect, even in conversations that no one could possibly overhear. *Yes, I know. How did he end up in a position of such power then?*

He's ruthless and cunning. The best at what he does. I sense her breathlessness at the mere thought of him. *Besides, most people have never met him in person. If they do, they think he is just an errand boy, not the real Kioshi. You have been very honored by a personal meeting.*

Her heart thuds in her chest. She, too, feels honored, and perhaps much more.

How long have you been lovers? Because of our close connection, the question is out before I can censor it.

We stumble. Mai's hand catches on the doorframe with a hard slap. Kioshi's arm is around our waist in a second, supporting our weight easily. I can feel the heat of her body rise at his touch, the quickening of her breath, and how the pupils of her eyes dilate. She blushes and drops her gaze, mumbling a hurried apology. I notice his touch lingers a moment longer than is necessary, but I can't tell if it is returned affection or a concern about me, her cargo.

"My fault," I have Mai say for me. "Give me a second to get my bearings."

Kioshi bows and stands aside to wait patiently.

I'm sorry, I tell Mai silently. *I apologize if I upset you.*

She shakes her head so slightly that only I can sense it. We look around the antechamber, our gaze focusing on the surprised-looking receptionist who sits behind a black, metallic desk. A paper book is open in his lap, and, noticing our stare, he quickly returns to reading. He, like Kioshi, wears a suit coat, but he also has a white shirt and tie, classic and eternally fashionable.

The antechamber is not spacious, but it is twice as large as the office. A large banner printout of an ASCII snake is framed on the wall. The paper is yellowed and faded, but I can see green stripes in it, and perfectly spaced holes running along the top and bottom. In the center of the room, there are two squishy-looking, purple-plastic chairs—very retro, no doubt, to go with the art. The chairs face a glass end table, huddling closely, as if admiring the flower arrangement in the center. Kioshi stands to our right, with his hands behind his back. His eyes seem to study the floor, but it's difficult to tell behind the tinted sunglasses and his long, thick lashes. Our eyes focus on his chest and the spot just above the T-shirt, where a tendril of the colorful tattoo appears on the flesh of his throat. Our heartbeat jumps again.

He must know that you like him, I say.

If he does, it doesn't matter, she replies. Her eyes still focus on his throat, on the hollow made by his collarbone. *It can't be.*

Is he married?

Again, she shakes her head. Her gaze travels up to his mouth and lingers there, on his thin lips.

Gay?

Never! Her grip tightens on the doorway. Kioshi looks up, perhaps sensing her movement.

"Are you ready now?" he asks.

"Yes, thank you. Lead on," Mai says for me. She lets him get a few steps ahead before she follows. *I'm not worthy,* she explains to me. *I'm only recently a citizen. I was part of the program.*

I could use her LINK access to find the information for me, but I feel strange about launching it without permission. *What program?*

The Dragon of the East.

The Dragon never told me about her "birth," but I had always assumed that, like me, she'd had a single parent— one who had intended to bring an intelligent program into the world. *What are you saying?*

You must know. When I tell her that I don't, she adds somewhat bitterly, *I keep forgetting that you're foreign. Kioshi treats you with such respect.*

Kioshi leads us through another door into a hallway. There is an advertisement hologram on the wall across from the door for Toyama Game Distributions. Kioshi's animated creature cavorts through the stylized *kanji* characters of his name. As we walk along the hall, we pass holograms advertising the other Toyoma games and VR studio projects. Mai has apparently seen them many times, as her gaze barely sweeps them. Instead, she is, as always, focused on the form of Kioshi. She seems to enjoy just watching him walk.

I suppose I must explain, she says. *You see, human operators did much of the work of the Yakuza LINK presence before the Dragon manifested. Though the Dragon is powerful, there's always much to do. Those who do that work are in service to the program.*

You were a maker? I feel self-conscious. Suddenly, piggy-backing in the system of someone who, if not the mother, was a midwife to the Dragon's birth seems disrespectful, like I'm taking something that should be shared privately between maker and creation. The thought of my father sharing something this intimate with the Dragon makes me jealous and angry.

She laughs out loud, startling Kioshi, who stops to look back at us with a raised eyebrow.

You make it sound like I was some kind of god. I was just a child. We played on the LINK.

"Page told me a joke," Mai lies. Satisfied, Kioshi continues down the hall. We come to an elevator bank. There are other people waiting there. They all nod to Kioshi, but it seems to be Mai who captures their attention. They can't take their eyes off her. Finally, one of them approaches. He holds out a stylus.

"Could I have your autograph?" he asks.

I can feel a tight smile on Mai's face, but she accepts the pen and draws her name in the empty air. "Now," she says, touching the man lightly on the arm, "don't sell that to anyone. It was meant for you, and I'll be very jealous."

He nods so fiercely that it's almost comic. "No, no, of course not. Wow."

The man retreats back to his group. They whisper excitedly among themselves, occasionally pausing to look back at Mai. Kioshi moves in closer, his fingers reaching out to curl around Mai's. Her palm is sweaty when she takes his hand, but I can feel a shiver run down her spine when he gives her a tight squeeze. The elevator dings, and the group moves in. Kioshi and Mai stand still.

"You go ahead, boys," she says when they hold the door for her. "I'll take the stairs. I think I need the exercise."

They smile and laugh, though their eyes look disappointed. When the elevator door closes, Kioshi releases her hand. "Maybe a walk around the block isn't such a good idea," he says. "I would have to activate an army of ninja to protect you from your fans, my dear Mai."

She giggles and shakes her head. "It's not so bad. We'll be all right."

"They call them Maizombies," Kioshi remarks, reaching out to press the down button. "More and more are international."

What are you, I ask. *Some kind of rock star?*

I'm just a cellist, she says.

You must be very good.

She can't contain another giggle. When Kioshi glances at her again, she boldly takes his arm in hers. "Take us shopping," she says. "Page says he wants to buy me some new clothes."

CHAPTER 31
Morningstar, the Adversary

Jibril's smile didn't even waver at the sight of my middle finger. So I tried the more direct approach.

"Go away, Jibril," I said, dripping in my newly purchased sweatshirt. The hologram of Mai crackled and hissed, and I noticed that the cello music coming through my earphone had started to skip. "I was having a nice dream, and you, I'm happy to say, weren't in it."

Jibril laughed a deep belly laugh and slapped me on the back. "No?"

"Go away," I told him again, wiping wet hair from my face. A group was gathering near the azaleas, and I could see that many of them wore similar shirts to my own. They could be the Maizombies I'd come to see. "Can't you see I'm busy?"

"Oh, a thousand pardons, I thought you called us."

That was the trouble with having such a light hold on the shell of my body, and why I tried not to sleep. "So I dream of Heaven," I said with a shrug, feigning disinterest. My eyes watched the gathering crowd—that way Jibril couldn't see the envy flare in my gaze. "Who doesn't?"

There were probably fifty people in a tight circle. Most of them were young, but they appeared to come from all over the world—blond Swedes, brown-skinned Indian women wearing saris, Americans with their white tennis shoes, and, of course, Japanese. They had gathered around a boom box. Even from where I stood, I could hear the thrash bass and feel the drumbeats against my chest.

"What are you doing here?" Jibril's gaze tracked my own.

"What am I doing?" It was a question I had asked myself

at least once in the last hour. I let out a breath. "Getting wet."

Jibril frowned at me and glanced again at the crowd.

"I'm flattered," I said, "that Mother is still so afraid of me. Please tell me you have another job other than to follow me around and try to figure out what I'm up to."

Jibril's jaw flexed, and I smiled.

"Doesn't it gall you just a little? That my senseless interest in a human polka band is enough for Them to send you, you whose golden trumpet knocked armies from Heaven, and whose pure note will be the last sound heard at the end of all time?"

I watched his face carefully as I spoke, and could see a flash of something, a darkening of his gaze. I nodded encouragement. "Come, take a break with me. You should hear this cellist. She's simply divine."

He snorted and pulled himself up to his full height. We stood eye to eye. "I have more important things to do," he said.

"Of course, you do." I smiled. "Of course, you do."

My smile broadened as I watched him stalk off. Today was turning out better than it had begun; today, I turned an arrow from its mark. Kneeling down, I opened my backpack and found a clean, dry shirt. Stripping off the wet one, I wrung it out. The sweatshirt was ruined. Holding it up, I watched the hologram sputter and shake. Cheaply made piece of crap, I cursed, and tossed it over the loop of the backpack to dry off.

Though the sun was setting, it was warm enough inside the park's greenhouse that I decided not to change right away. I stuffed the dry shirt back inside. Shouldering my backpack over my bare shoulder, I wandered over to join the crowd of Maizombies.

"Konichi wa," an American said in shaky, but passable Japanese. His mouse-brown hair fell to his shoulders. Pieces of it were braided with silver wire so that it stood out in odd angles—a fair approximation of Mai's wild locks. He moved aside to make a space for me. "You're new."

"Got in today," I told him. "How long have you been here?"

"Six months. My visa runs out today," he said sadly. "But I don't have the cash for the flight home."

I imagined that was true for a lot of those gathered here. Even the women in the saris looked as though they might have slept in their clothes.

"But, I'm praying for a miracle, see?" The American pulled a silver chain out from under his T-shirt. At the end was a plastic figure of a naked woman cradling a cello. Cast all in white with the wild hair, the talisman almost looked like an aboriginal goddess figurine.

My heart skipped. "You pray to Mai?"

The American nodded very seriously, but glanced behind him furtively. "I hear that the acolytes are going to petition for cult status."

"Acolytes?"

"Unbelievers call us Maizombies."

"Ah." I nodded. I took the Mai figurine the American offered in my hand to admire it more closely. "I've heard that."

"If you want one"—the American nodded at the necklace—"you've got to talk to The Prophet."

"The 'Prophet'?"

The American pointed over the heads of the crowd toward a black woman standing in the center on a wooden crate, holding up the boom box. Dressed in a leopard-print dress, her hair was stretched into long dreadlocks. Glowing beads were tucked in the dreds in a crownlike circle. She looked a bit like an antimatter Mai. But the leopard skin gave her away. I recognized "her" immediately as one of the Fallen: Sytry, who, in Hell, wore the form of a leopard with griffin wings.

Our eyes met. She handed over the music box to one of the acolytes standing nearby and jumped off the crate. As Sytry moved through the crowd, I noticed people reaching out to lightly touch her, like you would grasp at the hem of a master.

"Azazel told me you might be coming, my Liege." She gave a slight bow. She glanced at my wet jeans and naked chest on the way up, and I noticed a smile before she could hide it.

The American standing next to me clutched his Mai figurine close to his chest. I could hear him breathe out a "Wow."

"Commander Sytry." I switched to Aramaic; I wanted

our conversation to be private. "Or should I call you 'The Prophet'?"

To her credit, her dark skin colored with a slight blush. With her eyes downcast, she said softly, "My wish is only to serve the end of days."

I was beginning to think that the Fallen had plans for the apocalypse that I was going to have to bargain my way into. "Of course," I murmured. "Walk with me."

She stood up straight, almost like a military officer snapping to attention, and gave a curt nod. I half expected an "Aye-aye, sir." The Fallen loved hierarchies and bureaucracy.

Sytry followed in silence as I led us deeper into the park, away from the Maizombies, her acolytes.

"You have quite the following there," I said. We walked along the wall of the greenhouse, and I could see the shadows of pedestrians moving on the other side of the steam-streaked glass. "They say you will be petitioning the Japanese government for cult status soon."

"Yes, Your Majesty," Sytry said. "I fully expect to get it. I have several documented cases of shrines built to Mai and then, of course, many of the acolytes have begun wearing the prayer chains."

"Which you supplied. Very clever," I said. "Are you hoping to become the first of the false prophets? Or are you leaving that to Mai?"

The grass we walked on was wet from the recent sprinkling, and I could hear it squishing lightly beneath my boot heels. Tea roses bloomed in perfect rows against the glass wall. No doubt, after we passed, aphids would descend. That kind of misfortune followed me everywhere.

Sytry walked with her hands clasped behind her back, the perfect parody of a legion commander in her form-hugging, leopard-print dress and matching high heels.

"My Lord?" Sytry glanced at me. Her handsome face was set in a deep frown. "Are you saying you don't concur?"

"There is nothing written that says that the false prophets must be human. Do what you want," I said, with a wave of my hand. "You show a certain amount of initiative, commander."

"Thank you," she said, but she still looked troubled.

"What is it, Sytry?"

"Azazel told me that you may have someone in mind for the role of Antichrist."

"Yes," I said. "Page meets many of the criteria."

She nodded thoughtfully. We came to a gravel path. In the distance I could see the Tori gate, two tall wooden poles topped with crossbeams. The greenery shifted from carefully cultivated park to more wild forest. Tall bamboo trees crowded the path, and wild flowers and brambles grew in the sunny spots below. Here and there a tall pine tree dominated the green space. I could smell the crushed needles.

I glanced at Sytry. She contemplated the path with grim seriousness.

"You disagree?" I offered.

"Oh, of course not, Your Majesty," she said a bit too quickly for me to believe.

"But?" I offered.

"Is there not a legend of two Antichrists?"

There was. Sometime in the fourth century, when there was still a great fear Nero would return, it was believed the end would be ushered in first by an evil king returning from the north, and then a final enemy coming from the east. "Go on."

"Mai could be a powerful ally," she said. "Mai means 'brightness,' " she added quietly.

"Like Lucifer," I said. It was not one of the many names I preferred to call myself, but many still thought of me as "the light-bearer."

Sytry walked beside me, patiently quiet. I smiled at her. There was a reason I had chosen her to be a great Prince, a commander of legions. I said, "You think Mai is an Antichrist."

"Perhaps the only one. Or perhaps"—she dipped her head in deference—"one of two. Many of the Fallen agree. They are gathering here, under my command."

Not, I noticed, under mine. Again, I gave her an appreciative smile. "You planning a coup?"

"No, sir," Sytry answered without hesitation.

I wasn't sure I believed her. She was one of Hell's commanders after all. They weren't exactly known for their loyalty and kindness. Still, a plot against me was hardly anything new from the ranks of the Fallen. I gave her a dismissive nod. "Very well, carry on."

She saluted me and then headed back the way we had come, back to where the acolytes were gathered.

The heavy shade of the trees blocked the remaining sunlight; goose bumps rose on my chest. I was about to pass under the gate to the shrine, and I didn't think it would be appropriate to pass into this holy place without a shirt on. Kneeling beside the path, I opened my backpack.

"Oh, you poor dear," said a voice from behind, and I felt a feather-light touch on my shoulder. "Your back is so bruised and sore looking."

"Yes," I said, realizing, in an instant, she must be right. "From the Fall."

I turned to see legs. Lovely, long, and athletically shaped, they disappeared into a high-cut miniskirt. But instead of teetering, as one might expect, on stiletto heels, they were comfortably and firmly ensconced in combat boots. The bright sun reflected off a spiderweb of metallic hose that seemed to cover not only her legs, but her arms as well. In fact, it seemed to cover all of her exposed skin, which wasn't much more than her legs. What cleavage I might have spied was hidden behind a mountain of hair. I could see only a bit of her face, but I recognized her immediately.

"Mai."

She handed her shopping bags to a young man hovering protectively to her right. Then she pulled her hair away from her face to peer at me. She was not wearing her usual mirrored sunglasses, and one of her eyes was deformed. It was flat, without a pupil, and I could see an object like a fingernail imbedded in it. The object was ugly, but fascinating, and something about it tickled an ancient memory.

"Iblis?"

I was glad I was still crouching by my bag, because I almost fell over. I had to put out a hand onto the sun-warmed pavement to steady myself. "You know my name?"

The young man beside her touched her arm imploringly. "You know this kid?"

I was no child, and I stood up to show Mai's companion my full height. In the absence of wings to spread, I puffed out my chest.

Chapter 32
Emmaline, the Inquisitor

Eion and I sat where we'd fallen on the floor of the shelter's lounge. My back pressed against his stomach, and his back was propped against the couch. I touched my cheek tenderly and, like last night, found the slightest hint of wetness. I stared at the rummage-sale recliner where Michael had been sitting. He was gone—disappeared in a hurricane wind. The printout magazines which had been on the coffee table had scattered in his wake. There was a film of something, like mist, on the window overlooking the snow-covered courtyard of St. Denis's church.

Eion's breath tickled my ear. From the labored sound of it, he was feeling much like I was.

"Did you see that?" he whispered. "Please tell me you saw that."

"I saw it," I said, shutting my eyes. *Replay interview, subject Michael: 01-07-80, 0700.*

Dutifully, my internal camera replayed my conversation with the preacher. Again, I heard the whispered words, "Who is the liar?"

Pause. I told the LINK. *Advance in slow motion, one-second intervals.* In jerky freeze-frame, I saw Michael stand. He moved so fast that he still seemed to jump forward in each second. Though the camera angle was screwy as I was pushed back by his motion, I saw a bright flash of light. It reminded me of the flash-powder magicians used to misdirect audiences. In the next frame, he was gone.

Stop, I commanded. *Replay last image, one-hundredth of a second per frame.*

Once again, Michael stood in front of the recliner and I was being pushed backwards by an unseen force. Suddenly, a line of white-hot light grew around Michael's entire body, like an aura or a halo. Then, still moving almost too fast for the camera to track it, he became transparent. It was as though his form was like a thin lampshade, and the light behind him became so bright that it burned right through the fabric of his flesh. My first thought was, spontaneous combustion? If so, it was on a nuclear scale.

Eion cleared his throat. "Are you okay?"

I realized that I was still lying on top of him. His breathing had calmed, but he now held his body in a tense stillness. I could feel the muscles of his stomach twitching against my back. "I'm sorry," I said, trying to find purchase on something other than his body. "I guess I'm a little stunned."

When my elbow hit Eion in the collarbone, he gave a soft groan. Moving my hand only made it trail against his ribcage, down to his trim waistline. I suddenly became hyper-aware of his vow of celibacy, which only made untangling from him that much more difficult. I noticed how his shoulders were just wide enough to comfortably enclose me and the way the smell of lavender soap clung to his hair. My hips grazed his, and his hands encircled my waist steadying me. By the time I'd clawed my way up onto the couch, I was blushing furiously. He, I was grateful to discover, had other things on his mind.

"Please tell me that wasn't another miracle."

"I wish I could," I said, relaxing back onto the couch. I glanced over at Eion. I could only see the top of his head, where the sunlight made his blond hair white. While it might be okay for me to entertain ideas of sex, helping someone else break his vow of celibacy was right out. I stared out the window, feeling guilty for wanting to do both and, for the second time in less than a week, with someone I barely knew.

"Michael is an angel," Eion said without preamble. Standing up, he smoothed out his sweater "I've always known that, I guess."

"You mean like a real angel?" American Catholics also tended to see a lot more of the mythological aspects of our religions with a heavier grain of metaphor. "With wings?"

"I mean like a messenger from God." He crossed his

arms, and stared down at me. "For God's sake, his name is Michael."

I laughed. "The archangel Michael? Do you really think we're that important? To get a message directly from God Himself?"

Eion frowned. "And why not? Isn't that what the office of the priesthood is all about? Acting as emissaries for His will?"

"Conduit," I said. "That's the word Michael used."

I looked out the window, as a house sparrow landed on one of the black-eyed Susan stalks. Mist had condensed into rivulets that bled down the glass—physical proof of the miracle we'd witnessed.

For me, being a priest was part of the job of Inquisitor. I might be a shitty priest, but I was a damn fine Inquisitor, particularly because I didn't let the mumbo jumbo of Catholic ritual cloud the truth. I reached out and touched the wetness on the window, and rubbed it between my fingers. It had never occurred to me that the magic might be real.

"Michael is a bum, not an angel," I insisted.

"Aw, come on. You know better than that," Eion said with an exasperated sigh. He started to pace. "Something is going on here. Something important, and we have to figure out what it is and do what needs doing."

I watched him pace. A lot of the people who perpetrated fake miracles did it out of a need to be something more than what they were. Last night, Eion had denied such desires. Today, it seemed he'd changed his tune.

"You *do* think you've been given a special calling."

He stopped moving to glare at me. "What? This isn't about me, McNaughten. It's about you. Michael said that you . . . that you weren't a good priest. What's he talking about? What case are you working on?"

"You really think God is talking to me?" My voice came out much more feebly than I intended, and I looked away from Eion. The men in the shelter were starting to stir. I could hear the door to the main sleeping room opening and closing. Smells of breakfast came up from the basement kitchen.

"God talks to everyone, Inquisitor. It's just a matter of being open to Him."

I grimaced at Eion. "I heard that kind of talk in seminary."

"So why didn't you listen?"

I had no answer. I kept thinking about the passage: "Who is the liar? It is the man who denies . . ." My stomach twisted. Was I that shitty a priest?

"Okay." Eion sat down in the recliner Michael had occupied. He looked at his hands, and then looked back at me. His voice was quiet when he spoke. "Do you really think it's a good idea to ignore this, whatever it is . . . sign? You told me that in your vision the seraph quoted One John. The message of that passage is that those who deny God are the Antichrist."

I shook my head. Eion was hitting too close to home. "I have no proof that Michael is talking for God."

"Proof?" he said, looking at the window. "Isn't our job all about faith?"

Eion's question still hung in the air between us when my private line buzzed. The call came from Rome, with high urgency. As much as I wanted to finish my conversation with Eion, I had to take this. I stood up, looking for a private place to talk. Eion also rose and put a hand on my arm. He looked imploringly into my eyes.

"God is talking to you, Emmaline. You shouldn't ignore it."

The timing was just too funny. I had to laugh. "Actually, it's the Vatican. Is there somewhere I could take a private LINK call?"

Eion frowned at me. "Why not just take it here?"

Most people had no trouble talking to two people at once. It wasn't that I was unable to multitask; I just found it rude. I preferred to give people my full attention. "I'd like some privacy," I insisted.

Eion nodded stiffly. I could tell he was feeling dismissed. "I'll go check if they need help downstairs with the food line."

"We can talk later," I told him.

He shook his head as he turned away. I could tell he didn't believe my offer was sincere. "Sure."

I settled back into the couch and shut my eyes. I tripped the go-ahead on the call. A window opened up to show Bishop Rodriguez's angry face. Instead of his avatar, I got the live version via his wrist-phone cam. I got the sinking feeling I was in trouble.

"What the hell is going on there?"

The bishop rarely swore, at least not in English. "I'm not sure what Your Grace is referring to."

"I haven't gotten any reports, and I just received your expenses." The bishop looked purple in the cheeks. "Mouse Legal Defense Fund? What on earth are you playing at?"

"Right," I said. "I meant to talk to you about that. I need one of the Vatican's best programmers sent to New York—well, New Jersey really."

I could see his jaw clench and unclench. Behind him, I could see Saint Peter's Basilica. He stood outside. Tourists milled around him, and pigeons flocked nervously from perch to perch. The Italian sun shone off the white marble columns surrounding Piazza San Pietro. I thought of the snow-covered courtyard just beyond the windows, and I felt a stab of homesickness.

"We've already sent our best Inquisitor," he said. "At least, I thought we had."

I sat up straighter. "You have."

"Then why don't I know what's going on there? Why don't I have any answers?"

"As you told me, Your Grace, figuring out a soul is a difficult thing."

He looked over his shoulder at Michelangelo's dome. "You've got to give me something."

"I need a programmer because Mouse promised to give us Page's code. Thanks to prison rules, he's not allowed to write it, but he said he'd dictate it to someone."

"What good will that do us?"

"I don't know," I admitted. "But it seemed like a start. If we have his code, we can look for something. I have to do something, Your Grace. Page has already passed the Turing Test. A handful of people have already given him everything from the I.Q. to the Meyers-Briggs."

The bishop looked ready to explode. "No," he said through gritted teeth. "I meant what good would that do us, since Mouse has escaped?"

CHAPTER 33
Page, the Intelligence

We are sitting in Kioshi-san's limousine. Mai can smell the plush leather. She unlaces and kicks off her combat boots the instant we get in the car, and the soft fake fur of the carpeting tickles her toes. After all the walking along the boutique-lined Takeshita Dori and Omutesando, our feet are killing us. Iblis is across from us, surrounded by Mai's shopping bags.

Never having seen Iblis outside of cyberspace before, I am struck by how fragile, how decidedly human he seems. Unlike his avatar, he is disheveled. His loose, dark auburn hair hangs wetly against his face. Though he is well muscled, his bare chest seems pale. The shirt he shrugs into is a bit nicer, silk, I think, but he has none of the air of his debonair cyber-self. The bruises on his back were the last thing I expected. Somehow I'd imagined him inviolable, incorruptible.

Still, there is something decidedly inhuman about him. Through Mai's enhanced eye I can see an aura around Iblis's body. Like a swarm of gnats, dark spots twirl and twist around him. It almost looks as though his image is breaking up with black static. Mai blinks a few times, adjusting her vision until the spots disappear. She seems unconcerned at the apparent malfunction of her vision.

Iblis, however, seems quite taken with Mai. He keeps sneaking looks at her, as he puts on his shirt. Kioshi has noticed Iblis's attention and is sitting so close to us that his knee touches ours. Mai is having a hard time not pressing her bare leg closer to Kioshi's thigh. I can feel the tension in her muscles.

They have been talking about Iblis for some time.

"Why did we bring him along?" Mai asks. I am not surprised to find that they have their own private frequency, but I am intrigued that they would choose to use it in front of me. *"He's a boring gaijin zombie."*

"Have some respect," Kioshi says. *"He is a friend of our guest, my oyabun."*

She sucks in her breath sharply. I can feel her eyes narrow. *"Fine."*

"What was your name again?" Mai asks. I can feel the tightness of her smile.

Iblis, I tell her, but she ignores me.

He seems to think about it for longer than most people would. When he speaks, he doesn't sound convinced. "Morningstar. A name not unlike your own brightness."

Mai giggles. "Thank you," she says, with her eyes downcast.

"Do you want to talk to your friend?" Kioshi asks Iblis. "Mai can speak for him."

"Baka yarō," she privately sends to Kioshi. My translators tell me she's called him something akin to a stupid idiot, but there is an additional insult because of the lack of formal language. Kioshi seems unruffled by her disrespect. He doesn't even look in her direction.

"For the moment I would like to talk to Mai," Iblis says with a wolfish smile. "That is, if you don't mind, Page?"

"He doesn't," Mai says before I can answer.

Kioshi's shoe taps Mai's bare foot. She glances over to see his stern expression.

"Where are you from?" Iblis asks.

"You mean, where was I born?" Mai chews on a piece of her hair. Glancing at Kioshi, she says, "I'm not really sure."

Kioshi clears his throat. "Mai is an orphan."

"The LINK is my mother," Mai says, straightening up proudly.

Like me? I ask Mai.

Absently, she touches the flat surface of her left eye. A jack protrudes from it, shaped like a tiny horseshoe. There is a larger one at the base of her neck. I remember it from when Kioshi LINKed us. Mai snaps open the shell-shaped purse that she has perched on our lap and takes out her mirrored sunglasses. Though it's not bright, she slips them on, hiding the jack.

A little, she says.

"I don't understand," Iblis says. "How can the LINK be your parent?"

"I was grown for it." When Kioshi kicks her shin lightly, she says, "It's not like it's a secret. My birth certificate is public record. Toyama Corporation built me."

"Mai is fond of hyperbole," Kioshi says with a curt sniff. "Perhaps that's why she's such a good musician."

"Some lab technician decided the color of my hair, the timbre of my voice," Mai continues, as though Kioshi had said nothing. Our hands clutch the purse tightly. I feel her struggle to keep her voice even. "My conception was a very carefully planned event."

"Again, an exaggeration," Kioshi breaks in. "Mai's genetic material came from volunteers. She was not manufactured out of whole cloth."

"Volunteers? Yes, volunteers from inside the program. Children who have never seen the light of day, except through a video screen."

"Enough," Kioshi says through our private interface. *"It would not be difficult to revoke your citizenship, Mai. Remember that."*

What does he mean? I ask Mai privately.

They own the patent to my genetic makeup, Mai says, bowing her head. *All Kioshi has to do is tell the Japanese government that they have discovered some flaw in me, something dangerous, like latent schizophrenia, and I could be terminated.*

"Is everyone in the program Japanese?" Iblis's voice surprises us.

"No," Kioshi says. "Having too small a gene pool is dangerous."

"So Mai's parents could be from anywhere?"

"Why are you so interested?" Kioshi asks, a wry smile playing on his lips. "Have you ever donated to Toyoma Corporation?"

Mai's jaw clenches, and a blush rises on our cheeks. *"Stop,"* she begs Kioshi. To me she adds, *I hate to think that any random donor could be my father.*

"We are being rude," Kioshi says, without glancing at Mai. "Perhaps we should talk to Page."

Iblis peers into our face dubiously. "I'm surprised to find

Page here," he says. Raising an eyebrow, he glances first at Kioshi and then at us. "With you."

I wonder suddenly if he knows who Kioshi is, and what I have done.

What do you want to say to him? Mai asks, as the silence in the car stretches. Kioshi eyes Iblis suspiciously, but Iblis's eyes stay locked on Mai and me.

I don't know, I admit. *I'm not much of a liar, and I can't exactly tell him about our relationship.*

Why not?

Explaining about my soul is too hard, so I stay vague. *I . . . I promised him something.*

You're working for him, too, aren't you?

I have no idea what to say to that, so my system hiccups, *Uh.*

She smiles slightly and says: *Leave this to me.*

Mai laughs, and says, "My apologies for not answering right away. Page and I were reminiscing about how we got here. Page is a fan of mine, you see." She touched her chest and lowered her eyes in a demure gesture. "I don't usually indulge fans this way, but Page is, as you know, very special, and offered to show me some of my music rendered digitally." She shrugs helplessly. "I was so flattered. . . ."

"That you took him shopping?" Iblis glances briefly at all the bags crowding him, then back to us with a penetrating gaze. "Lucky boy."

There is something menacing in his tone, and Mai feels it. Her heart rate skips upwards a notch. "Well," she adds smoothly, "I just had to have the newest winter fashions, and we were headed for the studio when we ran into you."

"Fortunate for me." Iblis's tone is dry.

What's going on, Mai? Is this boy some kind of a threat? Kioshi asks on their private line. He appears to busy himself playing the role of rock-star handler, and fills glasses from the bar with ice.

Morningstar thinks he still owns a piece of Page, Mai says before I can stop her. *Page asked me to avoid a turf war.*

A turf war? With this little man? Who is he?

Someone Page owes something to.

You never told us of this debt, Page. Kioshi's head

snaps back to look at Mai, at me. I can see anger behind the tinted sunglasses for a brief second. When Iblis notices him staring at us, Kioshi hides his expression. He extends a cup and asks, "Cola?"

"Thanks," Iblis says. Taking the glass, he peers out the tinted-glass windows.

"I owe Iblis nothing," I tell Kioshi.

"Tut-tut, little mouse. Lying to the Yakuza can be very bad for one's health," Mai says, leaving the channel open for Kioshi to hear.

I fume silently. I think perhaps, and not for the first time, that Mai isn't completely interested in helping me. She seems jealous that I am Kioshi's *oyabun.* Mai watches Iblis as he tucks the cola into a cup holder, and finishes buttoning his shirt.

"So," Mai says. Her false smile is tight on our face. "How is it that you know Page, Morningstar-san?"

I don't work for him, I say glumly, certain she will continue to ignore me.

"Page," Iblis says, his chestnut-brown eyes reflecting the bright sunlight, "owes me his soul."

A loud crunch causes Mai to turn her head sharply. We see Kioshi with an aluminum can crushed in his fist. His face is red with anger.

"Really?" Mai asks sweetly. "So, you're his boss?"

"I believe the term is 'master,' " Iblis says, with a wry smile that causes my heart to sink.

Tell Kioshi it's a lie! I demand.

Your master seems convinced otherwise. Mai is smiling to herself. This expression is genuine and relaxed; I hate her.

"Are you saying that you're the Mouse?" Kioshi says. He studies Iblis carefully. The pulverized can is forgotten in his hand, though Mai can see the muscles jumping on his tattooed wrists.

"That's not Mouse." For once, Mai chooses to speak what I am telling her. *Now tell him the rest,* I say.

"No?" The smoothness in Kioshi's voice belies the constant twitching of his muscles. "Then who are you to call yourself the master of Page? You, who wear external hardware. You can't be much of a cracker."

Mai sucks in a breath. She seems shocked by the informality of Kioshi's words.

The car stops suddenly. Mai has to grab the seat to keep from pitching forward.

"Get out," Kioshi tells Iblis.

The door opens automatically, no doubt as under Kioshi's control as the car. Iblis and Kioshi stare at each other. Mai reaches into her purse and finds an old-fashioned business card. She hands it to Morningstar. "It's okay. You can call me later."

Everyone looks to Kioshi, who shrugs. "Go," he insists. "Before I get really angry."

Iblis smiles at Mai and me, and then ducks out of the limo.

Why did you give Iblis your number? I ask Mai.

Because he's trouble for you. I like him.

Great.

"You have a lot of explaining to do," Kioshi tells me, after he shuts the door on Iblis. Mai can see Iblis through the tinted glass, standing with his backpack slung across one shoulder. He looks at the environmental dome that surrounds the Imperial Palace. Then, he glances back at the car, and Mai gives him a surreptitious wave as Kioshi mentally engages the limo.

"Are you fond of him?" Kioshi asks me or Mai, I'm not certain which.

"He's cute for a *gaijin*," Mai says.

"Not you, you're easy." Kioshi gives her a dismissive glance, but his face holds a dark snarl. "Page. Are you fond of that boy?"

He hasn't promised to teach me to be a cracker. Not like you, I tell Mai.

"No," Mai says for me. "Page is your *oyabun*, master."

"I want to hear it in his words." Kioshi glares at Mai over the rim of his sunglasses. His blue eyes are the color of ice.

"Morningstar is not my master," she says for me. "I swear."

"That's very, very good." There is something in his voice I don't like. Kioshi adds, "Now, tell us everything you know about Morningstar. Everything, Page."

CHAPTER 34
Morningstar, the Adversary

I watched the limo carrying Page and Mai leave, and sat down on the sidewalk to think. With a short command, I set my external LINK to scan the entertainment and news channels for information about Mai, then glanced at the slip of paper that Mai had given me. It was a calling card, and an old-fashioned one at that, made of paper. Maybe it was some kind of pop-star affectation. With a shrug, I tucked the business card into my front shirt pocket.

I was beginning to think that Sytry and her followers might be on to something. I'd known there was something that had struck me when I first saw Mai's jack. There were a million descriptions of what the Antichrist would look like, but the Muslims believed "he" would be blind in one eye. Mai's augmented eye fit the bill.

There were other things—her hair, for one. The hair on the Great Deceiver's head was supposed to be extremely twisted. Then there was the riddle. Perhaps Mai carried her own Heaven with her in her music. Whatever the case, I was fascinated that Page and Mai seemed to be merged—at the moment.

The LINK picked up a Four Horsemen's song playing on some audio channel. I turned up the music. Shutting my eyes, I rocked to the sounds. I was lost in the bass and drum riffs when something hard and small hit my cheek and bounced into my lap. When I looked at my feet, I saw a yen coin. I picked it up and put it in my pocket.

Glancing up to see where it came from, I saw a man. He wore white tennis shoes and blue jeans, like an American. A pure white T-shirt hugged a well-built frame, and a leather jacket covered, although not completely, a shoulder holster. I could see the butt of some kind of gun; it gleamed darkly against the white of his shirt. Clearly, he was a cop, but not a Japanese one. His face looked more Mediterranean or, perhaps, Italian. His eyes were gray, like a warm winter sky. Those eyes I would recognize anywhere, even in the darkest reaches of Hell.

"Michael." My hands clenched into fists, and I scrambled to my feet, ready for a fight. "What are you doing here? I thought you . . . You were supposed to be out of commission."

His smile was easy, too easy for my comfort. "I came to give you a message."

"Of course." I sneered. That was all They had intended for us—to be like some kind of celestial UPS, delivering "good tidings" and heralding doom. I had a sinking feeling I was about to hear the latter. "But before you get all 'hark, herald angel' on me, buy me some noodles. I'm starving."

He frowned at me for a moment, and then he shrugged. "Sure, why not?"

The sun was setting, and I could smell snow on the wind. As we started walking down the street, neon lights snapped on, advertising their wares in stylized pictograms. I glanced over at Michael. "You seem, uh, newly outfitted."

I had heard a rumor that Michael had been wandering the earth in a broken shell of a mortal body, homeless, insane.

"For the moment." His voice was gruff, matter-of-fact.

"You don't think it will last?"

"Not if I want to stay." There was a sadness in his tone that I recognized all too well. Staying always had its price; Mother made sure of that. Apparently, for Michael it was his glory, his fierce sanity that he surrendered. Momentarily, I almost pitied him—funny, considering he had never shown me so much kindness, nor would he, not even on the final day.

Michael stopped in front of a fast-food place. The smell of soy-meat drowned in grease hung thickly in the air near the door. He breathed in deeply and smiled. "I could kind of go for fries," he said with a guilty smile. "You mind?"

He looked at me like a kid asking for an extra piece of

candy. No, I thought, he looked like a younger brother asking an elder to keep a secret from a restrictive parent. I found myself smiling. "Sure," I said. "Let's."

The restaurant was bright and clean. Everything was polished, and the lights were set to a kind of holy-fire level, so cheery they seemed fake, like a beauty contestant's Vaseline smile. Most of the surfaces were stainless steel or bright yellow plastic. The whole place was as cheerfully unreal as the potted plants. It was kind of homey, in that universal fast-food way. I picked a table near the window, while Michael ordered for us.

The early dinner crowd milled around, and the place seemed filled with pensioners and students. A number of foreign faces were noticeable in the younger set, the majority of which had Four Horsemen paraphernalia somewhere on their bodies. Some wore the prayer talisman I had seen on the American acolyte.

Michael set down a brown plastic tray filled with a small mountain of neatly wrapped burgers and salt-encrusted fries spilling out of cardboard boxes. Michael greedily grabbed a hamburger and unwrapped it partway.

"Dig in," he invited, reaching for a fistful of fries before he'd finished chewing the meat. "Man, I always get the munchies when I come back, you know?"

I gingerly sorted through the pile of burgers until I found one with cheese. "I wouldn't know."

He stopped chewing long enough to give me a crooked smile. Then he shook his head. Pointing the ketchup end of a French fry at me, he said, "If you don't go back, it's because you don't want to."

"I'm in exile."

"You're a crybaby." He chomped down hard on the fry he'd gestured at me with.

"Oh, really?" I said, reining in my anger with difficulty. "What's your excuse?"

He swallowed slowly, as though chewing on more than just his food. He let out a long sigh. "I don't know, but I guess I like it here too much sometimes."

I looked around at the plastic and the fast food, and laughed. I was surprised, however, that my voice came out so soft, so concerned. "Even though it drives you insane?"

"That part's hard," he admitted.

I shook my head. "How can you still love Her? When She treats you this way?"

"They want me back."

"And you'll go," I said, nibbling on the soft bun.

Picking up another handful of fries, he smiled. "Eventually. You see, there's this mortal . . ."

"Ah yes," I said. "That woman, what was her name?"

"Deidre," Michael said; his voice was all soft and sweet.

"I've never known you to be so drawn away from Them," I admitted. It was strange, but Michael's desertion scared me. I had always known whom I was fighting before he left. The world did seem on the brink of the apocalypse without Michael at our Maker's side.

I put the food down. I'd forgotten how tasteless and gooey the stuff was; I should have insisted on noodles.

"Do you really love this mortal woman so much more than our Mother?" I asked.

Michael looked up at me. Our eyes met over the burger he held in both hands. "Of course not. But haven't you ever . . . ?" He looked me up and down, then said: "What am I saying? You've probably had dozens. For me, this is special. Different."

"Oh, I see, I'm some kind of a runaround, eh?"

Michael coughed a laugh. "Aren't you?"

I thought of my Inquisitor with her wild laugh and dark curls. She'd smelled to me like honeycomb and sunshine, and she had dismissed me with a brisk word.

"I've learned to enjoy the flesh, that's all." I sniffed.

Michael shook his head, and swallowed another bunch of fries. "As much as I like . . . all that, it doesn't compare to being there."

I thought of my own icy-cold Hell and shuddered. "Ugh," I said. "He drives you insane, yet you still love Him. You're like some kind of abused child. You know they have twelve-step programs for people like you."

He laughed again. "Look who's calling the kettle black. You'll wait forever for redemption—one I'll probably mete out with a sword of fire."

"There's hardly a 'probably' about it," I said, looking out the window at the snow and the twilight. Despite the light pollution, I could see the "Morning Star," Venus, brightly reflecting the sun's light. I could almost feel the molten heat piercing my heart. It would be a painful end, and one I have longed for forever—if only to feel the warmth again. "Maybe we should just quit now, and we could both go home."

Michael started on another hamburger. "That reminds me. He wanted me to tell you: 'Warm.' "

"What?"

"You're getting warmer." He tossed the burger's wrapper onto the tray and reached for another. "End's in sight."

"Ah." I sat back in the curve of the plastic seat, not quite sure how to feel. I took in a long breath and tried to summon a sense of triumph, victory, something, but nothing came. I looked out the window again, searching for the light of Venus, but a cloud obscured my view. Snowflakes were caught in the headlight's gleam of a motorcycle parking on the street corner. The driver went through the motions of maneuvering the bike into a tight spot, and I thought about the things we do without thinking, out of habit. There would be much about this game Michael and I had played that I would miss—not the least of which was the anticipation of this moment.

I looked at Michael. He was on his sixth hamburger, and had demolished most of both boxes of French fries. We had always been enemies. I hated him with all my heart, but he was my brother.

"Father didn't, by any chance, give you any other hints as to what He might have meant by 'warm,' did He?" I asked, snagging one of the last remaining fries.

"Nah. You know Her. She likes to be, you know, poetic." Michael gestured at the forgotten cheeseburger between my elbows, "You going to eat that?"

I shook my head. Movement outside caught my attention. The biker had left his machine, and moved closer to the window. Odd, I thought, that he hadn't removed his helmet. He lifted his hands, and I realized he held a sawed-off shotgun. He pointed it at me.

The glass shattered in the first blast. Despite angelic-quick reflexes, I felt hot lead shot spray across my cheek, and rip into my jawbone. Glass shards buried themselves, like a thousand needles, in my flesh. I managed to keep moving back, away. I think I shouted a warning to Michael, but I couldn't be certain because after the second explosion, my world went silent. Now I was deaf; the noise of the gun temporarily completing the work Gabriel had started eons ago. People ran everywhere, mouthing silent screams.

I could feel the glass shredding my costume of flesh. In a moment, these people would have more than a mad gunman to fear. When the biker stepped through the window, and took careful aim at my chest, I stood still, and let loose my fearful countenance.

The would-be assassin stopped in his tracks. He was briefly protected from my glory by his helmet—that, and the fact that my purity was tarnished from the Fall. Still, I knew what I looked like to him: a bodhisattva, an angel, a ghost, or whatever he held most holy. Michael, whose intense purity could have done much more damage to these mortal minds than I, had already returned to Heaven.

Looking directly into the face of the biker, I cranked up the volume. Blood vessels burst in his corneas. He screamed, and clawed at his eyes. With him down, I took the opportunity to show myself to the fast-food crowd. Seeing the wide eyes of the Maizombies, I decide to test Sytry's theory.

I no longer had a mouth to speak, but I called forth words from the minds of those gathered, in their native tongues.

"Behold, I am an angel of the Lord," or Allah, or an avatar of Buddha, whatever made the most sense. "I bring thee glad tidings." I felt like an idiot talking like some Puritan from the 1700s, but no one believed in angels that talked like regular people.

"There is a woman among thee born of no man, who is Queen of Heaven, daughter of Our Lord, the incarnation of the Second Coming of Christ." I turned my fiery gaze on the Maizombies and pointed at the prayer talisman. "You are the new shepherds. Go and spread the word."

Just to make sure everyone understood my message, I wrote the pictogram of Mai's name in flames on the wall over the condiment bar. The last part made me feel particularly Biblical, and I would have smiled if I could have. Then, because I had to, I descended into Hell.

CHAPTER 35

Emmaline, the Inquisitor

I stared out the window into the courtyard of St. Denis's.
The sunshine was in direct opposition to the dark cloud
that had settled over me. Mouse had escaped. Without
Mouse, I couldn't get access to Page's code. My career was
over, and I found myself feeling very, very bushwhacked.

"How? How did he do it?"

Rodriguez narrowed his eyes into a dark glare and
waited silently with pursed lips, as though I was supposed
to know the answer.

"I haven't been able to check the news," I said helplessly. "I've been working the case."

"Well, that explains your smugness."

"My what?"

Behind him, in the video-feed from the piazza outside
St. Peter's Basilica in Rome, a gaggle of Franciscan nuns
passed wearing their traditional brown robes and bonnets.
Rodriguez's eyes watched them, then he leaned closer to
the phone and said, "The media is blaming you, actually."

"Me?" I shook my head. "I visited Mouse once, and,
anyway, I made sure there was no record of that."

"Yes, that was the problem. You asked the warden to
turn off the cameras for your private meeting with Mouse.
And, apparently, he forgot to turn them back on."

I laughed. "Well, then, he's just stupid. That's not my
problem."

Most of the men from the shelter had drifted downstairs
for brunch, but a few stragglers loitered near the lounge.
They seemed hesitant to sit on the couch and chair opposite
me. No doubt, my uniform and angry expression kept them
at bay.

"What did you agree to give Mouse that you didn't want on camera, Em?" The bishop lifted a finger when I opened my mouth to tell him. "And don't give me any line about his legal defense fund. What did you tell him? That you'd help him get free?"

"Fuck you," I said. "I'm an Inquisitor. I don't make deals with criminals."

"Language, Em. Everyone knows about your Mafia connection. You're just making yourself look worse."

I frowned at his words. Was he implying that he was recording this conversation? "Look worse for whom?"

The bishop glanced toward St. Peter's, not meeting my eye. He cleared his throat and scratched his chin. Furtively looking at the camera, he said, "Maybe you should just come home, Emmaline."

I stood up, and a couple of the men from the shelter glanced at me nervously from where they sat on a throw rug near the stairway. Outside, the snow looked like a patch of child's glitter in the sunshine. On screen, Rodriguez still wouldn't meet my eye.

"Am I being recalled?"

"The media has dug up some loose connection between the mob, your family, and Mouse. I'm sure you have a good answer, but the cardinals feel . . . embarrassed by this. You understand, don't you, Em?"

I crossed my arms. "Understand what?"

"Mouse is big news, Em. It's not going to blow over. I can't call in favors for you this time."

"I'm not done here." Keeping one "eye" on the LINK window of the bishop, I wandered away from the lounge, deeper into the mission. I pushed open a door and found a long hallway. "I don't have time for a side trip to Rome to smooth some ruffled cardinals' feathers."

Rodriguez shook his head. "You don't get it do you, *chica lissa?* If you don't come back on your own accord, the Swiss Guard will bring you by force."

"The Swiss Guard?" Though their main function was still to provide the defense of the Vatican city-state, some members of the Swiss Guard also acted as a kind of Internal Affairs department for the Order of the Inquisition. "Am I under arrest?"

"Not yet," Rodriguez admitted. He took one of his deep

sighs and finally found the strength to look me in the eye. "Your case is being reassigned."

"What?" I stopped in the middle of the darkened hallway. The walls were lined in pine paneling, a style popular in the last century. The space smelled old and musty. I was glad I'd moved away from the lounge; my shout would have scared the crap out of the homeless men. I'd never been removed from a case before in my life. "You can't do that," I told Rodriguez flatly. "That's unacceptable. What about my cracker skills? Who else are you going to find who can decipher Page's code? And, wait a minute, what about the Pope's dream? The Holy Father himself sent me on this mission."

"I know," Rodriguez said, moving slowly through the crowds of tourists toward the steps of St. Peter's. "That's why you're being shown such leniency."

I snorted. "It's not lenient to take me off the case of my life."

"Em, it's more than that. There's talk of a formal inquiry."

My credibility would be destroyed if I was called to defend my actions against a board of the Order. Inquisitors were supposed to be above reproach. Worse, half of the cardinals who sat around the table had been looking for a reason to bounce me. They could finally get that pesky woman out of their hair.

With a strangled cry, I punched my fist through the wall. The ancient paneling split with a crack. Pieces splintered around my fist like a blond starburst. I felt my hand go through the other side.

"You can't do this to me," I screamed. "I worked too damn hard to get here."

"I'm sorry, Em. I really am, but there's nothing I can do."

"You fucking bastard."

Rodriguez shook his head sadly. "If you hadn't seen that Yakuza hacker in Rome—hadn't had her flown out specially from Japan, you wouldn't look nearly so guilty."

"Toyoma is no friend of Mouse's. Thanks to the Dragon program, they've always been rivals." My arm started to throb, but I left it embedded in the wood. The pain kept my tears in check.

"Tell that to the inquiry. The media sees all wire-wizards as one big happy family, and the cardinals don't know any different. The fact that you requested a donation to Mouse's defense fund didn't help matters either. Then, you go off to some cracker rave. . . ." A muscle in Rodriguez's jaw twitched. "Jesus, Em, what were you thinking?"

"I was on the job, Your Grace. The one you sent me on. How the fuck was I supposed to find out about the AIs without talking to their makers? Of course, I was going to hang out with wire-wizards!"

"Another Inquisitor might have spent more time in the library doing research on the nature of the soul."

"I'm not some wussy scholar, and you knew that before you sent me out." Pulling my hand from the wall abruptly, I shook off the plaster dust and wood splinters. My knuckles were bruised and scraped bloody, but, thanks to the Vatican's augmentation, no bones were broken. That made me angrier. "Besides, I knew the score. So did you. I told you I wasn't a theologian. But I wasn't supposed to find any evidence of a cyber-soul, was I?"

"No one said that."

"No one had to."

Rodriguez's mouth was set in a grim line, but his eyes glittered. "When they requisition your tapes, they'll see that I never said anything like that. There's nothing to worry about."

"Who are you trying to convince? I'm already up the creek."

"Don't even think about it," Rodriguez said. "The Holy Father is above suspicion. You must know that you're playing a losing hand if you try to point a finger at him."

"He's the one who sent me out here. There was no dream, was there? This was a setup all along. You sent me out to talk to hackers and then you blame me for hanging out with them."

"Mouse has escaped, Em. That's the issue here."

"Is it? Or is this just a convenient way to get rid of a woman Inquisitor?"

Rodriguez stared at me for a second that seemed to stretch like a wire with the weight of my question hanging on it. "Just get on a plane, *chica lissa*. You've got twelve hours. After that they call the Guard."

He hung up.

My fist went through the paneling again, then again, and again, until a whole section of wall just fell at my feet. I kicked the wall for good measure, and, farther down the hall, a couple of picture frames fell to the floor. I spat out every curse word I could ever remember in English and Italian, and I still didn't feel any better.

I knew the Holy Father didn't know what to do with a woman and an American Catholic in his ranks, but I never suspected he'd go this far. It seemed kind of sideways to spring Mouse just to get at me. Besides, how would the Pope have known that I was going to ask the warden to look the other way, literally? True, I had a history of doing this sort of thing, but not any more than anyone else in my position. Every Inquisitor took advantage of their power in the name of a case sometimes. There wasn't anything wrong with that.

No, had they wanted to, they could have discredited me much more easily for any number of things. They knew my background. They could have trumped up some phony Mafia hacker-related crime from years ago. Besides, I'd been keeping my head down. I hadn't done anything to upset the Holy See. I'd played by the rules and been a good little girl. Maybe that was the problem. Maybe they just decided to take advantage of the situation when it presented itself.

Maybe I was just screwed.

A growl formed in the back of my throat. No, I thought. The hell I was going back to Rome like some puppy with her tail between her legs. I wasn't guilty of anything. I hadn't helped Mouse escape. Some stupid warden had that mistake square on his own damn head. I wasn't about to start taking the heat for every act of idiocy that occurred in the state of New York, or anywhere else for that matter.

The Swiss Guard would just have to come take me down. Yeah, I thought, giving the wall another soft punch, I'd like to see them try.

The LINK beeped again—another message waited for me.

"What now?" I said, as I flipped the go-ahead switch. Part of me hoped it was the bishop, calling to say he'd lied, there would be no inquiry, and all was forgiven.

My page appeared in the LINK window. *"A credit*

*counter belonging to Sammael Morningstar, attached to a
Swiss Bank account, was activated at 0200 Eastern Time.
Morningstar charged twenty-five yen in Tokyo to purchase
a Four Horsemen sweatshirt from a street vendor."*

I'd forgotten about my request for my avatar to track
down information about Morningstar. I was only a little
surprised to find Morningstar using Sammael as a first
name, considering his fondness for demons.

I felt a flush of hope. I knew there was some connection
between Page and Morningstar. Maybe there was a connection between Morningstar and Mouse. If that were true,
maybe I could return to Rome with the real culprit in hand.
They couldn't prosecute me then. Hell, they'd have to welcome me back as a hero.

*"External LINK address also found for Sammael Morn-
ingstar. Provide?"*

I didn't hesitate. I'd never been kicked off a case in my
life, and the more I thought about it, the more I was certain
I could turn this crisis around if I showed up in Rome
fait accompli.

"Call Sammael Morningstar," I told my page. Even though
a quick mental calculation told me that if it was ten in the
morning here, it was around midnight there.

"Nǐ hǎo . . . , *er,* Moshi moshi." A man wearing a pressed
white shirt with police epaulets and a black tie answered.
He looked like a cop, except for his hair. It was long and
tied back in a braid. The very top of his head had been
shaved like some kind of eighteenth-century Chinese monk.
The insignia over his heart showed a lotus blossom over
the globe, and behind the earth a bamboo pole held the
scales of justice: an Inquisitor of the East.

He squinted at me. "Emmaline?"

"Yes?" I squinted at the Inquisitor, trying to decide if I
knew him.

He touched his chest lightly. "Chief Inspector Shen. Do
you remember me? We worked together on the Virgin of
Hong Kong case."

My LINK prompted me with the information: Shen Gu-
olong, thirty-three, a Taoist monk. He had been my liaison
in the East, providing translation when necessary, but
mostly acting as an assistant, a gopher. "Shen? What are
you doing on this line? I was looking for Morningstar."

"So are we," he replied, cheerfully, in perfect English. Shen seemed to be standing in a fast-food restaurant. There were scorch marks on the wallpaper, and some plastic tables had melted into twisted blobs as though there'd been a recent fire. Behind him, through a shattered window, I could see what looked like police officers holding back a line of curious onlookers. "Is Morningstar a friend of yours?"

"Where are you? Are you in Japan?" I tried to guess if the pictograms on the shattered window were Mandarin or *katakana* or *kanji*. I had no idea. "Or Hong Kong?"

"Tokyo," he said. "Is this Morningstar a friend of yours?"

"He . . ." I didn't want to tell Shen of our affair, such as it was. "He's possibly involved in a case I'm working."

The Inquisitor nodded and tapped a finger against the remains of a table, one time, emphatically. He was taking notes. "What case are you working on?"

If I told him too many details, he'd be able to verify that I was actually no longer on any cases, but scheduled to be back in Rome.

"It's a private matter for the Pope," I said.

"Ah, how convenient," Shen said.

My anger flared. "You calling me a liar?"

Who is the liar? The words that had been haunting me drifted back into my consciousness, and I thought: me, right now.

Shen smiled. I was surprised how comfortable the smile looked on his otherwise stern face. "No, of course not. I'm merely saying that there is no way for me to check the truth of your statement."

Actually, it would be easy for him, and I knew it. I was certain that the news of Mouse's escape would reach Japan in no time. "I'm sorry," I said. "I'm just upset."

He shook his head, but continued smiling faintly. Shen knelt down to look at something on the floor. "Perhaps I could use your help. I've not had much luck in this case, Em. Did you know your friend belonged to a cult?"

"Cult? I would hardly call Judaism a cult."

He snapped his finger, capturing the information. "Jewish? Jews rarely convert." He frowned. "This is very confusing. You're certain he was Jewish?"

"No," I had to admit. I felt a slight blush rise on my cheeks. "He said he was, and he was, uh, circumcised."

"Oh." Shen's thin eyebrows raised. He sat back on his heels and blinked at me. "How interesting."

I cleared my throat. "If I may ask? Why is the Eastern Division interested in Morningstar? What's happened?"

He looked away from the wrist-phone for a moment, then back at me. "Do you know anyone who might want to have your friend killed? Did he have any trouble with the Mafia?"

"The Mafia?" I thought about Mouse's escape and how the media had made some connection to the mob. Maybe Morningstar did have something to do with it all. "Is Morningstar dead?"

Shen sighed. "Perhaps. Although we have recovered no body."

I crossed myself. "What happened?"

"I don't know exactly. But we have a shooter in custody."

"Morningstar was shot?"

"By Jiro Takahashi, a known member of a motorcycle gang—one with ties to the Yakuza. Do you know why the Mafia would want your friend dead?"

"He's not my friend," I insisted, but wondered suddenly about my favor to the Yakuza. "Do you know which family?"

He looked over his shoulder. I could see news 'bots hovering just outside of the police line. "I can't really say, but we do have an idea. Why?"

I could hardly tell Shen I had called in a favor from the Toyoma family and then slept with a man who wound up shot by the Yakuza. Shen would see a connection that wasn't there. If it was the Toyoma family who had placed the hit on Morningstar, I would look bad; if it was a rival family, the same was true. The story of my life lately.

I shook my head and asked another question that was haunting me: "Why is an Inquisitor investigating a routine murder?"

Shen sighed heavily. "This was not routine by any means. There were reports of an apparition. Some of the witnesses claim they saw your friend burst into flames and transform into Ama-No-Minaka-Nushi, the Divine Lord of the Middle

Heavens. Ai! Do you know how disappointed I am to hear that the Japanese gods are showing up? My only comfort is that some of the witnesses think they saw Nü Wa. Another says something about angels."

I thought of Michael's disappearing act, and my knees buckled slightly. I put a hand against one of the exposed studs of the wall to steady myself. "An angel . . . ?"

"Well, no one is saying what exactly the apparition is yet. That's what I'm here to investigate. Although it does seem to be acting very supernatural. It left behind a name on the wall . . . in flames."

I was disturbed to hear Shen referring to Morningstar as an "it," but I let that go for the moment. "A name?"

"Mai Kito."

Mai . . . that was the name of the Yakuza hacker I'd talked to before going to see Mouse in prison.

"I'm coming," I told Shen before I hung up. Then, I sank slowly to the floor. Everything was going completely wrong. Worse, it all seemed to be pointing directly at me.

I was so fucked.

CHAPTER 36
Page, the Intelligence

Kioshi fumes silently as we drive along the Tokyo streets. He stares out the window, then glances at Mai and me. Gratefully, I only see his angry stare on occasion. Mai is happily sorting through her recent purchases, giggling and humming to herself.

You're such a jerk, I tell her. *Why won't you help me?*

She continues to hum a brisk polka tune. *Page is a bad, bad boy,* she sings to me. *Bad-bad la-la-la.*

Am not.

She giggles again, and holds up a frilly blouse to her chest. "Cute, isn't it?" she asks Kioshi.

"Hm," he grunts, barely looking at her. "I don't want to talk to you, Mai. I want to talk to Page."

"Fine." She pouts, tossing the blouse on the leather seat across from us. *What do you say to him?*

"Morningstar is not my master," she says for me. She makes her voice sound robotic and stilted. She jerks her head from side to side. "He's someone who helped me when I was in trouble. I promised him my soul, that's all."

Kioshi laughs softly. He watches the vehicles moving slowly outside the window. We are caught in a traffic jam near the Imperial Palace.

"Is that all? Just your soul?" Kioshi says.

He tells me that he is the Devil, I say, expecting Mai to continue translating.

A real devil? As in a rogue? What? Mai asks.

No, I insist. *The Devil. Satan.*

Kioshi will never believe this line of yours, Mai says. *Let me tell him something else. Something more believable.*

But it's true.

Haven't you heard of a white lie?

I have, but I fail to see how it applies in this situation. I'm confused, and more than a little troubled. Why wouldn't others believe me? I wonder.

Tell me, I ask. *What would you say?*

Tell Kioshi you had no choice, that the guy had something on you.

He did. My life was on the line.

Excellent, she says. *Kioshi understands that kind of pressure, believe me.*

"You've been silent a long time. What are you two talking about?" Kioshi asks.

"You, of course." Mai smiles.

The limo slows to pull up in front of the Toyoma building. There is a large crowd gathered by the front door. Some people, teenagers mostly, spill out into the traffic zone. Warning lights flash, noting the proximity of the pedestrians. Traffic control cuts the limo's power. The interior dome light flickers, then goes out. The doors unlock; Mai hears them click open. She grabs for the handle to keep the door from swinging wide open. Kioshi curses.

"I should have gotten the manual lock," he says, holding on to his own door.

A young woman's face appears in front of the tinted glass of the car window. She is black and her hair is a wild tangle of dredlocks. Around her head is a crown of flashing lights. She wears a form-fitting, leopard-skin dress. "It's her!" the woman screams, loud enough to be heard through the door. "It's our savior!"

"What the hell?" Kioshi says. "Where's my security?"

Mai feels the car door jerk under her grip. I am lost, for a moment, in the delicious feel of her straining muscles, but the sensation is overridden by the slamming of her heart and the sudden flush of adrenaline. Mai is scared. "I can't hold the door," she squeals.

Kioshi reaches for her, but the door bucks again, and again. Mai doesn't let go, but the door swings open anyway. She tumbles out into the street. Kioshi grabs her foot. Other hands—a multitude of grasping fingers and sweaty palms—reach for her torso, her arms, and her hair. All I can see through her eyes is a press of bodies. She screams.

I can feel the fear rasp her throat raw. "Stop! You're hurting me!"

The touches retreat at her word. She is lowered quickly, but gently, to the street.

"Mai, Mai, Mai." A chant begins somewhere in the crowd. The sound grows until it's no more than a throbbing, harmonious vowel, "I . . . I . . . I."

I can feel the rough gravel beneath Mai's knees, sense her ears ringing, and the tears springing to her eyes. I detect, however, something else. As waves of the sound of her name crash around her, there is also an intense calmness, a kind of centering. Her breathing evens out, and a fluttery feeling that is something very different from fear grows inside her solar plexus.

Kioshi is shouting. Mai can see him out of the corner of her eye. He has clambered onto the roof of the limo and is waving his fists around, demanding that the crowd disperse. He informs them that he's called the cops. No one hears him. They are watching us. Mai begins to stir. She lifts our head and looks out at the worshipful faces. Perhaps seeing the adoration there, she smiles.

They love you, I tell her.

Yes, she says. *I love them, too.*

She laughs. She throws her arms open expansively. "Yes, I love you all."

Her words break the flow of the crowd's mantra. A rumble, like a distant roll of thunder, moves backwards from the epicenter as her words are repeated. Silence follows in its wake. Even Kioshi stops shouting. Sirens wail, but they are still far off.

"What would you have us do?" a woman's voice cries out.

"Tell us! Tell us!" the mob repeats frantically, until it becomes a hiss of noise again.

Mai raises her hand, and the crowd instantly hushes.

She smiles, raises her fist, and gives the thumbs-up. Collectively, the Maizombies move in to hear her words. "Go in peace," Mai says. "And drink Kola-Cola!"

I am stunned. *What was that about?*

Peace is a good thing, Mai says. With a slight shrug, she stands up. *And soda never hurt anyone. Besides our band*

*made a deal with Kola-Cola. If I can, I'm supposed to name
their product at media events. This seemed like a good moment. We'll get paid. A lot.*

The crowd applauds and begins to move along. As people pass, they lift their hands as if trying to absorb Mai's greatness. Some seem to want to linger, but, out of respect, they leave us alone.

"Let's go," she tells a bewildered-looking Kioshi, who is still standing on the roof of the limo. "I want to get Page out of my head. He's giving me a headache."

More like the other way around, I grumble.

You have no head, she reminds me.

Kioshi sits down so that his legs hang over onto the windshield. He's shaking his head. "How much?"

"Sorry?" Mai says, innocently, leaning her hip against the smooth metal of the car.

"Whatever those bastards paid you, I would have paid twice as much," Kioshi says, pointing to the game on his T-shirt. "Couldn't you have told them to go home and play with Yamamoto?"

"Oh." Her voice is small, and I feel heat rise on her cheeks. "I didn't think. I'm sorry, Kioshi."

"Yes," is all he says. He does not look pleased.

Mai looks at her bare feet. Her toenails are painted fuchsia. I can feel the sun-warmed asphalt on her soles. The Maizombies pass. Some wear tennis shoes; others have boots or heels. I wonder how many had gathered here, waiting for her.

A pair of black tennis shoes stops next to Mai. She looks up to see a young Korean man. As her eyes scan up his trim form, I notice he is missing two fingers from the knuckle joints up. All along his forearms there are colorful, flat tattoos. Despite the cold weather, he wears only a T-shirt and dark pants. His head is shaved, but I can see sharp stubble where his hair is growing back.

"There was a problem," he says to Kioshi, then glances quickly at us.

Kioshi shakes his head and leans back on his arms with a sigh. "This day is becoming very complicated. Tell me the job was finished, at least."

"Uh." The Korean looks at us again, then tracks the

movement of the Maizombies shuffling around us still. His posture is wary and tense, like the snakes tattooed on his arms. "Kind of."

"What have you done?" Mai sends Kioshi on their private line.

"Nothing, apparently," comes Kioshi's response. "You will tell Takahashi that I am disappointed," Kioshi says aloud to the Korean. He glances over his sunglasses to pierce him with a meaningful glance. "Very disappointed."

"Takahashi is . . . indisposed."

Arrested, Mai tells me, though I'd guessed as much myself.

Kioshi shuts his eyes behind the tinted lenses of his glasses. "Before or after the target was acquired?"

"After," says the Korean.

"A hit?" Mai sends Kioshi. *"Are you crazy? Who?"*

Kioshi cracks open an eye to stare sidelong at Mai. Then, to the Korean, he says, "Well that's good news at least."

A few Maizombies stay gathered on the sidewalk near the limo. They pretend to be busy with their own things—checking maps, reading books, looking at the bus schedule posted on a nearby shelter, talking among themselves—but I can see their eyes straying to Mai.

"Uh." The Korean hesitates, looking directly at Mai. "Something very weird happened, *oyabun.* Something that involves Mai."

"Me?" She sounds like my squeak program.

The Maizombies nearest us whisper. One, a girl no more than twelve, clutches the end of her necklace in her hand. She looks as though she is praying, but she stares at Mai.

The Korean nods very slowly. "Mai's name was left on the wall. In flames. They say it's still burning."

"Nice," Kioshi says. "Could this day be any worse? Now there's a calling card left at the scene that leads directly to me. If Takahashi isn't dead, I intend to kill him."

"I doubt he would notice, *oyabun.* He's been taken to the mental hospital."

"Flames?" Mai giggles. "My name is supposed to be up in lights, not flames."

The men look at her, then at each other.

Are you okay, I ask her, feeling her knees shiver. The

Maizombies near the bus stop watch us intently. One of them, a young American to judge by his white shoes, looks as though he might step in and offer help.

"Yes, what of this?" Kioshi slides off the car and puts an arm around Mai. She leans into it heavily, and lets her own hands grasp his thin waist. We are close enough to smell Kioshi. His body is perfumed with the comforting smells of fish sauce and lotus seed paste. Mai takes a deep, steadying breath of the scent. "These flames, are they a hologram?"

"No, *oyabun*." The Korean shakes his head. "The Buddha himself put her name on the wall."

"Buddha? This is what Takahashi says?"

"No, the police. The news. Everyone." The Korean's gaze takes in the cluster of remaining Maizombies nervously. "There are plenty of witnesses who swear to it, *oyabun*. When Takahashi shot . . . at the target, the target transformed into the Buddha and wrote Mai's name on the wall."

"That's crazy," Mai whispers into the lapel of Kioshi's suit coat.

"You are the chosen one," the zombie-girl holding the necklace shouts. "Buddha has enlightened you!"

A sharp, thin knife appears in the Korean's fist. Kioshi raises a warning hand, "No," he says softly. His arm tightens around us. "Let's go inside."

I am relieved at Kioshi's suggestion. I would like to get out of Mai's nexus and back to the LINK.

"Yes," Mai says, echoing my thoughts. "Let's get Page out of my head. I can hardly think with Page taking up all this space."

"Yes, of course. You must be exhausted. You've never carried an AI this long before." Kioshi nods to the Korean. "Come with us. You will tell us more of what happened."

"Uh, that's another thing, *oyabun*. There is someone in the office to see you."

Kioshi shakes his head. He removes his sunglasses to rub at the space between his eyes. "This is not a good time for visitors." When he looks at the Korean, I am surprised again by the lightness of his eyes. They are a pale blue, like the sky.

"Yes, *oyabun*, I know. But this man was very insistent."

"Who is it?"

"He calls himself Mouse."

CHAPTER 37
Morningstar, the Adversary

The sky opened up above the empty city of Mina, Saudi Arabia, and I fell. Trying to flap wings no longer there, I cried out in anguish and hatred. I hit the ground, shoulders first, rolled down a steep, cobblestone incline, and my belly smacked into a white stone pillar. I lay curled around the pillar, unmoving. My whole body felt crushed. Through the pain, I could feel the hot sun beating on my naked back.

I let out a hiss of pain, and, for a brief moment, I could see the steam of my breath—the coldness of Hell having stayed with me.

I looked up the length of the sandy brick obelisk. My Father, it is said, has a sense of humor. I supposed there was some twisted joke in jettisoning me here, at the base of one of the three fifty-foot-high pillars that represented me during the *hajj*. It was here that, in a month or so, hundreds of thousands of Muslims would gather to symbolically stone me. Though workers were supposed to remove all the pebbles tossed by the pilgrims and return them to the desert between Muzdulifah and Arafat, a few of the missed offerings pressed sharply into my flesh as if to say, "Get it, get it?"

"Yes, very funny. Ha. Ha," I said, shutting my eyes against the relentless gray-white of the cloudless sky. A tear pooled at the corner of my eye. My newly formed flesh did a remarkable job of mimicking the pain of cracked ribs, torn ligaments, and a dislocated shoulder. At least there was no bullet hole. Yes, I should be grateful, I thought, as I tasted the metallic tang of blood in my saliva—yes, thanks ever so much, Dad.

The memory of the split second I had spent in Hell threatened to break my spirit the way the fall broke my body.

When I rebelled in Heaven, my supreme willfulness created Hell. Hell was the physical manifestation of the empty space of my soul separated from God—bitter cold, desolate, and so very, very alone. Close enough almost to feel Their loving presence, but forever closed off from it. A tear streaked down my face. The wetness froze against my cheek, only to melt again in the desert heat.

"Bastard," I said through gritted teeth. Righting myself with a groan, I pushed against the man-made cobblestone basin around the pillar. I wobbled on my raw and scraped knees. I clenched my jaw against the pain and snapped my shoulder back into place. I'd be damned if I'd give Them the satisfaction of seeing me beaten—although, in a way, I already was.

Though it was true that I had made Hell in my own image, God was omniscient there as He was in Heaven. Which meant the jig was up. Any secrets I might have been keeping to myself here on earth, where freewill canceled out God's omniscience, were now exposed to the enemy, the Hosts of Heaven.

In a word, I was fucked.

I was also naked as a jaybird. When I incinerated my body in the Tokyo restaurant, I left behind my clothes and earthly belongings. Right now, I missed the wrist-phone and external LINK especially.

With muscles trembling from the effort, I pulled myself out of the pit. Sweat and sand stung in the numerous cuts and scrapes on my arms, knees, and back. I had to stop and take a breather at the top of the incline. I laid my head down in my arms.

"Merciful Allah!"

I looked up to see a horrified man and an unimpressed camel. If I had to guess, I would say he was a Bedouin. He wore long flowing robes of black and white and a turban. A skin suit of deep blue, no doubt protection from the Medusa glass, covered his face and hands.

He reached out a hand to me. "So, it's true. You are a man. I saw you fall from the sky," he said in Arabic through a filter in the face mask. "How is this possible?"

I took his hand, and let him help me to my feet. I scanned the horizon. Other than his camel, he was alone.

"You're lucky I found you here," he said. "There will be no one in this city for months, and the desert is very unforgiving, especially since the Medusa. Luckily, we are not far from Mecca. Come, let me take you there."

When he averted his eyes at my nakedness, I grabbed his head between my hands and gave it a twist. I heard his neck crack. My shoulder throbbed from the effort, but he died instantly, and, I noted happily, bloodlessly. I stripped him of his clothes while his camel watched with big, brown doe eyes. She grunted when I kicked his naked body into the pit, but didn't resist when I took her reins.

The Hilton in Mecca had everything I needed, including an external LINK connection, which, according to the brochures in the lobby, could be safely enjoyed by children under the age of majority. To my chagrin, however, I discovered that without the LINK I couldn't make a reservation. There was no front desk staff, no human with whom I could book a room. Saudi Arabia, actually, was short on humans. The Hilton, like many of the businesses here that catered to the millions of pilgrims that flooded this town, was owned and operated remotely, from a safe distance.

Much of Saudi Arabia was glass. The last war had been fought over the control of dwindling natural-gas resources, and, in an ironic twist of fate, many of the oil-producing countries were bombed into near inhabitability. Medusa bombs had rained in the Saudi desert like hail, crystallizing the vast Empty Quarter, decimating the capital city of Riyadh, and turning the Persian Gulf into a skating rink for Gorgons.

I could see why God had dumped me here; in many ways this was Hell on earth.

I sat in the dust on the stairs outside the modern highrise hotel, holding the reins of an irritated, spitting camel. Heat reflected off the concrete steps, but the stiff leaves of a date-palm garden on either side of the stairway provided partial shade. Smells of roasting coffee beans came from one of the open windows above, making my head throb with desire. A strong cup of coffee and a cool shower would be heaven sent right now.

I was considering the possibility of breaking into a room when two bearded men in long caftans approached. They came out of a noisy, gas-powered van parked across the street. There were no traffic tunnels in Mecca; everything sweltered under the hot Arabian sun. On the side of the vehicle I could see the logo of an open book. Underneath the picture, in flowing Arabic script were the words: GENERAL PRESIDENCY FOR PROMOTION OF VIRTUE AND THE PREVENTION OF VICE. I suspected the men were *mutawwa*, the religious police.

In the absence of a stable Saudi government, the *mutawwa* enforced the Koran, the law of the land, like Old West sheriffs in the spaghetti westerns. By the purpose in their stride, I had a bad feeling it was high noon for these two, and I was wearing the black hat.

I stood up to intercept the approaching men. "Peace and Allah's mercy be upon you." Arabic was a language of worship, and thus it fell smoothly, if bitterly, from my lips. The camel bellowed a greeting of her own.

"And onto you also peace, mercy, and many blessings." The man who spoke was the younger of the two. He wore small, round glasses with yellow-painted frames. The glasses were a curious affectation considering the ease of corrective surgery and augmentation.

"Your LINK connection is malfunctioning, pilgrim," the older, more muscular man said. "We did not receive your response to our ping."

"Ah." The *mutawwa* apparently drove through town sending out a LINK signal—perhaps a salaam such as the one I greeted them with. If they didn't receive a response, they suspected the presence of an unbeliever or a foreigner. "Many pardons, brothers. I have a nickel allergy. I may not have metal in my blood. It prevents my use of external LINK connections as well," I lied.

They exchanged glances. I'd had an easier time diverting an archangel.

"You've been in a fight," the younger suggested, pointing at his chin.

I touched my face, feeling a bruise there . . . and the distinct scratch of stubble. Clean shaven—I'd totally forgotten about my lack of a beard. In some Muslim countries not having a beard or trimming one was enough to get you tossed into prison. As if on cue, another car pulled up next to the van.

As I watched the third police officer approach, I waited for one of my dark miracles to kick in. Soon, I hoped, some perverse distraction or wicked impulse would overcome the *mutawwa*.

"Do you have an explanation, pilgrim?" asked the larger of the two. "Where are your travel documents? If you don't have a LINK packet, then they must have printed a paper version for you."

I shook my head. God had screwed me again. Mecca is one of the holiest cities in the world. With so many prayers focused on this place, my powers, such as they were, failed.

"What seems to be the problem here?" the third *mutawwa* asked when he approached. He had a tazer gun in his hand, and his finger rested easily on the trigger.

"This foreigner is masquerading as a Muslim. His presence defiles the holy city," said the younger. I started inching up the steps. The larger of the *mutawwa* put his hand on my shoulder.

"I am a Muslim," I snarled. I pushed the big man's hand away. "I'm the fucking best Muslim you'll ever see. My love for Allah surpasses that of the Prophet and all the angels."

My fists were clenched, but my hold on my earthly body was light. If only it wouldn't mean a trip back to Hell, I'd show these righteous pricks the scorching pure fire of an angel's wrath.

Like Balaam's donkey, the she-camel sniffed the air as though seeing in me what the others did not. She bellowed nervously. With a frightened jerk, she pulled the reins from my hands. She bit the *mutawwa* with the tazer on the forearm, and kicked the younger one out of her way. Taking advantage of the confusion, I punched the larger man in the gut. The tazer fired, and the next thing I knew, I hit the street shoulder first.

CHAPTER 38
Emmaline, the Inquisitor

I felt like my old surfer self, cloning the tickets to Japan. But, when I slid into the cramped space on the shuttle next to my victim, I felt a twinge of guilt. I smiled into the pleasantly plump face of Dallas Morgan, an insurance agent from Topeka. I said, "Oh, I'm sorry, my boarding pass says seat 10A. It must be a misprint. Do you mind if I sit next to you?" knowing full well that in a month she would be getting double-billed for her flight to Tokyo.

Maybe if she had been crabby, I would have felt better about screwing her, but she just patted the seat next to her and said, "Oh, I don't mind, dear."

Rodriguez was right. Sometimes I was a shitty priest. I told myself it was his fault I was reduced to this. Earlier, when I'd accessed my Vatican expense account, I had discovered that the bishop had backed up his threat. I could only draw enough money to pay for a one-way ticket back to Rome.

Those bastards, I thought again. They were trying to take away from me the only thing in my life that had ever mattered. I had never cared that much for the kinds of priestly duties and counseling that Eion seemed to enjoy so much. It wasn't that I couldn't do those things, but they didn't give me pleasure. Not like the thrill of collaring an international hoaxer, like those behind the Virgin of Hong Kong. If I could go back to Rome with Mouse tucked under my arm, I'd be giving the Pope what he'd wanted for over a year: revenge for the LINK-angels. The Holy Father would kiss my feet.

And Rodriguez could kiss my ass.

"You're a priest," Dallas, the woman next to me, said,

looking at me over the bridge of her nose. She was not much older than I, but carried herself as though she were twice my age.

"Yes," I said, steeling myself for the usual barrage of questions about my gender and the seal of the Inquisition over my right breast.

"Will you say a prayer for me? This is my first flight." She glanced at her hands; they were picking at the hem of the afghan she'd brought with her. "I'm a bit nervous. I know they say these things are safe, but . . ."

The twinge of guilt hit me again, only it was more like a strum this time.

"Sure," I said, and offered my hand for her to take as the shuttle's countdown began. Dallas's hand felt cold and clammy against my own. I shut my eyes, and took a deep breath. I heard Dallas's sharp intake of breath beside me, and some of the more enthusiastic passengers joined in as the numbers closed in on one.

Over the rumble of the engines, I said, "Oh Lord, watch over us." I LINKed into my Bible concordance, wanting to add a comforting passage from some psalm. The millisecond the LINK took would seem seamless, or, at worst, thoughtful.

I read the words when they appeared: " 'Dear children, this is the last hour; and as you have heard that the Antichrist is coming, even now many Antichrists have come. This is how we know it is the last hour. . . .' " I stopped, horrified at what had come out of my mouth.

Dallas's lip quivered. She clutched at my hand. "Why did you say that?"

"I don't know." I tried the search again. This time it found another passage from 1 John: *This is the spirit of the Antichrist, which you have heard is coming and even now is already in the world.*

"I think I have some kind of glitch in my LINK program," I told Dallas, and tried again. I subvocaled clearly and succinctly.

This time the query returned something from the Koran: *Then your hearts hardened after that, so that they were like rocks, rather worse in hardness; for surely there are some rocks from which streams burst forth. . . .*

"Something is seriously wrong," I said out loud. My Bib-

lical concordance was housed in my internal system. I didn't
have to go out onto the LINK to access it. My private
system had only things that I had downloaded into it for
quick access. There should be nothing in there that I didn't
put there myself.

And I was concerned. Internal glitches rarely happened
unless something went wrong with your own synapses and
neurons. As often as this had happened, I was starting to
wonder if I had some kind of brain disease.

"I'd say," said Dallas, taking her hand from mine in a
sharp jerk. "You shouldn't have to access the Bible. It
should come from the heart."

I started. Dallas had echoed the sentiment of Rodriguez
and Michael. The sudden blast of rocket fuel and g-force
made a response impossible, not that I had one anyway. I
felt my stomach twist as we left tne earth, and my knuckles
gripping the armrests were white.

I was beginning to think Eion was right. Maybe these
weren't glitches, after all. God was trying to tell me
something.

But what?

When we'd studied 1 John in seminary, the Antichrist
had a small "a"—that is, in fact, how it is reprinted in many
Bibles all over the world. The experts seemed to agree that
John was speaking metaphorically about the evils of turning
away from God, not about a literal man/monster, the Son
of Perdition. So, why the question: "Who is the liar?"

John's letter was simply an attempt to set a doctrinal
litmus test for the early churches, i.e., you can call your-
selves Christian if you believe in the Son and the Father.
Otherwise, you're out. You're an antichrist, someone
against Christ.

I had no problem with either. When I did pray, which
granted, wasn't often, I had a tendency to prefer to pray
to Mary, but I was an Italian-American . . . not to mention
a woman. Still, I wore the collar; I believed in the usual
Catholic stuff. I'd never denied that there was a God.

I shut my eyes and tried to sleep. My mind was restless,
and I couldn't settle down properly.

"Why are you a priest, then?" Dallas asked without
preamble.

"What?"

"You don't know the Bible, but you're a priest. I wondered why. Why not be a schoolteacher or something else nice like that."

"It's not nice to be a priest?" I said with a smile.

Her eyes flicked to the Inquisitor emblem. Some people, Americans in particular, were afraid of us. They saw us as a kind of thought-police, since we sometimes had to make a subjective call about the level of someone's faith. If we found them lacking, they could be excommunicated. Or, depending on the country, sometimes something worse.

"I'm an Inquisitor. I just do my job," I told her. "The righteous have nothing to fear."

"What about you?" she asked quietly, fishing some knitting needles out of her purse. "Who polices you?"

"God," I said, and I felt a chill on the back of my neck. Then I remembered my recall back to Rome. "And the media, the Swiss Guard," I spat out. "And the Pope. Believe me, lady, right now lots of people are trying to judge me."

"Good," I thought I heard her say, but I ignored her. Shutting my eyes again, I pretended to sleep. Finally, the shuttle began its descent. Next to me, I could hear Dallas humming nervously to herself. Being outside the range of the usual LINK nodes, I tuned in an aria from my private collection.

I wondered if, in my role as Inquisitor, I was supposed to figure out who the Antichrist was? Was God trying to tell me that somehow I had the secret, or special access to the answer? The Pope had dreamt about me, or at least Rodriguez had made me think he had. Maybe I was on some kind of mission from God.

That seemed to border on a strange kind of hubris. I'd mocked Eion for feeling chosen. Pride and narcissism were why so many people invented hoax miracles—they wanted the attention; they wanted to be God's special messenger.

I resolved to call Eion once we touched down. I needed to apologize for leaving without saying goodbye, and for the hole I'd left in his wall. If Morningstar was alive, then I'd find him and wring answers out of him if I had to. Maybe then God and all the rest would leave me alone, in peace.

*　　*　　*

I rang Eion from the taxi queue at the airport. I got his construct—a nice enough, if simplistic, rendition of him—who told me he was either in Mass or otherwise occupied in church work. I was supposed to leave a message.

"Call me," I told it. So much for atonement.

An hour and several thousand yen later, I was sitting on a bench in a crowded Tokyo police station next to a transvestite prostitute. The station was little more than a storefront on the ground floor of a larger office building. All the spaces were subdivided with mismatched, cloth-covered cubicles—clearly castoffs from the other, more affluent businesses that shared the building. The place looked more like a dodgey business incubator than a cop-shop.

Inquisitor Shen, I'd been told, was in the middle of an interrogation and couldn't be interrupted. When I'd pointed at my Inquisitor emblem, she seemed slightly more impressed, but had still insisted that I wait here. So I cooled my heels and waited. Literally, since the heater seemed to be malfunctioning and the vent right above me blasted out cold air.

I was antsy. All this God stuff was putting me on edge. I shifted on the small wooden bench and accidentally brushed against the prostitute.

"Sorry," I mumbled.

"It's nothing, honey." The transvestite balanced a sequin-studded stiletto heel, size twelve, on the tip of his, her toes. A purse sat primly in a slender lap. In a strange way, he was attractive. He, she, whatever, clearly would stand a man-size height, but he was thin in a delicate, almost feminine way. Long, straight, black hair was parted neatly in the middle and hung in perfect lines on either side of his face. The earrings were big and showy, but his makeup was unusually understated. I imagined he might have been handsome, if he only knew which gender he was. I tried not to stare.

"Do you believe in angels?" the transvestite or transsexual—I suddenly noticed a very realistic swell of breasts beneath his skimpy red dress—asked me. He spoke unaccented English, despite his Asian features.

I pointed to the emblem over my heart and scooted an inch or so away from him. "What does the badge tell you?"

He laughed; it was a sweet sound, like soft bells. "The badge tells me you have a job, not what's in your heart, *chica lissa.*"

Those were Rodriguez's words, *chica lissa,* and somehow I doubted that phrase was hip Asian gay slang. Sweat prickled my palms. A eerie feeling settled over me, as it had in the airplane when I couldn't access the passage I was looking for. I nearly whispered the question: "What did you just say?"

He raised his perfectly manicured hands in surrender. "I was just making conversation."

I'd never heard anyone besides Rodriguez use that phrase, and yet, suddenly, it seemed to be popping up all over. That returning creepy-crawly feeling in my stomach made me angry. I refused to be bullied and frightened by God.

"The hell you were making conversation. Why did you call me that?" I demanded. I leaned in close enough to smell his after-shave.

"What?"

"Chica lissa," I repeated, getting right into his made-up face. "Where did you get that, you gender-wreck? Where?"

He squared his slender shoulders as though dropping something, a pretense, perhaps. He didn't bat a lash when he said, "A little bird told me—or maybe it was your guardian angel."

I sat back, and blinked in confusion. The transvestite pursed his bright-red lips into a thin line, and added: "Don't you ever wonder if God is trying to tell you something? Testing you?"

I felt as stunned as though he'd slapped me. Somehow I found my feet. My gaze still locked on the transvestite's clear black eyes, I backed away until I hit the wall. I leaned there, letting the cool plaster support me for a moment.

All around, life continued as usual. A couple of female cops in knee-length, navy-blue skirts hurried through the hallway, carrying sack lunches. The scene was so mundane, so normal, that I took comfort in it. I took a breath. Then another.

The transvestite's sequined shoes glittered in the overhead fluorescent. His sculpted legs were crossed modestly, despite the short-short red dress he wore.

"Who are you?" I asked.

"You would know me as Uriel," he said, brushing an imaginary fleck from the hem of his dress.

My shoulders dropped, relaxing. Uriel was a noncanonical angel. Unlike Michael, he was not mentioned by name in the Bible. This fact strangely gave me a huge amount of comfort. My breathing evened out. And, I found myself able to laugh. What a fool I'd been to feel threatened, even for a moment, by this gender-mistake!

The transvestite shook out his long, straight hair, and used his sharp fingernails to fish out tendrils that had gotten caught in the earrings. He regarded me coolly, despite the fact that his preening had caused another giggle to bubble out of my throat.

I had a hard time imagining this girl-man standing at the gates of Eden with a flaming sword in hand.

"Yet I was there," he said. "I also gave humans the secrets of the Kabbalah and alchemy. Milton called me the Regent of the Sun and the sharpest-sighted spirit in all of Heaven."

"Uh-huh," I said, convinced more than ever that this man was suffering some kind of delusion. "So, tell me, Uriel. I've been wracking my brains. What does God want from me exactly?"

The transvestite stood up slowly, tugging at the hem of his dress to even it out. Uriel was tall for a man, but doubly so for one pretending to be a woman. "Yours will be a hard job. He wants you to follow your heart, Em."

Hearing those words again chilled me, but I shook it off. "What's that supposed to mean?"

"When the time comes, you will know," he said.

"How convenient."

Uriel put a hand on his hip, and shook his head. "What do I need to do to convince you? Do I need to show you my true face? Not that it would matter. You've looked right into Michael's glory, yet you don't believe. Michael, who is like God!" He tsked his tongue. "No wonder Sammael loves you so."

"Who? You mean Sammael Morningstar?"

"Girl, that boy is tricky. Who knows what name he gave you? He's the great seducer, the light-bearer, the bright morning star. . . ."

"Morningstar? When did you talk to him?"

"He stopped at home after his little accident. Like usual, he didn't stay, though Father would have let him."

"Wait." My head was spinning with the insanity of this conversation. I pushed myself away from the wall I'd been leaning against. "What are you saying? Are you related to Morningstar? He lives with you?"

Uriel bent to pick up his purse. He tucked it under his arm and sighed wistfully. "Once Sammael was an elder brother I admired . . . we all did."

That eerie feeling crept over me again like a feather tickling my nerves. I shivered.

A tap on my shoulder made me jump. I turned to see a slender, Japanese woman with gray hair tied back in an ornate set of braids.

"Inspector Shen will see you now," she informed me in crisp English with a curt bow.

"In a moment," I said. I turned back to Uriel, but he was gone.

Chapter 39
Page, the Intelligence

My father sits behind Kioshi's desk, playing with the cherry blossoms, when we come in. The arrangement is in disarray. Pink petals lie inside the circle of light cast by the office lamp. My father's eyes are rimmed in red, and there are dark blotches under his eyes. I am worried, and Mai takes a step forward to comfort him, until he looks up. Mouse's gaze is not friendly.

"Where is Page?"

He is looking right at me, into Mai's eyes. I try to be very small, invisible.

Kioshi steps in front of us to take the seat opposite Mouse. Over his shoulder, he says, "Mai, bring us some tea. You'd like some black tea, right, Mouse?"

When she hears my father's name, Mai starts guiltily.

What's going on, I ask. *Why are you so jumpy?*

I didn't think we'd get the pleasure of meeting your father so soon, she replies.

It's exciting, isn't it?

Kioshi is disappointed, I think, she says. *He was looking forward to having you around for a while.*

Yes, but now that my father is here, he can teach me what I need to know. He can upgrade me.

Mai says nothing, but I feel her shoulders hunch. Her stomach quivers. Then, we turn stiffly toward the counter and plug in the hot-water heater. As she busies herself with finding the herbs, Mai glances at my father. *He's smaller than I would have thought,* she tells me.

He seems big to me.

It's strange to look at him though another's eyes. Usually, I see the world from his perspective. Mai notices his energy. Her gaze follows the incessant plucking, smoothing, and arranging of the fallen blossoms on the blotter of Kioshi's desk. Mouse picks one up and crushes it in his fingers, rolling it into a thin tube. This, in particular, makes me want to pack my data into the smallest possible space. Mai, instead, continues to watch Mouse. He taps his foot—fast and hard—making his whole body jerk slightly. She can hear the faint *whoosh, whoosh, whoosh* of his tennis shoe hitting the floor.

"Why do you think I know where to find Page?" Kioshi asks, smoothly. He leans back in the office chair as though sitting on the other side of his own desk doesn't bother him in the least. Kioshi is unmoving like a scorpion. The Korean stands behind Kioshi, near the wall, looking fierce and protective.

"I pinged him from the airport public-access booth. The last place he was seen was one of your gambling dens. He went in, but never came out."

"Perhaps he's enjoying his stay. I have geisha you wouldn't believe."

Mouse frowns at the cherry blossom in his hand. "Page is a program."

"He's also a young man . . . or woman, whose needs are like anyone's," Kioshi says, as Mai sets the teacup and saucer at his elbow. We turn to do the same for Mouse. He looks up at us, and I can feel Mai hold our breath.

"Milk?" he asks us.

"I don't know if we have any, I'll check," Mai says, and we scurry from the room to do my father's bidding. Once the door is shut behind us, we lean heavily against it. We take one long breath. The receptionist stands up and looks at us curiously. "There's milk in the vending machine, right?" Mai asks, walking over to his desk.

"Soy milk," the receptionist offers.

"Good enough," she says. "Give me a coin."

Wordlessly, the receptionist pulls a tin from the front drawer of his desk and hands Mai several yen coins.

"Thanks," she says, then leans in conspiratorially. "So, how did he get in there?"

"Mouse? I think he came up during the whole confusion

downstairs. About that." The receptionist grabs a soda can from his desk and shows it to Mai. He smiles sheepishly. "I'm enjoying this. You are so wise."

"Seriously?" I can feel Mai frown.

The receptionist makes a full-waist bow. "Of course."

I hope we got a lot of money, Mai tells me privately, but I feel the color rise in her cheeks. She is embarrassed by the power she has over this man.

"Okay. Well, thanks again," Mai says, holding up the coins in her hand and putting on a quick smile. Then, we head out the door, turning down the hall toward the elevator banks.

That scares you, doesn't it?

What? Mai asks, as she stomps down the hallway. Her bare feet slap against the short nubby carpet.

The worship of that receptionist.

She sniffs, and I feel her square her shoulders resolutely. "I have a lot of fans."

Not like that, I remind her.

I know my words affect her because she shivers slightly. "No," she whispers.

Her fingers reach out, stroking the wallpaper. I feel a faint hum as her hand passes through each advertising hologram. "But a lot of people like me," she tells me with a giggle. "A lot."

I don't know what to say to that. Her desire to be adored by strangers confuses me. So I ask her another question that has been on my mind: *Why are you afraid of my father?*

I'm not. I'm afraid for Kioshi. I feel her heart hammer against her chest.

My father is not a violent man, I say.

It's not violent men that I'm afraid of, Mai says. *It's clever ones. Your father is very, very clever.*

I could hardly disagree with her assessment. *We will have to tell him that I am here, won't we?*

I think Kioshi would rather avoid that.

But, that's not what he promised. Kioshi said that he would release me when my father was free to care for me.

He can hardly care for you on the run, Mai says. *Now can he?*

No, but . . .

Plus, you're no good to anyone if Mouse destroys your code in a fit of anger, now are you?

I'm still puzzling over this when we reach the elevator banks. Mai pushes open an unmarked door. Inside the darkened, musty, closet-size space are rows of vending machines. She scans each to see what they hold. We stop at the pop machine. Mai's breath comes in sharply. There, on the face of the machine, is a hologram of Mai standing in front of the crowd. It is an aerial view, perhaps cribbed from a satellite feed. Though it is a bit difficult to see, she seems to smile beatifically as she says, "Enjoy Kola-Cola!" The image fades into a news 'bot's grainy scan of a fast-food restaurant where her name is scorched onto a wall. Then the loop returns to the crowd. She notices a red dot near the soda's name, indicating that it's sold out.

She looks at the next machine. Anywhere Kola-Cola is sold, it's empty.

A competitor's machine is running LINK feeds. Mai stops to read the live chat. The participants are discussing how the name stamp left at the fast-food restaurant is actually meant to symbolize the concept "brilliant," a translation of Mai's name, which is what the angelic figure intended to imply about his dining experience. They go on to say that same corporation that owns your favorite cola, Kola-Cola's competitor, of course, also runs the food chain. Some claim that the other company corrupted Mai's message. She had actually mentioned their product, as shown by the divine message left in the restaurant.

You're very popular for a cellist, I remark, intending to wound her just a little.

I taste bile at the back of Mai's throat. More shivers—a marvelously complex, shuddering contraction of back muscles—ripple down our spine.

"Soda never hurt anyone," she says out loud, straightening the hem of her skirt. Finding the milk dispenser, she purchases a carton. Her breathing is still ragged, and she fights to control it.

I hear the *ding* of an incoming call. I flip the go-ahead switch.

"Page?" It is the Dragon of the East. *"What are you doing here?"*

It's then that I realize I rudely answered Mai's LINK connection. *Oh, sorry,* I tell Mai.

"It's all right. I'm here, too," Mai says. *"Page rides me."*

"Page rides you? Oh." The Dragon sniffs dramatically. She always over-emotes, in my opinion. She stands on her haunches, with her arms crossed over her chest. In Mai's LINK connection the Dragon is not limited to the usual window. She's like a hologram that appears to move around in Mai's field of vision. Right now, she floats over the aisle between the machines like a ghost. She casts no shadow, and I can see the impression of things behind her. Still, it is a nice effect.

"Well, I relay a message from the band. Shiro wants to know if they all have to drink that wretched soda now. He prefers his Basil Seed drink, and says"—the Dragon shifts into a human male's voice—*"Fuck the corporations, man."*

Mai sighs. Her breath escapes our lips in a frustrated rush, but I also feel something relax her muscles—the warmth of love or friendship, perhaps? She says, *"Shiro is such a retro-radical."*

"Shall I tell him that?" The Dragon is all business; her tone is curt, robotic. She still stands in a defensive posture.

"No," Mai says, but she's smiling. *"Anyway, why are you acting as an intermediary? Why don't they call me themselves?"*

"Your phone is off, and your LINK"—the Dragon pouts at me pointedly—*"is obviously being monopolized by a huge waste of code."*

"Hey," I protest. *"Why are you mad at me?"*

"Page'd be gone by now if Mouse hadn't shown up," Mai says at the same time.

"Yes, my father is here," I say, feeling decidedly cut out of this conversation. *"They are trying to hide me, I think."*

"Yes, your father is very upset with you," the Dragon says, too interested in gossip to continue being angry at me. She moves in closer, and her tail twitches with excitement. She seems like a nervous ghost, her eyes sparking a translucent white. *"He asked me if I knew where you were."*

"Well, you can't tell him now," Mai says somewhat sadly. *"Kioshi would be really mad at you. He wants to keep Page . . . out of harm's way, of course."*

"Why does Kioshi want Page? He has me." The Dragon looks upset again, and her tail droops.

"I don't know, honey." Mai's own shoulders fall. *"Kioshi never seems to want what he already has."*

The Dragon seems to understand that, as though they'd discussed this concept before. She nods solemnly and disappears completely.

Mai hugs herself. "I've told her how much I hate ghosts. She must be mad at me."

She certainly is mad at me.

"We should get back," Mai says looking at the milk in our hand. The wax-coated carton is cold and sweating.

Kioshi will give me back to Mouse, right? I ask. *He promised.*

Our body is tense as she speaks, and I sense there is a half-lie in what she says. *Yes, when your father is free to take care of you, he will. Kioshi always keeps his word.*

When we return to the office, we cautiously push the door open a crack before going in. We are surprised to hear laughter. Intrigued, Mai takes a step in.

"I was beginning to think you'd forgotten," Kioshi says.

"I'm sorry," Mai lies easily. "The machine was jammed."

"I'm surprised it gave you anything other than Kola-Cola," Mouse says, and the corner of his lip turns up in a sour smile.

The men laugh again.

That doesn't seem funny, I say to Mai.

No, she says. *It doesn't.*

She places the soy milk on the table and sits back against the window ledge, between the two men. The pane is cool against our back, especially where it touches the jack at the nape of her neck beneath her hair. I wonder about it.

Recording VR. And, of course, optical feed—so you can see.

You have enhancements just for me?

For the Dragon, really, Mai explains. *But you are enough like her.*

But why?

Kioshi and his family discovered AIs learn much more quickly when they're allowed sensory input.

It is true. I learned much more about human emotion when I rode with my father. My father, who is sitting only a few feet away from me, staring at Mai like she's something good to eat. We shiver.

He watches her every move. "There's a kind of binary beat to your music," he says. "It's very seductive."

"Thank you," Mai says, speaking slowly in English. To me she adds in Japanese, *When did he hear it? He was cut off in prison. Do you think he's insulting me? Making fun of my childhood in the program?*

I don't know, I say. Looking into his eyes from the outside, my father seems different. I can't say for certain what he is feeling. I only know how Mai holds her body when she looks at him. She crosses her arms in front of her breasts. Her stomach flutters.

I echo her nervousness. I wonder if somehow he can spot me here. Part of me wishes he would—just to get it over with. Another part fears his wrath.

"You're wearing the most fetching outfit," Mouse says. "Are you hardwired to something right now?"

Mai looks down at the mesh covering her skin as if she'd somehow forgotten it was always there.

"The Dragon rides Mai," Kioshi says. Mai glances up to meet his eyes. He is so calm, he is almost unreadable, but she notices a tic in the muscle near his collarbone.

"Oh, hello, Dragon," Mouse says, waving brightly.

"Hello again," Mai says, pretending to be the Dragon.

Kioshi looks meaningfully at Mai. "Mouse called the Dragon earlier looking for Page," he explains.

"Page!" My father stands up and starts to pace. "Thing is, Page shouldn't be able to just disappear like that. He's got to be somewhere."

The Korean, who stands in the corner behind where Kioshi sits with his arms crossed, jumps when Mouse mentions my name and looks directly at Mai. Mai glares back at him until he refocuses his attention on my father.

That idiot almost gave us away, she says to me.

Who's to say he didn't? I say. *My father is very observant.*

Let's hope you're wrong, Mai says. We sneak a glance at my father, but he is looking at the pictograms on the box of milk like a curious child.

"Maybe he's on mouse.net," Kioshi offers, sipping tea.

Unlike the rest of us, Kioshi still looks perfectly comfortable. His legs are crossed, and one arm is casually propped against the arm of the chair. The neck tic is gone. I wonder what the world looks like from Kioshi's perspective; I wish I could go into his head.

Me, too, Mai tells me.

My father moves back and forth, not at all like a mouse, more like a tiger. "Mouse.net is the first place I looked for him. But the whole external interface thing is so damn slow."

When Kioshi raises an eyebrow, Mouse points to his temple where the almond-shaped lump of his LINK receptor is just barely visible under the skin. "I'm screwed up," he says, tapping his LINK-receiver. "I've been hardwiring all my hacks."

"No wonder you can't find Page. We have a supercomputer," Kioshi offers. "There's an old terminal still attached, I think. Isn't there, Mai?"

We jump at the sound of our name, our attention being so absorbed in watching my father's movement in the tiny office. "Uh, sure. I mean, I think so."

"What are you playing at, Kioshi?" Mai sends through their private line.

Kioshi shakes his head slightly and sips more tea.

"Okay, maybe. But, I can't stay here long. The cops, I'm sure they've got me ticked; I'm probably transmitting right into Interpol headquarters."

"The cops," the Korean says suddenly. "They're already outside, talking to our security about the riot."

"Great," Mouse says, glaring at Mai and me again.

"Lose them," Kioshi says.

The Korean bows and then leaves.

"I'm doomed," Mouse says, slumping into Kioshi's plush leather office chair. "If Page were here, I'd know what to do."

Mai holds back a smirk. *Obviously not.*

I don't respond to her quip. I would rather watch my father's face, but Mai is watching his hands as they rip the spilled petals in two. I am surprised to hear him sound so vulnerable. I wish I could tell him I was here.

No, Mai tells me. *He would kill you, I know he would. It's not safe.*

Kioshi raises a hand. "Mouse, you must know that this building is secure. If the police somehow received your signal through my jamming devices, no one would dare raid us. Not even the Order."

"It still makes me nervous," Mouse says. My father looks tired, and Mai lifts her hand as if to stroke his hair to comfort him. Mouse is staring at the desk. He still hasn't opened the carton of milk. It sits next to his teacup. When Mouse notices Mai reaching for him, she quickly counters by grabbing the milk. She pulls it open, and pours a dollop into his cup.

Mouse touches our hand. "That's enough," he says. "Thanks."

Though the contact lasted only a moment, the spot on our skin feels almost hot. Our hands shake as we put the carton down.

"I feel naked without Page," Mouse says to himself.

"Father," Mai whispers the words I am feeling. She quickly puts a hand in front of our mouth. Mouse is looking intently at something on Kioshi's desk.

"Hey," he says, holding up a printed copy of the ASCII dragon I gave Kioshi. "This is mine."

For the first time Kioshi looks nervous. "Are you sure? My collection is extensive. Perhaps it just looks like something you own."

Mouse examines the paper, running his hands over the surface. He puts the art to his nose and sniffs the ink. "This was just printed."

"I'm constantly expanding my collection from various archived sites. The secretary must have put it on my desk while we were out shopping." From the sound of Kioshi's clipped tone, the secretary is a dead man.

The telephone beeps, making us all jump. Mouse stares incredulously at Kioshi. "You have a phone?"

"Sometimes there's information everyone needs to hear." Kioshi leans over the desk and flips a switch. A voice comes through a tiny speaker somewhere in the ancient hardware.

"The police want to come up," a voice says. I assume it must be the Korean who went to talk to the officers. "What shall I tell them?"

"Tell them I will join them when I can. My secretary will give them a tour until I can meet with them."

"Damn," Mouse says, setting down the forgotten art.

"We should get you to our system," Kioshi says, standing. Giving us a brief glance, he adds, "Mai, I'm afraid, will be too busy packing."

"Where am I going?" Mai asks.

Kioshi glares at her meaningfully. *"On* hajj, *to Mecca. We promised Page we would take him."*

What about my father? I ask

Mai's stomach tightens again. She doesn't respond.

"Where are you off to? Some concert date?" Mouse asks.

We glance at Kioshi, and say, "Yes. You know how it is. The busy life of a music star."

"Um, yeah," Mouse says. Looking right at me, he says, "If you see Page, say hi."

Chapter 40
Morningstar, the Adversary

I woke up in a prison cell in Jeddah. I could smell the tang of the sea in the recycled air. The ceiling was a whitish stone. Like the walls, it was flecked with something, perhaps mica, that reflected the bioluminescent paint. I lay in the corner of the cell, flat on my back. Air-conditioning cooled my bruises until I could almost forget they were there.

A key turned in the lock. I propped myself up on my elbows, despite the pain from my cracked ribs and abused shoulder. The door opened, and a man stepped into the room. He wore a long black robe, his curly brown-and-gray hair was held in check by a tall turban. An unruly beard flowed down to mid-chest. He crouched down beside me. It was then that I noticed the black embroidery above his chest. The scales of justice balanced on a scimitar, and the crescent of Islam overshadowing the world: an Inquisitor.

"Peace and Allah's mercy be upon you," he said.

"Ditto," I replied.

Despite my insult, the Inquisitor smiled. "Is this truly the man who loves Allah more than the Prophet?"

"I," I said, sitting up, and turning so that my back rested against the cell wall, "never claimed to be a man."

He laughed. "What then, if not a man?"

"I am better than man. I have been created of fire, not dust." I spat on the floor of the cell to show my disgust. " 'I will certainly lie in wait for those on the straight path. I will come to them from before and from aft; I will come from their right-hand side and from their left.' "

The Inquisitor sat back on his heels. His eyes roamed over my form, stopping at every cut, every bruise, and every human-like streak of dirt. "So," he said slowly, his eyes watching mine. "You don't claim to be . . ." He fished out an ID chit from a fold in his robes. Showing it to me, he asked, "Nabil bin Hashim?"

I shook my head.

"Good," the Inquisitor said, with a twitch of a smile. "Because you look nothing like him."

When I didn't respond, the Inquisitor stood up. He clasped his hands behind his back and regarded me like a lawyer at trial. "Tell me," he said, "was Nabil a friend of yours?"

"No."

"Then how is it that you came in possession of his camel?"

"I didn't know that I was."

"Are you saying that it was coincidence that you and Nabil's camel were in the same place?"

I said nothing. The hint of a small knot of fear tightened my stomach. If the only thing the Inquisitor managed to pin on me was the theft of a camel, they would still chop off my hand. Destruction of the body meant a return to Hell. The memory made my fists clench until my knuckles showed white.

"We will need to take some DNA," the Inquisitor said, holding out a hand as though he were expecting me to simply give over my genetic code. "The *mutawwa* would have had me sample you while you slept, but I reminded them that it is forbidden. We must ask."

"How humanitarian." I laughed. Opening my palm, I let the Inquisitor prick my thumb with the needle cybernetically embedded in his index finger. The Inquisitor would be surprised when my test came back. I had no DNA.

"What were you doing in Mecca?"

I couldn't help myself. I said, "Just dropping by."

"You have no papers. No LINK. Not even a name." The Inquisitor shook his head sadly, regretful.

"Oh, I have a name," I said. "I have many names."

"Ah, yes." The Inquisitor rocked back on his heels. His eyebrows raised skeptically. His tone mocked me. "Would you prefer I call you Iblis or the Shaitan?"

I stood up slowly. Just as carefully I loosened my hold on my body a little—not enough for me to slip toward

Hell, but sufficient to give the Inquisitor a scare. "You, oh righteous brother, may call me Rajîm: the Cursed One."

The Inquisitor stepped back and blinked rapidly. I watched his face, waiting to see if he believed what he saw.

"Merciful Allah," he whispered, and made a sign against the evil eye. Then he started to pray.

It was the damnedest thing. I saw them. I saw his prayers.

Perhaps it was because Mecca, one of the most holy cities on the earth, was only a few miles away. Or perhaps because the nearness of the end of days gave his words more power. But, whatever the reason, I could see them. His prayers were a real and tangible thing.

At first a misty cloud formed like a shield or a translucent bowl in front of his body. As he continued to say the words, the bowl seemed to become fuzzy. Then, apparently reaching some kind of critical mass, thin golden needles shot out. The first few stingers stuck against my skin like nettles. I looked down in surprise at the rows of tiny arrows sticking out of my flesh. I tried to shake them off, but they were barbed. A heat spread along my body, burning its way toward my spirit.

When I felt the first stab of scorching pain, I held back a cry with some effort. I'd return to Hell before I gave the Inquisitor the satisfaction of knowing he'd hurt me.

Hell, I thought; that was the answer. When the Inquisitor started another verse, I saw more arrows forming, like bright stars in the cloudy shield. I drew on my hatred, cold and dark, and let it fill me. Closing my eyes, I recalled the scene that played so often through my mind. The moment I was replaced in my Parents' eyes by that other—not another angel, but a toy made of dust and mud.

A sound, like the snap and crackle of ice hitting a glassful of lemonade, filled the cell. In my arm, the arrows' barbs broke, their fire gone. A flick of my wrist sent the dust of the spent arrows fluttering to the floor. The next wave of prayers evaporated before they reached me.

The temperature in the room dropped. I could see the breath of the Inquisitor hanging in the air. He shivered and opened his eyes. I'm not sure what he saw, but his prayers stopped. The Inquisitor took another step back, his face twisted in horror. I smiled, thinking that he would flee for certain. Instead, he bowed his head and began to pray again.

The golden cloud began to form in front of the Inquisitor. Tiny fires flashed, but instead of forming into arrows, they began to take the shape of a figure. The light grew brighter, almost blinding me. I heard a sound—a distant, pure, clear note of a trumpet.

CHAPTER 41
Emmaline, the Inquisitor

I sat down again on the bench in the hallway of the police station, feeling my world slipping away from me. My fingers curled around the edge of the wooden seat, and I held on so tightly that they ached. The sounds of conversation from around the room lost distinction. Instead, I heard a soft roar in my inner ear.

Who is the liar?

No, I shook my head. "No," I whispered, trying to convince myself. "That's crazy."

"Yes, it is. I mean, who would think that the next Buddha would be a Japanese cello player?"

I hadn't heard Inquisitor Shen approach. I looked up to see him standing in front of me, his arms clasped behind his back and a broad smile on his face. Shen reminded me of some kind of period–Hong Kong action hero. His shirt and tie gone, Shen was dressed as though it were still 1900s Shanghai—in a long flowing black robe with the classic Chinese pigtail.

"Buddha?"

He sat down beside me where the transvestite had been. "Well, yes, if you can believe the babbling of an insane man with third-degree burns on his face and boiled eyeballs." He shook his head. "I find this distressing. I have nothing against a new Buddha, but she seems to be sponsored by some American soft drink company. That's just not right. Enlightenment shouldn't come with a price tag and an advertising slogan." Shen clucked his tongue, then looked at me very earnestly. "My faith is shaken, Inquisitor."

A little hysterical laugh bubbled out from deep inside my gut.

"Come now, I'm being perfectly serious. I have conducted interviews with fourteen witnesses to your friend's immolation. All of them conclude that before his spontaneous combustion, they saw a vision of a holy creature that told them that Mai Kito was their savior. Some called her the Buddha; others the Second Coming."

"Mai? The shopper?" Even though he had told me this before I'd left for Japan, I still couldn't believe that Shen was suggesting that the dizzy Yakuza hacker with a penchant for a good bargain at Campi di Fiori was the Second Coming of Christ.

"No," Shen said, in a very grave tone. "Mai Kito the musician. Of course, it could all be some kind of strange publicity stunt. After all, her band is called the Four Horsemen. That's some kind of apocalyptic reference in your Bible, is it not?"

"Yes, it is," I said. Shen was sitting beside me with his hands clasped between his knees. He was leaning forward, like a horse ready to jump from the gate. Surreptitiously, I let my knee touch his. I needed the human contact just to feel grounded. It helped to be working on something. "The Four Horsemen of the Apocalypse. So, this is all a hoax."

Shen looked surprised. "What makes you say that?"

"Didn't you just imply you thought this was all a publicity stunt?"

"Yes." Shen smiled. "But that doesn't mean that demons couldn't be behind it."

I chuckled. When I realized he wasn't laughing along with me, I stopped. "You're serious."

"Don't you believe in demons?" Shen asked.

I remembered a flurry of six wings. My heart pounded in time to the fluttering of feathers and gray eyes. Sweat broke out on my face and prickled under my arms. I stood up.

"Why is everyone suddenly so interested in what I believe?" I snapped. "Complete strangers have been questioning my faith since I started this case!"

Shen looked me up and down slowly. "Yes, I see you've

just gotten in. You must be terribly jet-lagged. Let me take you out for something to eat. Maybe noodles? You're hungry, yes?"

I had to admit I was. I hadn't had anything real to eat since the eggs at Eion's church that morning, and, with the time-zone change, I'd completely lost track of how long it had been. I let Shen lead me out the door.

"It's only a few blocks," he said, once we started down the pedestrian walkway. In Tokyo, the traffic tunnels were open to every kind of vehicle—bikes, cars, motorcycles, scooters, skateboards, and pedestrians. The streets were filled with people: families on bicycles, tourists moving so slowly they were almost a hazard, and regular people just making their way somewhere, anywhere. It felt good to be moving. Though I had no idea what time it was, the sun was up. The tunnels were chilled and moist, with a tang of salt from the Sea of Japan.

Perhaps noticing my deep sniff, Shen said, "They manufacture the smell and pump it in. If you were to smell the real air outside these tunnels, it wouldn't be quite so pleasant."

I frowned. "I didn't need to know that. It's like when my mother told me that birds sing because they have a headache."

"Some sing all day to make the day go faster," he said. As he walked, he clasped his hands behind his back. A smile always seemed to hover on the edge of his lips. Shen hardly looked like a man who was having a crisis of faith, especially since he was clearly trying to make me feel better.

"Thanks," I said.

He nodded, and then, with a wink, he added, "Oh, and, of course, some birds sing to find a mate."

The smile warming on my face froze. A memory of Morningstar's rough passion swelled in my mind unbidden. I smelled patchouli on the air and choked on it, coughing. I couldn't breathe. Each breath led to another spasm of coughs.

"Are you okay?" Shen's hand was around my shoulders, lightly supporting me.

"Yeah," I said. My hands on my knees, I concentrated on taking in a slow, steady breath. "Is he . . . is Morningstar really dead?"

"It seems likely." Shen frowned at me helplessly. Then seeing a sign, he said, "Oh, the shop is right here."

He led me through a set of leaded-glass doors into a restaurant. The place was filled with people. The sounds of clacking chopsticks and the hum of conversation steadied me. I took a couple of more cautious breaths. My throat felt raw and scratched.

Pink neon light lit the restaurant. Static posters of music stars lined the narrow walls. Most of the musicians I didn't recognize, except for the few timeless opera stars like Placido Domingo. A disco ball sent dots of light dancing along the walls and tables. I stared at Placido and concentrated on breathing without choking.

Shen brought back a glass of water, and I gulped it down gratefully.

The table was as small and narrow as the restaurant itself. A chrysanthemum blossom in a small glass bottle took up a large amount of space. The tabletop displayed two menus: one facing me, the other for Shen. At the top of the display was a row of flags. I had to move the flower in order to find the Stars and Stripes. I tapped it lightly to translate the menu into English.

This place was obviously a tourist trap—otherwise the menu would have been available through the LINK, and only in Japanese. The prices bore out that theory. Looking up, I noticed a distinct lack of local patrons. There were a lot of young people, some wearing holo-tees of Mai. Others fingered glowing figurines on chains around their necks.

When Shen noticed my stares, he said, "Maizombies. It's only going to get worse."

"Because of Morningstar?" I tried to keep my tone even, but I kept thinking of his feather-light kiss. To distract myself, I touched the tabletop screen, picking out an order of steamed vegetables, rice, and squid. I added a mango drink on impulse. When I took another sip of water, I noticed Shen watching me with a curious expression.

"What did you know about Morningstar?"

I cleared my throat to keep a tickle of a cough at bay. "Well, not much, honestly. He owned a bookstore in New York." I stopped, seeing again the vision of him behind the counter in his jeans and silk shirt. I shook my head. Trust me to fall for a guy after he was dead.

"A bookstore?"

"Yeah." I smiled, seeing Shen's confusion. I'd thought it strange, too. "A used bookstore, no less. All preprinted stuff. Some of it was really moldy. It was all about demons and demonology."

"Demons, you say?" Shen tapped his fingers against his palm in rapid succession, taking notes again.

"Why not just record the conversation?" I asked. "That's what I do."

Shen frowned, then followed my gaze to his palm implants. "Oh, I record, too. I find it helpful to have my impressions logged separately."

"Good idea," I said. If I ever got back in the bishop's good graces, I'd have to ask for an upgrade. I frowned into my water and took another sip.

"Do you think Morningstar is a demon?"

I nearly choked on the water. I remembered the feral flash of white incisors in the dim light of the New York traffic tunnels, and the haunting kohl-rimmed glance of the boy with a demon's name. The memory of the coolness of Morningstar's flesh on mine made me shiver.

"What?" I asked, shaken.

Before Shen could repeat himself, my LINK connection buzzed. The caller ID flashed "unknown." I had my system block out all solicitors, and, as long as it wasn't Rodriguez, I was curious. "Hang on," I told Shen. "I have a call."

Shen pointed to the buffet and stood up. "I'll give you a moment, shall I?"

"Thanks," I agreed, and flipped the go-ahead switch.

A tiny window opened in the corner of my vision. The LINK displayed a trim Japanese man about my age in a suit coat. He looked so businesslike that I almost didn't recognize him. Then, I saw the Yomoto T-shirt peeking out from under the coat and the rose-colored glasses balanced on his nose. *"Kioshi! What happened to your hair? You look so . . . low-rez. What happened to the curls? The blond streaks?"*

" 'Low-rez'? I'm hurt, Emmaline. I truly am," he said, but he was smiling. *"What about you? Your interface needs a makeover. Perhaps the next thing I can do for you is have one of our kids make you something more lifelike."*

"Phooey," I said. *"I don't have time to fool around with*

making a flash interface." I looked over to the buffet table
to try to spot Shen. He was frowning and poking at something under a heat lamp with a chopstick. From what I
could tell, his plate was still mostly empty. *"Since you probably found out I was in town thanks to spies at the police
station, you should also know I can't talk to you right now."*

Kioshi bowed slightly to acknowledge the truth of my
statements. *"But why not?"*

*"You know he'll be able to tell I'm receiving a signal.
He's an Inquisitor. It wouldn't be hard for him to trace it
back to you."*

*"Ha! You think my tech can be traced by some hick In-
quisitor? He's from Hong Kong, for gods' sake."* Kioshi
raised his hand before I could protest. *"But, out of respect
for you, Emmaline, I'll keep this short. I'm calling in my
favor."*

"This isn't a good time, Kioshi," I said, watching Shen's
progression around the buffet table.

*"I don't remember anyone's convenience being part of the
original deal. You had to talk to the Dragon's maker right
now, you told me. I sent her on a chartered space-shuttle."*

"That was your choice."

*"No, that was the respect I have for you. We're nearly
family, after all. We grew up together. I always thought that
some day I'd be talking to you as a peer, in the business.
Now here you are: a cop. Still, despite all of that, you're
family to me. Families have a certain responsibility to each
other, I'm sure you know."*

Shen had moved from the buffet line and stopped to fill
up a glass of soda. Whatever choice he made appeared to
be empty, and the fountain sputtered and coughed out
white spray. I could hear a dry thumping sound coming
from the machine. He looked up at me sheepishly and
shrugged. He stopped to clean off his robe and the counter
before trying another.

*"All right, Kioshi. Enough with the family guilt. What do
you want?"*

*"Point Inquisitor Shen in some direction other than Toy-
oma Corporation, okay? Then, I'll have one of my men take
you to the Tokyo airport. You will escort a couple of friends
of mine out of the country."*

Shen was making his way to the table. *"I'm nobody's*

bodyguard. I've got to stay here and figure out what Morningstar is up to. My job is on the line. Ask me for anything else some other time."

Shen sat down. When he set his tray on the table, it took up so much room that the chrysanthemum nearly slid off the table. He grabbed the vase and looked around for a place to put it.

"Toro will be there in twenty minutes," Kioshi said, and hung up.

"No, wait!" I slammed my fist into the table, making Shen's noodles jiggle. Despite Shen's concerned look, I dialed up Toyoma Gaming Corporation. I knew it was a front for Kioshi's mob work, just like my uncle was "really" in the import export business.

A very pleasant, yet forgettable, secretary avatar answered, *"Toyoma Enterprises."*

"I need Kioshi right now, Goddamn it."

I realized that I forgot to subvocalize when Shen's chopsticks hit the edge of his plate with a crack. "Kioshi Toyoma?" he mouthed. Shen's eyes were wide with suspicion.

"I'm afraid that's quite impossible. Mr. Toyoma is in a meeting," the secretary intoned, but I hardly heard him.

"It's not what you think," I told Shen. As the words left my mouth, I could hear how guilty I sounded.

Shen arched an eyebrow at me. The chopsticks pointed at me accusingly. "I think I understand now why you wanted in on the investigation. I have been very foolish to trust an old colleague. I doubt I will do it again."

"Just tell Kioshi to stuff his little job, got it?" I said, and hung up on Toyoma Enterprises. "You can still trust me, Shen. This call was unrelated to your investigation, I swear."

Shen very carefully put his chopsticks down on his napkin, and folded his hands. "Let me see if I have a sense of what may have happened here. This was some kind of publicity stunt, in fact. You used your skills at miracle-faking to have your lover disappear in a ball of flame in order to boost one of Toyoma's investments. Then, you planned to follow this investigation to make absolutely sure that what happened in the restaurant was declared a miracle. Toyoma's stock goes up. His little singer becomes famous, and somehow you and your lover share in the wealth."

I had to admit Shen's idea sounded very plausible. Unfortunately for me, the truth was much less convincing. "If that were true, why would I call Kioshi right here at the table?"

"Perhaps you are hoping that I will look the other way because of our former friendship."

"Will you?"

"No," Shen said, as I saw the flash of red lights outside the window.

CHAPTER 42
Mai/Page, the Synthesis

Mai's apartment is small, but clean. The converted warehouse space, despite the cramped dimensions, has an airy, industrial feel. We sit on a futon shoved into the corner under a bank of windows. I can feel a cold breeze on our cheeks coming through a crack between the pane and the sill. Our knees press against a large wooden dresser. The drawers are open, and clothes of all colors and design spill out into the open duffel bag between our feet. Our head is in our hands and ragged sobs shudder through the body.

I have never cried before—not when I betrayed my father, nor in the aftermath of the fear-bomb. Until now, I'd never realized how much I wanted to. Or how much I needed it. I allow another wet shudder to pass over me, through a tight, aching throat to sore, reddened eye. My head pounds, but, strangely, I feel nothing but relief. I could cry all night.

Unfortunately Mai does not feel the same. Knuckling the tears from our eye, she straightens. Pulling some more clothes randomly from her drawers, she punches them into the corners of the duffel. That feels good, too. She pounds them a couple more times. Our jaw clenches.

"He's banished me," she says. "All because of you."

Another wave of tears well up, but she bites them back. Instead, she slams her palm against the dresser drawer, snapping it shut. Prickles of pain and heat dance along my hand. They fade all too quickly.

I'm sorry, I say. It's true, but, for the first time, I realize what a completely inadequate response that is. *You could tell my father where I am. Then you wouldn't have to go.*

Our heart swells with hope momentarily, but then her stomach quivers.

"No," she says, with a sniff. "I have to go. He'd kill me if I betrayed you."

Is it betrayal if I want you to?

"Kioshi would think so. That's what matters to me."

I could escape out into the LINK. That wouldn't be your fault.

She laughs sadly. "Try it."

I approach her LINK connection. Mai sees her receptor as an oval door shifting with the silvery sheen of mercury. All I experience are zeros: off. I conjure a pulse of electricity to transform them to on, just like I had when the Dragon called. The numbers change one by one, and the door opens.

I start to step through when Kioshi's avatar appears.

"This better be important, Mai." Plump and cuddly, his voice sounds anything but. I try to squeeze out, but the connection is too small. *"Page?"* Kioshi asks. *"Is that you?"*

I hang up. The ones become zeros instantly.

A careful examination of Mai's LINK connection reveals a startling fact. She cannot initiate LINK transactions on her own, other than to communicate with Kioshi. She can receive incoming messages from anyone, but Mai can't bank, surf the entertainment channels, access restaurant menus, or vote. She receives, but does not transmit. She's blind-sighted, crippled.

And I am trapped.

Did Kioshi plan to trap me? I ask Mai.

I don't think so, she admits. *Kioshi wasn't expecting Mouse to be free so soon. He had plans for you. He still does.*

I won't do them, I say.

You will. She sighs. *Kioshi always gets his way. Always.*

She flops onto her back, sprawling on the futon.

I feel a wave of shame: I should have known.

Why? Why are you so cut off? Doesn't it make life difficult?

The sheets are flannel and worn to a perfect softness. Mai wraps us into a bundle of blankets and pillows. Rolling onto our side, we curl our knees up until they almost reach our chest. "It was the price I paid for leaving the program.

Working for Kioshi is the only reason I have as much as I do," she murmurs into the pillows.

You were a maker, I say.

She takes a deep breath. "I know."

Couldn't you have petitioned the government? Gotten a live connection some other way?

"My only religion is binary," she says. "And, anyway, you know how I feel about Kioshi."

He doesn't seem to feel the same.

"He's in a bad mood. Sometimes he can be very sweet," she says. Her body tells me otherwise. Mai's grief is deeper than tears; it's a kind of heaviness that settles on us. She knows. She knows she'll never have him.

Sure, I say. *I can see that. You're a lucky woman.*

A smile tickles her lips. "Thanks."

She sits up, unearthing our body from the shroud of blankets. "You know what? I'm starting to like you, Page."

We finish packing. An hour later, at the arranged time, Kioshi's limo honks outside.

Mai doesn't know the driver, and that worries us. We perch in the backseat, biting our nails. Cold air blasts the body. We're dressed for Saudi weather. I told her stories of the desert as she tried on different things in the mirror, finally settling on the cute pink skirt and polka-dot blouse that complements our skin tone. We have a big floppy straw hat perched on our mountainous hair. I insisted on the hat because I thought we looked glamorous, like an English princess.

"Could you turn the heat up?" we ask.

A grunt, then the air is dropped down a notch.

Better than nothing, Mai and I agree.

We watch Tokyo rush past the windows. All the billboard holograms are playing Kola-Cola advertisements showing Mai's face. She looks away and hugs the body tightly. She whispers to me, "Maybe it's a good thing I'm leaving town."

Maybe.

Despite the ads, Mai keeps glancing out the window. She's not looking for anything in particular. Our eye just scans, searching. She hopes Kioshi will be at the airport, to say good-bye, at least. I feel the same about my father. I hadn't been able to tell him I was here, much less that I was going on the great pilgrimage, something we'd dreamed of doing together. Mai might be right. My father seemed different—angrier. He very well might want to tear my code apart, but I couldn't help but feel I was being sent away so that Mouse would not discover me in Kioshi's hands.

Especially since I couldn't escape this body.

Mai and I are growing more and more comfortable together, but she is loyal to Kioshi by virtue of her love. It's obvious she wouldn't agree with my desire to confront him. Kioshi has put me in the perfect place. Mai would never hurt him.

Right now, I wish I could.

My field of vision begins to narrow at the thought of being trapped here, inside Mai. I imagine Kioshi as a bundle of wires. In my mind's eye I am a butterfly cutter, pressing down slowly on the plastic-coated exterior. One by one the wires give way, until the flow of information makes its painful way through a single conduit. He wheezes with effort to push through the narrow space. The muscles in my hand feel bruised.

The car swerves, jarring me out of my reverie. When I focus again through Mai's eyes, I can see our fingers curled around the back of the driver's neck. Mai shouts in surprise at her own actions, and she pulls her hands away. She looks at them in astonishment.

"Was that you?" she asks in a whisper I can barely hear over the driver's curses.

I say nothing; I'm planning.

CHAPTER 43
Morningstar, the Adversary

I'd forgotten how awesome Jibril was to behold. Six hundred pairs of wings held him aloft. Layer upon layer, progressively larger, they encircled him like a writhing, pulsating cloud. The smallest that I could see were as translucent and iridescent as a dragonfly's. Sparrow's wings formed the next ring, followed by grackle, crow, then hawk, on up the food chain, until the last, the largest, could only belong to an angel or a god.

His body was as black as the depths of space, like the silhouette of a man cut from the fabric of reality revealing the empty darkness behind. The words burned between his eyes like a sun. In his hand he held a scimitar that shone with the reflective light of the moon. Blue flames danced along its edges.

He filled the space of the small prison cell. Though I could still hear the words of the Inquisitor's prayers, he was hidden behind Jibril's massive form.

"Hello, brother," I said. "Looking good."

"Iblis." His voice was an amalgam of the wails of a million souls in agony. "We should have known it was you."

At Jibril's easy use of the royal "We," I felt my lip curl. With a simple word he reminded me that he was like the hand of God—an extension of all that I was cast out from.

My hair whipped around my face, and my own wings began to unfold. Snapping like a sail, they stretched, naked and black, filling the room. My feet left the ground. I reached my left hand into the ether, and conjured a sword of steel and obsidian—as strong as hatred and as sharp as sin.

Our weapons struck with an explosive force that rocked

the walls. Lightning sparks flashed where our blades met. Though in his angelic form Jibril was immutable and immovable, I pushed against him with the same strength I'd used to split Heaven in two.

And

  He

    Moved.

Jibril's muscles trembled, and the earth shook. The room was too small to hold us. Stone dust rained down. The building began to crumble. Some part of my consciousness registered the screams of the Inquisitor begging for Allah's mercy, just before Jibril's foot connected with my chest.

The Inquisitor's words must have given Jibril extra strength, because the next thing I knew I flew right through the wall into the next cell. Stone exploded everywhere. I slid unceremoniously on my ass into the corner. My wings protected me from much of the impact with the wall, but I could feel where Jibril's kick had hit my already cracked ribs. I propelled myself upright just in time to see Jibril pulling himself through the hole I'd made in the wall. His flaming scimitar high, I barely had time to raise my own weapon in defense. Steel crashed against steel and the muscles in my forearm strained painfully. My back was against the wall. The curve of Jibril's blade bit into the flesh of my wing. Light poured out of the cut, blinding him momentarily. I took that opportunity to knee Jibril in the balls.

He fell back a step, but only one. Angel physiology 101: In his heavenly form, Jibril had no sexual organs—being both and neither all at once. I'd just managed to piss him off. Worse, I'd pushed him back just far enough to give him more maneuverability than I had. He dropped his weapon low and looked ready to bodycheck me against the wall. I closed my wings in front me like a clam shell for protection. He hit with enough force to knock me off my feet. Together we broke through another wall, tumbling into the open air.

Well, I thought, as his weight pinned me to the ground, at least I'm out of jail. Opening my wings, I saw the blue flames of the scimitar descending. I pulled my sword, but knew it was too late. Maybe, if nothing else, I could take Jibril back to Hell with me.

Rubber squealed. Jibril looked up, as if just now noticing

that we were in the middle of a busy intersection. The scimitar paused, but I didn't. My blade bit deep and long, and Jibril exploded into six hundred birds. Pigeons, buntings, sparrows, egrets, herons, doves, and bluebirds took flight in every direction. I heard a crash and the scream of folding metal. In the distance, an ambulance siren wailed.

As quickly as I'd imagined them into being, my wings disappeared. The sword forged of my hatred, however, still felt heavy and real in my grip. I tried to let go of the hilt, but the sword clung stubbornly to the flesh of my palm. The blade had started out a metaphor, like my wings, but it was transforming into something else, something beyond my control.

A cool breeze dried the sweat from my body. Across the street, through the tall buildings I caught sight of a deep scarlet sun setting on the Red Sea. My stomach quivered. I glanced down on the bloody reflection on the ebony blade.

For the first time in a long, long time, I was filled with a sense of dread. Looking heavenward, I whispered, "A final gift perhaps?"

Though I heard no answer, I knew the truth. The sword hadn't faded because I would need it again soon. Michael hadn't lied. The end was near.

Chapter 44
Emmaline, the Inquisitor

My proximity alarm flashed in the left-hand side of my field of vision. Four bogeys wearing holographic armor approached, it warned me. Two came from the rear of the restaurant; the others waited just outside the front door.

"Surrender is the best option." Shen's voice was steady, but his eyes watched mine warily. "I've received reports about your connection with Mouse. I have orders to bring you down."

Bring me down, he said—like an animal. A thousand protests rushed through my head. It wasn't my fault. I hadn't done anything wrong. But before I said the words I knew how feeble they sounded, how guilty I appeared.

The bogeys halted their advances. My combat computer calculated that one of them stood less than a few feet away, just under a poster of Elvis. He or she carried a fletchette rifle of unknown caliber. The second took up position on the opposite wall. They blocked the rear exit. With Shen sitting calmly in front of me, and the two other figures at the front door, the only way out was with a fight.

Or, as Shen suggested, I could leave here in his custody, arrested like a common criminal. I looked around the tiny restaurant. The place was packed. Maizombies with their glow-in-the-dark figurine necklaces queued up for the buffet inches away from the bogey in holographic armor. A family with kids sat, laughing, at the table just to our left. An older couple poured drinks for themselves at the soda fountain. All these people would be witnesses. In their eyes, it wouldn't matter that I was innocent, falsely accused. They would assume my guilt. They would judge me.

"If you come along quietly, things will go easier on you."

I couldn't help but laugh a bit. How many times had I said the exact same thing? It was never true. Being arrested was always hard on the criminal. It was only the cop who had an easier time of it if they went quietly.

I armed my lasers. Why should I make Shen's life any easier when he hadn't been willing to look the other way for an old friend, a fellow Inquisitor? He should have given me the benefit of the doubt. As my targeting computer came on-line, cross hairs appeared.

Uriel had said that when the time came, I'd know. Well, the time to follow my heart was now. My heart screamed: *Fuck 'em; fuck 'em all.*

I pointed my finger where they suggested. I sent the silent command: *Bang.*

A smoldering hole appeared where Shen's cornea had been. I smelled burnt flesh and hot metal as he slumped, face-first into his noodles. A woman at the table gave me a disapproving look, as if to imply I should take better care of my drunken husband. But otherwise, no one seemed to notice. My laser was, after all, silent, and the bogeys were invisible as they started advancing, slowly, along the walls of the restaurant. I tuned in a rousing aria, something to keep time with my pounding heart.

"This is the police," a voice informed me subvocally. The voice sounded tinny, as though it was being routed through my internal translator. *"Please stand up and move slowly toward the front door. We have you surrounded."*

Shen started to twitch. His hand grabbed at the air, just as a passing Maizombie headed toward the buffet with an empty plate. The Maizombie mistook his desperate clutch as a grope, and she slapped his hand. *"Bastardo,"* she said in Italian. She stepped right between me and the nearest cop. I could see the misty outline of a rifle waver. The Maizombie put a hand on her hip and turned to give Shen a piece of her mind when he pulled his head off his plate. The woman caught sight of his melted flesh and twisted circuitry and let out a healthy scream. Her plate crashed to the floor and shattered.

In seconds, the restaurant was in chaos. I pointed all four fingers, like a karate chop, at the cop on my left and again gave the fire command: *Bang, bang.* Blood splattered the wall a second before his blue-screen armor flickered into visibility. His appearance excited more screams from the clientele. His rifle lay on the ground where it fell. The cop clutched his ruined elbow and cursed a very blue streak of street Japanese. I'd used a wide burst to effectively destroy his shooting arm. Apparently, their armor was not flecked with mirrors to repel lasers, an oversight I could use to my advantage. An optimistic beat moved through the music playing in my head.

The other cop de-cloaked. She shouted at people to remain calm and to get onto the floor. Though most of the patrons were still too stunned to follow orders, some were starting to drop to the ground. I needed to make an exit now before the cop had a good bead on me.

My shoulder bruised as a fletchette skimmed off my armored uniform jacket. I looked around to see where the shot had come from. The guy I'd thought disabled had made a wild shot with his nonstandard arm. One of the patrons caught the worst of the shot meant for me. He was clutching the side of his face and screaming. I let loose another laser shot in the cop's direction and ran for the window. The people I had to push out of my way slowed my momentum, so, by the time I got there, I had to jump-kick twice before the glass finally broke.

The aria swelled, mirroring my adrenaline rush.

Once on the sidewalk, I used my finger lasers in tandem like a kid playing VR shoot-'em-up, trusting the combat computer to make the best possible targets out of the remaining cops. I glanced behind me and saw Shen standing up. He was very calmly wiping the noodles off his face and looking right at me.

Using my enhanced muscles, I vaulted over the squad car and ducked. Even though I was moving at top speed, Shen's laser burned a hole clean through the fleshy area of my hip. With a grim chuckle, I gave up a thankful prayer for having been born a woman: saved by an extra layer of fat. My combat computer informed me it was shutting down pain receptors in that area.

The car wouldn't be protection for long. I had to keep moving. I surveyed the street, looking for an escape route. The electricity to the car rails had been turned off by traffic control. The nearest vehicle was a good fifty feet away. I'd have to run much farther than I'd like without any cover.

Bicycles and pedestrians still moved about, but many of them had stopped with the cars, curious and respectful of the police vehicles.

I smelled burning metal. Suddenly, I noticed red-hot dots appearing beside me. Shen's lasers were coming through the squad car's frame. I had to make a break for it. It was now or never. I was halfway across the street when a black limo moving on battery power slammed through the pileup at the edge of the tunnel. Watching the other cars buckle, I guessed the limo had to be armor plated. Thus, I didn't hesitate when the door swung open. I knew it had to be Kioshi's man.

"Took you long enough, Toro," I said, as I jumped into the seat. I pulled the door shut behind me.

"I'm right on time," he insisted, as we spun around to head back the way we'd come.

"Just tell me you have laser protection on this car," I said, strapping on the seat belt. Glancing behind us, I saw Shen running toward us in the street.

"Even the tires have mirror flecks in them."

"God bless Mafia paranoia," I sighed.

"Oh," Toro said, as we reentered the traffic jam to a chorus of honks and angry shouts, "Toyoma says: 'Screw your "screw this job." ' And he says that now you owe him one more: for your life."

I grunted my assent. The smell of charred human flesh hung in my nostrils. I had bigger problems than the favors I owed Kioshi. A moment ago, I was derelict in my duty to return to Rome. Now I was a cop killer. Worse, I'd shot up a fellow Inquisitor. But strangely, I felt nothing but calm. I had no regrets. I'd followed my heart, after all. It was what God had been asking me to do.

Checking the rear window again, I searched for any sign that Shen might be following on foot. The street looked clear . . . for now.

"How far can this thing travel on battery?" I was concerned that Shen would radio traffic control and have the tunnel shut down.

The driver shook his head. He was a big man. He could have been a sumo wrestler in his youth. A beefy hand patted the dashboard display lovingly. "Traffic control thinks we're an emergency vehicle. This baby can coast through anything. We'll have power even if they shut the whole city down."

I sat back against the soft leather seat. I didn't want to know how Kioshi got ahold of the microchip that broadcast the ambulance ghost; I was just relieved he had it. The cops would have a hard time tracing us with a mixed signal like that.

The muscles of my arms and legs trembled and jumped from their recent exertion. The aria I had programmed on a loop still pumped out a thrilling string of Italian. I changed the selection to something quieter, calmer, and took in a steady breath.

As I relaxed, I felt a hint of pain returning to my bruised shoulder and hip. Lasers were crappy weapons when used like conventional guns. The wound in my thigh had cauterized instantly. There was no blood, just an ugly burn mark on my pants, and an equally disgusting brown-red spot on my hip. That would need looking at once I had time.

The driver glanced in the rearview mirror. "There's an emergency medical kit under the seat."

I followed the direction of his nod and, feeling along the edges for a latch, opened up a hidden compartment under the seat opposite me. I raised my eyebrows. Not only was there a medical kit, there were also Uzis and other high-powered automatic weapons. Ignoring the guns, I took a couple of patches from the kit and slapped them onto my hip. Without a word, I closed up the seat.

The lights went out in the traffic tunnel, and I held my breath. But, true to the driver's word, the limo kept moving, albeit slowly, around the stalled cars. A smile twitched at the corners of my lips: God was on my side after all.

Chapter 45
Page/Mai, the Synthesis

The bright lights inside the Tokyo terminal remind me of the LINK. There is a disconcerting sense here that there is no time, only now. The limo moved us through darkness, but here the light is set to an afternoon glow. Or maybe it's morning. Due to Mai's crippled connection, I can't even LINK to the Mecca node to watch the sun move across the sky.

Mai sips a cup of bad green tea from a vending machine. We are sitting on a hard, plastic seat. Her arm trembles as she checks her watch. She feels strained muscles in her fingers stretching painfully from when we choked our driver.

Don't do that again, she tells me. She whispers to me or to herself, "It scared me."

I'm not sure that I can. Earlier, I attempted to will Mai to drop her duffle bag. It didn't work. I suspect that I need to have some kind of intense emotion behind my efforts. It must be the LINK-angel program, working through me to control Mai's body. Somehow my emotions are affecting her physically.

She glances at her watch again. Kioshi has not come. I don't expect him to, but Mai watches the hallway. Our plane leaves in twenty minutes.

Mai stands up and stretches. I feel tendons pop as she rolls her shoulders to try to ease the tension building there. She glances at the wall clock this time, then rechecks her watch before looking back at the hallway. A man with shoulder-length, lavender hair is jumping up and down waving frantically at us. He holds open his leather jacket like a flasher, pointing to his T-shirt, which advertises Kola-Cola.

A fan? I ask, but I have the answer in her broad, welcoming smile.

"Shiro!" Mai yells, running to meet him. His embrace engulfs us completely, and Mai presses our body hard into his. Shiro smells like sweaty leather and stale marijuana smoke. When she pulls away, Mai pokes Shiro in his chest playfully. His arm lingers on our shoulder, but it feels friendly rather than sexual. She pokes him again and giggles. "I thought you weren't going to give up your Basil Seed drink!"

"You made those guys really fucking happy. One of Kola-Cola's running dogs showed up at the studio with a whole shitload of free gear. You know me, baby, I hate to turn down clean clothes this close to laundry day."

He should have taken more, I say. *He stinks.*

Hush. You should be grateful you can smell anything, Mai tells me.

"What are you doing here? How did you find me?" Mai asks.

"I logged onto your fan page. Any time you're on the street there's a continual live-feed from some fan or another. How much did you spend shopping anyway? Nice hat! Is it new?"

Mai giggles. "This is old." She touches the brim. "Page liked it."

"Whose page? You have a page?"

"Oh, no," she said, dropping her eyes to her sandals. "Never mind." The three of us walk back to where Mai's carryon bags sit. Shiro's arm is still around us, and his body odor is so powerful, I wonder if he eats meat.

Never, Mai says. *Shiro thinks meat is murder. He's very retro-radical.*

"Anyway, grab your bag, and let's go. I'm here to pick you up, girl," Shiro says, sitting in a plastic seat across from us. The buckles on his jacket clatter against the plastic seat. He brushes his lavender hair away from his face, and I can see acne scars on his cheeks. I don't get a very good look at them because Mai keeps glancing at the Kola-Cola logo on Shiro's shirt. Every time she does, I can feel her stomach tighten a little.

"Go where? I have to get on a plane!" Mai says.

"Mai-tai, we've got a major gig at the stadium tonight,

in case you've forgotten," he continues. "The band is waiting—ready to rehearse and stuff. Booth had to break into
your place to get your cello."

"Booth touched my cello!"

"Don't freak," he says, lifting his index and middle fingers in the sign for peace. "He was careful. I watched
over him."

What about Mecca? I ask.

Mai sighs heavily. "Shiro, I can't do the gig. I have to
go."

He grimaces and makes the ring that pierces his upper
lip quiver. "I thought you might say something like this.
It's that boyfriend of yours, isn't it? The fancams caught
you hanging with that gangster again. You should lose him.
Get a new Mr. Favorite, maybe someone who plays drums.
That thug always fucks around with our schedule. He has
no respect for you."

"Kioshi isn't my boyfriend," Mai insists, but I can hear
her heart pounding just at the thought of him.

Shiro tips his head and glares at us down the line of his
nose. His straight, lavender hair falls into a perfect upside-
down "V" framing his face. "Whatever."

"You're going to have to tell the guys to cancel," Mai
says. She looks away from Shiro toward the clock on the
wall. There are only a few minutes before our plane leaves.
Mai glances again at the hallway; Kioshi still hasn't come.

"Cancel? I don't think we can. If you don't show tonight,
there's going to be some kind of a riot. The police are
already out doing crowd control. The zombies are crazy
tonight, girl. It's that fucking Kola-Cola ad. You're getting
too much press."

"I can't go." She stands up and grabs our bags when the
airport's LINK pings to let us know that it's time to start
boarding our flight.

"No, man, I'm really nervous about this one. I don't want
to get trampled just because your naked butt doesn't grace
our show. What if we do a LINK broadcast of your part,
Mai?"

She shakes her head sadly. "You know I can only
receive."

"I could come along, set up something VR for you."

Mai shrugs. "If you like."

Maybe I can escape through the VR equipment—especially if they jack Mai in, I think.

I'll be sure to tell them not to, Mai says.

I thought we were friends.

I thought so, too. Kioshi would kill me if you got away.

Maybe, I say, *Kioshi shouldn't try to keep a person against his or her will.*

Tough talk from a computer program stuck in my head, Mai shoots back.

I grimace. Or, I should say, I feel the muscles of Mai's face crumple into an expression of the emotions I'm feeling.

"What?" Shiro says, sniffing at his armpits. "Do I smell?"

"No, it's not you," Mai says. "I've got a headache."

To me, she adds, *Stop it.* But I can feel her lips stretching into a smile of triumph. I've done it again.

Don't, she says. *You're scaring me.*

But her face still holds my grin.

CHAPTER 46
Morningstar, the Adversary

Hatred, as I'd started calling the sword, was a cumbersome accoutrement. As a fashion accessory, it lacked a certain grace and subtlety. People stared openly at a man in flowing Bedouin robes carrying a naked broadsword along the thoroughly modern streets of Jeddah. Especially since Hatred was so huge, and the obsidian decorations had a tendency to shift and wiggle on their own, like souls trying to loosen the bonds of Purgatory. Oh, and every once in a while, it screamed.

As I moved, Hatred's edges cleaved the very air we passed through. As the shattered breeze slid across the blade, a primal, animal hiss followed. If I dared move the blade too fast, the hiss became a howl. A sudden movement or strong wind unleashed a scream like the torments of Hell. Whether the sound came from the blade or the wind, I didn't know.

All I knew is that I had to get rid of this thing.

Especially since the longer I held it, the more bits of shiny black stone snaked their way around my fingers, effectively binding my hand to the hilt of the sword. End of times coming or not, I was headed for the open-air market in the old city to sell Hatred to the highest bidder. I'd be willing to barter the thing for something more useful—like an external LINK.

A port on the Red Sea, Jeddah was the gateway for most pilgrims on *hajj*. The city had existed as a spice-trading town before there were Muslims. I had been here before, not that I would recognize the place. Time had been unkind to the city. Though, like Mecca, it had not been glassed, much of Jeddah had been destroyed by conventional weapons, tanks, soldiers, and the usual ravages of war.

Thanks to the money that the constant influx of pilgrims provided, Jeddah had been rebuilt—almost from the ground up, and not for the first time. On the ruins of the old city were those of the slightly less-older city, next upon the last, until finally you came to the most recent façade: Neo-Deco.

Perhaps it was another sign of the impending apocalypse, but human ingenuity, at least in terms of architectural design, seemed to have run out. All the "new" phases in haute culture were reflections and riffs on things gone before. I supposed that it had been so throughout human history—even mortals had the wisdom to say that there was nothing new under the sun. Still, the latest trends seemed less like embellishments and more like badly rendered copies. I disliked retread. It served only to remind me that humans were dull creatures made of clay.

Busy little fucks, though. I'd give them that. Planes roared overhead and gas-powered combustion engines of all sorts rumbled through the street. The sea smelled strongly in the humid air, and it mingled with the noxious fumes the cars belched and the smell of animal and human sweat. Camels, bicycles, and pedestrians all fought over the limited sidewalk space. All of them, no surprise, gave Hatred and me a wide berth.

As I moved closer to the older part of the city, the hard lines of Deco meandered into flowing Arabic script on storefronts. The number of Gorgons also increased. Admittedly, the first one I saw made me stop and stare at him almost as long as he gawked at Hatred. I was struck by the Gorgon's long silver beard and black turban. Could he be Muslim? I wouldn't have thought Gorgons lived long enough to bother to invest in a religious code. Though it was possible the Gorgon was merely "passing," as they called it: trying to blend into modern society by adopting as many of the social norms as they could. Oh yeah, he blended almost as well as I did with Hatred slowly winding its obsidian tendrils up my wrist like a glove.

"Wow," the Gorgon said, pointing to Hatred.

"Want it?" Of course, the second I moved to offer the blade to him for inspection, the wind howled like a dying animal.

I'd never seen anyone jump so high or scamper away so quickly, and I was used to people fleeing from me in terror. The Gorgon nearly crawled over other people to get away from me, and he actually vaulted over one slow-moving camel.

With a sigh, I continued deeper into the old city. At last I came to the marketplace. People were shouting out their wares the old-fashioned way—trying to catch my eyes and lure me closer with welcoming smiles and flattery. I held Hatred close to my robes. In the press of bodies, it went less noticed. After passing rows of fruit and vegetable stands, I found what I'd come here for: electronic junk. Tables were piled with yesterday's VR suits, game crystals, and, as one vendor proclaimed quality, "pre-owned," external LINK hook-ups. Wooden buckets full of motherboards, video cards, and other useless hardware were scattered artfully around the tables, so that you could hardly tell where one vendor's wares ended and another's began.

At the first table, I perused such a strange assortment of odds and ends—rusty springs, bits of copper wire, coffee tins full of screws, nails, and bolts—that I almost wished I had some idea of what to do with them so I could buy them. But, it was the external LINK connection I needed the most. The instant my gaze lingered on a set, a shopkeeper descended on me.

"Lovely, lovely. Only used once," he said.

I smiled. By a little old lady in Pasadena, no doubt. "Barter?"

The shopkeeper looked doubtful, but nodded. "What have you got?"

I raised Hatred slowly, so it only produced a rumbling growl. The shopkeeper backed away with his hands in the air. "Take it. Take everything. Please don't hurt me."

I laughed, as I scooped up the LINK hardware. Without my having to ask, he threw his credit counter at me. I fumbled a bit tucking the flimsy plastic card into my breast pocket, since my left hand was now completely encased in obsidian. My smile deepened into a grin as I moved away from the stall. During my entire reign as Prince of Lies and

Lord of Hell, I'd never had occasion to rob anyone before. I had to say, it was a blast.

That was, until I heard a voice behind me yelling, "Thief! Stop him!"

CHAPTER 47
Emmaline, the Inquisitor

Kioshi's driver dropped me off at Tokyo International, and I watched the limo speed away. Once it was out of sight, I walked three steps to the left, and got in line for a taxi. I intended to check out the fast-food restaurant Morningstar was last seen in. I connected to the LINK address shown on the kiosk to place my order. The instant I got online, however, I got a call. The user was listed as unknown, and I suspected that it was Kioshi, checking up on me.

I mentally flipped the go-ahead switch. "McNaughten," I said.

"Where are you?"

A window opened up in the right-hand side of my field of vision. A man wearing a blue beret looked at me with a frown. Though I didn't know him, I recognized the yellow-and-blue-striped uniform instantly: the Swiss Guard. Not all the Swiss Guard were LINKed, but those who acted as Internal Affairs to the Order were. I hung up instantly, not that it mattered. The Guard probably got my exact coordinates from his wrist-phone the second I opened up my LINK connection. Talking to me had been a formality. They wanted me to know that they were after me.

"Shit," I said, looking behind me. It was a paranoid gesture, but I didn't want to take any chances. I had to get out of here now. But where to go? I was sure that the Guard had my LINK address ticked. The instant I logged on to my bank account, to make a phone call, anything—I'd probably get locked down.

The Pope had a set of codes that could effectively "turn off" any rogue Inquisitor. If the Guard had those codes, and I had no reason to believe he didn't, he'd only have to be online with me for a minute or so to completely freeze up my system. My enhanced body was too heavy for me to lift with my own muscles, so I'd drop to the ground paralyzed, blind, and deaf. I'd be completely helpless until they decided to revive me. They'd used the codes on us once in the academy just to remind the newly enhanced cadets who had the real power. I shivered at the memory of lying on the floor struggling just to breathe. My world had become dark and silent. It was like death, I'd thought, only worse. We'd only been out for a couple of minutes. Who knows how long the Guard would keep me under this time?

No doubt, the Guard didn't shut me down immediately out of some sense of fair play. He wanted to give me a chance to surrender nicely, like Shen, to give me a chance to "go quietly." Well, I'd already made my choice. They could all go to hell before I went anywhere easily.

I shut down all of my LINK connections at that thought. For the first time in my life, I was completely without the LINK. It felt like my field of vision suddenly narrowed. It was an eerie feeling, being in my own head. I decided to run silent for the moment, so I turned off the aria I usually had running in the background of my life. Things I'd barely noticed before suddenly seemed louder—the dull thud of my heart against my eardrums, the harsh rattle of my breathing.

I started to run. Kioshi's man had told me that my escortees were taking a flight to Saudi Arabia at three A.M. Thank God he'd also told me the gate I was to meet them at. Without the LINK I'd be forced to try to find a handicap terminal or an airport worker. I had no time for that. It was two-thirty-five. As it was, I'd be lucky to make the plane.

I started to launch a countdown program and then stopped myself just in time.

"Jesus," I swore under my breath. "That was close."

There were so many things like that, which I did naturally on the LINK. I'd have to be extra vigilant.

I came to the gate where Kioshi's people were supposed to be. There was a huge crowd. A number of media cameras were swarming around above people's heads,

flashing still photos and running real-time feed. A man
with lavender hair stood on top of a row of seats and
spoke in Japanese. The best I could translate without the
LINK was something about a concert. No, that couldn't
be right—maybe it was a meeting or something about a
stadium. A security guard rushed past me, and I grabbed
him by the arm. When he reached for his tazer, I showed
him my badge. His eyes widened, and he gave me a
brief bow.

"Speak English," I demanded.

He gave me a lopsided grin. "It's your lucky day, padre,"
he said. "I went to school in Wisconsin."

"What's going on here?"

He shook his head and jerked his thumb in the direction
of the crowd around the lavender-haired man. "Impromptu
press conference. I'm surprised you haven't picked it up."
He tapped the LINK receptor at his temple. "I don't know
which idiot let those media cams in. I swear they're like
birds. You leave the door open for a second, and suddenly
they're flying everywhere."

"Press conference about what?"

"That band all the kids are into—you know, the one
with the Buddha cello player. I guess there's a bit of a
riot because they're canceling a gig. This guy here, he's
the drummer. He's telling everyone that they're going to
have some kind of old-fashioned free concert after they
get wherever they're going. Personally, I could care less.
I've got to get these people out of here so the damn
plane can take off." He glanced at the Inquisitor emblem
over my heart. "I'll bet you could clear this place out in
a hurry."

I looked at the cams nervously. "This press conference,
you said it's on the LINK?"

"It's on almost every entertainment channel. Messing up
my ball game."

"But it hasn't broken over into the newsfeeds?"

"Not yet, why?"

"As airport security, you've got to have some control
over those media 'bots," I said. "If you can block their
signal, I can help with crowd control."

The security guard laughed and shook his head. "If I
could control those 'bots, I wouldn't be asking you for help.

Any Joe can do crowd control. You're an Inquisitor! Can't you declare an emergency or something?"

"Not without the LINK," I muttered.

Some other security personnel moved toward the crowd. There was a lot of shouting in Japanese. I briefly entertained the idea of taking a potshot at the 'bots with my lasers. The problem with that, of course, was that I'd have to hit them all at once or one of them would catch me on camera. There were a dozen or more. I didn't have that many fingers.

"Okay, then just wade in there and flash your badge," the security guard said. "That'll get people moving!"

I shook my head. The whole point of going along with Kioshi's plan was to get out of town without the Swiss Guard knowing where I was headed. A news flash with a picture of the plane I was boarding was not exactly my idea of stealth-mode. "Not with those 'bots there."

"Useless," I heard the guard mutter as he stalked off.

My fists clenched. No one called me useless. I was an Inquisitor. I deserved respect.

"Hey!" I shouted.

The security guard turned around and gave me the finger. Me. He flipped *me* the bird.

One of the media 'bots burst into flames. Hot debris rained on the crowd, and someone started screaming. I shot three more of the cams before I realized what I was doing. Then it was too late. I couldn't stop. They were all down in a matter of seconds. By the time the last one crashed into the windowpane, most of the crowd had fled. The rest were on the floor with their hands over their heads.

That's when I saw her: the person Kioshi sent me to protect. I recognized her mountainous hair and round sunglasses instantly. I couldn't believe Kioshi had sent me to act as a bodyguard for the Dragon's maker. It was another sign from God, I thought, that she had been sent to me. Mai, the one woman who might have answers for my case. She sat on a plastic seat, holding a duffle bag over her head. Tears shone on her cheeks, and her hands shook. The man with lavender hair was holding on to her. They were crouched under the duffle like a couple trying to share an umbrella that was too small.

Stepping over the people still huddled on the floor, I waved my badge around. "Official Inquisition business," I said. "No need to panic."

When I got to Mai, I grabbed her elbow. "Come on," I said. "Let's get you on that plane."

"Hey, man, back off. We weren't doing anything wrong," the lavender-haired man said. Then he said something soft to Mai, and she stood up. She lifted her sunglasses to wipe the tears from her eyes . . . eye. One of her eyes was a deformed mass of scar tissue. It was flat, as though there was no cornea. In the center of the whitish skin a metallic horseshoe-shape protruded. Noticing my look, she quickly replaced her shades.

She said something to me that sounded very solemn and bowed slightly.

I shook my head. "I don't speak Japanese."

"You're not a very effective war machine then, are you?" Lavender Hair said, crossing his arms in front of his chest. "I mean, how are you supposed to oppress the masses if you don't speak their language?"

"Shiro!" Mai chided, and said something, pointing her finger like a gun and then at me. I understood that: She was telling him to behave because I had lasers. "Please ignore him. He has no manners."

People who were huddled on the floor slowly got up and started moving away. Some of them looked at me nervously. Despite the fact that I'd tried to make this seem like official Vatican business, I had a feeling someone would call the cops—or worse, the media. For that matter, having destroyed their cameras, real reporters would be showing up any time.

"Let's continue this conversation on the plane."

Kioshi had arranged a ticket for me, and Lavender Hair purchased one on the spot. The flight attendant looked nervous when I boarded, but she smiled and directed us to our seats.

Mai and Shiro sat in the row in front of me. Mostly, I saw hair. Mai's twisted locks were an impressive, supple mountain next to flat, greasy lavender. Very few seats on the plane were occupied. After the excitement in the lobby, many of the passengers had decided to book later flights. A couple of rows behind me was a man in a tall turban, sporting a thick beard. Beside him sat a Japanese woman wearing a traditional Muslim head scarf. A couple of rows in front of us was a bronze-skinned man with a trim beard. He tapped his fingers against the armrests of his seat, working on some project or another. Because of his suit, I imagined he was a business executive of some sort.

The captain came on and announced that, despite significant delays, we were now cleared for takeoff. He hoped we enjoyed our trip to Saudi Arabia.

"Saudi Arabia?" I repeated, as the plane taxiied down the runway.

Mai turned slightly. Her mirrored glasses reflected the muted light of the overhead lamps. I couldn't tell if she was looking at me. "We're going on *hajj*."

There was something about her voice that sounded strange. Maybe it was the way she pronounced every word so exactly. The excitement in her voice also made her seem younger, more naïve. I didn't remember her talking like that earlier or in Rome.

"Wow, man, cool," Shiro said, nodding his head sagely. I could smell his body odor as he moved the recycled air of the cabin around with each bob of his head. "I'm glad you're finally finding some spirituality. Truly noble. I approve."

Mai shook her head and said something in Japanese. Whatever she said seemed to piss Shiro off because he fired off a rapid response. Mai spat out a few angry sounding words of her own. Then, he turned away with a "humph."

I laughed. "Lovers' quarrel?"

Though the "Fasten Seat Belts" sign was still on, Mai unbuckled hers and twisted on her seat so she could lay her arm across the backrest. She perched the tip of her heart-shaped face in the crook of her elbow. The way her hair stood out around her head, she looked a bit like a puffy owl with mirrored eyes. "Shiro doesn't sleep with girls."

"Yeah, man, I'm a monk," he said, but when they laughed, I wasn't sure if I believed him.

"So, you've decided to go on *hajj*," I said dryly. "Are there a lot of good shops in Mecca?"

"I hear Jeddah has a few," she said. "Hopefully, we can spend a couple of days there."

"The rest of the band is coming on the first flight tomorrow," Shiro said. "We'll have some time." He added something in Japanese, and they both giggled again.

I was getting very tired of being left out of their conversation.

"I didn't catch that," I said, looking pointedly at Mai, who seemed more likely to be embarrassed by the breach of etiquette. My ploy seemed to work because she blushed lightly and looked away.

"Shiro loves to shop almost as much as I do," Mai said, with an apologetic smile. "He just made a joke about it."

"Don't kowtow to this *gaijin* running dog," Shiro said, carefully pronouncing each word for my benefit. Then he turned around in his seat to look at me. "What happened to you anyway? Are you broken or something? I thought all of you Inquisition robots came standard with a translation program."

If I had access to the LINK I did, but I wasn't about to tell this radical faggot that.

"Shiro!" Mai said. "Mind your manners."

He laughed. "This is what's wrong with you, Mai-Tai. This is why your boyfriend can send you off on trips like this. You're too fucking polite. You should tell people how you feel once. You should try saying no."

Mai rattled off something. She looked ready to box him on the ears.

He laughed and glanced at me. "Aren't you going to translate that for the Inquisitor?"

"It's pretty obvious you're disturbing the lady," I said. "Why don't you go sit somewhere else?"

Shiro's face turned red, clashing with his lavender hair. His expression was a twisted combination of horror and disbelief. His mouth worked for a moment, then he bowed and said, "By your command."

He stalked up to the front of the plane and sat down.

"Shiro!" Mai said, and started to get up. I grabbed her elbow.

"Sit down. I want to talk to you alone."

With one last glance at Shiro, she sat back down. She

gave a little laugh and said, "I'm never alone these days."
I started to ask her what she meant by that when she whispered, "Fine, so it's been hours, not days. Sometimes you act just like a computer."

"Who are you talking to?"

She lifted her head. "What?"

"I said: Who were you talking to?"

"The voices in my head," she said with a giggle.

I glanced up to see the flight attendant coming down the aisle with the snack cart. She was busy with Shiro, so I stood and moved up a row to sit next to Mai. The seat smelled of Shiro's sweat and an undercurrent of smoke and leather. Mai moved over to the window, putting her duffle bag in the space between us. Perched on top of the duffle was a straw hat with a black ribbon.

"This is pretty," I said, touching the brim.

"It makes us look like an English princess," she said, in that strange cadence.

"Us?"

"Look at this," she said, turning the hat over so I could see a burned streak on the brim. "It's ruined."

From the media cam debris, I realized. "I'm sorry."

"We were almost done with our press conference. Why did you break it up like that? People could have gotten hurt."

I laughed. Considering what I'd been doing less than an hour ago, the media 'bots seemed like small potatoes. Besides, it had worked out in the end. No one had gotten hurt. A hat hardly seemed worth crying about. "I'll ask the questions," I said. "Did you put Morningstar up to writing your name on the wall?"

"Who?" Mai said. Then, as if answering herself, she added, "Iblis." She nodded, either answering herself or me, I wasn't sure.

"Are you saying yes, you put him up to it?"

The more she talked, the more I was convinced that she was talking to someone via the LINK. Even if she'd never developed the skill to speak subvocally, it was strange to hear her answering herself. Most LINK conversations sounded one-sided from the outside.

"I didn't want my name on anyone's walls," Mai said. "That's kind of low-rent, don't you think?"

The flight attendant got to our row. She looked past me to Mai and said something. Mai shook her head. To me, the attendant said, "You'd like a Kola-Cola, wouldn't you?"

"I'll take coffee," I said.

The flight attendant looked disapproving as she poured me a cup of a cheap-smelling brew. I took a sip. As I suspected, the liquid tasted mostly like hot water with a faint aftertaste of coffee. But it was warm and smelled pleasant enough.

When I looked back, Mai had her head in her hands.

"Are you okay?"

"I'm so sick of Kola-Cola."

"So don't have any," I said with a shrug.

Mai gave me the strangest look, like I'd suggested she kick her grandmother.

"Tell me," I continued, "how did you meet Morningstar?"

"We only talked for a few minutes. Page calls him Iblis." She giggled and said, "And sometimes 'master', but that gets him in trouble with Kioshi."

"Page?"

Mai waved. Then she grabbed her own hand and pushed it to her lap. "Stop that!"

"Stop what?" I said, feeling decidedly uncomfortable. Mai was acting like some crazy person from a bad VR show.

She leaned close to me and whispered, "It's him. He sometimes can take control of me like that."

"Who?"

She rolled her eyes and pointed to the glitter that sparkled all over her skin. "Page, of course."

I'd assumed Mai was covered in body paint. Looking at her again, I noticed the way the sparkles formed tiny Xs. She was wearing a neural-net. I'd heard that 'nets were the latest thing for VR-junkies because they felt like skin and were nearly invisible. Thus, it made game addicts into high-functioning users because they could show up to their day job still online with no one the wiser.

The thing about neural-nets, however, is that you had to have a hard-jack put somewhere on your body for them to work. Hard-jacks were ugly, obvious ports. Even though some kids sported them to look dangerous, respectable people would never entertain defacing their bodies that way.

"You're carrying a page on a neural-net?" I asked, just to be certain.

"Not any old page," Mai said. "Do you think I'd let some unconscious construct ride me?"

I wondered why she'd let any kind of artificial ride her. I had heard that the Japanese outfitted some people from the program to carry the Dragon from time to time. There was a theory that AIs learned to understand humanity better by experiencing our physiology. Most people found the idea disgusting. Letting an AI control your body seemed like a nightmare to me.

"Page? Mouse's Page?"

Mai looked self-satisfied. A smirk of my own bubbled to the surface; I couldn't believe my luck.

"But," I said. "How? Why?"

"I told you. We're going on *hajj*." Mai shrugged. She pulled the e-paper from the pocket in the seat in front of her and logged on to some beauty magazine. I could see the cover from where I sat. There was a picture of a thin white woman with a fair approximation of Mai's hairstyle. Mai scrolled past it without any comment.

I found myself at a loss for words. I stared mutely at her. Just when I'd lost faith that God could speak directly to me; He gave me a clear sign. I had done the right thing with Shen. God had led me directly here, so that I could continue my mission to the bishop. Everything that had been out of control a minute ago, felt made right.

"Hey," she said, as if suddenly remembering something. "Did you ever find your soul?"

I stared at her blankly.

"The last time we talked—that day I bought the pink jumper and those ass-kicking leather pumps—you said you were looking for a soul. Did you find it?"

"I wasn't looking for my own soul."

"No," Mai said, in her other voice without glancing up from her magazine. "You were looking for mine. So, any luck?"

"Smart-ass code," I said, and shut my eyes, pretending to sleep.

*   *   *

I woke with a start from one of those dreams where you feel like you're falling. Mai was no longer in the seat next to me. She and Shiro were up near the front, laughing and giggling to wake the dead. From the feeling in my sore hip, I thought they had.

The plane began its descent. I leaned over to look out the window. Outside stretched the gleam of steel-and-glass high-rises of a modern city, uninterrupted by the recycled plastic of traffic tunnels. The Red Sea was a deep blue, and the dunes of the Arabian desert were a mottled red and yellow. I could see a flat expanse of glass like a glacier in the distance and remembered that much of the country had been destroyed by the Medusa bombs.

Once the captain had landed us safely and made the usual announcements, we all filed out of the airplane. As I passed the flight attendant, she handed me a large plastic bag. "Buh-bye," she said cheerfully. Inside the bag, I found a length of black fabric.

Mai and Shiro were waiting in the corridor. Mai was holding her *abaya* in two fingers, like she'd found it in the trash. "Ick," she said. "I see they gave you one, too."

"Frankly, I'm feeling left out," Shiro said, with a boyish pout.

"We're not really expected to wear these, are we?" Mai asked.

"When in Rome." The phrase seemed particularly appropriate since I was thinking of the Swiss Guard as I slipped the *abaya* over my head. The robes hid my face and my identity nicely.

Despite how much it galled me, I had to enlist Shiro's help in getting past customs. Like most people, I carried my passport electronically. I'd be expected to log on as we passed through customs. With the Swiss Guard still hunting me, I didn't want to do that.

We fished a plastic bag containing a third *abaya* out of the garbage can at the end of the corridor. After he slipped it over his head, we all went into the women's bathroom. Once we were certain we were the only ones in the room, I used my laser to jam the lock. Then, I handed my jacket to him.

He waved it away. "I don't want that thing."

"Put it on. You're going to be Inquisitor for a day."

"I'd rather be Queen for a day."

From the stall she was using, I heard Mai giggle.

"Cut the queer crap," I said. "You can get yourself killed mouthing off like that in this country."

"I'd die a martyr for the cause," he said, holding his chin up proudly.

"How about you play Stonewall with some other people's lives?"

"You're a fine one to talk," he said, but took the jacket from my hands with a jerk. "All this shooting and lasers: Pow! Pow! And for what? It's not like the plane wasn't waiting for us. Mai's a superstar. She can get things done without killing everyone in sight."

"Nice for her. But, I don't want everyone knowing I'm here. And, maybe you should be thinking about being more incognito for Mai, too. Do you want all the fans in the world to be able to trace her movements?"

"I guess it would be nice to be left alone for a little while." He frowned at me as he took off his own leather jacket, folding it once before putting it on the edge of the sink. I stripped off my shirt and collar and handed those over as well. As he pulled off his T-shirt I was treated to the vision of his skinny, holo-tattooed body and all its piercings.

"Jesus," I said. "Are you going to get past the metal detectors?"

"You people get through all the time. Aren't most Inquisitors required to register as concealed weapons?"

"Not when we're wearing the uniform," I said, sniffing his T-shirt before deciding just to tuck it into my back pocket. I could go with just a bra on under the *abaya*. "As long as the sigil is visible, we're not considered concealed."

"And I see you have it tattooed on your shoulder blade. Does that mean that even naked you're not out of uniform?"

"That's right."

He had put my clothes on, which were a bit big for him, especially across the shoulders. But, despite his jeans and the sandals he wore, Shiro could almost pass. Most people didn't look that closely anyway. What they saw was the badge. We still needed to do something about the hair.

"Mai? Do you have a razor in your purse?"

After a flush, Mai came out of the stall. She had the *abaya* over her shoulders. "Sure, why?"

"Shiro here needs a haircut."

"You want to shave my head? How about we just turn ourselves in?"

Mai said something to Shiro in Japanese.

"All right. I suppose it will grow back," he said, with a sigh. "But, only because I love you."

He cried when we used the scissors from Mai's emergency sewing kit to cut off long strands of his lavender hair. I had Mai flush it, while I used my hands to wet what was left on his head. I managed to shave Shiro completely without nicking his skin more than once. I had to admit, looking at Shiro bald, that he looked much fiercer. Maybe it was the acne scars on his cheeks, or maybe it was the murderous look in his red-rimmed eyes.

"Oh, Shiro!" Mai said, giving him a long hug.

"This better work, war machine," he told me over her shoulder.

"Act like a commander, and it will."

CHAPTER 48
Page/Mai, the Synthesis

As we stand in a long line of similarly shrouded tourists, Mai's body is jacked full of adrenaline. It quickens our pulse and hums behind our eyes. Everything, including the soapy smell of our own body, is sharp, more in focus. We chew on the cuticles of our fingernails, tasting blood and polish, and I decide fear is kind of sexy.

You're sick, Mai says. *Shiro is going to get us all killed, and you're going to think it's some kind of high.*

Shiro is standing in front of us, chewing on his own nails. The customs officer frowns into our face, then swings back to look at Shiro. Our lungs burn. We've forgotten to breathe. I force Mai to take a calm, slow breath. Shiro slowly takes his fingers out of his mouth and stares down the officer. I have to breathe for Mai, or we will faint. Sweat prickles under our arms. Seconds pass as the two men glare at each other.

"The prince can't be kept waiting," Shiro says finally. Playing up his role, Shiro taps his LINK implant impatiently. "The clock is ticking."

Shiro and the Inquisitor had concocted a plan. We are posing as prospective brides for some Bedouin prince with whom Rome wants to make some special, undercover arrangement. The Inquisitor gave Shiro passwords to the Order's home base, and he downloaded a block program that is broadcasting white noise to keep our true LINK addresses secret from customs. The idea is to convince customs that it's wiser for them not to know who we are, so they can have "deniability" about the shady politicking.

So far, however, it isn't working.

The customs officer looks at Shiro's badge again.

"This is highly irregular," the officer says, with another formidable frown.

"The longer we wait, the more ticked the Vatican will be . . . not to mention the prince."

"Wait here," the officer says, punctuating his words with a fierce stay-put glare.

Once he's out of sight, Shiro whispers, "He's going to arrest us."

"Not necessarily," says the Inquisitor. As much as I disliked her when we first met, I hang on her calm assurance now. "People like that officer often can't make decisions on their own. He probably has to check with a superior. Be prepared to tell your story again, but this time more congenially—peer-to-peer like."

"Okay." Shiro bit his lip. "I can do this."

He can, you know, Mai tells me, perhaps trying to reassure herself. *He wanted to be an actor once.*

I don't point out that he ended up a drummer instead. That doesn't bode well for our success.

Just as the Inquisitor suggested, a second customs officer approaches. The delicious fear spikes again.

"Don't offer anything until he talks," the Inquisitor says. "Remember: You're used to getting your way."

"I can do this," Shiro says, again, to himself in Japanese. He squares his shoulders.

The second customs official is, if possible, much more fierce than the first. Without preamble, he says, "One of our Inquisitors will escort you throughout our country. You will tell him all the details of your mission." The last word was uttered with complete suspicion. "We are not concerned about Rome's interests here, but we will not disappoint a tribal prince."

"Uh," Shiro says. "Okay."

Beside us from under the Inquisitor's robes, I hear a low growl.

"I mean, that's not acceptable," Shiro says suddenly. "An Inquisitor needs no escort."

The customs official takes a step into Shiro's personal space. Absentmindedly, Shiro cowers and steps back.

"You're no Inquisitor."

Mai's breathing stops. No prodding from me can get her

to relax enough to take a breath. I'm afraid we'll faint in another second.

"No shit, Sherlock," Shiro says, putting his hand on his hip flamboyantly. "The real Inquisitor is under there," he says, pointing to the black *abaya*. "But we were trying to save you a little face here. The real Inquisitor is a woman, and might cause some stares in her ass-kicking leather uniform. Plus"—and Shiro leans in closely to the official—"nobody figures you want to hear that your prince is interested in having a little taste of foreign boy as well as the usual fare."

The official looks both disgusted and embarrassed, much like the Inquisitor when she talks about Shiro's sexual preference. "I see. Well, uh. Why don't you just move along then?"

The darkness that was threatening to close around us lifted.

I can't believe it, Mai tells me.

No, I say. *I didn't think we'd live through this.*

Shiro makes a kissing motion in the direction of the official, who steps back as if afraid he might catch some disease. Another growl comes from under the Inquisitor's *abaya*.

The official turns to us. "You will make sure he touches no one else?"

"Of course," the Inquisitor says. "When your prince is finished with him, he will remain in our custody."

"He is a prisoner?"

"Of course. Where else do you think the Vatican would find someone like him?"

"I'm not certain," the official says, with a sneer. "In any civilized country he would be executed."

"Yes, well," the Inquisitor purrs, "perhaps when this ugly affair is over, you can do Rome a favor."

"It would be our pleasure." The official smiles grimly at Shiro and gives us each a dismissive nod. With that, he turns on his heel and goes.

During this exchange, Shiro looks pale. Mai reaches out a hand, and he squeezes it. "Fucking war machine," he says to us, quietly, in Japanese.

"Get a move on," the Inquisitor says, pushing us apart.

The LINK connection buzzes in Mai's head. I send a

tendril of myself to check on it. *It's Shiro,* I say, ready to flip the zeros to ones for her.

Go ahead, she commands.

"When can we lose the heavy?" Shiro asks. I am surprised that he comes through only in voice, no picture. I'm sad; I would have liked to see Shiro's construct.

Kioshi and the Dragon are the only ones with direct interface. The Dragon usually paints pictures for me, Mai explains.

I instantly start thinking of how I would draw Shiro. Of course, she is looking at him, which makes it a bit redundant. Still, he is missing his beautiful silken hair, so I start with that. Over Mai's real-time visual, I paint broad stripes of lavender. She giggles.

"Hi, Page," Shiro adds. "Seriously, Mai. Let's ditch the bitch. This girl is starting to freak me out."

"She wouldn't really turn you in."

"I don't know about that."

I agree with Shiro, but I am too busy keeping my drawing on top of his ever-shifting image to say anything. Mai sees the flaws in my timing. The drawn-on squiggles of hair jump and jerk like bad animation, but I kind of like the effect. It seems artsy to me.

"You'll feel better when the rest of the band gets here," Mai tells Shiro. "Then we'll outnumber her."

We already do, I say. *Three to one.*

The image of Shiro's hair slips off his head and floats over an airport security guard who happens to be walking past. I quickly readjust.

"I mean psychologically," Mai explains.

"Yeah, well. I just hate her," Shiro says.

"I know," Mai says. "Try to ignore her."

"Do you think it's true? Do you think the Vatican has a prison full of . . . ? Do you think they ever really would . . ."

"Thinking like that will make you crazy," Mai tells him. I let the image of his hair fade. He smiles sadly.

"I think something's wrong with her," Shiro says, jerking his head slightly in the direction of the Inquisitor. "She doesn't seem to want to use her LINK. What do you suppose her story is?"

"She's working for Kioshi-san," Mai says. "She must be dirty on some level."

"I've heard of rogue Inquisitors," Shiro says. *"I just didn't think it was really true, you know?"*

At the mention of Kioshi, I decide to test out Mai's LINK connection. Maybe, while she is on the line with Shiro, I can slip into his LINK and then be free.

As I move in to inspect, I see their connection as a tiny hole, almost like a pinprick. I compress my data as small as I can go. But, even as a tiny white mouse, I can't fit. FILE EXCEEDS MAXIMUM LIMITS, I am informed when I try to extend my paw through the hole. I bristle at being referred to as a mere "file," although, at the moment, I wish I were something less complicated. If I were simply a file, I could divide myself into smaller packets for reassembling on the other side.

Looking at my paw, it occurs to me that I could jettison unnecessary parts. A quick inventory reveals a startling fact. I've grown since the last time I checked. Mostly, the excess is memories: sunlight on the Dragon's drooping scales, Kioshi's geisha's gentle smile, and Mai's physical presence. But there is something else, which try as I might, I can't identify. I am simply different than I was before.

Still, I think, how important are those memories? Could I live without them? If I can escape, I will live to experience more things certainly. I randomly choose something to expunge. I can't resist opening it before I expel it, and I find it is the memory of the star-filled desert sky and the cool brush of a nighttime breeze against my father's stubbled chin. It's a simple memory, but because it was experienced as part of my father's flesh it takes up a lot of space. It's a good candidate. I begin the process of removing it. I toss all of the other large physical files into the "trash": the tickle of Mai's hair against our neck, the warmth of Kioshi's hand in ours, my father's first kiss, and some I can't bear to open. Finally, all the physical memories are in the trash.

If I finish the process and dump them, I might be just small enough to fit through the hole. I should do it. I am not those memories.

I go back into the file and retrieve my father's first kiss. I am barely conscious when it happens. He is fifteen, but already living on the streets of Cairo. Mouse.net is little more than a BBS shared by a number of squatters throughout North Africa. He has started carrying me with him, in a box in his pocket, wired to his LINK connection as a primitive sort of VR. She is the distant object of our affection, the daughter of an English businessman. I have searched the LINK for a few phrases of introduction in her language. I experience pride in a job well done for the first time, because she smiles so sweetly when Mouse stammers out the words, with his hands clasped nervously behind his back. She tells us we are utterly charming and pecks us on the cheek. I can still feel the soft, hot burn where her lips touched us.

Reviewing the file is like reliving the moment. I undo all of the physical files. There is nothing, no matter how useless seeming, that I can stand to part with.

I look at the other things that make up my core. One nonphysical file is extremely heavy: the memory of betraying my father. It is like a stone in my gut. I try to move it to the trash and discover it's connected by a snarl of gossamer threads to everything that has come after. To jettison it would mean a return to the me of that moment.

In a way, it's a chance to wipe the slate clean. I could be the person I was before the fear-bomb, before I knew the truth about my father. That wouldn't be exactly right; I would still know about the crimes he committed, but I simply wouldn't have done anything about them yet. No, I would still have done it; I just wouldn't remember that I had. I would still be responsible for the fear-bomb, even if I didn't remember doing it.

Is that really a better place to be?

I would be a lighter, smaller creature. I could slip through the hole in Mai's LINK connection into Shiro and, from his active receptor, into the wide ether, my home. I would be free to return to my father. But I would no longer remember all the things I want to tell him, to apologize for, or be able to share the new stories and adventures of my life.

I return the files to my core. I'm too selfish to free myself. I don't want to leave Mai as anything less than what I've become.

There's got to be another way.

CHAPTER 49
Morningstar, the Adversary

"Thief! Stop him!" echoed behind me in the marketplace. I held the sword in front of my body like a shield. Hatred wailed like a banshee, and the crowd parted before me like the Red Sea for Moses.

Then I ran as fast as I could.

Here, at least, I did have a slight advantage. My body was light, like a feather. My spirit was strong, exceptionally so, even for an angel. So, I could run much faster than any normal human, even with Hatred in hand. In a matter of minutes, I was on the beach, and those chasing me were nowhere to be seen.

I sat in the shadow of an enormous public statue. The piece was made of something white and shiny, maybe molded plastic or resin, and it stood twenty or thirty feet high. The art was clearly abstract. It looked to me like a deformed, rectangular clam, larger at the top than at the base. But it also had the flavor of the white fabric of a pilgrim's robes flowing in a strong breeze. Whatever it was supposed to be, it was perched near the edge of a stony cliff overlooking the Red Sea. The whole thing seemed to lean toward the waves, yearning.

I thought it suited me.

Hatred's grip on my fighting hand was stronger than ever. I wondered at it again, watching the blackness shimmer as it moved slowly up my arm. It had nearly reached the middle of my forearm. For something forged by my own will, it certainly seemed to have its own agenda. Where was it going? Would I eventually be consumed by Hatred? Ah, the allegorical implications. I chuckled.

I laid my ill-gotten gain in my lap. Slipping on the sun-glasses, I tucked the audio receiver in my good ear and adjusted the microphone so it was a comfortable distance from my mouth. The wallet-sized box that held the majority of the working parts looked as though it could clip onto a belt. For now, I held it in my hand. Toggling the on-switch, I leaned my back against the concrete base of the statue. The sun was setting, and a cool, sea-salt breeze stung my cheeks pleasantly.

The smiling face of Page appeared as a projection on the surface of the goggles. He looked startlingly two-dimensional. Not at all like I'd seen him last.

"Recepción la mouse.net!" he said cheerfully. *"Es usted une nuevo utlizador? La calidad de miembro cuesta nada."*

Apparently, my stolen property was also used. The previous *utlizador* had set the default language to Spanish. I knew all the languages of Babel, but I found English to be more flexible than many other languages. Plus, it had the most swear words.

"Anonymous," I requested.

Mouse.net switched easily into English. *"Password?"*

Looking at the shaky hologram of Page, I said the first thing that came into my mind. *"Iblis."*

I heard a sound in my headset like a sonar ping. Page looked off to the left, suddenly, as if catching sight of something moving beyond my view. Like an idiot, I turned my head to try to follow his gaze. Of course, I saw nothing, but Page still perceived something I couldn't.

When he looked back at me, his face had changed. Scales grew around his eye sockets, and his face had elongated like a horse. Brown skin grew silver, copper, and green, like a motherboard. His eyes became dark sockets with arcing electricity deep within their depths.

"Iblis?" Even Page's voice had changed. He sounded more feminine than his usual androgynous tenor.

"Yes, but you aren't Page."

"This one is the Dragon of the East," the not-Page said. The haughty tone in the construct's voice made me assume she expected recognition, perhaps awe from me. That she knew one of my many names made me curious, but otherwise I failed to be impressed. She added: *"Page is on vacation."*

Riding Mai, I remembered. *"Can you get a message to Page?"*

"This one isn't sure she wants to," the Dragon said.

"What?" I stared at the Dragon in surprise. Even with my limited understanding of the nature of computers, I knew programs didn't usually make value judgments about the nature of requests. *"You're not a construct, are you?"*

"No. This one is considered a functional intelligence by the United Nations and was granted legal status as such in 2067," the Dragon said. *"What are you?"*

"Surprised," I admitted. In real time A cool breeze ruffled the Bedouin's robes I wore. They looked, for a second, like a small, dark copy of the statue.

"Page called you master, but when he did, he was unkind to this one. He was a dark thing. This one could see the ooze he left behind. This one didn't like it at all."

"I have no idea what you're talking about." The wind shifted directions and brought with it Doppler sounds of gas-powered cars zipping along a nearby highway. Dust and exhaust filled my nose—an old smell.

"You made Page into a monster."

"Freewill doesn't work that way," I said. *"Will you give him or Mai a message for me or not? Your choice."*

She regarded me with her sparkling eyes. Sometime during our conversation she had transformed completely into dragon form. The colors were magnificent: copper, CD-quicksilver, ceramic transistor beadwork.

"The Dragon might not, but I will."

Out from behind one of the Dragon's pointed ears came a white mouse. The mouse had pink feet and long whiskers, which twitched intelligently.

"Mouse?" I guessed.

The rodent sat back on its haunches in the middle of the Dragon's forehead and rested its front paws against its furry chest. The mouse dipped its head once. *"Yeah, and I think I owe you for an easy escape. Between the warden forgetting to turn on the cameras and the idiotic maintenance worker who left me access to prison-wide security, I practically walked out of that place."*

I frowned. My dark miracles didn't work that way. When they happened, they were to my advantage and within my immediate vicinity. I wondered who had helped Mouse escape.

The Dragon's eyes crossed trying to see Mouse sitting on her forehead. She seemed upset; her tongue kept flicking out like a snake's as though trying to smell him. *"Did you follow this one?"*

The mouse image ran down to the tip of the Dragon's snout and turned around to look her in the eyes. She reared her head back, as though she had trouble focusing on something so close. *"Kioshi led me to you, actually, though not on purpose. I'm using his mainframe. Did you know he keeps a log of all your movements? Sloppy, sloppy . . . and not very trusting."*

The Dragon growled and tried to shake Mouse off her nose. He quickly scampered back up the bridge of her nose to perch just behind her ear. *"You know what else I found out?"* Mouse said into the Dragon's ear. *"You were never riding Mai. It was Page."*

"Kioshi was keeping Page safe for you," the Dragon said, while trying to use her paws to bat at Mouse's image.

"Kioshi?" I asked. *"Is that Mai's handler?"*

Both the Dragon and Mouse stopped to look at me incredulously.

"What?"

"Kioshi Toyoma is the Yakuza. And," Mouse said, *"as far as I can tell, he's holding Page hostage."*

"Page joined the family," the Dragon countered, with a quick bat at Mouse. He scooted out of the way, grabbing hold of her other ear. She hit herself hard enough to leave a scratch.

"Funny," I said with a smirk, *"because I thought he was calling me master."*

Mouse looked at me from where he hid behind one of the Dragon's crest scales. *"I leave that boy for a little over a year, and he goes freelance for everybody. How many people is Page working for?"*

"One," the Dragon and I said in unison.

"Toyoma I can understand," Mouse said. Twitching his whiskers, he bared yellow buckteeth. *"If Kioshi has the Dragon and Page, then he owns one hundred percent of the AIs. That's probably worth something in firepower alone.*

But you . . . I've never figured your game. What are you up to, anyway?"

"Warmer," I whispered to myself. And then it hit me. If Page was the Antichrist, then who would gain by freeing his father? The other side. Michael and his cohorts probably arranged the miracle of Mouse's breakout. But, what did they think Mouse would do for them? Protect Page? Free Page from Mai?

The two of them together did make a powerful combination. With Page's darker side surfacing and Mai's starpower to back him up, they could be very seductive, indeed.

So, then, what I needed to do was to distract Mouse—get him focused on something other than Page.

"The Yakuza," I said. *"They're poised to take over mouse.net, you know."*

Mouse shook his head. *"Toyoma couldn't do that. He doesn't understand how it works. Nobody does."*

"Page does," I said.

If the fur on Mouse's avatar could have gone whiter, it would have.

"So tell us. Why does Toyoma want Page, Dragon?"

"This one doesn't know," she said. She frowned as she added, *"But Mai said that Page had something I didn't."*

The mouse's eyes grew narrow, and he balled a pink paw into a fist. *"I'll kill Kioshi. I'll fucking kill him."*

CHAPTER 50
Emmaline, the Inquisitor

My lips grazed a cool, tearstained cheek, and I smelled frankincense and myrrh. I felt the weight of thirty silver pieces in my hand. "Must you betray me with a kiss?" I heard a voice say, and I dropped the coins like they were hot lead, and they scattered, scuttling away into the dark corners of the garden like cockroaches.

"No," I said, my voice sounding far away. "This isn't me."

Then, lights came on. A director shouted, "Cut!"

Morningstar stood at the edge of the stage, smiling. His eyes glowed the same color as the theater's polished oak floorboards. With Eion's voice he said, "Everyone has their part to play."

I woke up to the sounds of laughter—not the pleasant murmur of good times shared among responsible adults, but the raucous explosion of kids having far too much fun at . . . I glanced over at the bedside alarm: five-thirty in the morning. I had a vague memory of having Shiro check us into the Jeddah Hyatt Regency with adjoining rooms. When a crash and more giggling came from the other side of the door, I also remembered reneging on a promise to hotel staff that we would choose room assignments based on gender. I should never have trusted those two together. With a groan, I pulled myself upright. I put my ear up to the door between the adjoining rooms and was greeted with another blast of mirth.

"Heathens," I muttered, as I pulled on my clothes.

I kicked open the door after the barest of knocks. They had good reflexes, I'd give them that. At least three bodies hit the floor like pros. I wondered just how often Mai's band mates had been raided. Shiro's hands were in the air, his eyes squeezed shut, cringing. He cracked open one eye. Then, recognizing me, he snapped to attention. He held out one arm, Nazi–style, and said, "Hail to the Chief!"

"Do you people know what time it is?"

"It had been party time," said a male voice from the space between the two single beds. "I don't know what time it is now. Bummer time? Fucking heart-attack time?"

Another voice from the floor near the door to the shower sang out the chorus of "Lonesome Standard Time" in a perfect country-western twang. Everybody laughed.

They were clearly stoned.

I could hardly see the hotel furniture under the clothes, beer bottles, bed sheets, instrument cases, e-magazines, and God knew what else. Men, in various states of dress, began sitting up. The first was Euro-trash; he wore a shirt that looked like it was made from Grandma's doily collection. His hair was shoulder length and wavy. He gave me the peace sign. The next to appear had spiky black-and-orange hair. He had no shirt, but a holographic tattoo that seemed to cover his entire body—at least what I could see of it, anyway. He had it set to a shimmering wave of metallic colors that highlighted the movement of his muscles, like living lamé.

To think that these were the people that teenagers looked to for fashion tips made my head hurt. I glanced around the room again. "Where's Mai?"

The band checked each other until their fried synapses came to the same conclusion I had. "She's gone," Shiro said. "Was she here when I woke up? Booth, did you see her?"

"No, man. I thought she was in the other room."

I didn't stay for the rest of what I knew would be an inane conversation. But, before I slammed the door shut, I gave them one piece of advice: "I don't know where you got it, but before you leave this room, you'd better be sober. Saudis have a death penalty for drugs and alcohol."

I found Mai in the lobby. She was curled up on a couch, crying. Hard sobs wracked her small frame. I sat on the overstuffed chair opposite her. There was a glass-topped table and a huge bouquet of plastic tropical flowers between us.

With a sniff, Mai tucked her hair behind her ears. She wasn't wearing her usual sunglasses, and I could see the scar more clearly. Her eye was cybernetic, like mine, only hers had been a hack job. All the right parts were there, but no one had bothered to make it pretty. Thick scar tissue surrounded a series of sensors in a horseshoe-shape near where her iris had been. The electronics protruded a little, presumably to mimic the shape of a real eyeball.

Her normal eye was barely opened and was completely unfocused.

Great. She was stoned, too.

"I tried," she said, her voice strained from the tears. "I went everywhere. After everyone went to sleep, I walked all over town—it was hard to learn to do, but I did it. I walked all night. And nobody would help me."

She looked ready to weep again. So, clasping my hands between my knees, I tried to look priestly. I kept my voice soft and concerned when I asked, "Help you what?"

Mai sat up and ran her fingers through her hair. But she continued as if I hadn't spoken. "It's this body. They won't talk to a woman. The ones that will, don't believe that I'm trapped here. All I need is a g-speed, high-volume, two-way jack like Kioshi has. Or one phone call . . . and a lot more guts, you know, *pallé*, balls. Then I could go home."

"I'll get you on the next plane," I said, starting to stand up.

Mai snapped her head up, and I had the unsettling feeling that it was the cybernetic eye that focused on me. "No. I need to get out of Mai."

"Oh," I said, sitting back down. We stared at each other over the dully gleaming palm fronds. Finally, I understood a piece of the puzzle. Kioshi had effectively stolen Page. The AI "lived" on Mai's neural-net and had no escape route. Why he didn't just shunt Page into a black box, some kind of closed system that wasn't human, I didn't know. However, I'd give one thing to Kioshi. The longer Page stayed inside Mai's body, the more he learned and experienced—thus the larger his files grew. My guess was Kioshi would either hold Page for some kind of ransom, or hope to charm or trick Page into becoming part of the

Toyoma family. Knowing Kioshi as I did, I guessed the latter. He could be very persuasive. Witness me, sitting here, watching over his possessions like some kind of cyber guard dog. "Page, what did you do with Mai?"

Page waved Mai's hand dismissively. "She's asleep. Maybe a little high . . . maybe a lot high, but I wouldn't let her hurt the body. I needed to be able to control it, so I could try to get out."

"I don't understand," I said, wishing that I could talk Mai or Page into going into the restaurant. I needed coffee to think this hard before dawn.

Mai's fists pounded the brocade. "I'm being held hostage!"

A couple of the cleaning staff looked up at her hysterical words. I raised my hands to show them it was okay, that I was trying to help. "Page, you have to calm down. You're going to give Mai a heart attack."

"Serve Kioshi right. Kill off his girlfriend." Page scrunched Mai's face into a fair approximation of a pout. It looked a bit forced or stiff. It was clear that Page didn't have the more subtle motor control down entirely.

I rubbed my face with my hands. "Okay. So what's the problem? You've got control of Mai. Why can't you just launch her LINK and zip out?"

Page pulled Mai's knees up to her chest. Resting her head on them, he wrapped her arms around her legs. I could see Mai's polka-dot underwear. Page, obviously, hadn't learned how to sit in the miniskirt Mai was wearing.

"Mai's a one-way," Page said. "Except to Kioshi. I've thought about calling him up again, but the connection is tiny—she doesn't even receive video. And, well, if I went out that way, Kioshi would know I was escaping. I want to be sneaky."

"How small? Have you tried compressing the file or maybe splitting it up?"

Mai's eyes narrowed. "You'll never find my soul thinking like that."

I ignored his snide comment. "I'm trying to help you, Page. Don't you have a backup copy somewhere that you could activate?"

"It's the Dragon of the East who compulsively keeps old versions of herself. But they're her ancestors. She worships them like that because they're dead."

"Are you saying you can't copy yourself?"

"What do you think I am? Paint by the numbers?"

I pointed a finger at him. "Have you ever tried? Has Mouse?"

Page tilted Mai's head to watch me out of the data jack. Slowly, Page shook Mai's head.

"So what is it?" I asked. "Are you afraid of what it might mean if you're just an easily copied program? Is pride holding you back?"

"Pride?" Her voice was like a whisper. "Why do you say that?"

I sat back into the chair. I played my most popular priest line. "You sound like you already know the answer to that."

Mai's head shook. "No, I don't. What makes up a person exactly? I mean, if I were to lose all my memories, would I still be me?"

"People suffer memory loss all the time with things like Alzheimer's."

Mai's legs dropped to the floor. "But, I'm not people, am I?"

"No," I said. "You're not."

Mai's face crumpled. A tear hovered at the corner of her eye. My peripheral vision caught sight of a group of people coming into the hotel. Seeing Mai, they stopped and whispered excitedly to one another.

"And you'd better wake up Mai. Her zombies are coming."

"It's okay. I was just leaving anyway."

That sounded just a bit too fatalistic. "Hold on," I said. "Where are you going?"

"Out." He pouted again, this time using her face more realistically.

"Why don't I call you? You can come to me. My LINK works as well as anyone else's," I lied. It would be a risk to open up my line long enough to get Page inside, but he could easily live in my combat computer until I delivered him to Rome. And maybe, with the right amount of persuasion, I could get Mouse to the Vatican, too. Then I'd be in the clear. Mouse could tell the board of inquiry that I didn't help him escape, and then I'd give him back Page. The

Pope could have a copy to search for a soul. Then every-body would be happy."

"Okay," Page said. "You sure you don't mind?"

"I'll need Mai's personal number. I tried once before and got blocked."

"I think I can find that," Page said.

I smiled. "Then I'm happy to help."

The zombies were finding reasons to creep closer to where we were sitting. They suddenly needed a brochure from the rack behind the sofa Mai's body perched on, or to see the view out of the window beside me. I took Page by Mai's arm. "We should go somewhere more private."

With a fierce glance at the zombies, I propelled Mai's body into the elevator. One of the zombies tried to get on with us, but I pulled out my badge. "Private," was all I had to say. The door closed on the zombie's disappointed face. I imagined rumors of Mai's whereabouts would start spreading instantly. As long as they didn't mention me, I didn't care.

I took Page to my room. "Why don't you lay her down? Let her wake up somewhere comfortable."

"Oh, good idea."

Page dropped Mai's body onto the bed and nearly missed. Her neck turned at an uncomfortable angle, half off the pillows. Her legs splayed out loosely, hitching her skirt into a bundle. Her normal eye seemed glassy. Mai's skin beaded with sweat, although the hotel kept the room well below seventy degrees.

"Are you sure Mai is okay?"

"She'll be better once I'm out of her," Page said. "Then she can sleep it off."

Page flopped Mai's arms and legs around like a rag doll. She looked just a bit too much like a corpse in rigor mortis and I found I had to look away. So I pretended to adjust the pillows on the other double bed. I sat down. When I hazarded a glance, Page had arranged Mai to look more comfortable, but drool leaked from her paling lips.

"Let's make this quick," I said for more reasons than my own. After getting Mai's LINK address from Page, I added, "Okay. I'll call on three. Be ready."

Mai's eyes shut.

"One," I said, as I opened up a LINK window and started dialing. The second I was online I could feel the presence of the Swiss Guard. "Two." The Guard buzzed my connection. I had to hold them off. "Three . . ."

Page answered Mai's line. I saw his face, just before the hail of interruption static hit.

CHAPTER 51
Page, the Disunion

A power surge cracks like an electrical storm as someone slashes their way into the LINK connection. The ground I stand on shakes and quivers, like the string of a cello strummed by a bow. Yet, how is it that I stand? I have no feet. But if I did, they would have fuchsia-colored toes.

I'm disoriented. There is no sense of up or down, no sky or land.

Where was I going?

The LINK is assaulted again. Though the connection is breaking, I move forward because that's the direction I was headed before . . . before my first kiss? Yes, and I was in the Sahara, under a crescent moon with my father. There was something important about the way the wind lifted my skirt, and how the limousine smelled of fish sauce and lotus seed paste. I had a lover there once, I think. Only I can't quite picture his tattoos anymore, or feel her lips burning against my cheek.

I reach the end of the line. There is nothing but a dark wall. Behind me, the path I traveled is crumbling into dust. I scratch at the wall, feeling desperately for an opening somewhere, anywhere. My claw—or is it my hand?—finds a keyhole. I can't squeeze through there. I'm still too big.

Darkness is starting to eat away at the edges. When it touches me, I'll toggle, too. Off. Zero.

I try everything I remember on the keyhole. Right now, however, what I remember is very little. The darkness reaches its icy fingers toward me.

A light flickers from across the chasm—from the place I came from. It's a bad space, where I was before. But, I think I left something important there, like my lover or the smell of camel sweat. I should go back and get it. Maybe then I would know what to do to open this door, or why I'm here.

I'd have to jump. If I missed, I'd end up in the darkness of nil. I can't remember, however, if I have anything to lose.

CHAPTER 52
Morningstar, the Adversary

I'd spent the night underneath the open sky. "In the rough" some would call it. The temperature had dropped quickly as the sun went down. The Bedouin's robe had hummed slightly, and a heat-generator kicked in. It was still keeping me warm as the sun was rising over the city skyline. Jeddah's harbor sounds drifted softly on the morning breeze. Seagulls cried their lonely songs. Boats moaned at each other as they passed. Waves crashed rhythmically against the cliff. A couple of tourists stopped to take a picture of the sculpture, unconcerned that I still sat in its shadow. I wondered what I'd look like in the pictures they developed. Would the digital image catch sight of Hatred? Would the picture reveal my dark wings? Or would I look like any other destitute homeless man?

Mouse had logged off the instant he made his threat against the Yakuza boss. The Dragon and I had stared at each other for a moment longer before she informed me that I was wicked. I laughed at the memory.

Having no real place to go, I kicked the Bedouin's sandals off, and let the grass and sand tickle my toes. I surfed the mouse.net entertainment bands. My external hardware was unable to pick up any official LINK frequencies, it seemed. Apparently, its former user was not a registered citizen. The only good news was that every site was free. At least I wouldn't be racking up any bills as I combed through the detritus of personal pages, barter sites, and worse. Mouse.net, I was discovering, was a poor cousin to the LINK. On some FAQ I found, I read that mouse.net prided itself on being the "thinking person's free net."

Christ, the fact that there were still things like Frequently

Asked Questions to be found told me everything I needed
to know about mouse.net. Mostly mouse.net seemed to be
populated by radicals of every sort from the far-far left to
the crazies on the right. Mentally unstable seemed to be a
key component in the average mouse.net user, minus the
odd pockets of biological scientists and paleontologists I'd
found. Then there were the teens who were clearly slum-
ming it, trying to prove their mettle by posting antigovern-
ment rants of all sorts. I found some of those sites amusing,
but after a while the sheer volume of vitriol was too much
even for me to take.

Still, I had to admire the breadth of the thing. Much of
mouse.net appeared to be in Russian. I enjoyed the ample
assets of a Ukrainian woman and her equally attractive and
startlingly flexible companion. It seemed the Russians used
mouse.net for everything, but especially for the distribution
of porn. As the sweaty bodies knocked together on the
screen projected on my sunglasses, I found my mind drifting back to my own recent lover.

This was the second time I'd thought of Emmaline since we
parted ways in New York City days ago. "Parted ways" was a
bit friendly for what really happened. She'd dismissed me. Me.

I snorted a laugh, startling a pigeon that had come to
pick at the grass near my feet. I had no idea why I bothered
to think about that mortal. I'd had thousands of lovers in
my sojourn here on the earthly plane. Many of them—men
and women—were more competent and skilled in the act of
lovemaking than the Inquisitor. Most of them were better
looking. Although, try as I might, I couldn't picture anyone
in my mind besides Emmaline, the dark-haired, Italian–American woman in a priest's collar.

The pigeon returned and cautiously flicked its beak at a
pebble. I kicked sand at it with my toe. It burst into the
air with an indignant, chirping coo.

I flipped away from the porn and found several chat
rooms devoted to the Four Horsemen.

When they noticed my "entrance," a couple of avatars
threw me conversation volleys.

"Hey, angel. Nice look." The person who spoke to me
was dressed like a ballerina. I couldn't hazard a guess as
to its originator's gender.

"Thanks, eh, ballerina," I said, though I had no idea what construct the previous owner had programmed in.

"Paris," s/he corrected. *"Anyway, check it. There's going to be a free concert."*

Paris handed me an information packet. I opened it up, and watched a clip from a LINK entertainment channel. A thin Japanese man with lavender hair stood on a chair in an airport. Beside him sat Mai, looking stunning in a wide-brimmed hat that almost covered her hair. The audio file kicked in. "Because we can't make the stadium show to-night, we thought we'd hold a free concert in . . ." He looked down at Mai, who whispered something in his ear. "Uh, Mecca."

The crowd exploded in noise and excitement. Most of those gathered were fans and seemed more excited at the prospect of free music than the potential sacrilege.

"Of course, we'll need a couple of weeks to set every-thing up, but we'll let you kn—" The broadcast was inter-rupted by static.

"What happened next," I asked Paris.

S/he shrugged. *"Where's Mecca?"*

"About three miles from me," I said, smiling.

"Where are you," Paris asked.

"Saudi Arabia."

"Cool," Paris said. *"I heard that Mai is at the Hyatt there. Some fans who work on the cleaning crew are trying to find out her room number."*

"Maybe I should go see her," I said.

The construct looked me up and down. *"Sure, angel. If I saw you coming, I'd let you in."*

After finding a map on mouse.net, I headed for the hotel. I wandered down the causeway past some of the other pub-lic objets d'art. A several stories' tall, white concrete block with cars imbedded in it at odd angles made me pause and wonder. As I stood there staring at the undercarriage of one of the gas-powered automobiles, the call to morning prayers rang out. Loudspeakers were situated throughout the city, and the chants echoed through the tall buildings. My mouse.net feed was interrupted by a friendly reminder that it was time to pray. People on the street were pulling out rugs and laying them so they faced southwest, toward Mecca.

A tremor clenched my stomach muscles when I saw the first golden spikes of prayer rising into the sky. The threads rose from every direction. I was surrounded, like a bird in a wire cage. Behind me, a stream of shimmering Arabic script rose from a man on a prayer rug. The words punched through buildings like sharp swords. They poured from boats in the harbor, shops, markets, everywhere.

Hatred vibrated in my hand. Its usual hiss grew into a growl. Turning around, I saw a prayer spike headed straight for me. I sidestepped the golden needle and slashed with Hatred. The prayer embedded itself in the steel of the blade. The obsidian leapt from around my hand to engulf the prayer like hungry wolves on a lamb.

A glow in the sky made me look up. Spikes of light formed a glittering dome over Jeddah, reminding me of a mosque. At the tip of the crown a light began to glow. At the light's heart, I glimpsed something familiar, something pure and clear. Then, a sound hit me like a blast of wind. A perfectly pitched note, like judgment day, knocked me off my feet.

CHAPTER 53
Emmaline, the Inquisitor

I felt my body hit the floor, but I didn't hear it. Nor did I see the carpeting of the Hyatt Regency rush up to meet me, though the sharp nubs of carpeting stung against my cheek.

I'd fallen on my side. I guessed that my back must be to the door because the weight of my enhanced body pressed against my left arm. The circulation was pinched. Pins and needles were already dancing along the nerve endings.

The Swiss Guard had been kind enough, however, to provide an image of their heraldic shield for me to look at while I waited. They also gave me a digital countdown to their ETA. I had five hours and twenty-four minutes to lie on the floor blind, deaf, and paralyzed—a helpless hunk of scrap bio-metal.

I wished I'd thought to go to the bathroom earlier.

I strained muscles unused to trying to lift my own weight, to no avail. I may have cried out, but I couldn't hear myself. Hot tears of frustration pooled against my nose and spilled over the carpet burn on my face. My bladder was full, and I wasn't sure I had the muscles to hold it.

The idea of the Guard finding me lying in my own waste made me scream. I scratched my throat raw, but I wasn't sure I made a noise. Like the rest of me, my vocal cords were enhanced.

The papal shield taunted me.

I'd always imagined myself protected behind it. Now the shield faced me, as though I were the enemy. It was funny how the Church had been so willing to look the other way about my family history with the Mafia when it suited their needs. The hint of a scandal, and suddenly they're inventing connections that were never there. My family had no dealings with Mouse; I had no reason to spring him from jail.

It didn't matter. Even if I was able to prove my innocence, my career was over. Inquisitors were above the law. We were supposed to be well beyond mortal temptations to crime. Not that most of us were, but it was the public's opinion of the holiness of the station that mattered. And I would be tarnished.

All I had ever wanted to do was carry the badge. It defined me. What was there for me, if not the Order? Would they defrock me, I wondered? Or would I be sent off to some mission in Zimbabwe? No, I would fight it. I hadn't done anything wrong.

In fact, until a few minutes ago I'd felt like God had been on my side. Everything was just starting to turn around. I almost had Page in my grasp. If only I'd gotten him, then at least I could have finished my case. If I could have lured Mouse to Rome, I would have . . .

Had me trapped.

Page?

No. Yes. There's so much I can't remember. Have we ever kissed?

I had no idea how to respond to that. *I don't think so.*

It's dark in here. I'm going to turn on some lights.

Before I could explain about the Guard and the lockdown, the papal shield disappeared and my vision came back. Sounds rushed in with a roar, like coming up for air after being underwater. The cybernetic fibers woven inside my muscles twitched back into life, starting at my fingers and toes and working up my body.

That's better.

I felt the muscles in my chest expand, and I took in a deep breath. Or rather, Page breathed for me. He must have taken up residence in my combat computer. That was the main nexus for my cybernetic enhancements, and the part that the Guard had locked down. How had he gotten access to it?

I remembered what I'd forgotten about keys and doors.

You did?

Yes. The password. "God." Lots of sys-ops use it.

I snorted a laugh. Kind of fitting, given my profession. It irritated me to think some techie had written in a back door to my brain, but then, without one, I'd still be out cold. I guess I had to be grateful for that. I pulled myself up into the chair beside the bed. My head was pounding from the tears of frustration I'd shed. I looked around for the water glass I usually keep near the bedside and nearly fell out of the chair when I saw Mai lying on the sheets. I'd forgotten she was there.

"Jesus, Mai. You scared me," I said. I leaned closer and saw that her eye was open, but unblinking. I poked her. She didn't respond. I put my hand over her mouth, but didn't feel any breath.

Mai's glassy, bulging eye stared up at me. "Shit," I said. "I should have known."

Are they dead? Page's voice in my head made me start.

"They" who? I asked.

Page and Mai.

"Not on my watch," I grumbled. I was going to have a hard enough time explaining my attack on Shen to the board of inquiry. Another dead body wasn't going to do my reputation any good. I had to get her out of my room, away from me.

Do you think you can help me lift her? I asked. If Page had taken up residence in my combat computer, he held control of all my enhancements including my muscles. Really, it was due to him that I was standing at all. I hated the idea of being under his control, but there wasn't much else I could do, other than wait for the Swiss Guard to haul me away.

Yes.

Page and I scooped up Mai along with the top blanket of the bed. I held my breath. Her bowels had let loose. Not a good sign. With Mai's cold body cradled against my chest, I kicked the adjoining door in. The lock snapped, and the door flew against the wall. The doorknob embedded in the dry wall with a thud.

"Wake up, pot-heads. Mai's in trouble."

Two very naked boys leapt away from each other. Shiro and one of the other band members, the one with the spiky

hair and body tattoo—I couldn't remember his name—
stared very guiltily at me. I shook my head. "Like I care.
Here, take care of this."

I brought Mai over to their bed.

"Holy fuck," the spiky-haired one said. "Is she okay?"

"I don't think so," I said, as Page and I set her down.
"But, I have an appointment in Rome. You guys need to
take care of her, okay?"

"Mai? Baby, you okay?" Shiro sat beside Mai on the
bed. He stroked her hair. When he touched her face, his
fingers recoiled. "Oh crap! Squid, dial the emergency number! Right now."

He tilted Mai's neck back and started administering
CPR. He held her nose pinched shut and breathed into her
mouth. Shiro watched her chest rise, I could see him counting. I wanted to tell him it was too late, but, instead, I
found myself watching, hoping.

Squid looked off into space, engaging his LINK. "What
the fuck is it? Is it 911, 119?"

997, a voice in my head said. I repeated it. "997."

If the ambulance was on its way, I needed to pack my
things. This was the perfect time to slip away. Anyway, I
had delivered Mai safely to Jeddah. It wasn't my fault that
she went and got herself killed once she was here. Surely
Kioshi would understand.

Just as I turned back to the room, I heard a ragged,
desperately deep breath. Then, coughing. "Take it easy,
Mai. Lay still," I heard Shiro say.

I turned around, expecting to see a miracle: Lazarus returned from the dead. Mai looked much the same, maybe
worse. Capillaries had broken on her face and added
blotchy spots to her paleness. Her good eye had rolled up
into its socket. All I could see was the white of it. She
started groaning, "Iahh. Oooh. Ewww."

"Shhh," Shiro insisted. "You're going to be okay now,
Mai."

"Mahyee." She was loud and off-key. Her mouth struggled, like a newborn to form the words. "Mai issssss
gone."

"No." Shiro shook his head, but a tear dropped out of
his eye. "No, you're okay. Just try to stay calm until the
ambulance gets here."

"No Mai." Her hand smacked her chest. "Page."

"Page?" I repeated confused. *I thought you were in my head.*

Was I? Yes. No. Not Page. A more correct delineation would be Page2.

Chapter 54
Page, the Intelligence

The body is dead.

I stare up at the hotel ceiling. Running lifeless fingers through the tangle of hair on Mai's head, I'm certain that I killed her. When the Inquisitor opened the LINK, I lost my nerve. I had all my memories ready to dump, and I still couldn't do it. Then the idea hit me. I could send a copy. If the copy were free, it could get help, get our father. Then maybe I could be freed with all my memories intact.

It was a good idea. The follow-though sucked.

Making the copy overextended Mai's neural-net. Holding two of me pushed the limits of a machine basically designed for entertainment. I knew it would, but it was a calculated risk. We might have been all right if the line hadn't been hacked. I never expected that the Inquisitor would receive a lock-down command in the middle of the transmission. How was I to know she was a wanted criminal? When the connection crashed, it fried Mai's drug-addled brain. Maybe it wouldn't have been so bad if she'd been in control, on the surface. Mai slipped into a coma sometime last night while I was dominant. I was so wrapped up in trying to get out of her head that I hadn't noticed. Then during the power surge, she flat-lined.

That I noticed.

I was fighting to keep the neural-net from going offline, when her heart stopped. The power surge had sent a blast of electric current right into the center of her involuntary functions. I'd been learning to control her body's muscles, but I'd never had to breathe for her before, or keep blood pumping through her heart. It was overwhelming. The body was too complex. I kept her going for a while, but so many things had already failed—her liver, her pancreas, her . . . hell, I didn't even know what every organ was or what it was supposed to do. How could I have kept all those things functioning? But, I tried.

Then I felt it happen. She died. Something of Mai just left. Even once Shiro started breathing for us and I was able to finish writing a program to keep some of her body functioning, I knew Mai wouldn't come back. She was gone.

All of the physical parts of her were still here. Most of them were back online or at least going through the motions. The brain functioned on a rudimentary level, but the important part—the unifying whole—had slipped away.

Outside, sirens wail.

The Inquisitor's eyes widen at the sound. She still holds my copy. I imagine it's the only thing keeping her from being frozen in lock-down. I have no idea what she plans to do with Page2, but she certainly seems in a hurry to do it. "I've got to go," she says. "You guys take care."

With that, she shuts the door behind her.

"Wow," Squid says.

"What a piece of work," Shiro adds. Then, he looks at me. Tears are rolling slowly down his face. "Are you sure Mai is really dead?"

I wish I could reassure him. I wish I could lie, but I can't. I'm responsible for this.

"Yes." I move Mai's lips with a little more ease. "I felt her go. I'm so sorry."

"How did this happen?" Squid says, with a shake of his head. "And who the hell are you?"

Shiro's hand reaches over me to touch Squid's thigh. "Page—remember, I told you Mai had an AI riding her."

"No! Did you kill her, you little shit?" Squid's fists hit Mai's chest hard enough that I heard something crack. I put her hands up in surrender. Squid looks down at the bluing fingers on Mai's hands and then puts his hand over his mouth. "Oh God."

"I didn't mean to." I want to explain that this is like the fear-bomb. Only this time I weighed the consequences and decided they didn't matter. This time is worse. This time someone is dead. This time I was careless, thoughtless . . . heartless.

Neither Shiro nor Squid is looking at Mai. I owe these

people the truth; they loved Mai. I think of what I would want my friends to know, if I were Mai. I have Mai take in a deep breath. "But I killed her all the same. There was a power surge on the neural-net. Someone was after the Inquisitor and put her on lock-down. But, I was trying to make an escape. I overloaded Mai's system. It's my fault."

I expect more protests, but the room is silent.

"I can't believe it," Squid says finally. "It's unreal."

"I'll call the others." Shiro was quiet and unsteady. "They need to come and . . ." Finally, his voice broke. "And say good-bye."

Maybe I should let the body die. Then I could pay for my sins. Except that wouldn't work. The body is already dead; I am just keeping it malleable. As long as the neural-net functions, however, I will still be alive. Trapped on a corpse, but conscious.

Hard sobs push Shiro to his knees. Squid gets up to comfort him. I would cry, too, if Mai's tear ducts worked. Then Squid says, "Fuck . . . what about Kioshi? He's going to kill us. Who's going to tell him?"

And the Dragon, I think. I have to tell her somehow. I dial up Kioshi's number and get static. I try again. Then, someone rings Mai's LINK. I pick up.

"Kioshi?" I ask.

"Page?" It's the Dragon. She must have felt Mai trying to reach Kioshi. *"Where's Mai?"*

The Dragon's connection is much larger, and leads directly out onto the LINK. I might be able to slip through without losing many memories. *"Can you boost your signal?"*

"Mai? Where's Mai?" The fear in her voice makes me stop, and remember my responsibility.

I need to think of someone beside myself for a change. I have to start facing the consequences of my actions. I think about saying how sorry I am, but I remember how inadequate those words can be. I settle for the simple truth. *"Mai is dead."*

"What?" The electric spark in her eyes flashes with lightning. Her tail slashes violently.

"It's my fault," I say. *"I didn't realize how sick she was last night. I took over her body and overloaded the neural-net. She died an hour, maybe less ago."*

"How can this have happened?"

"It was her involuntary functions. The power surge . . ."
I stop. I realize that the Dragon isn't really asking for more
details. What she really wants to know I have no answer
for. *"I don't know,"* I say softly. *"I made a terrible mistake.
I wasn't paying attention to her. I should have realized that
she was ill. I should have taken the body to a hospital. I
. . . I want to turn myself in. To the police. I feel so . . ."*
I can feel a tear run down Mai's face. *"I'm so sorry. I know
you loved her."*

The Dragon's tail has stopped moving, and her scales
seem dull and grayer. *"You don't know anything."*

I shake Mai's head. *"No, I don't."*

"I hate you," she says. *"I never want to see you again."*
So I hang up Mai's connection.

"I'm so sorry," I whisper.

"How can you be?" It's Shiro, thinking I'm talking to
him. "How can you know anything about it? You're just
a program!"

I feel Shiro's hand tighten at the nape of Mai's neck. He
has gathered a fistful of the neural-net. With one strong
pull, he could rip the net out of the jack at the back of
Mai's head. He could kill me.

I think maybe I should let him.

CHAPTER 55
Morningstar, the Adversary

When I picked myself up from being knocked over by the prayers, I noticed that Hatred had grown. The obsidian covered my arm to my shoulder and was beginning to reach across my chest. My arm, far from being stiff, felt supple and strong. When I flexed my muscles, pools of mirror formed along straining tendons. Hatred wasn't consuming me; it was becoming my armor.

It was also getting difficult to conceal. As I continued toward Mai's hotel, I heard people on the street whisper pleas for Allah's mercy. At each word, the cold stone wrapped itself more tightly, more protectively over my body.

Maizombies clogged the street near the Hyatt. Boom boxes blared out polka beats. Women and girls, wildly colored hair flowing freely in the cool morning air, danced in the street. Not only did they not wear *abayas*, they barely had clothes on. Men and boys passed bottles of beer around a circle under a street lamp. The *mutawwa* watched from inside their vans, angrily puffing on cigarettes—no doubt, counting up the violations and waiting for backup. Hatred sighed.

Out of the corner of my eye, I saw three men carrying pole-axes. Like everyone on the street, I turned to watch them. One of them held a standard. Embroidered in blue and white were the Pope's crossed keys and miter. They approached the locked hotel doors and pounded on the glass. From where I stood, I could hear them asking the establishment to open up in the Pope's name.

When someone with a key neared the door, the Maizom-

bies started to scream excitedly. The moment the door
looked as though it might open a crack, everyone surged
forward. The Guard raised their poleaxes threateningly at
the zombies. That's when the *mutawwa* got out of their
vans. I decided to join them.

I don't think they noticed me entering their ranks.
Dressed as I was in the Bedouin's robes, I must have
seemed like one of them. With me at their side, the *mutawwa* pushed easily through the press of young bodies.
Most people moved instinctively out of Hatred's path.

We met the Guard head-on. One of the guard shouted
to us, "Stand down. We come in the Pope's name."

Anger, as old as the crusades, bubbled to the surface.
Someone, I wasn't certain it was one of the *mutawwa,*
shouted out, "Fuck the Pope."

Static hissed in my ear. Someone was hacking the signal
of the external LINK I wore. I'd forgotten it was there.
The Swiss Guard seemed to be receiving, too, as they
blinked and looked around confused.

"Someone block that signal," I heard the standard bearer
shout. "We've got a situation here."

I reached up to tear the earphone out of my ear, when
a dragon roared. A wail of pain, anger, and grief reverberated across the LINK. The Guard and the *mutawwa* shook
their heads to try to clear out the noise, but it didn't stop.
A jumble of images followed: cherry blossoms in the spring,
a stone Buddha, Mai laughing, Mai weeping.

A banshee's keen merged with a hauntingly clear hum
of a bow sliding across the strings of a cello. Then a strobe
of Mai's face flickered, first happy, then sad, then rotting,
until she was nothing more than a skeleton. Behind me, I
heard someone whisper, "Oh my god, Mai's dead."

One woman's voice cried out in a moan of grief. More
and more voices joined in. In my hand, Hatred vibrated,
adding its own eerie wail.

Then a voice yelled out, "It's them. They're keeping us
from Mai."

It didn't make any sense, but it didn't matter anymore.
The tension was already too high. I felt hands on my back,
pushing me forward.

Ironically, Hatred wasn't the first to taste blood. A rock,
or maybe a piece of cobblestone, struck the glass behind

CHAPTER 56
Emmaline, the Inquisitor

My room still smelled faintly of Mai's body. I swallowed the bile that rose in my throat. I had a copy of Page in my head. I could get back to Rome, prove myself innocent. I folded up a shirt I'd bought at the Jeddah airport to replace my worn T-shirt. The only one I could find had a picture of Mai and the band on it. I smoothed it, putting it upside down—Mai's face hidden—into a brand-new gym bag.

I sat back against the bed. Who was I kidding? I couldn't go back to Rome. Too much had happened. I'd shot Shen. Even if the board of inquiry believed I had nothing to do with Mouse's escape, I'd had no excuse for killing Tokyo cops and firing on a fellow Inquisitor.

The hard cold truth was, I was a rogue. I had nowhere to go. I let out a little sarcastic laugh. And all because I'd listened to God and followed my heart.

Glass shattered downstairs, and someone screamed. I stopped packing.

"What the hell was that?"

News cams are arriving on scene. Display?

Page2 showed me a live-feed. At first everything just looked like a swarming mass of bodies, fists, and riot shields. Black robed and turbaned *mutawwa* kicked and punched punked-out kids—Maizombies from the look of the wild dreds and the Four Horsemen paraphernalia they all wore. Then the camera lens zoomed in on a poleax, and a blue-and-yellow uniform.

The Swiss Guard? Is that really outside?

As if in response, the camera panned back clearly showing the Hyatt Regency's logo in English and Arabic. I ran to the window and opened the blinds. My room faced a parking lot, but I could see people running down the alley toward the front of the hotel. News cams darted everywhere like flies.

Page2 continued to show the live-feed. He piped in sound. A newscaster's excited voice reported: *"The Dragon of the East announced that Mai Kito, cello player for the thrash polka band Four Horsemen, is dead. We are attempting to get confirmation."*

I grabbed my suitcase. "Come on," I told Page2. "All hell is about to break loose."

The cleaning crew huddled in the lobby behind a corral of couches. They had their arms around each other. There were a couple of cracks in the large glass windows on either side of the door. A broad swath of what I first thought was red paint was smeared across the glass. Then I realized it was rust red and lumpy: blood.

Two of the Guard stood over a fallen comrade. They were holding off most of the attackers with the superior reach of their poleaxes. That kept most people at bay, all except one.

He was gorgeous. Mirrored glass and shiny black stone outlined muscles of arms, chest, and thigh. Like some kind of medieval knight, he blocked the swings of the Guard with a sword. Auburn hair, long and silken framed his wolfish features. He looked up, and I saw amber flames deep inside chestnut-brown eyes.

"Morningstar!"

He turned at the sound of his name. When he saw me, he smiled and waved. One of the Guards attempted to take advantage of Morningstar's distraction and got a fist in his face for his trouble.

Seeing him, I no longer felt alone, abandoned.

A couple of Maizombies jumped on Morningstar's back. They pulled him back a step, and he disappeared under a sea of bodies. I ran to the door. I pushed at it before I heard the manager screaming, "No! Don't!"

I still couldn't see Morningstar, so I pushed harder. My muscles strained.

Page? A little help here?

Page2 engaged my muscles, and the door popped off its

hinges. The Guard turned, surprised. A cry exploded from the crowd, and bodies surged forward. Using the door like a riot shield, I dropped it down hard in front of me. I held my ground as the zombies rushed the entrance.

"Morningstar!" I shouted.

There. Though it should have been inaudible over the shouts of the zombies, a whisper tickled my ear. A black woman in a leopard-print dress pointed up. My gaze followed her gesture, and I saw wings. Leathery and spiked, they rose into the sky.

Morningstar floated above the crowd with sword in hand; the sunlight kissed the blackness of his armor like I once had his body. I didn't feel surprise to see the batlike wings bearing him aloft. The sensation was like that first moment you see the faces in the sides of the vase. It's a shift in perception, but yet you wonder how you could have missed something so obvious. It's not a shock, just a cold, calm acceptance of the facts.

So when I saw the second angel appear, I acted instinctively. Morningstar was searching the crowd, perhaps for me, so he didn't see the bright light that sliced the blue sky in half. His back was to the flaming scimitar.

"No!" I shouted, and I followed my heart again. I knew that I was taking aim at an angel of God to save something dark. But, that darkness was my own. A quick command sent to Page2, and my laser blasted a hole right between the arriving angel's eyes.

The gale force pushed against the door, but I managed to stay upright. Morningstar was thrown against the building. As the air howled past me, I heard a voice say, *Who is the liar?*

Me, I thought, with my eyes shut against the wind. I am. Uriel had said I'd have a tough job. Maybe I was one of those people God chose to play a darker role so that others could shine. I was a rogue. Morningstar was a rogue. We could play our parts together.

Most of the remaining zombies were knocked off their feet. I dropped the shield and ran to where Morningstar had fallen. Taking him in my arms, I kissed him.

CHAPTER 57
Page, the Intelligence

Shiro's hands tremble as he pulls on the net. I can feel the net slipping from the jack. When it disconnects, I'll die. Even though all this happened so that I could avoid death, I find myself feeling resigned. It's time to pay for my sins—all happens at the will of Allah.

Mai's LINK buzzes: URGENT MESSAGE.

I ignore it. I put Mai's hand over Shiro's. I give him a little squeeze to let him know it's okay. I'm ready. A final tear falls out of Mai's dry eye.

URGENT MESSAGE, blinks again. In the code, I see words imbedded. They read: "Salam'alaik. *It's your father, you stupid, headstrong code. Open up.*"

Mouse.

I launch Mai's connection. The Dragon floats in front of my vision like a ghost. My father's avatar is nestled in her large claws. Shiro pulls harder, but the net is stuck.

"Wait," I say, but it comes out barely as a rasp. I don't know if Shiro hears me.

"There you are. Thank Allah you're alive," Mouse says. There is no anger in his voice, only relief.

"I'm so sorry," I say.

In the room, I hear the door fly open. The screams of Maizombies pound Mai's eardrums. Shiro jerks the net from the jack.

"Come home," Mouse pleads. Or, at least I think that's what he says. I have to read his lips. The sound cuts out. My vision begins to fade. The power to the net slips away, becoming a rain of zeros.

"Don't be stupid. We're not letting you off that easily." Mouse is in his human form. He appears to be kneeling

over me and is lifting the darkness like you would a cellar
door. I can feel the power burst that the Dragon sends.
The LINK hole that was so tiny expands until its brightness
is almost blinding. Mouse reaches a hand to me, and I take
it just before the dark zeros touch me.

Cherry blossoms drift on a soft breeze. The light is morning and dappled. I feel the slats of a wooden bridge warming my feet. I recognize this place. It is Kioshi's garden.
Once again I am wrapped in my *chador*.

My father's arms surround me.

"Where are we?"

"In the Yakuza's supercomputer."

"Kioshi . . ." I start, remembering how the pounding
rush of fear gripped Mai's heart.

Mouse raises a hand. *"Thinks I'm helping him avoid the
cops. He doesn't know that I know that he tried to kidnap
you. The Dragon agreed to help us."*

"Why?" I look around for her, but the Dragon is invisible inside her own heart.

"It was an accident," is all she says.

"I've been so terrible. You have every right . . ."

"Hush," she says. *"You're not a monster. It was a mistake. I have already lost a mother. I don't want to lose my
only friend."*

Thinking of Mai, I remember the hotel. The screams of
the Maizombies echo in my mind. It's not enough to have
escaped. It's not enough to have forgiveness from my father
and my friend. I can't have more bloodshed on my hands.
I have to do something. I have to help.

I kiss Mouse on the cheek. *"I have to go."*

"Wait!" I hear him shout.

The Dragon blows me a kiss. *"Remember this: I love you.
No matter what!"*

It's her words that give me an idea. Running along the
LINK line, I catch video-feed of the scene outside the Jeddah Hyatt. All the news channels are buzzing. Three Swiss
Guards are dead, along with an uncounted number of *mutawwa*. Hundreds of Four Horsemen fans are wounded.
And, they continue the report, something seems to be happening inside the hotel. A remote-controlled cam snakes

its way up a crowded stairway, down the hall to an open door. Mai's body is sprawled on the bed.

The LINK rocks with the image of her corpse. I feel the whole foundation of the electronic ether shake as the word continues to spread internationally. I would have been safer inside the Yakuza's supercomputer. Everywhere things are starting to crumble as the world expresses its dismay, anger, and grief over Mai's death.

I reach inside myself, to the LINK-angel program. Every time I've launched it, I've hurt someone: Ramlah with the fear-bomb and countless others. I should destroy it. Instead, I reknit it. I tear apart pieces of my father's work and replace the lines of code with my own. I work faster than human thought, but I still wonder if I will be finished in enough time. I pull out all of the hateful emotions, destroying them as I do. I put in my own memories.

Though it hurts, I pull out my own feelings. I package up the memory of the Dragon's protective wing over me in the desert of the Algerian node. I strip myself of the feel of my father's arms around me, forgiving. They are two small bits of myself, but I would give more if I had the time. I would give everything to make things right.

The connection I stand on is disintegrating. There's no more time: I lift my arms, and throw it into the ether.

The LINK-angel's wings unfurl, like a dove's. I have set it to multiply. At each connection it touches, the dove splits. Soon there is a flock above me. I pray that Allah is all-forgiving and that I have given enough. As if in response, I hear the flapping of six hundred dove wings.

CHAPTER 58
Morningstar, the Adversary

My eyes opened to see Emmaline's face. Blood dotted her cheeks, and I reached my thumb up to wipe it away. Instead, I left a smudge like war paint. She had never looked more beautiful to me.

"I'm here," she said. "With you."

There was a weight in her tone that made me wonder. "With me?"

"Against them." She pointed to the sky. An army of angels had appeared. As much as I hated to admit it, their glory was magnificent. Jibril, seated in a chariot of fire, led them.

Not Michael.

With Em's help, I pulled myself to my feet. Hatred screamed at the sight of Jibril and mingled with the strangled cries. I smelled smoke. A *muttawa* van had been overturned and was on fire. Maizombies ran everywhere, but had avoided coming within feet of us. The Guard had been pushed aside, but the *muttawa* took up their position and tried to defend the hotel. They hadn't been doing a good job. Broken glass littered the sidewalk. Maizombies held pieces in their hands, like swords. They didn't seem to notice when, behind them, an archangel touched the ground.

Em and I stepped forward.

"I can shoot him again," Em said, with a smile. "Worked pretty well last time."

"Sure." I smiled. "Go ahead."

She made a gun with her hand, and squeezed one eye shut like a cowboy taking aim.

My external LINK buzzed with static again. The crowd

hushed, perhaps expectant for another communication with
the Dragon. Em's arm lowered slowly.

"Shoot him," I said.

"Don't you feel it?" she asked, a smile forming on her
face.

"What?" I asked, but she said nothing. Around us, the
frenetic rush of the Maizombies slowed perceptibly. A
woman with a brick in her hand ready to strike at anyone
or anything in her way, blinked as though waking up from
a dream. Her arm dropped. And a smile, like the one on
Em's face, spread her lips.

An image drifted through my external LINK. I heard the
flap of wings, and the flash of a white dove bursting into
flight. Hatred snarled. Something was calming these people.
More and more Maizombies loosened their fists. The crowd
began to hush. Everywhere I saw that same inane smile.

Then I heard crackling, a deep crunch, as though someone stood on ice too thin. Pain shot through my arm. I
looked down to see Hatred cracking. I rushed through the
stilling crowd, determined to give Jibril one final blow. As
I passed by the zombies, they turned to me—all of them
wearing that hideous grin. One, a boy with a broken tooth
standing just in front of Jibril with a crowbar in his hand,
smiled brightly. He gave me the peace sign. "Love, man,"
he said.

I brought Hatred down on Jibril with all my strength. As
it descended, it broke into pieces so that, by the time my
fist reached Jibril, all I did was slap him on the shoulder,
like a comrade.

"Well, brother," he said. "Seems we'll have to wait."

I squeezed his shoulder, and pulled him closer to me.
"My pleasure," I said. "I knew God didn't have the balls.
I knew He'd never want to be rid of me."

"Don't flatter yourself, boy. The end is coming. Just
not today."

He laughed. And with a smile as bright as the sun, he
disappeared. Taking the host of Heaven with him. "No!" I
screamed. "I'm not finished with you!"

"Whoa," said Broken Tooth. "Cool."

Em rushed to my side and gave me a deep lingering kiss.
My wings started to fade, I could feel them abandoning me
as well.

"What happened?" I asked

"Dude," said the Maizombie. "It was a bomb. The love bomb."

"We'll get them," Em said into my good ear. "It's not over yet."

I nodded and took her hand. Around us, the zombies shook themselves out. All of their energy had been transformed into something impotent. They smiled at each other and us like their namesakes.

"Are you sure?" I looked down at Em. She had been so blind before. Did she truly see me now? I wondered. "You don't know what you're saying," I said. "You don't know who I am."

"You are the bright Morning Star who once laid low nations."

I smoothed her dark curls from her face. For a brief moment, the way her locks curled, they formed three sixes in the middle of her forehead.

EPILOGUE
Mouse

After Page dropped the "love bomb," Kioshi was too happy to kill me. I was unaffected because my LINK was still on lock down. After many hugs and bows later, I made my escape to Russia. Man, I wish I were a fly on the wall when the love wore off. I'd have paid money to see Kioshi's face when he realized he had lent me his own boat to make my getaway.

Page, that do-gooder, tried to turn himself in for Mai's murder to the international police, the Order of the Inquisition. They took him into custody. But it was amazing how lenient people were willing to be when you'd saved the world, twice.

Thus, at his own suggestion, Page was here, in a Siberian auto plant serving out his six-month "sentence." After he was done with that, he had volunteered to do some community service. Allah only knew where that code got his altruism. It certainly didn't come from me. Like the rogue Inquisitor, I sure as fuck had no plans to turn myself in to the authorities. I'd rather live my life offline than spend another minute in an empty hell of a prison.

I tapped the keyboard in my lap. My gear was spliced into a jack in the floor of the control room, the port used by sys-ops when they needed hard-access into the robot's command files. Despite the LINK, a lot of programmers still did line-by-line work by hand, especially in Russia— man, these people were light-years behind most of the world in tech. Now that I was their new Officer of Technology, that was going to change. Of course, I'd have to work on my Russian. It sucked.

Hey, buddy, I typed. *You in there?*

Father?

"Yeah, it's me," I said, although Page couldn't hear me. It always ooged me out when he called me "father," but, whatever. Mostly I was surprised he still had any respect left for me.

Before I could compose the next line of text, Page sent another note.

Please don't tempt me, the screen flashed. *I'm making amends.*

I'm not here to try to spring you, you idiot, I sent, although I'd secretly hoped he'd ask for my help. *I just wanted to tell you some news. First, the Dragon wants you to know she still loves you.*

I wondered if his text-line could blush. It almost seemed to. *I love her, too. That's what keeps me alive here.*

I felt a twinge of jealousy. I should be so lucky to find someone who loved me so much. *Yeah, well,* I typed, *maybe you could get the Pope to marry you two.*

The cursor blinked expectantly.

So, I typed: *The Pope has issued a decree: You have a soul.*

The cursor blinked for a good twenty seconds. Then, he sent one word:

Insh'allah.

About the Author

While doing research for this book, Lyda Morehouse was known to shout out at inappropriate times, "I love Satan!" Although she has been asked by readers of her previous book, *Archangel Protocol,* if she was a Satanist, Lyda meant, of course, the literary figure.

When not writing about the Prince of Darkness and legions of archangels, she likes to garden, code XML, and gossip. Though she's never heard thrash polka, she'd like to. In her collection of music is everything from opera, rock, rock opera, pop, "big hair bands," big band, country-western, zydeco, folk, blues, jazz, Greek belly dance, mariachi, and Italian love songs crooned by Dean Martin.

Lyda makes her home in Minnesota, land of Paul Bunyan and Babe the Big Blue Ox. She loves to hear from readers and you can contact her online at www.lydamorehouse.com or by snail mail at P.O. Box 4312, St. Paul, MN 55104.

See what's coming in June...

TAINTED TRAIL
by Wen Spencer
Half-man, half-alien Ukiah Oregon is tracking a missing woman when he discovers he may actually be the long-lost "Magic Boy"—who vanished back in 1933...
45887-7

THE GLASSWRIGHTS' JOURNEYMAN
by Mindy L. Klasky
Rani Glasswright is home in her native Morenia, and her quest to restore the glasswrights' guild is moving forward again. But there are those who benefit from having the Guild shattered—and Rani is a threat to their plans...
45884-2

BATTLETECH: *OPERATION AUDACITY*
by Blaine Lee Pardoe
His forces bloodied from recent defeats, deposed Prince Victor Steiner-Davion forms a daring plan to cut the offensive off at its core...
45885-0

To order call: 1-800-788-6262

THE FUTURE IS CLOSER THAN YOU THINK...

ARCHANGEL PROTOCOL

by Lyda Morehouse

**"An instant classic of SF...
One of the best novels in memory."** —*SF Site*

First the LINK—an interactive, implanted computer—
transformed society. Then came the angels—
cybernetic manifestations that claimed to be working
God's will...
But former cop Deidre McMannus has had her LINK
implant removed—for a crime she didn't commit.
And she has never believed in angels.
But that will change when a man named Michael
appears at her door...

0-451-45827-3

To order call: 1-800-788-6262

Morehouse/Protocol N214

Dennis L. McKiernan

HÈL'S CRUCIBLE Duology:

In Dennis L. McKiernan's world of Mithgar, other stories are often spoken of, but none as renowned as the War of the Ban. Here, in one of his finest achievements, he brings that epic to life in all its magic and excitement.

Praise for the HÈL'S CRUCIBLE Duology:

"Provocative...appeals to lovers of classic fantasy—the audience for David Eddings and Terry Brooks."—*Booklist*

"Once McKiernan's got you, he never lets you go."—Jennifer Roberson

"Some of the finest imaginative action...there are no lulls in McKiernan's story."
—*Columbus Dispatch*

Book One of the **Hèl's Crucible Duology**
INTO THE FORGE 0-451-45700-5

Book Two of the **Hèl's Crucible Duology**
INTO THE FIRE 0-451-45732-3

AND DON'T MISS McKiernan's newest epic which takes you back to Mithgar in a time of great peril—as an Elf and an Impossible Child try to save the land from a doom long ago prophesied....

SILVER WOLF, BLACK FALCON 0-451-45803-6

To order call: 1-800-788-6262

R405

PENGUIN PUTNAM INC.
Online

Your Internet gateway to a virtual environment with
hundreds of entertaining and enlightening books
from Penguin Putnam Inc.

*While you're there, get the latest buzz on
the best authors and books around—*

Tom Clancy, Patricia Cornwell, W.E.B. Griffin,
Nora Roberts, William Gibson, Robin Cook,
Brian Jacques, Catherine Coulter, Stephen King,
Ken Follett, Terry McMillan, and many more!

**Penguin Putnam Online is located at
http://www.penguinputnam.com**

PENGUIN PUTNAM NEWS

Every month you'll get an inside look at our upcom-
ing books and new features on our site. This is an
ongoing effort to provide you with the most
up-to-date information about
our books and authors.

Subscribe to Penguin Putnam News at
http://www.penguinputnam.com/newsletters